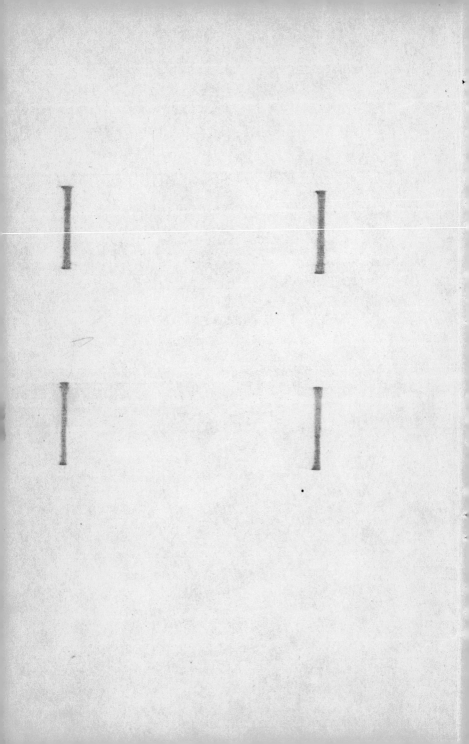

# NONE BUT THE
# LONELY HEART

RICHARD LLEWELLYN

# NONE BUT THE
# LONELY HEART

L77N

THE MACMILLAN COMPANY
*New York* · *1943*

SET UP BY BROWN BROTHERS LINOTYPERS
PRINTED IN THE UNITED STATES OF AMERICA

DEDICATED TO
THE QUIET CITIZEN

590483

". . . Wealth to us is not mere material for vainglory but an opportunity for achievement; and poverty we think it no disgrace to acknowledge but a real degradation to make no effort to overcome. Our citizens attend both to public and private duties, and do not allow absorption in their own various affairs to interfere with their knowledge of the city's. We differ from other States in regarding the man who holds aloof from public life not as 'QUIET' but as 'USELESS' . . ."

PERICLES, 490–429 B.C.


". . . Where in former ages, the laws and customs established by Lycurgus formed man into a model for martial exploits, and a perfect instrument for war, he is now trained, by other laws and customs, to be the instrument of a despotism which renders him almost, or altogether, unfit for war. And where the laws and customs of Athens trained the young mind to acquire as high a degree of partial rationality as the history of preceding times records, man is now reduced, by a total change of laws and customs, to the lowest state of mental degradation . . ."

ROBERT OWEN, 1771–1858

# NONE BUT THE LONELY HEART

# CHAPTER I

ERNEST VERDUN MOTT thought it was dead funny, how a blanket over bent knees, with the sun on it, gets like a lot of little grey trees growing over a couple of smooth mountains, with hundreds of camp fires all along the top burning curly hairs of light. Beyond where the sun had took a clip of his shears along the shadows, thousands of them there little flashing white bits fell out of the dark part and rolled about in the light, just floating round, they was, turning over and over, regardless as a shower of millionaires.

Waking up of a morning was a proper game, because nearly always it was a few minutes too soon, and it was no use of getting up for the sake of getting up, and giving yourself a dogs life for nothing. Else it was so late you had no time to catch the Workmans, so you might just as well turn over and make a morning of it, and have done with it, even if it meant a couple of minutes worrying about getting The Sack. But down there in the warm, getting The Sack never seemed to matter so much, and anyhow, never mind what you felt about it, everything all round you stayed the same. Even if the world came to a end this afternoon, them there little white bits would still fall out of the dark parts if the sun stuck his nose in the window and started clipping along the hedge, so it was no good of worrying about nothing.

But the sun never woke Him up, so it must have been old Ma Chalmers's fault again. Nobody could kip down while she was scrubbing her back yard. Why she done it, wearing her poor old bones out, morning after morning, year in and out, was a proper puzzler, because the railway come along the end of the garden and covered everything over proper comic with smuts, Jim Glass's pigeons next door was no ladies nor gentlemen, neither, and to cap the lot, there was the gas works just down the end of the road, and what come up out of that, when the wind was right, was a fine old prize packet. soot, steam, smoke, and stinks galore, and all of it free.

So the old girl had her work cut out all right, but never mind even if it was coming down a right old soak of rain, Ma Chalmers would be there with both her buckets, one pouring while the other was filling, and her pal, the brush, and that there little bit of red rubber hose for the cracks what the whiskers always got stuck in without doing their selfs too much good.

Brush, brush, brush, that there brush kept on swearing through its teeth, proper savage, it was, digging and biting at the concrete, getting its moustache all sort of curled up and bent at the ends there, and you could hear old Ma come shoving up behind, then more sloshings of water going on, and water splashing in the free bucket, making a flat doh-ray-me as it come up the brim, pouring over the sides and down the drain with a lot of sad little widdles, as though it was right sorry to miss the trip across the concrete with the brush chasing after it. And brush, brush, brush, always that there brush, brush, brush, till you just laid flat on your back and looked up at the ceiling, pretending you was deaf, or else you tried to kid yourself you was somewhere else, or enjoying the whole performance and trying to find some new sounds to add to your collection.

But all the time, whatever you liked to think you was doing, Ma Chalmers was hopping about her back yard hanging on to her brush, till you was nigh on sweating for her, and hoping she lasted out. Her black apron with all them little pink buds on it was tucked up around her waist, what you could get both your hands round, and there she was, flapping her plimsolls through the wet, stumping on her heels through the deepest puddles, with the laces wriggling about behind her trying to catch up with the laceholes. It was a waste of time trying to go to kip. Somehow or other, them laces kept on getting in your eyes.

When she went in the scullery there was always a moment what was just like going inside of a church. A load of quiet got in tow with a few minutes of time and out come a bit of peace, just after the bumpy goodbye of the closing door. Ma Chalmers never had it in her to slam anything, though come to think of it, there was that time when she slammed the piano lid on His fingers and give Him a blue nail for not doing His scales proper, but then she give Him a big apple to shut His row.

His face looked a bit more healthy, but that was only because He was so far from the glass. Feeling fingers found a couple of new pimples on His chin and what felt like the start of a nice old boil just behind His ear, so He was all right in the looks department for at least a week. It seemed to be years since His face had been clear. What was worse, all the little visitors left sort of small holes as never got filled up, like holes in the road dug up and left with a red light in front of them. You could hardly rush about getting off with brides when you knew your dial was like a pepper pot, and it never give you no heart to try and make the best of yourself, neither, because never mind how nice you tied your tie, one look at yourself would tell you to give over, and stop wasting your time.

Some said it was grub as caused it, but Ma had the same as Him and she never had no pimples nor nothing else, so far as He could see, so it was a proper mystery to Him how they happened. And they always seemed to come up in the night, that was the funny part of it. Look in the glass at night, and thank your lucky stars you was getting clear, and here you was in the morning, looking like Joe Rotten. But it was all the same, after all, because a lot of things happened inside of you as never ought to, and nothing you could say or do never had no effect.

It was like as if a couple of you was at it inside of you, one of them known, which was You, and another one as did the dirty on You behind Your back, like dishing you out a load of pimples, or working You a couple of boils, but he never come out in the open where You could get a good bash at him. It was a funny kind of a do, and the more you started thinking about it, the worse it got, till you thought you was going barmy or something, and give up.

The green plaster girl on the window sill looked as if she was wearing a sunny waterfall. Proper lovely she was, even though she was as naked as the day she was born. People often said as everybody was ugly with their clothes off, but not this girl. She was a proper marvellous shape, she was, and He reckoned all women ought to be like it. But Ma was so fat you could even hear it, and Ma Chalmers was that there skinny she proper put your teeth on edge. So was all the rest of them, as far as He could tell, all shapes and sizes except right, like this girl.

Nine shots a tanner it cost, and five in the bull won it. He wished He was there when Ma see it first time out, the morning after He put it there, but she never said nothing for weeks, and then she only called it a filthy thing, but she never meant it. She only tried to make Him think she thought it was a disgrace for a girl to be caught with her clothes off, but she never did nothing about it. She even dusted it when she done the room, so she must have thought something of it.

The gas oven door in the kitchen whacked shut and shook everything in the house. The case of birds from South America blinked a lot of light and made a lot of noise rocking about on the washing stand, and stood still again. A nice lot, they was, and they ought to have been very pretty when they was new, but they must have brought their own moths with them because they was going bald, and if you shook the cases, a lot of very queer looking little white Things come out, and had a look round, sort of nosey, like, and went back in again.

The smell of fried bacon was creeping about the place, so Ma was going to start shouting any minute.

It was time to think about getting out of it.

A rare old lark it was, gone through every morning as far back as He could remember. And even when He was out of it, it was easy enough to nip back in again.

And that had been done, too.

First, the time had to be right, not too early nor too late. Then if it was too cold He had to think about it. If it was too hot, He had to lay down and think how hot it would be to wear clothes, and what a shame it was some blokes could get up at ten of a morning and get in white trousers to go and play tennis instead of going to work. Anything was good enough to think about, as long as it had nothing to do with getting up, and the further off, the better.

The girl on the window sill come in for a lot of it because she was somehow nice to think about, without making a nuisance of herself, like going and telling her brother, or some bloke with her, about Him looking at her. She just stood there and let Him look.

He felt it was a bit barmy to think about her as somebody real, but after a bit she stopped being green, and only a foot or so high, and come up as though she was the size of a proper girl, and after He looked at her for a couple of minutes she seemed to shine long splinters of coloured lights, red and blue and pale yellow, as flicked in and out all round her, like as if she was doing it herself on purpose to keep Him staring at her.

He liked to feel His eyes going hot, and round, and dry, because then He knew He was losing His self without trying, and she was starting to be the woman He wanted her to be, somebody to muck about with, if she let you, instead of something to just think about.

She got more and more like Ada every minute and the bedroom was bright with the lights of the Fun Fair. She had lip rouge on her mouth, and red glue stuff on her nails as flashed when she give you your change, and made them look like red beetles what you kept on wishing was crawling all over you.

Ada come alive out of the green plaster, then. She was with Him, herself, standing in front of Him like the girl on the window sill, looking up at the ceiling with her hands down her sides and kind of half bent over backwards. White, a shiny sort of pinkish white she was, all over, only it was healthy looking, like as if somebody was holding a white light behind a smooth ground glass window. Her smell was near Him, too, the smell He loved, what He leaned over to catch whenever she passed quick, and there was enough of a draught to blow it His way. Warm sort of smell, it was, something to do with her hair, or something.

Them red beetles was flashing and crawling all over Him

making Him feel proper drunk, turning the bedroom into a loud roaring of hot rhythm and smiling lights, and Ada was with Him, fluttering her eyes at Him so He could see the blue water of them, with the pale blue stars shining away inside of them, and all the time she was looking at Him, them red beetles was creeping faster and faster, and the faster they went, the rougher they got, and the nearer Ada come, holding her mouth out to Him, making him reach out to try and get hold of her, but not far enough to disturb the beetles.

Then Ma had to go and spoil it all again. Time after time she done it, as if she knew all about it.

"Ernie?" she was yelling, and from the sound of her, she must have been shouting for a minute or two, "Ern? Time to make a move. Dinner's on the table."

She was always spoiling it.

She spoiled everything.

Her and Ma Chalmers's wireless set would spoil anything.

Never mind how much He tried to lose His self, one or the other would come up with something to bring Him back to His self, leaving the part of Him what He liked best out in the air somewhere, sort of crying and asking Him to come back.

"If you're more than two minutes getting down here," Ma was saying, in her morning voice, the one with the tired lace all round it, "you'll fight the birds for it, my lad. Sheeps heart and bacon's hard enough to get ready without having it mucked up by going cold. You just start looking round yourself, up there, fore I come up and shift you. Two minutes, that's all."

The kitchen door slammed and bounced open again, and He heard the knob fall off and roll along the linoleum in the passage till it come to that little hole by the parlour door. Then it turned over on its back, like it always done, and looked up at the ceiling with one square eye, very calm, as if it had folded its arms and said, well, here we are again.

But Ada had gone and the green plaster girl was back on the window sill, without the bright waterfall of hair, because the room had gone grey and all them there little white bits was hiding in the dark, somewhere.

His eyes was sore, and dry as marbles, but they went wet in no time. Looking up at the ceiling was like looking at a pond full of hot water. But He was hungry and it was time to get up, or lose His dinner, and there was no two answers about that, angry or not.

Somehow the blankets went back without any trouble at all, and all over again He felt proper surprised it was so easy, when earlier on it seemed a safe bet He would never know what it was to get out of bed that day, or any day.

Freezing draught slipped inside His shirt and brought Him out in a right old rash of goose flesh. Even after His trousers was on, He could still feel the hairs on His legs stiff as grass blades with cold, and having to thread a broken shoelace kept Him longer than He wanted, so the shivers got Him, and when it come through the hole at last, after He wet it a dozen times to get the bits to a point, it come sprouting up like one of them palm trees.

No two ways about it, He wanted some new shoes, too. Patent leather ones looked all right for the first week, but after that, they started turning over at the sides, with a lot of little cracks coming out all over them, so they was no cop to wear, and not much of a buy, neither.

But come to that, He wanted everything new. He was sick of thinking about it, and what He would get if He got the chance. And the more He thought about it, the more He wanted, and the less likely it seemed He would get even a clean shirt that week, never mind a new one, because Ma had stopped washing till her pains was better, so He was stuck.

While He turned His collar inside out, He went to the window and had a look at the day, but it was just like it always was. The express come by while He was watching, and all the white puffing come over the fence and covered everything except the fork end of Ma Chalmers's clothes prop, so it stuck out like a catapult. The window was a bit dusty and rain had made a lot of little clear curly roads in it, so what with that and the way the glass sort of bumped about, Ma Chalmers's garden come off none too well when the smoke blew off.

It was all concrete, for a start, laid by Pa Chalmers to save him digging it the year before he rolled up, and a proper mess he made of it.

There was circles and squares left open down the middle in a kind of pattern, and in them, Ma Chalmers had planted privets, and something else as never come to anything except a lot of weeds and marigolds. The marigolds was all right, in fact they was pretty but He never did take to them, because they kind of stared at you hard orange yellow, a round wide stare piled up with frill after frill, one atop the other. He always felt them looking at Him, and weighing Him up in a quiet way as made Him feel proper uncomfortable. Of course, it was soppy to think of flowers doing a thing like that, but there it was. He never got on with marigolds. You had to look at too many at the same time, till you could feel yourself going bosseyed and starting to worry.

Looking over at their own garden, He felt His mouth stretching up, trying to make Him laugh, because that there tore up branchy tangle was such a right mess. There was boards out of the fence as had gone on the boiler fire when Ma run short of coal, so the fence looked like a old girl giving you a grin with some of her teeth out. Everything grew where and how it liked, mostly grass and dandelions, except by the dustbin, and there was a bald patch all round that, and a wavy path as went almost straight to the scullery door.

The dustbin was older than He was, just about ready to give up, and bashed about by dustmen till it had no idea what shape it ought to be. So the lid never fitted, and just sat on the top of it, on the skew, like an old girl wears her hat after a nice fat skinful. Year after year it had been give a load of stuff only the flies seemed to want, so it got its own back by blowing a sweet breath of murder at anybody as went near it, all except the flies, and they loved it. They seemed to go barmy when they got near it, and if they flew into you, they hit you a wallop as if they meant it, like young bullets, and buzzed like sewing machines, they did.

The green plaster girl was cool in His hands and as His fingers smoothed her, He watched the grease fade into the plaster, leaving no mark except a sort of shadow. He wished again that women was born small enough to put in your pocket, so that you could take them out and smooth them whenever you wanted to, instead of all the palaver you got with them in the ordinary size. He wished again that He could blow his own breath into her and make her alive, like the bloke as done it in the Bible, but when He tried, it only left the steam of His breath all over her face, and a funny sort of clay pipe taste in His mouth. And anyway, more than a look at her face was enough, because her mouth was a kind of cut and her eyes was little holes, so there was nothing much to work with, all in all, and when He put her down, the little rocky platform, what she was standing on, kind of rang a little bell.

It sounded same as that there one in the little house atop of the red corrugated roof of the Brotherhood sometimes done of a Sunday morning, or when somebody was getting turfed in.

Far from helpful, that was, because it made her seem about as far away as they was, and He wanted her nearer. He wanted her alive. There was nothing in the world He wanted more than somebody just like her, alive, to talk to, and touch.

So there He was, looking out of the back bedroom window, with puddles steaming hot on the rims of His eyes, wishing He was over there in bed along with the other half of Him as called Him back to the warm, feeling the dampish hang of clothes on Him, and a big toe what was strangling itself through a hole in His sock.

He wanted to smash the window and reach out to tear Ma Chalmers's garden up, flinging lumps of it over the roof tops, pulling down the hard things that come between Him and somebody to talk to and put His arms round and look at, and sort of fall in love with. While His hands rubbed the wet off of His face He knew why people kissed dogs noses.

"Ern?" Ma's voice sieved up dull through the floor. "If I

have to come up there and shift you, you'll know all about it, I can tell you."

Hate of her come up in sort of blisters all over somewhere inside of Him, and His face was a funny colour when He looked in the glass to comb His hair. It come back sudden while He see His eyes red in the corners and silver round the edges, that morning Ma come in with it over her shoulder, like as if she was carrying a oblong load of flashing electricity, and put it down where it was now.

"Mind how you go with this," she said, and shoved her hair up back inside her hat. "Cost me two quid and me fares to Kentish Town and back, it did. Bit of Queen Anne glass, it is. Best one I seen, so watch yourself."

But she never got a customer for it, and her voice hung about the room ever since like old Christmas paper chains. So He looked at His self in it, through patches and blobs of yellow and grey where the flies had been having a go at gardening, going back a couple of hundred years, wishing He lived Then instead of Now, and making His tie worse by pulling the threads out of it where it was frayed, trying to hide the ring round the top of His collar by wrinkling it up where the dirt on the other side was showing through.

But it was no go, because the glass had seen a bit too much in its time, and said so, out loud, never mind the blobs or the flyblow. No good come of kicking it, neither, because it only shivered and He had to catch it and put it back against the wall, proper careful, case Ma saw the marks in the dust where it come from. Then the band would play, for sure.

Pulling some of the fur collar off of the comb, He looked up and caught sight of His self, yellowish down one side of His face, dark and no shape at all on the other, like them Italian prints Ma had in the shop.

It was easy to see where there was craters in His cheeks because the yellow light was all round the rings of them, and climbing up the sides of the spots. Over His shoulder, what He could see of the bedroom made Him almost afraid to turn round. It was so quiet, not a safe quiet like in a cinema when the organ stops and you wait for the big picture to start, but that kind of a one when some bloke just looked at you and told you to come outside, and you find yourself wondering whether to take him on, because your pals are all round you and looking at you, and hoping you will, or whether to kick him and chance your arm, or just laugh and pass it off as a joke, like. It was the same sort of quiet as the fluff was in under the bed, quiet as grey sky, yet you only had to even reach for your shoes, and there it went, flying about, not quiet at all, really, but just watching out for you.

So was the room, and everything in it. It was against Him, so was everything else, and what was more, all of the people what had ever looked at their selfs in the glass was looking at Him, and they was against Him, too. He could feel the looks of them all round Him, like as if they was on the end of pea sticks, pushing Him about with them. So He started getting angry again like He always done when He could feel the place trying to get Him down, and sort of frighten Him with grey, watching quiet, and little squeaks and creaks as if something was just waiting to jump out and slosh Him one.

There was only one way to answer. Kicking a bedstead never done no harm to the enamel, but it done Him a lot of good, so it come in for a couple of good hearty ones with the flat of the heel, and each time He kicked it, it grunted all over and give itself a bash against the wall for luck.

Any case, a frayed tie was nothing to worry about. Plenty of artists went about like rag bags and thought nothing of it, and people thought they was all right. And after all, a dirty shirt shows you know what it is to work. So pimples or not, He could still look everybody in the eye, and not worry what nobody said behind His back.

Looking at His self to make the best of it in the glass while He done His hair, He was pleased to see again where He was like the statue on old Nick Falandora's desk, about the face anyhow, only His mouth was a bit wider, His nose was squarer at the tip and He done His hair different, of course. So all in all, it was enough to give Him a bit of heart, any rate.

"Go on," He says to His self, "you ain't fell down and broke your blinding neck, have you? Give your self a treat, boy. You're walking about like a wet dream, you are?"

He was surprised to find His self being cheerful even though He never knew where it come from. One minute He was proper in the dumps and it looked as if it was all over, and the next, up come the cheerful part of Him and He only had to say a few kind words to His self, and He was all right again. But it was funny where it come from, just the same.

He thought while He was going downstairs how every day was always the same, and seeing the door knob lying in the hole in the lino only made it kind of more certain. The same things, the same smells, the same feeling, day after day. Nothing ever changed, except the weather, and you knew what to expect there, so it never worried nobody. Everything else was always the same, people and all. So was Ma.

## CHAPTER II

As far back as He could remember, Ma had never been no different. She was always in black for a start, and always wore a hat in the shop. Sometimes she wore it in the kitchen and the feathers always got caught in the gas bracket and either got burnt a bit, before she knocked the flame off, else they busted the mantle.

And she always sat with her back to the window, so she always looked like a black shape as let in bits of light here and there, and made the kitchen look that much smaller and darker. But however she sat, whether He could see her or not, He always felt the roll of her eyes finding Him and fastening down on Him as if they had hooks.

He felt as if she was afraid of Him, not afraid of what He could do to her, or anything like that, but what she was afraid He might do for His self. He never quite got the hang of it, and she never said nothing. So it just went on, with them eyes of hers following Him about in the shadow of the kitchen under the darkness of the cartwheel hat.

Sometimes they made Him feel a bit awkward, like when He come down late of a morning, or if He come home late and she had to come downstairs and let Him in, but generally speaking He felt all right about it. He felt she was frightened about Him, and it give Him a sort of feeling that He was a bit better than what she was. It might have been something to do with Pa, but after all, he went west at Verdun before He was ever born, but He had the idea. She never got tired of giving it out as they never got on, like, because Pa was always playing her up, or so she said when she had a few more than usual. But anyway, He never asked her what she was worried about, or what Pa had got to do with it, and she never said nothing, so He let it go at that. After all, it was no good of

13

Him starting a lot of excitement for nothing and disturbing the peace, what there was of it, so He never said nothing, neither.

He found a way, after a long time, of getting her all right, sort of having a laugh and talking as if she almost enjoyed it. That was funny about Ma, too.

She never talked much, and when she did, she shouted the place down, and as for laughing, which was very rare, she nigh on busted the windows. Funny sort of laugh it was, and all, very high and trembly, and proper loud, and she always finished up holding her mouth with one hand, and the two halves of her blouse with the other, shutting her eyes tight and holding her breath as though she thought something was going to happen to her, somehow.

So when He come in the kitchen, He done a couple of dance steps and stopped with His behind stuck out, pulling the horriblest face He could, with His hands over his head as though they was holding one of them strings of flowers like them girls with fluffy skirts, as dance in square shoes, rush about with, soppy as you like.

"Ta ra, ching," He says, like a band giving a bloke a good start. "Spirit of the morning. Here you are, Ma, all in one piece, in working order. How much?"

Her eyes come at Him over the top of the newspaper, and she chirped something out of her teeth, like sparrows round a plate.

"No bid," she said, and He was glad to hear her voice was coming round His way, sort of friendly like. "Go and get your dial washed, do."

"Ain't I lovely, eh?" He says, and hopped out in the scullery with His hand on His hip, seeing His dinner, with brown bubbles round the edges, on the shelf in the gas oven.

"Proper dream," she said, talking to the newspaper, not Him. "I see they got Ma Pearson, then?"

"Ma who?" He says, trying to sluice His face without wetting His cuffs, but as fast as He pulled up one, the other come down, till come to a finish they was both dripping, and His eyes was fried up with soap through trying to see what He was doing of.

"Ma Pearson," she says, after a bit, and He knew she was doing no more talking till He was sitting at the table. She liked talking quiet sometimes, in a very one string kind of a voice, thin, not too much tune in it, as though everything she was talking about was a waste of time, but underneath you could almost see the red excitement of her, and you knew then as one of her loud fits was coming on and just about ready to sprout.

"I don't know what they lob in this here rotten soap," He says, when He snapped His fingers from the heat of the plate, and reached for the mustard. "But I'm looking at you out of a couple of blinking furnaces."

"Shouldn't ought to shove so much on, then," she says in the same voice, so He knew she wanted to talk about Ma Pearson, never mind if the soap bored holes through Him.

He waited a bit, till He could feel her getting a kind of froth on top of her, hoping He was going to ask about Ma Pearson, but He kept on chewing, and dabbing the mustard in a sort of pattern round the next piece of meat, knowing just how long to keep her hanging about, and the exact second she was going to slam down the newspaper, shove the table away and pull herself up to go out.

Ma Chalmers turned the wireless on and the bloke come hollering through the wall as if he was standing behind the wallpaper.

"What's up with Ma Pearson, gel?" He said, like as if she might have only knocked a wart off of her hand, or something.

Ma kind of shook up and down in front, and her cheeks got fatter as her mouth come wider, but it never opened. "Gone and got herself jugged," she says, as though it was the biggest surprise in the world to everybody but her. "Course, I told her what would happen months ago, but do you think she'd listen? Course not. She knew it all. Well," she says, and kind of pulled her chin in, "she knows a bit more now, poor cow."

"Jugged?" He says, and it was a proper smack in the eye, because Ma Pearson was always round there, and a quieter bit of goods never come through a door. Four foot nothing, she was, with a long macintosh as buttoned to the neck what she was never knowed to take off, and a hat like the finish of a old wood fire.

"Got her Friday, they did, and she come up on Saturday," Ma says, getting as much juice out of it as a cat with a lump of haddock skin. "Three months, hard, and her costs. She would do it posh."

"Blimey," He says, proper up in the air, He was. Ma Pearson had five kids round in Basson Terrace, and the old man was on night work at the goods yard. So they was going to be in a right mess, because the eldest was only eleven, and he was a mug, by all accounts, sacked off the milk round for getting his book wrong, and no good at lighting a fire, even. The eldest girl was no more than eight, if that. "They're going to be in a bright pickle, ain't they? What's she been and done? Crowned the old man, has she?"

"Shoplifting," Ma says. "Some place in Aldersgate, if you ever heard of such a fine thing? I warned her, I says, you work on your own, I says, and you'll be inside in no time, I says. Asking for trouble, I says. And now she's got it. Three months of it. Soppy looking lump."

Ma Chalmers got tired of hearing the news and turned off on some organ somewhere, so it come through the crack at the top of the window like a swollen inner tube, till the kitchen was proper shaking with them low notes as sounded as if they was having a ride on hot treacle.

He chewed on the sheeps heart more than He would have in the ordinary way, and put a potato in to keep it company, not because He was so hungry, but to make sure He was sitting there and able to, which was more than what Ma Pearson could do. It was all right to be nice and easy at the table with the chair holding His back up, and plenty of dinner still on the plate, with a lump of bread ready to wipe up the gravy, seeing the grey sort of brown stones of Wormwood Scrubs coming up behind the sugar pot, and the clock showing all the hours of the day up on the mantelpiece, ticking away there, not caring about the minutes it was giving Him, and getting gladder every second as they was His minutes, what nobody could get off of Him, because He never done nothing.

"She must be up the blinking pole," He says, while He was forking the last lump of bacon. "Think she'd have a bit more sense, wouldn't you?"

"Well," Ma says, very sorry like, looking at it a long way off, "I told her. Can't do no more, can you?"

"That's right," He says, "quite right, that is. Proper barmy. Ought to have knowed better, she did, woman her age."

"Her age?" Ma says looking over the other side of the paper, and giving it a shake up, like as if it done the job itself. "Some of them didn't ought to be allowed out without a keeper, they didn't. Ain't as if she wasn't told, I mean. I wore my self out trying to."

"And that's the thanks you get," He says. "Three months in quod. Serves her right for being a thief."

"Who?" Ma says, a bit high, and her eyes come round at Him with a smack like a ball coming off of a lamp post.

"Who we talking about?" He asks her, quick, because everything was going so nice, it was a shame to go and spoil it by doing it all wrong and putting her off.

"Ma Pearson," Ma says, as if she was taking it to pieces somewhere inside of her to see what sort of a sound it was. "And you called her a thief."

"Didn't you say she got three months?" He says, sort of as if she was being proper unfair. "What she got it for then?"

Ma counted about three, looking at Him like she would some of that there grey stuff, as comes out of the cracks in the scullery table.

"Shoplifting," she says.

"Well, blimey," He says, kind of bubbly in the adam's apple, because of a lump of gravied bread stuck half chewed in and out of His throat, "ain't shoplifting thieving, then?"

"No, it ain't," Ma says, and give the paper a bash as tore a page right down. "It's only taking your rights from them as has more than they can handle."

"That's right," He says, very fast on the ball, and sort of trying to come round her way and laugh her out of it. "She got three months for trying to do herself a favour. But the coppers wouldn't have it, and shoved her in the cooler. What a girl, eh? What a bride."

But He could see she was narked, and her hat was shaking, although she was as quiet as a mouse and not moving a finger.

"All she done," Ma says, in a sort of rainish kind of a voice, "was get a few things she couldn't afford, that's all. Like you go in a hop field and pick hops or in an orchard and pick apples. She didn't take much. She never was much of a hand at it. No heart for it. I told the soppy little cow what would happen to her if she worked on her Jack. So they got her and now she knows. But she's no thief, let me tell you that."

But there was something as kept on wagging its head inside of Him, as said a shoplifter was a thief whichever way you looked at it. Besides, Ma looked as though she had some more to say, and He knew if He kept quiet, so would she, which would start a lot of nasty feeling, so He tried to think of a way of putting it as might do the trick for both sides.

"Well, look here, Ma," He says, kind of chatty, like, "if shoplifting ain't thieving, what do you reckon it is, then? I mean you couldn't have everybody trotting in and coming out with a few quidsworth on the sly, could you now? I mean, you'd all go bust, wouldn't you?"

"How?" Ma asks, and He could see she was thinking of something about as heavy as a iron plank to hit Him with. Everything inside of her was working overtime to find the right answer, and it slowed Him up a bit, because the last thing He wanted was trouble. The two half crowns He wanted to borrow was shining each side of her, and He could see if this went on He was doing His self a bit of no good, and just talking His self out of money.

"Well," He says, and puts on a lot of pretend stuff, kind of looking at the newspaper with His eyebrows up His forehead, and cutting up His voice with a sort of laugh, trying to get His self dragged out of it somehow, "I don't know. They got to pay the rent, I suppose? And the blokes as work there got to draw their rock of ages to get the roast and boiled of a Sunday, ain't they? How they going to pay out if everybody's hopping in and snarvelling the goods as fast as they can stick their hooks in them?"

"Look here," Ma says, not so quiet, neither, "you talk about something you know something about. Don't go giving no advice to them as don't want it, nor no funny ideas, see? We can do without it. Shoplifting ain't thieving, and that's it. A thief pinches anything going because he's born a thief. But shoplifting's different, like Ma Pearson is. And if you must know," she says, and she looked bang at Him, with white all round her eyes, the size and just about the colour of brandy balls, "so am I. And I've been on it for years. So that's it."

If somebody rolled a couple of dozen ice cold pickle jars down His bare back, it would have been nice beside a wallop like that. But He see, quick, like a big yellow flame, same as when you light a fire with paraffin, why Ma Pearson and Ma Sutcliffe and a few more of them was always round there.

All the same, He had to say something cheerful because them two half crowns was just about up the spout, and that would mean standing about the billiard saloon or on the corner, instead of going to the pictures with Ada and taking her to the cafe afterwards, and seeing her home.

After all, it was no business of His if Ma was a shoplifter, and besides, even if she was, she had enough sense not to get knocked off by the police. She was no Ma Pearson, with a shiny grease line round the top of her collar and bits of hair hanging out of her hat all round her face, what she was always pushing out of the way with a funny sort of hand, as had the nails all cracked, and kind of purplish and white on the back. Proper smart, Ma was, and knowed for it. Which was why everybody come round the shop when they was down the drain for a nicker or two.

"You're different," He said, and He was surprised His self,

how His voice kind of come up as if He knew every word was true. "I mean, everybody knows you're the best buyer round here. They can't do you. They wouldn't even try. Besides, it's none of my business what you do. Nothing to do with nobody, it ain't. So we come out where we started."

Ma was rolling little balls out of the soft part as comes in the middle of the loaf, and looking at them as if she was deaf. But He knew from the way her head was sort of turned that she never missed a word, and somehow, He knew she was pleased even though her face was like a stove lid for all the life there was in it.

She come alive, all of a sudden, and sent the balls running up the crease in the paper, and her fingers tapped on the black print like a jumping crab.

"You called me a thief," she said, and He knew them two half crowns was safe because of her voice. He knew He only had to push hard enough. "You want to be more careful, you do."

"Well, stone me," He said, and looked up at the damp bit on the ceiling, reaching out quick for the right words to bring them two half crowns safe in His trousers pocket, "who said you was a thief? Eh?"

"You did," Ma says, and slapped one plate atop the other to show how pleased she was, and started grabbing for the knives and forks.

"Go out of it," He says, pushing the chair back behind Him, as if He was so disgusted with the way things was going, they ought to call in the Navy, or something. "Now you're talking proper ridiculous, you are. Just because I try and make a joke out of it, you start getting nasty. I don't know. What did I ought to do, then? Say me prayers or something?"

Ma was like a big black island shutting out the light all round Him, and when she bent across Him for the spoons, He could feel in amongst the darkness how warm she was, same as when He was a kid, sleeping with her.

He knew she was waiting for Him to say some more, and He knew He had her on the sore, somewhere, but He never knew where, and while He was trying to think what it was, He could almost feel her crying out to Him to say something, and stop whatever it was hurting her, like a kid too young to talk proper, howling because a pin was sticking in it without being able to say where.

"I'd like to know how you'd got on if it hadn't been for me," she says, out in the scullery, in the sort of voice as got His eyes all screwed up. "I've done enough for you in me time, I know."

"All right, all right," He says, knowing He was in for about a quarter of an hour of it, from the sound of her. "I know all about it. But I'll be out of me Time, soon, and then I'll show you something. Told you before I'll pay you back. Hundred per cent interest, and all."

Ma made a sound down her nose and turned the tap on full, so that the loose washer started hammering like mad and the bowl started frothing over, till she turned it down again.

"Ain't it about time the landlord had a go at that there blinking tap?" He says. "Makes more row than the Great Eastern, it do."

"You try having a go, for a change," Ma says. "It wouldn't do you no harm at all, it wouldn't. You might be the son of a thief, but that don't stop you doing a job of work."

"Look here, Ma," He says, talking bigger than He felt, by long chalks, "my father wasn't a thief, nor you ain't neither. So give over. You're just talking daft, you are."

"Oh, no I ain't," she says, and she was so sure. "You can leave your father out of it, and all. You start thinking about me, for a change. You called Ma Pearson a thief, just because she's gone inside. All right. What am I? Now then. That's it. What am I?"

Time come down atop of Him like a ceiling full of red hot darts while He tried to think of the right words, and Ma Chalmers's wireless sausaged out squirts of organ like as if the bloke playing it had run out of music, and just thought anything would do as long as it was a row, not knowing what to do for the best, and playing between the cracks case he missed anything.

"You're all right, Ma," He says, talking quick and bright, like, and half shouting to try and lift the feet of the words out of the sliding glue of the organ, which come in useful, because making Him talk louder made Him feel more sure of His self. "Don't matter what I say, do it? Sides, I keep on telling you I was only joking about Ma Pearson. What's it got to do with me, I'd like to know? Good luck to her, I say. If they leave the stuff about where it can be knocked off easy, it's their fault, nobody else's. Any case, they can't make nobody out a thief till they catch 'em, so how you make out I called you a thief, I don't know. It don't stand to reason, now, do it? Be fair, Ma. Now, do it? Eh, Ma?"

It was all right, and it was washing. Smiles jerked up inside Him as wanted to rough His face like wrinkles in a carpet, but He knew the right time was later on, so He swallowed them back again and kind of gripped the skin round His mouth to keep it looking sorry and sort of a bit worried, like.

Ma was trying to follow the bloke on the organ in and out the tune, but she missed him every other note, till come to a finish, she started singing something she made up herself, as sounded like all one long hum, broke off here and there by breathing, and you could see her mind was made up, organ or no organ, she was going to peg out before giving in, even if it played twice as many notes a dozen times louder. Ma was going to have it her way, and that was it.

So while she was running rings round the organ, she was forgetting Him, and them two half crowns was as good as in His pocket, safe as houses. This was just about the right time to start putting His hat on, not too soon, else there might be some funny remarks about coming home late and waking everybody up, or that it was all right laying stinking in bed till the afternoon, but look at the way He flew out the front door.

If He left it a bit too late, she might start going on about the garden again, and how it never even knew what a spade was, or else some job or other of mending, or some nonsense what was all very well for them as liked it, and very nice for some, but not for Him.

Some blokes was never happy unless they had a hammer walloping away at something, or digging up a bit of grass, or fiddling about with a lump of wire or some bright thing or other. Sit up all night at it, some of them would, driving everybody barmy, and come to work next morning, proper wore out, and say they got a hobby.

He believed in letting things alone, like they was, and if they was broke, they was broke, and that was it. But Ma never seemed to get hold of it, somehow. She was always on the run, but she never seemed to get much done, especially when she had her pains, and if He had to start listening to all of them all over again, the cows would be home and dry before He got out of it.

His hat always bothered Him. He never see one in a shop as looked the same when it was on Him. It was proper strange, it was, how a hat would look real smashing on a wax bloke, but when it got on Him, it kind of started being a different shape. Pulling the brim about never did nothing to help, because as fast as it come the way He wanted it to be when He held it, it just sort of cockled its way back again inside ten seconds when He left go of it.

So there He might be, for ten minutes or so, arguing with a lump of felt as never said nothing, never swore, never got sweaty, and yet got its own way in the finish as sure as eggs was eggs. And getting proper savage with it never got you nowhere, neither, because if you pulled too hard, the ribbon round it started tearing again, and a bit more of that would make a right mess of it.

Then Ma would start off again about money growing on trees, and the other old one, about Him waiting till He had a go at buying His own clothes, and He would soon find out how to take care of them, and all that business.

So come to a finish, He shoved it on, and give the front of it a smack down and let it go at that. After all, people would just think He was one of them blokes as puts on a hat and thinks no more about it, a proper careless sort of artist or poetry bloke, as never give a sausage how he looked, and yet managed to look different enough to be picked out quick.

But even supposing the hat was all right, He was only putting it atop a load of pimples, a dirty collar, and five bob, when He got it, so there was a lot to get fussy about. Somehow it started Him off feeling a bit rotten again, not inside His self, but with things He knew and yet never found the right words for. It was funny how He could feel things so easy and yet not know how to put His tongue to it. He often thought about it, but not a lot of good come out of it. The feeling just got worse, that was all, so lately He got a bit more sense and give it the go by, and got on with thinking about something else, like Ada.

"Ma," He says, as if He was lifting every word on a butterfly, "how do we go for a couple of your nice little half dollars, today, eh? I'm so broke I'm three halfs."

"What, again?" Ma says, and it made you angry just to hear her say it. "I don't know what you do with your money, I'm sure. If I went on the way you're going, we'd be in a fine old pickle, we would. You're seeing a bit too much of that there Len Tate, that's what's the matter with you."

"Len Tate," He says, as though He was asking His self a question, but hanging on to it as long as He could to get the right excuse. Proper marvellous, it was, the way it sort of come without having to dig for it, as though there was a bloke shouting it in His ear. "I don't have nothing to do with no Len Tate, Ma. I meet him now and again, of course. I mean, he's always round the neighbourhood. Oh no," He come down a bit weighty just there, to try and give it a bit of stiffening, "I want it to get some paints with. I want to finish off the landscape while the light's all right, see?"

"No," Ma says, like putting a frying pan in the sink, "I don't see nothing, I don't. Where you going to get paints from of a Sunday afternoon, eh? Eh?"

"Old Nick Falandora," He says, as though He was being proper hard done by. But He knew He was on the wrong horse soon as He said it. Ma smacked the plate in the water and the dish cloth atop of it.

"Nick Falandora?" she says. "After all what your father done for that dirty swine, he goes charging you up for paints, does he?"

"No, Ma," He says, "he ain't charging me for ordinary paints. They're special ones, see? These old blokes, they got the secret of how to get them, you know, kind of secret dyes and things. Proper marvellous, they are. He's learning me, see? But I want these ones this afternoon to get this picture finished and sell it. Then I can pay you back a bit, see Ma?"

"I'll scratch him off a line or two tonight as'll learn him a thing or two, and all," Ma says. "When I think of all the years your father slaved down there, and what he done for them, and what he got for it, and what I've got, I got a good mind to go down there tomorrow morning and give him and Tomlin a piece of my mind what they won't forget in a hurry, I can tell you."

"Wouldn't do no good, Ma," He says, very tired. "For one thing, I'd get it served up for the next six months, hot, and as soon as I come out of my Time, they'd give me the boot. Sides, I want to know what Old Nick knows. Then I'll start me own business here. Don't you understand, Ma? You got to be cunning to get anywhere these days. You got to use your loaf, see? It's no good of me having a row with my bread and butter, is it?"

It was washing again.

He knew it was all right, because Ma was easy when it come to business, in pounds, shillings and pence, and bread and butter. There was no argument. Two half dollars to take Ada out would have started a riot, but to get things coming His way later on, that was a different story. Nor she never had the sense to ask for a look at the paints, neither, so He never made a mistake after all. In fact, it looked as though this new idea about the paints was going to do Him a nice bit of good, because it could go on for weeks and weeks if He played His cards right.

"Under the right hand vase on the mantelpiece," she says. "Five bob enough?"

"Well," He says, proper jumping somewhere inside of Him, "it'll cost me one and twopence for me fares to get there. But I can walk all right. Unless I get back late, of course."

"There's eight and a tanner under that there vase on the right hand side," Ma says. "Leave the shilling case I want it for the gas."

"Okeedoke, Ma," He says, "seven and a tanner for yours truly. I shan't forget you, Ma. You wait till I start up on me own. I'll show you."

"If you get back late," Ma says, talking over a lot of washing up, with slops of water and bashing of plates, "the key'll be under the mat. I ain't crawling out of bed after you again."

"Depends on how long Nick keeps me nattering," He says, and it was funny how everything come the colour of almost marigolds when He could feel them three half crowns in His pocket and think to His self how much more He could do with three than two. He could have a go at every machine in the Fun Fair, and not miss it, and get change from Ada every time in the bargain. Proper lovely to think of, it was, and He never knew how sorry He was for Ma till He come to say something nice to get Him out of it without too much of a hurry. "Well," He says, sort of slow, as if He was bleeding to death, "I suppose I've got to go. I could have had a go at that there garden this afternoon, and all. Only Nick said I ought to start this new stuff, so there you are. Can't do nothing about it. It's just got to be done in me own time, so I've got to make the best of it. So long, Ma. Shan't be late."

Ma was looking at the dishwater as if it was a lily pond. Against the white shiny stone of the sink, her fists was like bunches of red plums, but her arms was whitish, thick as legs, and pinched in where her blouse caught her a bit too tight above the elbows, and made a very wide white line where the blood got no room to pass proper.

"So long, son," Ma says, kind of twisting her head at the

water, "I'll leave you a drop of hot in the kettle to wash some of the paint off with."

He was through the passage and right on top of the kitchen door knob still sitting in the hole in the lino before she got it all out, and there was something about the way she said it as pulled Him up. It sounded as though she was on to something, but if she was, He says to His self, while He looked in the umbrella stand glass again, them three half dollars would still have been squatting under the vase alongside the shilling.

His hat still looked nothing like He wanted, but the money was there, just beginning to get warm against His leg, so everything was all right.

He give the knob a little kick, not loud enough for Ma to hear, just enough to send it in the corner out of harm's way, case He fell over it when He come in, because a china door knob is a slippery sort of thing to step on in the dark, and life was hard enough without coming in for a couple of busted legs or a double rupture, or some other fine thing. Especially His age.

Opening the front door nice and quiet, He had a good sniff at the air what was blowing at Him, but he never thought of nothing except Ada, only Ada, and three half dollars, and them red finger nails of hers and His big toe what was getting itself bit off sharp by the hole in His sock.

And for once in His life, the street looked proper marvellous, friendly as anything and full of this here funny sort of gold light same as what marigolds, the pale ones, is made of, somehow. Yet the sun was in, not out, and the only marigolds He knew of was in Ma Chalmers's garden. The shine, it was, not the colour, what was there, up and down the street, full of it, like as if all the lamps was alight. Proper lovely to be alive, and Him, it was, with music from somewhere beating up under His heels, and three nice little half dollars having a game in His pocket.

# CHAPTER III

THE LITTLE tobacco sign down at the corner was winking a lovely blue at Him, swinging away in the wind as happy as you like, bringing down lumps of sky every time it come up and dropping it in the road on the way down, with a whistle He could hear soon as He turned out of the door. All the railings both sides of the road bobbed up and down with Him as if they was all the same mind as He was, and even the gutterings at the tops of the houses all waved about as if they was in it with the tobacco sign and the newspaper placard, what had kicked itself loose from one corner, and told everybody no wire frame was going to hold it for long, because it was off on a sail the first minute it could, and anybody liking to join in was welcome.

The brewery down the end of the road nigh the gas works was smoking a large brick cigar, and blowing the smoke over the church steeple, what stuck the top of its nose in the air as if it had made up its mind not to notice anything, nor cough, even if it died for it.

Ma Fadden come off second best with her pots of fern in the front room window because they was all gone yellow, which was a bit of a pity, and no fault of hers, if you thought of the times you passed and see her giving them a drink, out of the white jug, what young Bessie was always fetching the beer home in.

Jim Salmons had give his front door a coat of orange in the week, and grained it up in dark brown and yellow, so it looked very cheerful, it did, for a Sunday afternoon, but sort of like a bad place on your arm as tries hard to heal up the same colour as the rest of you, but wants a bit more time to get over the raw look.

Across the road, all the doors was just about the same colour all the way down to the corner, all except Aggie Hunner's, and that was pea green with twelve months wear on it. But after all, she was knowed to be a bit off, with her hair cut short and low shoes, and a big fiddle she humped about in a green bag and practised on till twelve o'clock at night, till the neighbours had to crash on the walls with a boot to make her stop.

Her friends was a queer lot, and all, most of them like she was, but the blokes was a proper fancy lot, rolling up in cars for the most part, shouting and acting about in funny kind of queeny voices and having a rare old time, as if they was all out for the day. Specially down at the pub, where they always bought the beer in a bath, and a couple of floor buckets, like as though it made the evening, and a proper grand do was being had by all comers. If they knew what was thought of them, they might have took another place to have their parties in, but just the same, He often wished He was inside the pea green door among the laughing what was going on, just to see what they was doing, even though He thought they was a proper lot of mugs.

Dad Fitchett's gate was still broke, He see, but the top hinge had given up at last, so it just leaned against the fence, not tired, but just having a breather, like an old dear putting her shopping bag down in the middle of the pavement to catch up with herself, and rub her hand, like Ma Chalmers done, sometimes. Catch Dad Fitchett mucking about with a gate, and besides, it was easier to walk in.

Charlie Floom's barber shop was nice to pass because of the girl in the swimming costume looking at you to buy fags. Lovely drop of stuff, she was, and proper juicy. Old Charlie kept her there, even though she was fading a bit, to spite Ma Floom, because some bloke, and they said it was old Charlie his self, shaded her with a pencil, and when Ma Floom saw it in the window she nigh on give birth there and then. But old Charlie said it was his lucky mascot, and after it got round, the customers come miles to see the Girl Without One, because Ma had rubbed out the pencil, and the printing with it, so there was a bare patch where It Ought To Be, so you could think what you liked.

Poor old Ma Floom got her leg pulled something cruel when-ever they called in the pub of a Saturday night, and the jokes they made up for her benefit would turn your hat round. Ma always said she would rather be dead and in her grave than be Ma Floom with all them jokes. But just the same, Charlie done a smashing trade and had a car of his own, and all the kids went to the Poly, or somewhere posh, so they was all right for nicker, jokes or no jokes.

Merry and Bright, old Dad Prettyjohn called his shop, and so it was and all. It give you a shout soon as you got in the road, and though all the shops was the same, there was no miss-ing of Dad Prettyjohn's, because where the others was two stories, shop and upstairs, he nailed up boards along the gut-tering of his to make it look like three stories, and used the space for adverts what he got paid for, so his nut was screwed on right.

A fine old chuckle of colour it was, too, and lashings of it, no expense spared. Yellow and blue doors and windows, red round the sign, M. Prettyjohn, in what was gold leaf once, with a green lining, purple and white pillars up the sides of the shop to the top of the advert boards, and all the rest of the shop front filled up with posters for everything from soup to razor blades, except for two holes cut out for the upstairs windows, and there was red cloth geraniums in green boxes, with white diamonds painted round the sides, in both of them, and stained glass paper over the panes, so everything had a go.

Dad Prettyjohn was never knowed to wear a shirt, or collar and tie. He only wore a yellowish wool vest sewed down the front, with a waistcoat over it, always unbuttoned and held together with his watch chain, ratty sailor's trousers with a lot of wasted cooking on them, and old tartan slipslops with the toes cut out to give his corns a treat. He said he never see no use of lumbering his self up with a lot of clobber, and but-tons was always coming off, so he give it all up years ago and had no trouble since, and getting up of a morning come a pleasure stead of a handicap.

Proper lad, old Dad was, and look at you over his half moon

gold glasses, he would, and if he liked your looks you could have what you wanted. But if he thought you was a mug, or your face was the wrong shape, you got told your fortune in sailor's language, and out you went, big or small, never mind how much you wanted to spend. He made Ma laugh so much when she went in there for her groceries, she never knew how to get home, and when she did, she was proper weak and pie eyed with crying laughing.

Sid Boulby's Select Dining Rooms you could tell with your eyes shut, by all the warm smell of kind of years of pepper being shook over steaming spuds and cabbage, and thousands of knives digging in the salt and getting beat with the fork to shake it nice and smooth over the steak and kidney pud, and the dark bright green brussels sprouts very hard and nigh bitter with juice, and poached eggs like suns in skies of white glass, and thick rounds of toast dipped in big mugs narrower at the bottom than they was at the top with no saucers and pink rims, full up of sweet orange tea as scalded you. Give your guts a proper treat it did, to go past and niff, because you thought you could smell everything everybody ever eat in the world.

The windows was always steamed over, so it made the white enamel letters plainer than ever, even though some of them was missing. Good Pull Up for Carmen, was one, and Courtesy, Civility, and Cleanliness underneath it, and then Best cups of Tea in the District, All Pots, No Urns Used. On the other side, with the swing door in the middle, there was Good Nourishing Dinners for Working Men, Every Satisfaction Guaranteed, and All Fresh Meat, No Chilled, and Veg Bought Fresh Daily. Then across the top of the door, under Sid Boulby's Select Dining Rooms, was Under the Personal Management of Prop. He had a lovely business, Sid had, crowded out all day, he was, and the vans and lorries was waiting all round the side roads, sometimes down as far as the school. A nice smelling, clean, lots of grubsy place it was, and the sawdust still looked fresh even after half past two, after thousands of them had been in there for their dinners and come out again.

Ma Crann kept the newspaper shop at the corner with her

four girls, though how she ever got through a day, let alone a year, was a proper mystery. It was give out she had the cancer and no hospital would look at her, so she stayed in the shop when all the girls was out on their rounds or over at the pictures, looking like as if she had five minutes to go. All sort of dark right round her eyes, she was, and her teeth was all showing because her mouth never seemed to be able to get itself closed up because the skin was too tight, and she wore a little black hat all the time because all her hair had fell out.

# CHAPTER IV

THE HIGH ROAD done Him good to be in, with the tram lines sliding round the corner like butcher's hooks polished up special for the afternoon, gutters full of paper, and orange peel, and old apples, and cabbage leaves, and bits of boxes and crushed punnets from the market last night, and the pavements almost hid by blokes in their Sunday's best out for a stroll to give the brides a going over, to see if it was worth while taking them in the pictures for the night.

Proper cheerful crowd they was, and all, yelling out to their pals across the traffic, some of them, and chucking lumps of orange peel if they felt like it, just to show there was no ill feeling. Walking in threes and fours most of them was, because it give them more of a chance to chat the brides when they was spread over the pavement, like, and it worked, too, what was more. You could get off with a bride easy enough if you played your cards proper, but if you done it all wrong, you stood a good chance of getting a smack in the nose from one or the other of them, and it was no use of being sorry afterwards.

So all the jokes, and pretending to stop them passing, was all done very careful although it looked kind of loose and easy, and, as you might say, a bit rough. But the brides liked it all right, or some of them did, and they could do their fair share of slinging jokes about, too, to say nothing about a quiet bit of shoving here and there, as might have you sliding under a bus if you got careless, and took your eye off the job in hand.

It was a right treat to look in the Thirty Bob tailors shop on the turn in the road. It was so big, and everything was so posh and shiny, with lots of glass and brass, and so cheap, you was proper surprised every time you had a look round to see what they could do for the money. For two quid you could get a suit as made your mouth flush out, straight up and no larks.

Navy blue serges with lovely stripes, there was, and smashing nigger browns, and tweed sports coats in all the colours you could think of, all of them showed on dummies as had the faces of the film stars, all laughing, and looking right boys with their hats a one side, and giving you a proper sort of itch inside of you to get one and look like them.

But the trouble come when you had to make up your mind which one to have. So you just had to keep walking round the windows like everybody else was, and try to see your self in the blue double breasted serge, in the corner, with a proper lovely waist and high shoulders, or the grey double breasted, round in the passage going up to the main door, or else the nigger brown with wide fish tail lapels as come down to button with a link in the middle, or else the light sort of blue tweed plus fours, what you had to wear stockings with, or perhaps the blue sports jacket with smashing patch pockets and grey flannel trousers. And after a lot of that, and shoving through the other blokes all having a boss at them, you just give up and come out on the pavement again, beat, and in the sunlight out of the shady blinds, you saw your self as you was, sort of faint, like as if somebody had took a suck of you and breathed you on the glass.

But it was enough to turn you up, what you could see of your self, with your trousers nowhere near creased in two halfs, and your coat fitting you where it liked, and all sorts of black-ish creases chopping you up in bits proper ugly, and to crown it all, your lovely hat as looked like a owl's nest for all the good it done you.

So it started Him off feeling out of it again, specially because them there three little half dollars, what felt a proper mint down the road, up here was only a little bit of what He had to have to buy only one of them there suits, even the cheapest. And even then there was the hat to buy. And shoes. And a collar and tie. And the tie would have to sort of match the suit, like it said in the fashion column.

So by the time He come nigh the jewellers, He was proper down the dumps and feeling something wicked, He was. It seemed to Him that if He was helpless about getting even a suit for His self, there was a precious fat chance of getting Ada even to see He was alive, let alone talk to Him. And as for going out with Him, well, even to Him, it sounded barmy, three half dollars or not. 590483

And besides, looking at the diamond rings in marvellous orange velvet trays, all of a white sparkle, and pale bluish and reddish glitter, and flash, like a bride's eyes when she laughs and the light kind of catches the tears in the corners, only more of it and harder somehow, He knew He stood no chance of buying one of them, take the big one in the middle as never flashed at all, till you got your head one side of it, then it nigh blinded you with a white and green and red and blue handful of long flashing fingers as reached out through the plate glass and dug you gentle sort of lovely in the eye. Even if you felt sorry for your self not having it, or even ever seeing the skies above it, you had to like it, because it sort of left a hole in your very heart.

All the false teeth in the dentist show case looked yellower and bonier than He noticed before, and the pink gums was like icing on a stale cake. The top and bottom set, like a laugh without a face, was saying what a mug they thought He was, and a proper suit of machinery to stick in your gob, they was, too. It seemed to Him they was saying out loud how He ought to go upstairs and get a tooth jerked for a bit of enjoyment, and get a smile back on His dial again. It would have been a piece of cake to put a brick through them.

He was feeling proper wore out with misery by the time He got to the tobacconists next door to the Fun Fair, and although the pavements was full of people, they was all just a lot of shadows He somehow missed in the warm white sunlight, and all of them there little white bits was even smaller, proper powdered up, so they made a sort of sunny fog as all the talking shadows went in and out of, with more coming up behind to take their place, and He hated all the whole lot of them, and His self and all.

So He went inside the dark tobacconists, where some old

bloke was reading the paper behind the counter with the help of a shaky little blue and yellow feather sticking out of the gas jet, as tickled up the darkness and made it laugh all round.

"Afternoon," says the bloke, sort of chatty, as if he was lonely and ready to make a meal of it. "Lovely day again, ain't it?"

"Not bad," He says, and He was looking along the shelves full of every kind of fag you could think of, Russians, and Turkeys, and Gippos, everything, in all sorts of colours and lovely and tidy packed, with the bacca jars underneath in rows with big gold numbers on them, as was almost wore off, and the snuff jars on the side, out of wood, and shiny with wear. Soon as He see all them, He was worse off than ever, because His three little halfs was no use here. He could buy one packet of fags, the cheapest of them all, out of the whole lot. And that was it.

Then He got proper wild, He did, because He thought the bloke was looking at Him as if He was up to no good, so He had to put a Little Bit On to make him understand he was wrong.

"What cigars you got?" He says, knowing He was putting His foot in it, but something inside Him was driving Him on.

"Cigars?" the bloke says, and pulled his nose proper hard, looking round the shop as if he was made of them. "Well, as it so happens, I got a very lovely stock of them, but the wife's gone over to a friend of hers in Clapham, and took the keys with her. And you're the second one in here this afternoon after a cigar, and here am I, standing here like Joe Soap, and I can't give you one. Can't take your money, I can't. See?" He reached over and tried to get his nails in the crack of the cupboard door. "That's locked, that is. And here am I, Soap, turning money away. But," he says it very slow, with his head a one side and looking proper serious through his glasses, with his finger wagging about, "you just wait till she puts her foot through that there door. That's all."

And from the looks of him, it looked as if the old bird was going to cop a right packet, by and large.

"Okeedoke," He says, sort of tired, "I'll go down the road for some. What else you got?"

"I got a Burma cheroot," the bloke says, but the way He says it, you could smell it burning and turning everybody up, till somebody called the police.

"Not for me," He says, as if He knew them out of sight. "Got more respect for my guts, I have. No," He says, very man of the world, "best or worst for me. Nothing in between. Give us a large Woods."

"Large Woods, a gentleman," the bloke says, and picked up the half dollar as if it was just a half dollar and not the first of three waving its pals goodbye. It proper hurt Him to see it throwed in the till, and when the drawer shut with the sound of a bell in it, He could see the green plaster girl and heard her ring again. And almost as soon, them red finger nails come tearing at Him inside Him, and Ada was near Him again.

After all, there was a tidy bit of change to pick up, and two half dollars not even touched, twenty nice little smokes to the good, and all the afternoon to play about next door. There was nothing to be worried about, come to think of it like that, because even if He had the money, even a million pound, no tailor could make Him a suit that there very moment, and as for the diamond ring, there was bags of time for that when it was a case of getting engaged.

So there He was, just His self, a artist very near, or He would be when He was out of His Time, in a artist's clothes, sort of old and loose and easy, wearing one of them sort of careless hats what was a pal for years, as you could never find the heart to chuck away, case of bad luck. Putting it like that, He felt all right again, and even got cocky with it.

"Okeedoke," He says, "don't be too hard on the old duck, will you? She might have done me a favour, you never know. Sides, who's over in Clapham? Somebody taking her mind off of business? Got a lodger, have you?"

"Ah," says the old bloke, pulling his nose till it come up all red at the end, "ah, there you are, you see. I wish there was, I don't mind telling you. It'd save me a lot, a lot, mark you, of money, to get shut of her nice and quiet, like." Then he started laughing a bit, and his teeth was very pretty, what there was of them, a sort of creased brown. "But we've all got our crosses to bear, ain't we? It's a proper lark, all round."

"That's right," He says, and come out of it, in the sun again, lighting up a fag, thinking how it must have been to live in the dark all your life with a little yellow and blue feather flicking about under your nose, and the smell of cartons of fags mixed with snuff and menthol and packet shag deep in your head, a wife you wished you was shut of, and them teeth, as must have been lovely for the old girl, so no wonder she went off to Clapham.

He stood outside the Fun Fair for a minute, knowing it was there but taking no notice of it, and it was the same nice comfy kind of feeling you get when you got a big juicy beef sandwich in your fist, and you look round for a minute or two to feel how it feels to be hungry, and all the time your mouth is falling over itself, dying to have a go.

The trams come past in sliding blushes of scarlet and breathed on Him, so hard, the brim of His hat blowed up and stayed up, and so did the ends of His collar, and His trousers was pressed flat against His legs, while He was smelling that funny sort of tram ticket, people, hub grease and sparking electricity niff what you get aboard trams and nowhere else, what they leave behind them in a small chunk to hit you under the nose. But when you try to find it with a second breath the tram is down the road and so is the smell. And here you are, sniffing like a sooner, and looking a proper dream with your trousers wrinkled flat against your legs, and your hat turned up in front.

So He pushed it on the back of His head with His thumb, and sort of like as if He wanted it like that, with the brim up in front, not giving a couple of pennyworth what nobody thought. But as He went nice and steady towards the top step of the Fun Fair, He was watching out for somebody giving Him a grin, and His ears was on the end of long arms, listening for somebody being funny.

Although there was plenty of people about, and a lot of the right boys ready to take the mike out of anybody for anything, nobody never said a word, in fact, they was looking everywhere but Him, which was funny, because when He had a screw at His self in the glass on the side of the stairway going down, He give His self a proper shock, what with the look of His hat and the way the rotten thing was on, and His clock all dolled up with a collection of pimples and Christ knows what, and His collar all screwed up and His tie in rags, and Him looking at His self as if He seen something horrible come crawling out the wall.

This all had to be put right before He see Ada, so He dodged behind the weighing machine at the bottom of the stairs, and started pulling His self about, tucking things in here, and pulling things in there, and getting His marvellous hat a bit more like it.

But He knew, while He was doing it, He was over the wall. So all of a sudden, while a little sort of cloud come down very cold and heavy and fitted over His head, like a doughnut with a hole in the middle, He give up, and come out, and shoved the hat in His side pocket. He was a artist, that was what He was, and they could think what they liked if they wanted to, and even if they did, all they could say was He was untidy and a bit roughed up, and He could say it was His work as done it, and so it was, too.

But He was a bit rocky about Ada. It was what she said, and when and how she said it as counted, not nobody else.

So instead of going straight to her line of machines, He went the other way, round by the dart shows, towards the fortune teller, under the arch painted none too well to look like rock.

## CHAPTER V

EVER SINCE IT OPENED at eleven o'clock the place had been doing a smashing business, so now it was full of blokes, mostly, though there was a few brides about, as you could hear from the row they was kicking up, somewhere. All the loud speakers in the place was going as hard as they could, pushing out the jazz so the bloke as sung the words sounded like as if he was sixty foot high with a chest on him like corrugated iron, but you soon got used to it and it made things more kind of comfy somehow. It sounded sort of empty when it stopped a minute, and you see blokes looking round, hoping it would come on again quick. Besides, it was the best place to learn the words of the latest songs, because they was played so many times while you was in there, it was a piece of cake to pick them up.

All the dart shows was full, and it made Him kind of happy to see the colours of the dartboards, all lit by white globes, with the white stabs of the darts flying at them and the shining wire of the dividing lines, and all the lovely prizes grouped on both sides, china vases painted up with flowers, and big dolls, and clocks, and cases of spoons, and things. There was no doubt about it, you got your value there, but darts never was His pigeon so He always give it a miss.

Next up was the rifle range which was more like it, although He must have spent a fortune before He got any good at it. But He was good enough to get the bulls now when He wanted them, so that was why the bloke running it always waved Him off, kind of good natured, like, to stop Him having a go if there was nobody there. But if there was a crowd, He got a go for nothing, so that His card could be pinned on the board to show the mugs how easy it was. That was how He won the green plaster girl, and the alarm clock on the mantelpiece downstairs.

The bloke tipped Him the wink as He passed so He went over there, going through the blokes as if He was by His self, in a empty street.

"Here He is, gents," yells the bloke, "best shot of the district and all done here. Here's a man as used His loaf. He can take care of His self and His family, any time there's a bit of barney anywhere. Safe all over the world, He is, and respected. Kindly note the last word. Respected, I said."

He holds up the rifle like as if it was worth a thousand quid, in both hands, and handed it over very gentle.

"There," he says, "now watch the fur fly, gents. Quiet, please, while the shots are took, and I'll mark them through the glass. All paid and all weighed? Eyes down, look in."

There was something proper nice about getting your elbows set to shoot, where them points on the end of them can sort of miss hurting you, and then putting the rifle in your shoulder, while you close one eye and try to get the little black bloke on the end of it to stop wagging about between the V of the back-sight, all the time knowing them blokes behind you are watching you, and hoping you do it all wrong, to give them a chance to pass funny remarks.

But it was fruit cake with nuts to get the bulls home, and when He finished, the bloke never said nothing till he reeled the target in and had it in his hands, and all the time he looked like a bishop having a go at a shower of savages.

"There," he says, and holds it up where everybody can screw, "five shots a tanner, and all of them where they ought to be, in the little black hole of Calcutta. I told you who He was, and this is Him. Your fags, governor," he says, and hands over a ten, "and good luck to you. Who's next for a tanners-worth?"

He come out the crowd feeling a proper boy, and they was looking at Him as if they thought so and all, even though a couple of them had new suits on, and one of them got a double breast waistcoat like He seen up at the Thirty Bob, with a smashing shirt with sort of grey and red stripes, and two pins in his collar, one under the other, to kind of strangle his tie and keep it where he wanted it. He wondered why He never thought of it before.

Just round the corner was Madame La Zaka, a very umpty bit of stuff from somewhere or other, not young or old, but fattish, and always done up like a rabbit stew, with veils and things, beads and bracelets, and points on her slippers as turned up in front.

From the looks of her place, you might think it was a proper right hole for getting half murdered in, but once inside the black curtains, with a skull swinging about outside with a blue electric light in it, you was due for a nasty disappointment because the place was so small, a three cornered affair where two walls come together. By the time Ma Zaka was squatted, you had the wrong end of you sticking out the curtains, so all the time you was in there, trying to make out what she was on about, you was waiting for some bright herbert to take a first timer at you, and it sort of spoilt the proceedings.

So when you come out, you was as wise as you was when you went in, almost, and a bob worse off, but so thankful you missed the boot, it was worth twice the money for the feeling. She had a dekko at your hands in there, under a red light.

Then you come out in the main room, and it was a smasher.

Everything was shining white with light, glass, chromium, looking glasses, everything was sparkling, wherever you looked it was glittering, flashing, a real do of light as must have cost a fortune in electric light bills.

But the first thing about it was the happiness in the place. You had pals wherever you looked. The whole caboodle was having a laugh, or seemed like it, and it was easy to start a laugh, and have one yourself, even if you was outside the joke. Lovely to get in there, it was, and stroll about, whether you had the nicker to play a machine or not. You never see people looking so pleased with their selfs, except perhaps outside the cinema when the queue was getting ready to go in the nines when the first house was coming out, or else when you was inside, and the lights come on just before the big picture.

Enjoying their time, they was, and that was why He liked

getting in there with them, instead of hanking about outside where you was either driving your self barmy about something, or else somebody was doing it for you.

He went down the steps slow, like, feeling the smiles come on when He got to the bottom, not only because it looked and sounded as if everybody else was smiling, but Ada and them red beetles was just behind the first lot of machines, so it was a matter of seconds till He see her, and got that sort of hot jump in the guts He always got when she got near enough for Him to touch her, if only she let Him.

And the music was lovely, just right it was, slow, sort of getting hold of you with one hand and smarming you down with the other, like a bride going all soft and pressing herself up against you, till you never knew if you was going or coming. And the drums was just doing a whisper like a little drop of rain, and the tune was cutting through somewhere inside of you like a warm fretsaw made of sweet, red jelly, and some bloke was surrendering, dear, and not caring, like He felt about Ada.

Just exactly like He felt about Ada.

And there she was.

# CHAPTER VI

SHE WAS LOVELY, she was grand, a proper, right, straight up smasher of a bride, she was, and what was more, knew it, and glad of it, and bleeding good luck to her.

It done you good just to stand there and watch her, specially when she was quiet, and looking at something she was holding under the ledge, and when she turned the pages over she never give her thumb a lick like a lot of others done, but done the job right and followed the page all round till it come apart itself, and when she blew at it to help things along, the shape of her mouth went, like a flower or something, it was, sort of made you go all of a tremble very near.

Her hair was a funny kind of colour as you could hardly lay your tongue to. It was very fair, yellow, but not one of them dirty yellows, and not a yellow as walloped you in the eye, but yellow just the same, with a lot of polish on it, so it shone up like a quiet lovely light, and she done it plain so it come down sort of wavy, not curly, to her shoulders, parted a one side, so half or more of it kept getting slung across her face, and when she took a dekko at you like that, you nigh on had a go of heart failure. Blue eyes, she had, pale blue they looked, as big as two bob pieces, with eyelashes thicker than some blokes moustaches, and they come round at you on the slant, like as if she was wondering what your little game was, and how far she had to go before it come to sloshing you one.

The rest of her was all on the same level, more or less, plenty of it though not too much, in a manner of speaking, and all of it classy stuff, and she nearly always put it in a red wool jersey and a black skirt, fitted tight so as not to get caught up in anything. So when she walked, which she done very light, half of her going first and the other half catching it up and passing it, proper chase me Charlie, she just about laid you out to watch her.

She was a proper bramah, a smasher, a right one, growed in the garden.

It was dead funny to watch the blokes playing her lot of machines. You could see they was all, well all, that is, except the old blokes as had gone past it, as you might say, trying to play the one nearest to where she sat, about a yard from her, and if you wanted to see a fight, you only had to wait long enough, till some bloke had done about a tannersworth on it, played slow, and then some other bloke would get tired of waiting and if he was bigger or fancied his chance, he just come along and nipped his penny in before Number One. Then there was a scrimmage, or not, as the case might be, depending on Number One.

If there was, Ada just got up and walked down the other end, while the gents was having it out, and when the chuckers out had been in, and gone out again, she come back and sat down as if she never even shifted.

But while the blokes played that machine they watched her, sort of under their hats, or the peaks of their caps, and them as come out bare just had a good look now and again. Some of the flash boys just stood there and had a proper old dekko, and tried to be funny and make her laugh. Then she just got up and walked down to the next girl to ask her to keep an eye on the machines, and went down the Ladies for a few minutes till somebody give her the eye that the half hard comic had sloped, and then she come out, and sat down, and the game went on, as before.

She sat on a cane chair, she did, on a ledge about a yard high as run behind the machines, and she had a till as she give you change out of, because the machines only took a penny. You put one in a slot, and give a knob a pull, and five big silver balls come out, one after the other, what you shot up a little alley to try and hit some numbers. If you hit them right, these here numbers come up in electric lights and if you got over 30,000, you got a free packet of fags. But everybody knew them machines was cooked. You had as much chance of getting your fags as a five pound rise, but them machines took more than all the rest put together.

Ada done that.

There was a bit about two foot square cut out of the ledge where the till was, so you could see more of her when you played the machine opposite to her. You only had to get a bit to one side, and watch the blokes playing it, for a proper good laugh out of the way they capered about, not moving, except to play a ball, but just looking, and pretending they was doing everything else but.

It was the red jersey as done it. Proper caused it, that did. It was so tight, and showed up everything, like.

Ada did, Ada had the most marvellousest pair of tits, you ever see in all your puff, like tennis balls with spikes on, they was, that round and hard, and sort of handy, like, and the second you looked at them, you was blinded with science.

And that was what all the blokes was looking at, and of course, at what there was of her legs, if she crossed them and forgot to pull her skirt over proper. Then you see about a couple of inches of sort of pinkish whitish skin between the top of her stocking and the start of her drawers as had lace round the bottoms, so by the time you had your share of that too, you was just about right, and hit for a nice fat six.

So He always come in slow to see which way the wind was blowing, what competition there was, like, who was there, because He knew the regulars by heart, but some was bigger than others, how many was in the queue, and how long He was going to wait before it come His turn, what Ada was dressed in, and if she was chatting somebody.

It was almost never she even looked at a bloke, but sometimes she chatted a bloke she knew, but He noticed she never laughed or looked pleased with herself, nor He never seen her dive for the powder puff, like she would have done if the bloke was in her good books, as they say.

She was by herself, as per, reading something, as per, and dressed in the same old jersey, as per.

In fact, Ada was as per, and a joy to behold, as per.

While he was mucking about with one of the cranes, a sort of big glass affair with a pair of pincers on a arm inside of it, what you swung round to try and pull up some of the prizes, small clocks and spoons and things, a proper load of junk it was, He was trying to watch her, and see what He was doing of at the same time, but like all two jobs at once stunts, it never come off.

She looked up quick and see Him looking at her, and started reading again as if He was part of the wallpaper, and He was that there shook about, He started trembling, sort of, and dropped the whole lot what He had hold of, and lost His turn at her machine in the bargain.

So there went a tanner down the drain hole, and what was more, she knew He was there, and never even give Him eye room, never mind about the sort of little smile, well, not quite a smile perhaps, but a kind of nod and a sort of a kind of a friendly look in her eyes, same as she give Him last time, as He thought He might always get from then on, till it grew up in a smile as showed her teeth.

It was no use of Him trying to kid her no more, and He was past kidding His self, so He went across to the line of machines slow, not rushing it, as if time was no object, but the nearer He got, the more He felt her, as if she was as near as she had been that morning, and the closer He come, the more she seemed to hurt, till He felt His self sort of going all sloppy inside somewhere, and He was proper miserable, and yet happy enough not to want to be anywhere else.

It come His turn on her machine soon as He got to it, so He went through His pockets very slow, to make it last out, trying to make it look as if money was His second name, and when He come to the pair of halfs and the change of the third, He give it a good shake up to make it sound like a proper bank, and run his nail round the edge of one of the halfs to make sure He had hold of it, and not a penny.

It made a very nice noise when He picked it out and let the

rest of it all go, and He was feeling just about all right when He give it across the glass of the machine, and tapped it on the woodwork at the top to get her eyes off of the book, and on Him.

"Change here, please Miss," He says, as if He never seen her in His life before and never give her a thought even if He did.

She puts the book down on the floor, and while she uncrossed her legs to get at the till, she cocked one up higher than the other and He see right up her clouts for a split second or more, the wide parts of pale skin aside both of her legs, and straps as come down from somewhere and fastened her stockings with shiny round clip sort of things, and the little bit of lace round her drawers, all there, all old pals, all giving Him a shout, as if them and Him was in it together and voting for Ada.

The half dollar got swallowed by red beetles and one of them pressed the till and brought out the drawer. In went the half, and the red beetles scratted about in the pennies, three, six, took out a two bob bit, shoved the drawer shut, and come a bit closer to Him.

"Your change?" Ada said, with a question in it, as if she wanted to be sure He was the right bloke, but too tired to look at Him to make sure, and besides she wanted to get back to her book.

But though He heard her voice, and knew this was His chance to try and get another of them nice looks from her, He was looking at them beetles, and His eyes was sort of stuck to them, sort of proper stuck, they was, even though they was a matter of a couple of foot away.

Long, oval, with sharp points, they was, and red, redder than blood, smooth and shiny, moving about on the ends of her fingers, up and down while the pennies clicked and clinked between them, flat round brown pennies, so lucky to be in amongst them lovely red beetles, falling atop one another in a fine old game, enjoying every second of it, like Him, if them beetles ever got hold of Him, them long, shiny, oval red beetles as moved so slow on the ends of her fingers.

All of a sudden they stopped moving. They was quite still, shining quiet red, waiting.

The music stopped and all.

All you could hear was the sound of the machines being played, and somebody having a go on the rifle range, nothing very loud, sort of machiney sounds, whizzes and things, balls going along wood, and a bloke in the darts alley shouting out for customers, sounding from the size of his voice easy two inches high.

"What's up?" says Ada, and something inside of Him shot in two halfs like a busted lump of cotton, because there was a sort of a laugh in her voice and He knew if He done it right He could get her chatting.

"They're lovely, they are," He says. "Proper lovely. I never knew finger nails could be so lovely, straight up."

"What?" she says, sort of interested, and out of the sides of His eye He see a bloke coming up to play a machine, and blinded him for it, but the bloke went on one at the end.

"Them there finger nails," He says, still not looking at her, and knowing she wanted Him to.

All the beetles, both hands, turned their selfs up for Ada to have a look at, then the two big ones on her thumbs, all of them red, quiet, and shining. They moved again, spread out and waggled about a bit.

"Don't see much in them," she says. "Bit of red enamel, that's all." The beetles come at Him and plonked the change on the glass. "Here you are, half a crown, right."

"Wish you'd let me paint them," He says, quick, to get it in before the music come on again and drownded Him out, and what was more, before she grabbed hold of the book. He looked up at her and she was looking him smack in the eye, sort of weighing Him up, not in a nasty kind of a way, but like a goldfish as got in a tin of sardines.

"Paint 'em?" she says, and her eyes come full of stars

and bright blue sky. "I'll do all me own painting, thanks, mate."

"No," He says, on the ball quick as you like, "oil paints, not that stuff. On canvas. You know. Make a picture out of 'em, like."

"No, thanks," she says. "Couldn't waste me time."

"You wouldn't be wasting your time," He says, as if He was put out, and almost insulted. "You earn your living like this, and some of us earn ours other ways. Painting's my way of wasting me time, and it's me living as well. And I still say, waste of time or not, I'd like to paint your hands. And you, too."

"Lots of blokes would like to paint me," she says, "only it's the first time I've ever heard it called painting. Sides," and God stone the perishing crows, she was proper laughing, laughing she was, teeth and all, hair round her face, yellow over her bright blue skies, laughing with white teeth, no brown on them and no holes nor none missing, laughing proper marvellous, "who'd want to look at it when it was finished?"

"Art galleries," He says, and come up in a kind of blushing smile, about as pitiful as He could make it, not to look like He felt inside of Him, all frothing up and winning right the way up the street. "I shall be showing some of my stuff later this year, you know, up the National Gallery, and places, so I'm looking out for, well, you know, things as ain't done every day. Sort of unusual. I mean, there's thousands of us at it, so it makes it awkward, like. Some of us ain't as rich as we'd like to be, so we can't afford models, see? So it comes a bit hard."

She was caught, boy, she was there, just like Ma, dead easy when you knew how.

Her look was different, like the look on some old dears face when she sees a proper down on his luck beggar in the street, and her hand goes to her purse to give him something, and she stops with her finger and thumb on them two little crossed knobs as close it, wondering if she ought to give him a couple of coppers, not having too much herself, or save them for the gas.

"What," she says, "you mean you can't get nobody to paint, or something? Why d'you want 'em, though? I mean, you know what they're like, don't you?"

"Ah," He says, kind of giving it up, proper hopeless, "that's not it. You want somebody to sit still to paint 'em. You can't remember the colours of their faces, can you? Nor even the colour of their eyebrows or the shapes of their ears, and things like that. No, it's got to be done proper, or not at all. Can't have any half larks. It's art, like, but it's a business on its own. And a paying one, when you're in. But I ain't. And that's it."

"Well," she says, sort of from a long way inside of her, "I reckon that's a shame. But I can't see where I come in, just the same. Why me?"

There was a bloke coming up to spoil everything and He wished every machine in the place would fall atop of him, but he was coming up just the same.

"How about meeting you afterwards?" He says, quick and off hand, as though He was collecting her insurance and had His book out, ready for signing up. "Then I can get me canvas ready tomorrow and set me paints tonight. Time's everything."

The bloke was right atop of them, and here come the music, slow, soft, covering all the little sounds like warm satin bed-clothes.

She give Him one look, out the side of her eyes, while the red beetles was hid in yellow hair, pushing it out the way of blue skies and loads of stars, white teeth, with two sharp shadows on the shady bumps of the red jersey, and the yard of air between Him and her come full of little white question marks, like bits of paper flying about and hitting Him in the dial a purpose to make Him blink, while she looked at Him as if she wondered what sort of a lark she was in for, and if she went in, how she was going to come out of it.

She stood up and pulled the red jersey down, tighter than ever, and He closed His eyes while His guts was jumping about, opening them to look down at the change and pick it up, as if all the interest was off.

"Round the back," she says. "Half six, if that'll suit you?"

"Okeedoke," He says. "I'll be there. Thanks."

And instead of playing a machine, He went straight out of it, not even looking back, as if He had a lot to do and not much time.

# CHAPTER VII

TREMBLING, He was, trembling, and His mouth was proper sucked up, like as if it had been give a handful of sawdust as got stuck in His throat. He stood in the dark by the electric motor boats, watching them swing round and round, not seeing nobody, nor hearing very much except the music, and the scrape of the boats on the metal floor and the banging and crashing when they bashed against each other, and Ada's voice saying everything all over again.

But it was dead funny the way He could remember everything she said, and even her voice saying it and the way she looked, but He could no more bring her to mind than fly in the air. She was like Him, when He see His self in the window, a palish sort of a stain what was there, and real, but nothing much else.

The clock in the middle of the rock garden give Him more than three hours to go. He watched for a minute to see how long it took the hand to click down one, and it seemed like a hour on its own.

There was no sense of Him staying in the place, case of her finding out from somebody or other He was still there, and anyway, she had to pass where she could see everything if she went down the Ladies, or up to her tea, so it was a case of scarper.

But where to go to was another question and a different story.

For a start off, it was no good of going to the pictures, simple reason they was closed. A walk up and down the High Road was a marvellous idea for them partial to it, but He never see much sense in it, unless you was out to buy something, and then if it was a bit far away, it was brainier to take a bus than go roaming about.

There was nowhere else to go except the park, and that was

a splendid sort of a suggestion, because of all the places on earth He hated the sight of, the park was one. Just a lot of wore out grass, and a few round beds of flowers as seemed to hate the place as much as He done. A couple of pennyworth on the bus seemed a waste of time, reckoning where it would take Him, and besides that, it was chucking money away.

Outside in the sun, a bloke with glasses on a long bit of ribbon, all gone curly at the edges, was tearing about with a big black shiny cloth poster with The Wages of Sin is Death wrote on it in red paint, looking proper daft, he was, with a little brown bag what he took handbills out of, and a proper masterpiece of a small black hat with hardly no brim, as squatted atop a bush of hair. Looking proper hard done by, it was, as if it had been eat in, drunk in, and slept in, till it was proper fed up of the whole affair, and specially the bloke underneath it. All cockled up, and pinched in at the top, and polished up of grease and horrible, it was, and knew it, without being told.

He was almost down there when He see He was nigh on the park, so He thought He might as well go in for a kip on the grass as muck about in the road. It was dead funny how you might walk for a long time and not be able to remember what it was you was thinking about or anything else, and yet you found your way to places as if somebody was taking you by the hand in and out of traffic and dodging the crowds, but if you was give a thousand quid to tell somebody what was in your mind on the way down, they could stick to their money.

All His life, He thought to His self, while His shoes was getting dust in all the cracks, going over towards the pond, you seemed to sort of meet people and talk to them, so you knew them, then you thought about something, like clothes or what was for dinner, or if you was going out, and where you was going and who with, and what you had to spend, or else a girl, or things like that, and the rest of the time you was sort of hanking about, spare, not thinking nor nothing, or else if you did, not remembering what it was all about, which was just about the same bit of bread, only fried both sides.

# CHAPTER VIII

THE POND WAS blue as Ada's eyes and full of bright gold footprints as come and went while you was looking, like as if a load of nobodies was running about the top of it with their sunshine boots on, and having a rare time, and all.

The kids was proper enjoying their selfs round the edge, paddling in and sailing their boats and having a right lark all round. Looking at them, He felt a bit sorry for His self as He never had a boat to sail, but only because Ma was afraid He might fall in and get His self drownded, or spoil His trousers, which seemed to be about as bad. So all He ever had was a bit of board what He pointed at one end, with a couple of sticks shoved in the middle for masts, and square bits of newspaper for sails stuck over the sticks. It sailed about all right, but it was different, somehow, to a proper looking boat with a real sail and a name, and little brass railings and a rope ladder up the mast, and all.

There was a kid He remembered a long time ago, in a white sailor suit and a soppy looking straw hat with HMS something, a long word, it was, in gold on black ribbon round it, as had a proper marvellous boat, a red one with a sail nigh as big as hisself. He never forgot the look on that kid's dial when he see that bit of board humbling about with the paper sails all wet and slopped about the deck. Funny how a thing like that sort of sticks in your gullet for years, and other things just go. Still, He give him a quiet poke or two to be getting on with, and then some old tart with him, his nurse or his Ma, started yelling blue murder and chased Him as far as the lodge with her umbrella, and a fat chance she had of catching Him, too.

The grass was rotten to look at, yellowish and patchy, as if blokes had been playing football on it for years on end, and the flower beds still looked fed up with their selfs, and what flowers there was looked at you as if they was saying, well, this is all the thanks we get for coming up.

But laying down, and looking up at the blue sky, it was all that much better, because not seeing all the things what got on your nerves, you was sort of giving your self a proper treat, one way and another, and you soon come on to sleep.

At least, you would, if kids would only keep their selfs quiet, and people walking about would only remember not to come crashing about with their dirty great big hoofs near where you was laying down. Rock the world, they did, and sound like bleeding cart horses out for the day, to say nothing of the way they laughed, and honked, and shouted and generally created a proper uproar, not worried about you nor nothing like you.

Perhaps they never thought to their selfs what kind of murder was going through the heads of quiet blokes just laying down for forty winks round about them. They might have been surprised if they had, and if they only knew how many times their blinding kids had every bone in their bodies broke, and their necks screwed in the bargain, they might have got a proper shock, the noisy lot of bleeders.

Still, He must have dropped off after a bit, because He woke up with some kid ferreting about round Him, but when He moved, so did the kid, so he must have been up to some lark or other. His face felt as if somebody had been holding it tight in the soft part of their hand so it come out with a suck. His eyes felt all swole up and His mouth was proper tasty, so all in all, He wished He stayed awake, to say nothing of the time. The nearest clock was up the Town Hall, so the only thing He could go by was the light, and that was getting darker blue.

He got in a blinding panic all of a sudden, He did.

Even to think of losing the chance of seeing Ada was kind of more than He could bear. There seemed to be something wrong and wicked about it, if she went before He got there. And Him just standing there, dizzy, looking at the dark pond.

He pelted down the gravel towards the lodge, and He see His self all them years before doing the same thing, but Away from a bride instead of To one. It was dead funny how you done exactly the same thing years and years after, yet turned sort of inside out. The same, only different.

The parkie was standing outside the lodge in his Sundays best with polished buttons and a top hat, looking as if he was the King of China's brother in law at a tanner a look.

"What's up?" he says, when He come tearing up to go through the gates. "Can't you behave yourself? Rushing about, there. Anybody'd think you was mad."

"What's the time?" He says, as if He was deaf, but He hated the parkie and the creases in the arms of his brown coat with the shining buttons in rows down the front, like eyes, they was.

The bloke was so surprised he pulled out his turnip, like a railwaymans, thick chain and all, with a little engine on it, without even looking what he was doing of.

"Six ten," he says, as if he was ready to say he was sorry, and his thumb come down a couple of times over the glass, for luck, perhaps.

"Okeedoke," He says, "now I can walk. Promised to take the old dear to church, I did. Didn't want to be late."

"Ah," says the parkie, "now you're talking. But mind how you go another time. Knock somebody down, and let yourself in for some damages one of these here bright days. Then you'll look pretty, won't you?"

"Don't you fret your fat about me," He says, and made sure He was all right for distance. "Paid to look after the park, you are, what there is of it, and a proper right hole it is, and all. Why don't you give them flowers a taste of water, stead of standing there nattering."

"You cheeky young," the parkie says, and pulls his self in very sharp because there was plenty of people about to hear it. "I'd like to get me toe behind you."

"Go home," He shouts him. "That there hat's getting you down, mate."

Nipping on a tram for a pennyworth down to the turning was dead easy, and He watched the parkie looking at Him all the way round the corner. Funny how it was people liked to take it out of you when they got a set of silver buttons on their coats, specially if they could chuck in a top hat, and if there was a few people about, they was in their glory, they was, shouting and hollering, proper wearing their selfs out with it all.

Here come the turning, and the tram was just pulling in a bit to go careful over the lights when He jumped off, missing the conductor and saving His self a copper. It all helped, and it never hurt the conductor, so they was both well off.

Past the chemist, what had a funny smell of old iodine bottles and shaving soap coming out the door, then the twopenny library with a window full of coloured book covers, pretty, some of them was, and the shadow of Him tearing past, then the fish market full of empty stalls with the grey canvas covers roped up, then the fruit and vegetables, then three old houses all joined together, with one shoulder higher than the other, so all the window sills looked like eyebrows on the squiff. The doors was never closed because they was stuck where they was, and their jambs was bent as old man's legs.

There was the back door of the Fun Fair, just a door in the back of the building in a small back yard as had its fence along the road all covered with posters, and a double gate, broke off and splintery with rot.

Not much of a place, and the Gents, just inside, give off none too good in the way of blessings, neither, but it was the best place in all the world to Him, just the same.

# CHAPTER IX

SHE WAS WAITING by the door with a small black sort of coat throwed over her shoulders, leaning against the wall, proper tired she looked, with the yellow hair still shining even in the dark light, one leg crossed over the other, with the toe pointing straight in the ground. Her feet was small, in very high heels, and her legs was white. Very white they was, sort of had a polish on them, they did. And her hips, the way she was standing, bulged out one side, so you could lean your elbow on her hip bone, easy.

She was smashing, a proper smashing bride she was, no, straight up, no larks, a smasher, and He come at her very slow, the last couple of foot, till He could smell her, some sort of sweet scent, lovely it was, like a soft tune or something, and He felt His self going all kind of soppy and trembling, and things.

She never moved, not so much as a inch. She was just looking dead at Him.

Ada.

Smaller than Him she was, smaller than He ever thought, leaning there resting on her tired muscles after another day of it, watching Him from the dark of her hair, not trusting Him a second, and all He wanted to do was put His arms round her and hold her, not even tight, but just hold her, and stop everybody from coming anywhere nigh her, ready to murder anybody as said a blind word to her, or even looked at her.

He wanted to say something to her, whisper something, never mind what, and anyway, even though He started trying, the things He had to say never had no words, or if they did, they was a bit further off than He could reach, and all as come to Him was the yellow light of the lamp down the road, and the leaves scratching their selfs in the gutter, and her smell, like a little diamond crown, somewhere, and the old, salty, nosey smell of the Gents.

She was quiet, not a move, just looking.

He was quiet, too, because He was afraid if He moved, or said something, He might be doing it all wrong, and put her off, or something. So there they was, standing there inside a foot of each other, quiet as mice, just watching, hardly even breathing, waiting for something, and He felt as if He was on the end of a bit of cotton, hanging down from the clouds, by His self, nobody to talk to nor nothing, just hanging, and wondering what come next, feeling a funny sort of prickle all over Him, not like it was when the beetles started their larks, but like it was when you was waiting in the passage to go in and see the boss. Like that, it was, only somehow different.

If only she let Him just touch her sleeve, nothing else, only her sleeve or anything she ever touched, or even looked at. If only He could shove His arms round her while she was standing there and tell her not be tired or take no notice of anybody, never mind who they was. If only He could do something for her, anything, any blinding thing to make her believe in Him.

If only He could get her to believe in Him, only He was a bit tied up about what she had to believe in, and treat Him sort of like, as you might say, other brides treated their blokes when they was walking home, with their arms crossed, and their fingers crossed tight between them, or with their arms round each other, just before they stopped in the doorway, not saying a lot, but close to each other. Or if only He knew a bit of poetry, or something, just to make her feel more at home, or kind of sorry for Him, or laugh at Him, anything she liked, if only He could get her sort of more comfortable with Him.

The sweet smell of her, and them red beetles laying quiet in the dark there, somewhere, and the blue skies and stars of her eyes as He knew was there behind her hair, and the sort of hot light He could feel coming out of her, and yet not see, as if all round her it was coming out in waves and what was alight, and yet dark, hot, yet not hot to touch, but only to feel, and her so little and all, kind of started something inside of Him as made Him want to go mad and kneel down and start kissing the very pavement she was standing on.

"What you looking at?" she says, in such a different kind of a voice to what He thought it might be, He was proper surprised. She was quieter, sort of friendly, as if she really wanted to know what He was looking at, instead of sort of telling Him off for looking.

Something somewhere inside of Him opened up wide all of a sudden, just because there was something in her voice, something not in words, just in the sound, as touched somewhere and brought it open, wide, redder than her finger nails, so wide, so far, so hurting for her, for the touch and sound and smell of her, His heart started bashing away and knocking the breath out of Him, so He was proper in the cart for a breath of air. Nothing come in nor went out, and He started going sort of dizzy again.

"Nothing," He says, as if it was water off of a duck.

"Go on," she says, "tell us," and ah, Christ, boy, she was proper interested with none of that there funny sound in her voice. Not what she says, but the way. The voice.

"Looking at the sky," He says.

"What's up with it?" she says, not a move, though.

"It's purple," He says, still looking up there, and them eyes of hers was sharper on Him than the beetles.

"It's only the lights," she says.

"No it ain't," He says, still looking up there as if He forgot her, "that's a bloke called London, that is. He's tired after his day's work and he's laying on his back and taking his socks off before he goes to kip. That there purple's his breath, full of grub and wine and things. Ever had wine?"

"I've had a port or two," she says, and He knew she was showing her teeth again.

"That's red ink with sugar stuck in it," He says. "No. Wine. Proper marvellous it is. Get a couple of them inside you, and you'll start breathing purple and all."

"Where can we get some?" she says, but not a single move except her mouth, and He only see that because the light was shining on the wet of it wagging up and down.

"Ah," He says, and the two halfs in His pocket come up like a couple of cartwheels in front of Him. "That's a different story altogether, that is. I know where we can get a cup of tea, if that'll do you?"

"I'm dying for one," she says, and she moved as if she meant to start running for it. "The air ain't too nice round here, neither. Proper gets in your clothes, it do. Something to do with the bloke breathing purple, perhaps?"

"I don't know about breathing purple," He says. "It's proper cherry ripe, ain't it?"

But though He wanted to say a bit more because things was going so nice, He see she was looking the other way, as if she liked her joke, but not too much of it, so He said to His self, go careful boy, go careful. He see He had to box very clever, there.

"I get so sick and bloody tired of that there place," she says, and the words come bashing out and sort of stuck in the night on long sharp points. "I could murder every bastard in it."

He could have fell straight down the drain hole.

"What," He says, getting His toe on the ball quick and handsome, "me, too?"

"Yes," she says, "and you. All the bleeding same, the lot of you."

"Nice cup of strong tea for two," He says, "quick. That's me, and me barrow's outside."

"Wish it was," she says, and He could see He was all right; "my feet's just about wore off, they are. Proper giving me what for."

There was crying in her voice, so much, He could have picked her up and squashed her, proper squashed her, and got blood in her mouth.

But He walked along as if He never heard a blind word. And she was doing about two and a half to His one. Ada was walking down the road with Him, and He felt as if it was a dream in yellow light, but there she was, solid enough, with them long heels going clip pat, clip pat, her, in black, and red, yellow by herself, Ada, and He was arguing with His self whether she was, or not.

Music, or something, come up inside of Him, like them white organs come up in the pictures and a bloke plays on five or six sort of levels at once, all deep notes as shook the seats, and you thought it was proper marvellous how they done it, with drums and bagpipes, and thunder, and stuff, coming out all the time and making you feel proper pleased with your self.

"Must you walk so bloody fast?" she says. "Ain't going to a fire, are you?"

## CHAPTER X

HE SEE, first off, it was no use of Him trying to get her chatting and asking her a lot of questions to try and get things going, because she was proper tired and her feet was giving her gip, so He kept His mouth shut and saved her getting worked up in a bag of nerves. Ma got like it sometimes, so He was used to it.

When they got down the cafe, all she wanted was tea and a doughnut, and half His meat pie, so He was all right so far as the cash went, and what with that, and being with her, He was feeling marvellous. Everybody in there had a look at Him, and then at her, as though they was asking their selfs how He done it, but He made out as He never see them, nor never heard the remarks, neither.

Ada sat down just chewing and drinking, looking at the puddles on the table top and playing with the salt pot, far from home and eyes like saucers, proper dreamy, she was, and since He always done a lot of that His self, He kept His mouth shut because He knew how you got when you was well away inside of your self, somewhere, and somebody kept on talking at you and bringing you out of it, till it did, it nigh on drove you proper barmy, and you had to get hold of your self to stay civil with them, or else get up and half murder them.

So when He finished, He only sort of give her a look, and got up, and she come out with Him, without a word said either side, as if she knew all about it, and He took her straight round the pictures, stuck His half dollar on the brass sort of ticket machine, asked for a couple of One and Threes as if He never even knew what it was like in the Tanners, and they both went past the queue in the Nines as if they was all the scum of the earth, and floated upstairs and squatted smack in the back row, nice as ever you see.

It was a pleasure to be alive, it was, sitting up there in lovely sort of soft hairy seats, like velvet only the hairs was longer, with springs as made a bit of a squeaking row if you shifted from one cheek to the other, and a marvellous smell what they squirted out of long sprays, scent, it was, and a smashing picture in the bargain, and Ada, herself, her very own self, no half larks, no plaster nonsense, just Ada, next to Him where He could touch her, if He put His hand on the arm where her elbow was.

But all the time He was getting that funny kind of a feeling, like as if somebody was playing on Him somewhere inside of Him like a banjo, sort of twanging Him about till His skin come out all sort of hot and not exactly prickly, but kind of pins and needlesey, in a manner of speaking, like, only different, not like when your foot goes to sleep, but somehow warmer and better, as if He knew if He touched her, He might faint or get heart failure, or something.

She was quiet in the dark, there, as quiet as she was down the Fun Fair, just looking at what was going on, not saying a word, or moving her face, even. He could see out of the corner of His eye how her legs was crossed and her hands was on top of one another, and her hair come down straight both sides, so the light never showed nothing of her face but only shone on her hair and the whites of her eyes. But her smell come off of her, easy enough, even coming through the stuff they was spraying about the place, just like as if she was talking to you. Proper strange, it was, even though He paid One and Three for a seat, He no more wanted to look at the picture than fly in the air.

He just wanted to look at her, and think of them beetles and breathe her in, and think how soft she was if you put your arms round her, and how lovely and hot she was, when you could feel the heat coming out of her even a foot away from her. She seemed to be almost bouncing with heat as come off of her, like looking at a saucepan over a hot stove when the air shakes about. What with it all, and not being able to get over the fact that there she was, herself, her very own self, there, by the side of Him, the pictures was a waste of time and money.

But it was worth it to be with her, all said and done, and He still had enough over to see her home, and get about a bit tomorrow. So all in all, He reckoned He was lucky, dead lucky.

Out in the road, it was a bit cold so they put their best foot forward, as you might say, but when He started going down the turning where the cafe was, she pulled up.

"Half a mo," she says. "Where you going?"

"Down the cafe," He says, "get a cup of coffee, or something."

"No thanks," she says. "I'll have a supper waiting for me. I'll hop on a tram, if it's all the same to you."

"Course," He says, only there was a plunk inside of Him like you might hear if you dropped a lump of stone in a puddle. "Want me to come, do you?"

"No," she says, and her hair waved about, "it ain't far, and you've give me a lovely evening. I wouldn't bother you."

"Oh," He says, "it's no bother."

"Tell you what," she says. "See me home another time. Eh?"

"Soon?" He asks her.

"Any night you like," she says, and He see He was all right. "Okeedoke," He says. "Fine. I'd like to. See you some other time, eh?"

"Come in in the week," she says. "Don't make it too long."

"No fear," He says. "I want to paint you."

"That's what I'm afraid of," she says, and starts laughing again, proper marvellous. "Well, so long."

"So long," He says, feeling like the bloke as missed the last train by seconds, and gets there just as the red light goes round the corner.

The night turned upside down and all the lights in the world went out, but hair warmth with sly tickles felt round His face, a pressure pushed His neck down a bit, and while He was trying to make up His mind what was happening, a cushion either side of His chest, as He felt as plain as if they was two hands, pushed against Him with empty space below and a parting of soft touching as ended down at His foot where she trod on the toe getting strangled in the sock, and her mouth was on the side of His cheek pushing one side of His mouth up, a proper lovely, gentle, feel of her mouth, cool, almost cold, and scent going up His nose like when you drink ginger ale too quick.

She was gone a couple of yards back before He come round.

"Night," she says. "You've got lipstick all over you, mind."

"Okeedoke," He says, to her shadow going away from Him, stuck where He was, still not knowing which end He was standing on, and not much caring.

"Oy," she calls out, twenty foot or more away. "What's your monniker?"

"Ernie Mott," He says, and when it was out He could have kicked His self, because though He never thought about it before, it sounded soppy, specially shouted in the dark at the yellow lamp. "Ernest Verdun Mott, that's me full name," He says, quick, and it sounded a bit more like it.

"Mine's Ada Brantlin," she says. "Good night, Ernie, boy."

"Night," He says, and He wished He had the guts to call her Ada to her face, but they was missing, as usual, so He see her turn the corner, a running dark patch as got in the way of the shop lights and copped the white shine on her legs just for a tick or two, two small white curves, as done something inside of you to watch, white with light, criss crossing quick and gone.

He tried to remember her, but though He knew her voice and every word she said, and the colour of her eyes, and the way they went when she smiled, and the shape of her and every bleeding thing about her, He could no more get her standing there in His mind than fly.

So all He got was a sort of shape and sound of her somewhere inside of Him as hurt more than a sort of blunt splinter, nigh as big as His self, sticking in Him, and the cold wind bit Him in halfs while He was standing there looking at the lamplights, trying to bring her back beside Him, but if the wind had bit chunks out of Him and made Him bleed, nothing would have shifted Him, because the cold was getting its own back on Him for losing the memory of her, He reckoned, and it done Him a lot of good.

His teeth was rattling about regardless, and shivers was all over Him, having a fine old game, till He buttoned His coat, give the corner one last look as if it was all its fault, and turned round walking very slow down the cafe, trying to feel like one of them blokes in the pictures, where they go out and get pissed because the bride turned it in.

# CHAPTER XI

Soon as the cafe door shut behind Him, He knew He done it all wrong again. He should have gone home.

Len Tate and all the lads was sitting down round the machine and Bert Clivey was playing it.

"Ah," says Len, sort of proper surprised, but not really, "the boy His self. What a lad, eh? What a lad. What, me old Ernie, boy? How's it going, eh?"

"Not bad," He says. "Give us a coffee and a double nelson, Ted," He says to Ted, behind the counter, in a white coat gone a dark sort of new colour with a lot of dirt in it, with a tie what was the same width all the way down till it give up just before the top pockets of his waistcoat, and crossed its legs there, as if it was saying, you put me on, now get on with me. It must have been wore for years to get as cheeky as that.

He knew they was all looking at Him, even though everybody, except Len, had their backs to Him, but they seemed to stare the harder out of the backs of their heads than with their eyes. And they was so quiet, what was more, kind of waiting.

Even the ceiling looked as if it was waiting on something.

"Here you are, mate," Len says, and edges up on his chair. "Bags of room, Ern. Old Bert's just done twenty eight thousand, he has. Gets his fags on another five."

"What cheer," says Bert, giving Him a wink the same time he pulled the playing lever, very gentle and fancy, as if he had the whole secret of it off by heart, standing back with his hands on the woodwork, like most of them done, pressing down till his shoulders come up nigh as high as his head, watching that there ball like as if it had all the hopes of the world sliding round on it. Frowning, he was, screwing his face up, shoving one shoulder forward when it looked as if the ball was going to miss hitting one of them little numbers, wagging his hips about when a half inch miss come up, as though he expected to give his play that bit extra by chucking his self about, not that the ball ever took a blind bit of notice of him nor nobody else.

All the other blokes played up to it, and all, to give the game a sort of taste, as if it was science as got the numbers bumping up. So they moaned when there was a miss, or else sounded as if they was nigh on their death beds, and made a lot of sort of sounds if the ball scored and kept on scoring, sort of whistles, and hisses, and clucks and nattering, not to each other, because they never took their eyes off of the play, it was that important, but just to their selfs.

It sounded proper barmy till you started playing your self, then you found your self doing it and liking it.

While Bert was trying to explain how he come to lose, Len was up there starting, but he no sooner played his first ball than he looks round with his fag stuck on his bottom lip, and his eyes nigh closed because of the smoke getting in them, and looks as if he knew it all but he just wanted it put in words, so he could kip down nice and peaceful for the night.

"How she go, Ern boy?" he says, cheerful as you like.

"Who?" He says, very amazed He wanted it to sound, and it did.

"Ada," says Len, not moving that much.

"Oh," He says. "She's all right. Go round the pictures tonight, did you?"

"Yes," says Len. "See you in there. How was she?"

"All right," He says, but He could hear what was being got at in Len's voice, and specially by the looks on some of the dials round about there.

"Let you, did she?" Len says, watching the ball, and his eyes was like a bloke in a railway train watching houses go past, flicking side to side, nasty to watch.

"Let me what?" He says, knowing the answer, but Ada was still with Him, even though He could hardly remember the shape of her, and it was like bashing her in the dial to talk about her, specially when He could still feel her kissing Him.

"Let you pay for her," says Len, and all the blokes starts killing their selfs of laughing, as though it was proper funny.

"Course," He says, getting proper cold inside somewhere. He knew if He started sloshing somebody, all of them would join in and He stood a good chance of waking up in hospital. He could feel a boot kicking His face in, easy.

"Get your fish afterwards?" Len says, as if he never heard nobody laugh in his life.

"No," He says, because saying anything was easier than saying nothing. "She had a hot supper waiting for her. So she went home."

If He was one of them funny blokes on the wireless they might have laughed as much, but no more than they was now. They was dying, they was, proper howling the place down.

"If it been me," Len says, and his eyes was still flicking side to side, "she'd gone home with one, I can tip you. A proper hot one and all, and plenty of gravy. You're slow, Ernie boy."

"Perhaps I am," He says, and puts the cup down. This was His chance to get out. He knew if He stayed on to play there might be trouble. He was proper surprised at His self to find Him wanting to murder Len Tate. He knew He could, easy.

"So long," He says, and goes down to the door, slow like, still chasing the currants round His mouth, and taking His time. "See you tomorrow, Len boy. Night all."

"You want to take your pencil sharpener, next time," Len says, and he was a right looking shape from the back, with his head like a bump on his padded shoulders, and his hair shining in waves. None of the other blokes was looking at Him or the machine. They was all looking at Len Tate, waiting for the next bright bit, and He was frightened, proper frightened, case it come before He got outside. He could bear it if He never heard it.

"Talk about yourself," He says, and He give the door a good old bash as shook everything in the window, and made old Ted swear proper educated.

He hated the whole lot of them, He hated the cafe. He hated

even Ada and the thoughts of her, He hated the road and the night, the yellow mess the lamps made on the pavement, the puddles full of weak wet gold splashed about in the dark in front and a side of Him, He hated where He was going and what He was, and He hated His self without being able to say why, or even know how to put His tongue to it, except He hated all of it, bit by bit, and each bit on its own, and His self most.

He knew, quiet like, as He was getting angry with things again, but it never done no good. They was just the same before as after. Getting angry never done no good at all, but it made things all the worse, it did, and He found His self always the worse off for it, kind of washed out and wore out, fed up with the whole shoot and no heart for nothing.

So the only thing to do was try to be cheerful about it, and look on the bright side, and as Ma always said, count your blessings, because thousands is worse off than you.

He had the change of the three halfs, not much, as you might say, but He could do a lot with it, and nigh on half a packet of fags as would see Him through tomorrow. Ada had half His meat pie and come to the pictures with Him, and she kissed Him, what was more, and asked Him to see her in the week, soon as He liked, and see her home.

All of that, every single bit of it, happened to Him without dreams, or thinking, or anything, but just the same, it happened. That was His day and here He was, grousing at it just because a load of rotten minded bleeders was taking the rise out of Him. Taking the rise out of Him, as took Ada out and still had her scent sticking to Him, and felt them lovely round ones of hers shoving against Him, as see her legs running across the lights, with the cold of her mouth still like hot iron burning on His dial.

Come to a finish, He was more angry with His self than Len Tate, because after all, Len had the money, and played the machines twice as much as Him, yet he never took Ada to the pictures, poor old Len never, for all his new suits and his wavy hair, what he always combed in the Gents with a little comb in a case what he carried in his hip pocket. Len never even got eye room, leave alone a kind word.

But that was perhaps because you could smell the fried fish and chips a mile away from him. Proper funny, it was, how that stuff stuck to you. A slice of bread and scrape, and two niffs of him, and you was full up.

By the time He was outside the front door, He was feeling proper all right, and He hoped Ma had something tasty for supper because He was proper peckish. After all, half a meat pie and a doughnut and what all, since half two, or thereabouts, was all very well, but He was growing, and He had to keep his strength up, or else He might get like Joe Cadlin, with a face like a old man, full of lines, and running eyes, and so much of a shake on, he had to be dressed, even. No nourishing food, or something, the doctor said it was.

None of that lark for Ernie, boy, no fear, He was thinking, when He picked up the key under the mat, and tickled about for the keyhole.

When He shut the door, He stood in the dark of the passage, listening.

But London was quiet as a mouse, outside there. And Ma was asleep, upstairs. He could hear her tearing it up a treat.

So it was all right.

# CHAPTER XII

So IT COME a mad rush again next morning, late as usual, tearing about the place to find His coat and it was upstairs all the time. Ma stood there, front of the kitchen window, like she always done, just watching Him, with His breakfast on the table going cold, as per, and her holding the teapot a bit helpless so the spout come nigh low enough for the tea to spill, just showing what she thought of the whole performance by not saying a blind word. Looking on, that was all she done any time.

The fried bread and bacon went down in about four gulps, and the tea splashed down atop of it. His sandwiches was by His hat and all he wanted was His fare and enough for His fags and perhaps a bar of chocolate, if Ma got out the right side of kip. He was a bit shaky about getting even His fares, never mind the extras, so He never said too much, but when He rushed in the passage to get His hat and lunch, the money was there, extras and all, so He felt a bit nice about her and He reckoned He ought to say something.

"Ta, Ma," He shouted her. "Okeedoke, duckie. See you teatime. So long."

He flew down the road, taking no notice of Ma Floom sweeping the step, rushed in Ma Crann's yellow gaslight for His paper, and stamped about while Ma was trying to sort out the Sunday returns from the Monday's, what the girls left lying about after they took what they wanted for their rounds, grabbed what she give Him, seeing the way it trembled in the space between a jar of toffee and a pile of pattern books, and felt how wet her hand was when He put the penny in it, then He tore out and nipped round the corner, but it was no go.

He missed the last Workmans again.

So that meant double the fare and a bit more, and a nasty look from Old Nick for being late, not that He cared about that, much, but it started off the week a bit skewy.

Waiting on the corner, He tried to look at the paper, but it was still too dark, and the wind was proper rough, and it was too parky to hold anything very long. So He stuck His hands in His pockets and stood behind a lamp post, letting the wind go back and front of Him, and felt His self getting proper angry at the trams because they took so long to come down the road.

There was others waiting in the doorways round about, as looked nigh on as perished as Him, but nobody never said nothing because it was no use. They was always too glad to get on the tram, in the warm, to say anything about it then, and any case, it was no good of nobody saying nothing to the poor old conductor, because he had his job to think about, same as everybody else.

He liked getting upstairs in the tram because you could put your fag on up there, and it was always blue and warm with smoke and breath, so it was matey, like, and He knew a lot of blokes to say good morning to, and some of them was in a nice way of business, and all, going up in collars and ties and bowler hats, some of them.

But sometimes it was all right downstairs, and all, specially if it was a bit full and you had to stand, because then you stood a chance of getting squashed between a couple of brides, young ones, so their behinds stuck in you and you could feel their titties rolling about, even under their overcoats. That was a right treat, that was, but it never happened many times, no such luck. Generally it was a couple of beefy blokes with their lunch bags, or a office cleaner with a shopping bag that stuck in you, or swung against your legs and drove you barmy, specially if she was having a natter with a couple of her pals or the conductor. Then her breath come round the corner and knocked you boss eyed and nigh on turned you up. So generally He made a dive for upstairs because it was safer.

The same blokes was on board, and they all nodded, or give Him a wink, so He felt as if He was welcome soon as He sat down.

Putting the morning fag on was a bit of all right, and one

of the best feelings of the day. First of all you settled down after nodding some bloke or winking, according to how you knew him, or if you was old pals you said good morning or something, never mind how it come out, then you rubbed the breath off of the window and looked through the dark holes, and little roads made by the running wet, to see how far you was from where you got on.

That was to make sure you was moving, never mind how loud the tram moaned and squeaked on the rails, nor never mind if it rocked so hard you nigh slipped off of the seat, you always looked out to make sure you was moving, and find out how far you was from home.

Then you pulled out the newspaper and dekkoed the front page, but all the time you was looking at it, you knew you wanted a fag, in fact you was shouting the place down inside you for one. So you got to a bit of the paper as looked sort of interesting, and then you felt for the fags, nice and slow, and out they come in their little cardboard box, neat as you like, and you shoved one in your mouth, careful as you could not to wet it too much. Then you felt it there for a bit, and then you pulled out a match and scraped it on your boot, or on the floor, or where it was dry enough to come up a flame, and you took a nice long pull and let the smoke find its own way out. Smashing it was.

All the blokes done it that way. It was the only way to do it to get the best out of it. The old blokes with their pipes was hours over the job, in fact, it proper got on your nerves to watch them at it, scratting about in their pockets for their baccy tins, pulling out knives to scrape the bowls, shoving pipe cleaners down the black parts, till you asked your self why they bothered with the job at all.

Some blokes never even had their pipes going when they got off of the tram to go straight on the job, what with screwing baccy in the bowl that there delicate, you might think it was a silk shirt they was smoking, and then lighting up with about half a dozen matches, and then nothing happening, except a lot of noises like as if the plug come loose out of the hole.

It was funny about blokes as smoked pipes. Some of them just shoved some baccy in anyhow, lit it, blowed out enough in three puffs to blind you, and they was set for the day.

Other blokes tissfatarted about for hours, and never even got the bleeding thing sucking proper, never mind about smoking. And if you got next to them, what with their elbows digging you while they was hanking about with one thing and another, and grunting, and then dropping tools to blow their snitches, it was a right lark, specially first thing of a morning, it was, and you felt it all ought to be put a stop to, quick, before something got done about it, a murder or something.

About half way up, the blokes generally started chatting each other about the news, if there was any, and then you heard them as felt like it giving it big licks about politics, and one thing and another.

He hardly ever took no notice of it, because it never had nothing to do with Him.

Sometimes it come a bit interesting if you got in with the right blokes, but that was a funny thing, and all. The early trams was full of blokes what was proper politics mad. Talk the hind leg off of a donkey they would, and proper wear their selfs out about it. But the later you got on a tram, the less politics there was and the more sport, if a murder or a divorce, or something juicy, was out of it.

The lads on about politics was generally a young looking lot, not many caps amongst them, and hardly ever a packet of sandwiches. But they was all for the workers. Proper red they was, shout the odds, they did, but they talked such a lot of funny sounding stuff it got a bit of a nuisance listening, because you never knew one minute to the other what they was on about. So you just let them have their say, and done a bit of thinking on your own.

He was a bit surprised at His self the way He forgot Ada so quick. He never give her a thought between going to kip and now, and when He tried to call her to mind He come up against that sort of funny wall as stopped Him going any farther, like one of them bits of paper in a jar of jam. You got the cover off, all right, but you had your work cut out getting at the jam over that there soppy bit of paper stuck on the top there, what for, nobody knowed.

But thinking about her, her hair and the smell of her and things, soon shoved the tram and everybody on it as far as China, and He had to get up in a dirty big sweat to rush down the stairs and hop off, miles past His stop, in the finish, and without paying for His ticket, which was a pity.

It was always the same. You started thinking and got your self lost. You never knowed what you was thinking about because it never sort of stuck anywhere to get itself remembered, so there you was, squatting there in the stars, doing your self a treat.

Then you sort of come to, and you was all over the place, proper barmy, and late to start with, so by the time you come tearing round the corner, you was that much later. But it was no good of you trying to tell somebody you was late because you was thinking about the way some bride looked, so you let them get on with it.

He always come in out of breath when He was late, to let everybody see He been running like mad to try and catch up with His self, and He went on breathing like a engine for minutes after He got to His stone. So He started at the corner, and tore for the door, pulled the spring leaf open and let it slap about behind Him while He was doing His morning gallop upstairs, then along the main passage what was black as the ace, day and night, and in the front main, where the tanks was, and through that to the stones, where He was, just inside on the right.

Hat and paper in the cupboard, crayons out, take off the dust covers, and away we go, taking no notice of nobody, saying nothing, not even looking, just breathing nice and steamy, as if a bit of that made up for being late.

## CHAPTER XIII

THE BLOKES in there was all the same, pretty well.

There was Mr Surcell over by the window, elderly sort of bloke he was, not a bad sort, but he never had much to say. His Mrs was queer most of the time and he always went home early to do the housework, so he was a bit unlucky.

If you come on him while he was working, and sort of brought him out of his self, he looked up quick with a smile in his eyes, as if you come to tell him there was no need to get his hands rough with soda or whatever it was, no more, but when he see it was you, his face kind of put its lights out, and he started working again, and there was something about the way he was standing as made you want to put your arm round his shoulders and say, cheer up, mate, everything comes to a finish, like it or not.

On the other side was old Josh Pickering, funny old bloke, he was, with two grown up daughters on the stage as drove him proper barmy thinking they was coming to a bad end.

They was away, most of the time, so he was worrying about them, most of the time, and he looked at everybody as if they was one of them what he thought was after his pair of girls.

So poor old Josh was never very sociable and when he was, he generally ended up by talking a lot about morals, as if he was the only bloke left as had any. The trouble was he was a bit doubtful about what morals was, or so it seemed, because when Old Nick started on him, there was always a row, and in the finish old Josh said flat out, that morals was what kept you out of going to bed, or coming the acid, with some tart or other, and Old Nick said they was nothing of the sort.

So you never knew where you was with the pair of them, and morals was like talking the same sort of stuff as the politics blokes on the Workmans of a morning, all words and no sort of meaning, like reading a book upside down.

Opposite him was Les Fishmill, a bloke about thirty five or thereabouts, always telling everybody how he was frightened about the way his life was going away from him, day after day, and not much to show for it.

He went out in the Gents once, and found Les standing in front of the glass, sort of conducting a band, going through all the actions with a pencil, making them play very quiet one minute and proper loud the next, waving his arms, and carrying on there something chronic, and there was a look in his eyes as if something sweet inside of him was being pulled out by the roots.

Les give Him what was left of a packet of fags and told Him not to say nothing to the other blokes, proper plum colour, he was, and trying to laugh it off for a joke.

But no bloke gets tears in his eyes when he wants to play a joke, so He took the fags and never said nothing, not because Les asked Him not to, but because He thought of His mornings in bed, sometimes, and how He would feel if somebody come in and caught Him out. When He talked to Les after that, it was like as if they had a thousand miles between them, proper queer, it was, but not very comfortable for Him nor Les.

Jim Mellowes was a different kettle of fish altogether. He hated the whole place and said so, but he was so good at the job that if he started on one of his larks, Old Nick used to wheel him in to old Tomlin and get him a half dollar or five bob rise, just to keep him on. He was proper marvellous on colour work. Nothing got him down, from Chinese stuff, to birds and flowers for science books, and the way he stippled was a real masterpiece, it was that there close and made your mouth water.

But what he really wanted to do was play the piano. Round the corner at the cafe where they had their dinner, Jim played the old joanna round there for hours on end. He liked hot stuff and he could play it, and all, but when he played it his self, for his self, like, he went off on some stuff of his own, classic, as you might say. It was all right, but it was a bit sort of shivery. You never knew where you was with it.

There was one bit, something he called out of some foreign language or other, so as to let everybody know what they was in for, and dodge out while they had the chance, what he played one Christmas when they give a staff do for the blokes and all their wives and kids in the acid tanks room. While he played it, they was all talking and laughing, so in the middle he got up and banged the lid down, and called them all a bloody lot of barbarians and went out and got proper drunk, and had a fight with poor old Fatty Sanders, the night watchman, as never hurt a fly. Funny bloke, Jim Mellowes was, but all right, as you might say, when he was all right. But you never knew when.

Then there was Old Nick, but he was like a part of the place, sort of went with the smell of the tanks, and the weight of the stones, and the colour of the limewash on the walls, in a manner of speaking.

Come from a place near Venice, Old Nick did, and proper got on your nerves talking about it, and all. To listen to him, you might think it was the only place a bloke ever got his self pupped out of, instead of being some dirty little hole or other in Italy somewhere, where everybody was either screaming the place down singing operas, or chewing macaroni, or rushing about with one of them there curved knives stuck in their chops ready to shove in you when you got your eye off of them, somewhere, sort of careless.

Litho work, painting and singing was about all Old Nick was good for. But there was no doubt about it, he knew what he was doing of, line and colour, and when it come to mixing colour, there was only one in it. Even old Tomlin his self never stood a chance with Nick.

He was only a little bloke, but broad as a door, with a corporation as made him leave the top three buttons of his trousers undone, and all the buttons of his waistcoat, except the top one, so the waistcoat sort of fell in two halfs both sides, leaving all the wrinkles in his shirt showing in front, and the top of his grey wool pants, as never buttoned neither, and left little bits of their self on the edges of anything they touched, so you could always tell where Old Nick had been.

He knew he was laughed at about it, but he always laughed his self, as if it was the biggest joke out, and patted his old mary, as if them what was laughing was unlucky not to have one like it.

Proper funny face he had, and all, real ice creamo, black curly hair, white at the sides, all grease and long, past his ears, and a funny knobby sort of little nose, thick eyebrows curling all over the place, eyes like them little black buttons as give you a grin all the time on Ma's boots, and a big black moustache brushed up same shape as a W, with the ends nigh tickling his eyes, and about five chins always stuck out in a rare old prickle of whiskers. A proper barber's joy, he was, and if he ever come in the saloon, poor old Charlie Floom would have fainted, he would, specially if it was late of a Saturday night when all the lads was in there.

But Old Nick never seemed to care how he looked, even when he was going out, and he must have earned good money, too. The funny part about it was, on Sunday, when he took Mrs Nick and his kids to church, he was done up like a dogs dinner, he was, face shining, hair combed, frock coat, high collar, real posh he was, and a sort of thick shiny felt hat, like a fur only with shorter hairs and a hand tied bow at the side, pulled right over his ears. Looked a right boy, he did.

He come out of his office later on, like he always done, to look round and see if everybody was down to it, or if they was stuck somewhere. If he see everybody looked as if they was going along all right, he just strolled round from one to the other, starting at old Josh Pickering, and finishing up with Him.

You never looked up when Nick was coming.

If you did, he stopped dead, one foot forward, looking you smack in the eyeball, and you felt as if you was atop of a couple of sharp black points as went right through you like meat skewers, frightening the life out of you till the crayon proper shook about in your hand. You had all your work cut out to sort of give him a wink, and pretend you just looked up for the fun of it, and see him coming and give him the glad, because you felt like it, and you was going back to work, then and there, without a care in the world, and you hoped he believed you.

But you knew how you felt, all right.

So you just watched his feet coming up to your stone, out the corner of your eyes, while you was busy drawing, very slow they come, not to disturb you, like, and you waited till you could feel him breathing on you, then you stopped working as if you was fed up of him coming nigh you, and proper impatient for him to hop it so you could get on with what you was doing. Then you dropped tools and give him a nice big smile.

Here come the feet, all bulgy inside, where the bunions puffed out the black velvet slippers with white soles a inch thick, bit by bit, very quiet, no fuss or noise, till you see the ends of his trousers piled in rings round the bottoms, all stained with spots of colours, pretty in a way, greens and reds and yellows and purples, and then you could smell him, a sort of warm, fat, hairy smell, it was, a bit sweetish, some hair oil, or soap perhaps or something what he shoved on his moustache, something smelly in that line, it was, so you knew he was there without the telling.

And you could feel him looking, what was worse, picking out the mistakes, specially them as you tried to cover over with that bit of paper what you tested the end of the crayon on. But it was no use.

Off come the paper with one flip of his hand, yellowy brown it was, with square nails stained sort of reddish blue with all the colours ever used in the place since it opened, fat fingers, like bits of bamboo, and a thumb, bent in half, as come out of his hand with a corner sharp as a set square.

There it was, there the mistakes was, there you was, and there he was, and all the whole place was listening and waiting to have a laugh at you, with ears as you could see getting bigger and redder every second, till they come up the size of garage doors.

"So," Old Nick says, in his business voice, "what you do?"

Funny voice, Old Nick had, sort of low, coming out of his mary, with showers of crushed mixed nuts pouring through it all the time.

"Nothing much," He says, a bit cocky, to let the other blokes know He was happy as a bird on the kitchen table, not caring if they heard or not.

Old Nick looked at the drawing on the stone, and then at the master print what it was copied off of, giving his black W a brush up with his finger and thumb, touching it very light case he got the hairs twisted up. Then he got tired of that and pulled his eyebrows, and you could see some of the hairs falling out like little light ginger half circles, till they fell on the white of the stone, then they was black.

All the time his old mary was brushing side to side, gentle and slow, against the rough edge of the stone, and his pants was leaving their little trade marks stuck to the sharpest parts, till it looked as if the stone had suddenly started sprouting grey hairs, all fluffy like, and queer to watch.

"How long you been here, now?" Old Nick says, still looking at the stone.

He was a bit surprised, because if anybody ought to know, Old Nick did, because it was him as put Him there in the first place.

"Nigh on five year," He says, and the room went kind of cold all of a sudden and He started feeling that there hot, He could hardly abear His self. All you could hear was Josh Pickering's pen, stippling as if he had another five minutes left before he rolled up. Squeak like a load of mice, it did.

"Come to the office," Old Nick says, and the back of his trousers wobbled out of it, leaving the stone bare except for a head of old mans hair round the bottom edge.

It was that there quiet inside the room all round Him, He wanted to shout at them to spoil it. Every dirty bit of language He knew come up on the lift inside of Him, ready to shoot out and blind them. But it was no good. Nobody could cut their ears off, and even if they found their selfs without a pair, they could always talk, and wink, and dig each other with their elbows.

Old Nick's office was two partitions of wood and glass making a square with the corner of the room. All the glass part was stuck thick with notices, and pictures, tore out of books, what he thought you ought to look at, to do your self a bit of good at your job, all except one square, so as he could look out and see how things was shaping in the room, who went down the Gents, and how long they was gone. The walls at the back was covered floor to ceiling in jobs done on the firm, anything up to twelve colours, most of them was, some of them proper posh, what Old Nick done his self, and others, done by other firms, right messes, what he stuck up to give his self a bit of heart.

His table was a sight for sore eyes. It was piled high with books, all kinds, ledgers, receipts, bills, rolls of paper, prints, pulls, and pencils, brushes, paints, colour trials, nibs, paper clips, a wooden clock as never went, a towel as never even see the skies over a laundry and bits of soap, bottles of medicine, jars of tablets, Italian newspapers, and a picture of his Mrs, in a red velvet frame with cockle shells stuck on it. In the middle of the mess there was a statue of some old bloke as looked at everybody proper suspicious, with a kind of a night cap on, with tassels, and another statue, of a bloke with curly hair and a broken nose as looked like Him, sometimes, only not always.

Behind his chair there was a oil picture of Venice, with the high road full of water and the front door steps going down smack in the drink, and a lot of boats floating about spare, with sort of busted combs on the fronts of them, and little huts built in the middle.

Old Nick wagged his behind at the door and it slammed shut.

"Ernie," he says, "you lose seventeen and half hours last week because you late. Why?"

He was just like Ma at the window, big and fat, blocking out the light.

Funny how a question proper gets you down. Laying in bed in the dark listening to Ma lighting the fire and the trains shoving a thick rope of noise through the quiet, and green tram tickets dropping atop of blokes talking about the bosses, and the smell of newspapers in Ma Cranns, and Ada, and the way she showed up when she pulled her jersey down, there it was, the whole thing, but it was no good of Him trying to explain it like that.

"Seventeen and a half hours?" He says, and He screwed His voice up at the end to let the blokes outside know what He thought about it, "I only come here six days a week, Mr Falandora?"

"Two hours on Monday," Old Nick says, and he was reading it off of the blotting paper, writ in red pencil, "three and half on Tuesday. Wednesday, you missing in the morning altogether, and Thursday."

"I had a cold," He says. "I was ill all the week. It's a wonder I come in at all."

"So," Old Nick says, looking as if he just seen the ghost of Doctor Crippen. "I am very sorry." He looked like as if he was trying to think how it would feel. "A cold, uh?"

"That's right, a cold," He says, feeling proper hard done by, "and I had a bilious attack, and all. I ought to stayed in bed, be rights."

"Listen, Ernie," Old Nick says, a bit too quiet to be nice, "I tell you something. You had a cold since you come here. You bilious since you come here. You always a late. Never you come the proper time. This afternoon, you see Mr Tomlin."

The crushed nuts stopped pouring and Old Nick looked at his Mrs photo as if he never see it before in his life.

"What have I got to see him for?" He says, knowing as well as Old Nick why, but just asking in case He was wrong.

"Because I don't want you here no more," Old Nick says, still looking at his Mrs. "You no good to me and you no good for this work."

When Old Nick was put out, he always talked quiet and got more ice creamo than usual, sort of sneery, over his shoulder, as if you was a thousand miles away. If it got worse, he started shouting the odds, and pulling his hair, and chucking things about, and generally carrying on there something alarming, till you could use his eyes for hat pegs.

Funny how everything looked as if it was being boiled in hot water, but it was worse to have your self shaking about and not be able to stop it, nor nothing.

"No use to cry," Old Nick says, and turned his back in the hot water, "I had enough. See Mr Tomlin three o'clock."

"I ain't crying," He says, "it's my cold. And I ain't seeing no Mr Tomlin this afternoon, neither. If you don't want me here, I can soon find me self another job."

Old Nick was looking out the window, and the light shone round the friz of his hair just like one of them gold rings round them old blokes with beards on Sunday school texts.

"What you going to do?" he says. "What you want to do?"

"Going to be a artist, I am," He says, a bit too rocky for His taste, though.

Old Nick pulled his keys out and went to the drawing cupboard where all the finished jobs was kept. Down on the bottom shelf he pulled out a big canvas folio and clouted it to knock the dust off.

"Is you father's work," he says. "Look."

They was big sheets, they was, lovely hand rolled paper, sort of rough all round the edges, and proper talk to you to draw on them, they did.

It was proper real to look at them, and all, while Old Nick's bamboo stubs turned them over like as if they was solid gold, and think to your self, this was the Old Man's work what he done when you was on your way, or perhaps not even thought of.

He felt His self crawling all over, He did, He proper got a shock and a half when He see them, though.

They was all so smashing. He wanted to look anywhere but where they was, but Old Nick was watching Him, not the stuff, so all He could do was look, and keep on looking, and the more He looked the worser it got, like when you run after a tram and you know how much chance you got of catching it.

Black and white, pen and crayon, two, three, four colour jobs, etchings, water colours, washes, blotting paper sketches, odd bits of paper with faces on them, they was all there, and the more He see of them the colder He was sort of getting in the guts. He never knew the Old Man was so good. He knew he was good, but He never knew he was as good as all that. He was proper smashing.

"This work you father did when he was nineteen, twenty, twenty one, twenty two," Old Nick says, and puts his fists on the sheets and sticks his face about three inches away. "How old you are?"

"Nigh on nineteen," He says, as if it was something to be proper ashamed of, why, He never knew.

"When you father was nineteen," Old Nick says, "he was great artist already. Twenty one, his picture is in the Tate Gallery. You see this one? Is call The Girl in the Mirror?"

"No," He says, "I never heard of it."

Old Nick looked down a bit, and you might think he been walloped by somebody. Then he started packing up the drawings again, a sight quicker than what he undone them.

"So," he says, half way through, "Mr Tomlin, three o'clock, eh?"

"Shan't be there," He says. "Don't want to see him."

Old Nick stops tying up and looks at Him.

"You know what happens, eh?" he says, as if he was sorry.

"Got an idea," He says, getting a bit cocky again in case the blokes outside thought he was feeling sorry for His self.

"So what you going to do?" Old Nick says, still looking. "What you mother will say?"

"Don't much matter," He says, feeling He wanted to get in a swipe, somewhere. "I'll soon get another job. You're only getting rid of me because you'll soon be having to pay me man's wages, that's all. We all know that lark. Wait till I nearly come out of me time, then sack me. I never expected nothing else."

"Aha," says Old Nick, and he nods his head as if it was on a thin spring. "So." A lot more nods. "So." He finished tying up and even pulled the tapes out their full width, and a bloke only wastes a lot of time like that when he wants to think, and take his time doing it.

"Ernie," he says, with the ends of his moustache and his eyes over the top of the folio, "you father, he was my friend. I hope you would be like him. Fourteen, fifteen years I watch you grow up. I bring you here, in this place, where I start with you father and Mr Tomlin. I want you to take you fathers place. But you are lazy boy. Inattentive. Not serious. You are late. You go when the clock says six o'clock. But you father worked. You father was an artist. You are a shoemaker."

The blokes outside must have been proper killing their selfs after that lot. He wanted to stuff something in Old Nick's trap to stop him talking, or else get up and nail a board along the top of the partition.

"You say you like to be artist?" Old Nick says, and more crushed nuts than ever come pouring through his voice. "But you don't even take the trouble to see you father's work. Not even this, in this cupboard for years. You not interest."

"Nobody never told me nothing about it," He says, and He reckoned He had a good right to start slinging His weight about.

"Look," Old Nick says, and he gives his self a smack across the forehead, just to learn his self a thing or two. "You want to be an artist. Who you are study with?"

"Study what?" He says, wondering what was on.

"You got to study, no?" Old Nick says, and puts the fingers of one hand together and wags them about. "What school you go to?"

"Can't afford no school," He says, and He proper had him there, so He made something big out of it. "My Ma can't afford no schools. I got to make me own way, I have. Sides,

I wouldn't let her do no more than what she's doing now. I can't be hanging round her neck all the time?"

"All right, all right," Old Nick says, as if he was proper tired of the whole nonsense. "So you go to the National Gallery, no? Exhibitions, eh?"

"No," He says. "I never get the time."

"But you know these places, eh?" Old Nick says, and he screws up his eyes as if pepper got in them. "You study the schools? Italian, Flemish, German? You know? Who you study? Who you like? Who is you favourite?"

"I can't see no sense of having a favourite," He says. "Sides, Italians and that lot can't do nothing for me. That's their look out, that is."

Old Nick reached over the table, and grabbed a roll of stuff in brown paper, pulling at the string as come off in one snatch. All His stuff, it was.

He could see the mistakes, the rubbings out, where the colours run, where the razor scraped till it went right through the sheet. They was proper shocking, the lot of them, specially after the Old Man's stuff. He found His self trying not to look again.

"So, Mr Nothing To Learn," Old Nick says, and smacks the sheets with his hands as if he wants to push the lot of them through the floor out of sight. "Mr Shoemaker, what you do? You don't know how to copy something in front of your eyes. How you going to create something? Late in the morning, and six o'clock at night, with colds in your nose, no?"

He went off in Italian, proper giving it big licks, but he never said nothing as meant nothing to nobody with some common sense, so the blokes outside was that much worse off, and all.

"My Old Man was a artist," He says, right in the middle of Old Nick's rubbish, louder than him, so it went over the partition easy enough for them to hear, "so I'm going to be one, and all. And you nor nobody else can't stop me, see? And that's it."

That stopped the caper. Old Nick shut up, grabbed the folio

again, and slung it in the bottom of the cupboard. Then he looked out the window and the place was dead quiet.

A couple of trams was moaning at each other going round the corner.

"Ernie," he says, "you are small boy. Perhaps it is my fault. I should have spoke to you mother plenty of time ago. I think perhaps you get better. And you father was my friend. I try to be like a father, but when I talk to you, I don't see anything with sympathy. So, I can't talk."

He sounded proper sorry for his self. Wagging his head, there, and sort of holding hands with his self and shaking them up and down, real ice creamo all over.

"I tell you what we do, eh?" he says, and turns round, sort of smiling as if he never wanted to. "Instead to go in the caffee for you lunch, you come with me, and we go to the Tate Gallery to see you father's picture. Yes?"

If He could work His way round by boxing clever, there was a chance, He was thinking, of staying on the job. The thoughts of going back to Ma, and looking out the kitchen door while He tried to tell her what happened, was a proper how do you do. What she might have to say far from suited his fancy.

"Okeedoke, Mr Falandora," He says, not too cheerful, though, as if He was glad of the chance, but none too hopeful about things.

"So," Old Nick says, and turns round again. "Half past twelve outside, eh?"

"Okeedoke, Mr Falandora," He says, and out He goes, but He closed the door like as if it was made of new currant cake.

The blokes was all well down to it. Nobody looked up when He come out, so He knew they all heard it, every word.

He felt He wanted to shout at them, swear at them, anything, to make them look kind of not quite so bleeding pleased with their selfs. He knew they never liked Him, but it was only because He stuck up for His self.

Back at the stone, He see what He done as if He never see it before in all His life.

There was something wrong with Him, but there seemed to be nothing He could do about it.

Never mind how hard He tried, that there crayon in His hand never done what He wanted it to, nor never did, nor He never see where He went wrong, nor how to shove it right.

There was the master print, what He was copying off of, on to the stone, but even though it was right on top of the job, still it never come out right. His hand and the crayon was always that much out. Other blokes never had no trouble, yet as far as He could see, they was proper mugs in other ways.

Perhaps His Old Man was a mug, too, in his day, like Ma was always saying, yet he was a proper artist. The thoughts of the stuff in the cupboard proper turned Him up, because He knew He could never get nowhere near it. Perhaps you had to be a mug to be a artist.

He would have given anything if only He could have got that there bleeding crayon to do what He wanted it to, something proper smashing, something Old Nick would kiss his fingers at, like he done when he was pleased with his self about a job.

But something kept on telling Him He was kidding His self, even though He took no notice of it, and His guts was getting colder and colder till He was all of a shiver.

Perhaps He was a shoemaker, like Old Nick said. Perhaps it was no good of Him trying to be a artist. He was looking at the stone through hot water again, and them trams, as moaned while they went round the corner, was making the same noise as some voice inside of Him.

## CHAPTER XIV

HE RECKONED it was proper queer how you can walk about with a bloke what you want to talk to, and yet all the words in the world sort of went for a walk all of a sudden, and left you climbing up the wall for something to say.

He tried heavens hard, He did, to get hold of something to talk about, but everything as come sounded so luny, He give it up and lolloped along there, aside Old Nick, just looking about and saying nothing, and feeling that there funny sort of hot space between them as He knew could be froze off by words, if only He could bring them to mind. But there He was, stuck, and about as comfortable as the toe trying to crawl out of the hole in His sock.

Old Nick was none too cheerful neither. He was looking away most of the time as if he was walking about in some fairy tale of his own somewhere, with his guts poked out in front, and his overcoat done up on the bottom button as just about covered his trousers, and his hair blowing about in lumps because of the grease as kept it together, and a lovely big drip on the end of his snitch as never dropped once, not once, because He sniffed up just in time. Proper marvellous to watch, it was.

He was a bit surprised when He found His self turning up some steps in Trafalgar Square, but He never said nothing. It looked like a funny sort of a place to be going in, kind of grey and big churchy, with a lot of railings, but it was Old Nick's do, so He let him get on with it.

So it come a right shock to get inside there and see a big stone stairs with pictures all the way up both sides, and dirty big doorways going in rooms smothered in pictures, nigh on as big as a house, some of them was.

Old Nick stopped dead, just after they come through the turnstiles, like going in the Stadium early of a Saturday afternoon, it was, only quieter, and he starts breathing with his eyes shut, big breaths, like as if he thought he could smell something tasty for supper.

"Ah," he says, and he holds his arms out wide, looking up and sort of laughing without shifting his mouth, "the perfume of creation, the breath of the Good God, free. Free, free, free. Smell, Ernie. Breathe in, steal, take away to remember. Live for a moment among the giants of mankind."

He shuts his mouth sort of quick and his eyes went wrinkled shut, and when he looked up again they was red round the edges and he looked as if he was going to start howling.

"You father and me was always here twenty, thirty years ago," he says, proper sorry for his self, trembly, sort of. "We were young men. Young. Is pathetic, this word."

He looked up the stairs, shoving his bits of yellow bamboo through his hair to lay it down a bit, and swallowed half a dozen eggs, shells and all.

"You father, he said this," Old Nick says. "Live for a moment among the giants of mankind. The pioneers. The heart breakers. The broken of the heart. For every one of these what you can see, one hundred thousand must be painted, and burnt, and little men must try again. Try and try and try. And make prayers on their knees. Starve to buy canvas. Buy colours. Oil. Make brushes. Starve, starve, starve. Gods among men, these one. Painting with blood, these men. Putting their souls in the hairs of the brush. Not for a living, but because they got flowers growing in their hearts. The brave ones. The beautiful ones."

A couple of blokes in blue uniforms was looking at the pair of them, as if they was wondering which door they ought to sling them out of, or whether to call the police and make a job of it.

"What was up, then, Mr Falandora?" He says, a bit anxious, to try and get Old Nick off of it. "Couldn't they sell nothing, then?"

Old Nick give his self a clout aside the head, not very hard, like he done when he forgot something, and turned his eyes up.

"No," he says, and he wags his nut at the ceiling. "They got nothing to sell and nobody don't want to buy. Come on. We go in this way."

He rushed off up the big stairs, and following his coat tails was no lark, neither, because he proper shifted his self. Some old dear at the top coming out give the pair of them a look as if she wanted to see the manager about it. She had a funny sort of a hat on, like a purple pancake, and glasses with silver rims.

"Now then," Old Nick says, and he pulls up at a long narrow picture of the Virgin Mary with a baby in her lap, with a lot of blokes all round her, all done in cracked gold and red and black, by somebody as never knew very much about it. "This was painted nearly seven hundred years ago. You will see how men, these little men, started to work. Beautiful, eh? Beautiful."

"Don't see much in it, meself," He says, trying to say His best for it and give it credit due, but it looked as if some kid had been having a go, and none too bright at that, neither. Besides, He reckoned Old Nick might be leading Him up the garden to try and make a mug out of Him, so he went a bit careful.

Old Nick bambooed his hair again, as if he had visitors, and looked at the picture, and when he had enough of it, he looked up and down this here long room, sort of trying to say something as stuck in his gullet. Then he put his neck back in the collar of his coat and walked up a bit, pulling up outside a walloping big picture of blokes on horses having a go at each other with spears, and old fashioned swords, slashing the guts out of their selfs if they got anywhere nigh each other, but they was all born careful by the looks of them.

"How much you see in this?" he says, and the way he says it, you could see you had to box clever to come out the right end.

"It ain't bad," He says, quick. "But he bit off a bit more than he could chew, didn't he? Old Josh Pickering can draw a better horse any day of the week. And I don't go too much on his perspective, neither, nor that bloke's hat. Looks like one of the old duck's parlour cushions."

Old Nick had his cheeks sort of puffed out, and though his eyes was looking at the picture, he looked as if he was seeing outside of it, through the wall, like. There was plenty to look at, say what you like, so there was no need of him looking nowhere else. It was a bit sort of anxious, watching him, looking with them black onion eyes of his.

"Funny," Old Nick says, sort of sad and stretching it out a bit. "Very funny. I would like to know what is matter why I can't talk. With you father I talk for hours, for days, months, years. He was my best friend. With you? Impossible. So impossible, absolutely."

Waving his arms about like a chicken, he was, and the old girl in the purple pancake was looking at them over her glasses, proper terse. But He could feel His self getting angry again, funny sort of angry, though, kind of hopeless and far from home, lost, as you might say, like. He wanted to know why Old Nick could talk to the Old Man and not to Him.

"What's up with me, then?" He says, and He was surprised His self how loud He sounded. Old purple pancake seemed to shiver all over. "I'm all right, ain't I? I've only told you what I've thought of the bleeding things, ain't I? Well, then, what's up with that?"

"Ernie," Old Nick says, sorry like, "listen to me. Don't try to see things of our time in these pictures. Try always to see things in the time it is painted. Try to see the difficulty, how hard, what hard work. Try to see some poor man trying to draw somebody lying on the floor. Foreshortened perspective, eh? So how he does it?"

"Like we do it," He says, and He was getting angrier, even though He could see Old Nick wanted to be nice, but that made it sort of worser than ever. "It's hard for me, ain't it? Think I find it easy, do you? You ought to know."

"So," Old Nick says. "Why you don't study what these men do? Why you don't come here every moment you can? Like you father? Like me? Where you think we learn?"

"All right," He says. "Where's the Old Man's picture? Let's have a look at it."

"Not here," Old Nick says, and he turns round and looks at the white horse again. "Is in the Tate Gallery, this one."

"What are we wasting a lot of time here for, then?" He says. "I thought we come to see how good my Old Man was?"

"Is better to see how you father get knowledge," Old Nick says, none too sweet, neither.

"It was born in him," He says. "It was born in me, and all, if only I could get hold of the right bloke to learn me a couple of things."

Old Nick slewed round and dug his finger in His chest and that little bit of bamboo felt like the poke of a umbrella.

"Echo," he says, right off of the deep end, he was, poking away there. "Echo. Here he is. You. Youself. Nobody else. You don't work. You don't want to work. You don't want to learn. You make excuse for yourself. You dream."

His eyes come up in front of you like a couple of black balloons, but you could see your face in them, white, very small, right at the back there, looking dopey.

The crushed nuts was pouring through by the bag full, and his breath smelt of them little purple cachous what he was always getting his front teeth on, cracking them like dried peas. They smelt all right, sort of sweetish.

"You think you like to be something but you don't make anything," Old Nick says, proper loud and getting louder, "you give excuse. Cold in the nose, eh? Nobody can teach you. You want to criticise. So. Criticise like other fools. Criticise till you blind, deaf, dumb. Criticise till you are dead. But when you are dead, Mr Critic, this picture will still hang on the wall. These men will always be perfume when you and the rest of you are finish to stink in your tomb."

No use arguing there. Old Nick was sweating angry, he was. His old onions was washing about like a couple of loose ball bearings.

"That's a nice way to talk to anybody, Mr Falandora," He says, as if He was cushy how He was spoke to, only He wanted it knowed what He thought about it. "I'd have picked a row with any other bloke, but seeing it's you, I shan't say nothing. I ain't no critic, whatever it is. I'm only saying how I look at it, that's all. No harm in that, is there?"

Old Nick had hold of Him by the shoulders in two ticks. Strong as a lion he was, and so help us, he was as nigh on howling as made no difference. It come a proper surprise, it did.

"Ernie," he says. "You too much like you father. Please, don't remember nothing what I say. Go home. Forget to draw. Be happy, please. No use to talk. No use."

Old Nick shoved his hands back in his overcoat and looks round like as if he thought of bashing his way out through a wall. Tears was like little blobs of mercury in his eyes. Proper ice creamo, he was, and looked it.

"Goodbye, Ernie," he says, all of a sudden. "You father was my dear friend. Many things I wish, but I wish more I could speak to you like you father. Go home to you mother, Ernie. Tell her what I say. Eh?"

"Okeedoke, Mr Falandora," He says, but He was so surprised He never knew what He was doing of. "What shall I tell her?"

Old Nick was dead quiet. You could hear his mary curdling, and somebody squeaking about on the polished floor. He shoved his hands right down in the pockets of his overcoat and looked round at the white horse, but he never see too much of it. He looked like one of them funny stone things as stick out of old churches round the top.

"Tell you mother she was right," he says. "There is more of her in you than you father. You got what you call criticism, but no ability. You got eyes, but no hands. You think you know, but you cannot think to do. Mr Tomlin was going to tell you this afternoon. Better I should tell you now. So go home, Ernie. You are a boy. You are young enough to start a good job. Come to see me sometimes, eh? We shall talk about you father."

He was walking away, talking to his self, he was, passing the old girl in the purple pancake, and she never knew which of the two of them she ought to look at first. Proper nosey bit of goods, she was.

"Goodbye, Ernie," Old Nick says, down at the big door. "Come to see me sometimes, eh?"

"Okeedoke," He says, but He could hardly hear it, even His self. It seemed all wrong, somehow, Old Nick going off like that, saying goodbye and leaving Him all alone in this here great big picture cemetery. He come over ice cold.

He was Out.

"Is anything wrong?" says purple pancake, and her two front teeth come out like a pair of piano keys. Square and white, they was, and her spit made them shine.

"No," He says. "I just lost my job, that's all."

"Oh," she says, "what a pity. Was that horrid little man your employer?"

"As good as," He says, getting to like her a bit more because she was so sort of kind, and like getting your cold hands over a stove. "He was the foreman. Italian, he is."

"Never liked them," she says. "Thoroughly dirty lot. I don't think I should worry very much if I were you?"

"That's all very well," He says, "but what about me rock of ages, and the roast and boiled?"

"The what?" she says, proper soppy.

"Roast and boiled," He says. "Roast beef and boiled spuds. The grub. Me wages."

"Look here," she says, and she starts scratting about in her purse what was the size of a young cabbage bag, full of junk it was. "There's my card. Come and see me tomorrow and I'll see what I can do. Eleven o'clock?"

"Okeedoke, Miss Wilmore," He says, "how do I get there?"

"A bus from Piccadilly brings you right by the door," she says. "Where do you come from?"

"Just off the Kingsland Road," He says, "I can bus it all right."

"There's half a crown," she says, and here comes a half, as large as life and twice as nice.

"What's this for?" He says, and He sort of felt queer. It hardly seemed right and He knew what Ma might say.

"What's the idea, Miss? Come to that, why d'you want to get me a job all of a sudden?"

"I really don't know," she says, and first she looked half scared, then her piano keys come out again and she starts laughing. "I've never done such a thing before. But he was such a nasty little bin, I simply couldn't help it."

Well, He starts laughing and all, so there the pair of them was, laughing like a double of lunies round a pudding cloth, but He could feel His self a artist all over, being sort of well in with a old dear like this.

"Isn't it silly?" she says, and she looks over the top of her glasses to see if anybody had his eye on her. "Goodbye," she says, and the fingers of her gloves was wagging their selfs at Him while she was putting them on. "Tomorrow at eleven."

"Okeedoke," He says, and He felt so barmy, and kind of hot, and right up the pole, He could have bit his thumb off short and never felt it.

"Oh," she says, just going out of it, "what's your name?"

Ada came back all of a sudden and the doorway was full of red beetles, not so as He could see them, but they was there, and He wanted to run to the Fun Fair, quick.

"Ernest Verdun Mott," He says, in the dark at the yellow lamp.

"Oh," she says. "Thank you. Well, goodbye."

"So long," He says, sweating all over, He was, and glad to see the goings of her.

No sooner she went out the big door, than one of the blokes in blue come over from the side, somewhere. But He was thinking something about not being a artist, trying to make up His mind how He felt about it all, so He never give the uniform much of a thought.

"What's your little game?" this bloke says, and he stands there with his fists on his hips.

"Eh?" He says, getting cold again, and losing the laugh, quick. This was different.

"What you playing at?" this geezer says, nasty like. "I been watching you this last ten minutes, or so. Don't you come no begging nonsense in here, or you'll find yourself somewhere else, me lad. You sling your hook, quick."

"What are you talking about, begging?" He says, hardly no voice at all, high up. "Me? I ain't begging. I've just been sacked, if you must know. And that there lady give me a card to go and see her."

"We've heard that tale before," this geezer says, and gives his guts a shove round with both hands.

"Not from me, you ain't," He says. "But if you want one, I'll give you one. I ain't having that, not from nobody, I ain't. I might tip you, I'm a artist and I don't stand no lip from nobody."

"Go out of it," says the bloke, "you saucy little bleeder, you."

"You can't talk to me like that," He says, and He was just about set to take a first timer at them guts, but there was somebody coming up the steps laughing. "I'll see somebody about you."

"Yes?" says the bloke. "I'll tell you what. I'll give you two seconds to get your body outside, or else I'll give you a bloody good hiding. How's that, eh?"

It was no good of starting a row, and perhaps Miss Wilmore might not want her name dragged in. If He got on to Old Nick, he could only say he give Him the sack. And this bloke had his uniform on, and a shower of mates for witnesses downstairs. So that was it.

"I was going any old how," He says. "I didn't come here to do me self any good, anyway."

"Just you let me catch you in here again, that's all," this geezer says, almost yelling, he was, with six silver button eyes all staring upwards, down this here big room, and his voice sort of come back at you from three sides. Some old girl just come in with half a dozen or so brides with her, all about sixteen or seventeen, proper good lookers some of them was, and they was all looking at Him going out. "You'll go out a sight quicker'n what you come in, you good for nothing young lout, you."

"Go and get stuffed," He shouts him, just before He gets to

the door, and winks at the brides, but though they was looking, their faces never changed. Eyes, with girl's clothes round
them, that was all they was, and about as sweet as a lump of
kitchen soap.

So He went down the stairs quick as what He come up, and
out of it through the turnstiles with all the clicks, feeling the
light of the Way Out whitening His dial, and when He got outside on the sort of platform with big pillars, He stopped, because there was two lots of steps, one on the left, what Him and
Old Nick come up, and another lot on the right.

So He went down them on the right, because it seemed to be
more of a break, and when He finished passing some brides
who was having their sandwiches for lunch sitting spraddle
legged on the steps, there He was, in the road, out of work. But
though He knew them brides must have been showing a bit of
laundry, He was in such a tear. He never even looked back,
never mind up, nor wanted to.

## CHAPTER XV

DOWN THE PAN, He was, proper in the dirt, and nobody looked as if they cared twopence. They was all walking by, there, and none of them even give Him a look.

The buses come by redding and roaring, shaking the place about with their rubber feet, and taxis full of rich people was ducking in and out, so it was a proper game dodging across the grey road in sliding gaps between shiny black wings and head-lights, first this way, then that, and when He got on the other pavement at last, He was thinking a bit angry how it would be to smash up everything on wheels, so as to cross a road decent for once.

Looking round sort of empty, Five to Three of a Monday afternoon in Trafalgar Square, coming on to rain when the sun went in, with buses and taxis rushing about all round, and this here big pole of stone with a bloke on top, and some statues of lions or some bright thing or other, sprawling about under-neath, and a couple of fountains full of black water with bits of paper and matches sloshing about on the tops, a couple of old blokes kipping on a bench, some kids playing about with a lot of pigeons down the end there, and Him, standing there sacked, bust, on His own, not a blind sausage one way or an-other, and not one of them cared that much, not even that much, or even knew He was alive.

Feeling proper wore out, He went over and pulled His self up on the stone railing to have a sit down. The paper bag His sandwiches was in started rattling about, so He pulled it out. The brown paper was all stained darker oily brown with marg, and the sandwiches was a bit squashed of sitting on them, but they was all right, except His throat was too dry to swallow, somehow, like eating a load of gravel.

So He give over eating, and slung the lot down behind Him

to give the sparrows a treat, trying to get rid of the dry lumps in His mouth as best He could, till He got tired of trying, and spit the lot out.

It come up inside of Him, sort of sick and hot, somewhere, or perhaps it was sick and cold, making His head go round a bit, so as the buses come by in ribbons of red instead of blocks, and the taxis was black tapes, not squares, and the grey horse was a dirty thumbprint, and He was proper sick and cold, sick cold sick, and breathing hot petrol smoke come up fatty sweet and blue all round Him.

He was out of work, He could hear a voice telling Him as plain as the voices of the people passing Him. But they was all walking by, there, and nobody give that much.

They never even seen Him.

Even the tall bride with yellow shiny hair, and a green coat, and lovely long pink legs and a mouth as red as a bus never see Him, neither.

Out of work, He was, and nobody cared, even though He was a artist with flowers growing in His heart. He tried to think what else Old Nick said but whatever it was, it never seemed to mean much. Not here, anyhow.

Looking at a bus through a lot of hot water, listening to taxis calling out as if they was being kicked up the jacksie, and other people talking about things while they was going by, and laughing, some of them was, He knew, empty and far away like, none of them knew He was there.

Nobody even give Him a look. He was just a bloke squatting on the railings, looking up at the pale grey sky as had smudges of light blue here and there, giving everything a sort of whitish look, and making the red buses redder. Their windows was like a lot of eyes looking at you, and getting out of it as if they was afraid they was going to be asked for a couple of coppers to get a mug of tea, like Ted Framlin used to do, fore they picked him up off of the railway.

Nobody never found out how he got there.

His shoes was full of cracks, dusty with walking, and all

bumps where His toes fitted them, and they looked sulkier than He ever see them before. They seemed to know they was going to last a long time. They had to, whether they liked it or not.

He was out of work.

# CHAPTER XVI

KNOCKING ABOUT THE ROADS and looking in shop windows was a treat, for a couple of hours, anyhow, because there was such a smashing lot of things you could get if you had the nicker on you. He never come up here before, except of a Sunday, when the shops was all shut, so to see them all open, and all the rich people tearing about in and out of them, it sort of come a proper shock, because it was so new.

It was just like as if the films suddenly come real all round Him. He see a marvellous sort of pink nightdress what you could see right through, like thin fog, it was, as might have fitted Ada right down to the ground. He kept it in His mind for later on when He had a job, like, and a bit of brass to spare. He kept on thinking of it every time His mind come on to Ma waiting at home, there. He stuffed it deep down in His mind where He could hear her voice.

He could hear her crowing over Him, and telling Him I Told You So. Every time He thought of it, and heard her saying it, plain as the traffic, it proper turned Him up. So He thought of the nightdress and how Ada would look in it, because it was nicer to think about, and from that, He thought of Ada, and He kept on wanting to go down the Fair, and get near her to feel that funny sort of unhappy, smiling feeling all over alike, as you might say, and yet He knew He was down the drain till He got a job and started earning a bit of dough.

He had to have a few bob, now, or else, if she wanted Him to see her home, and they went in the cafe for a cup or two of something hot, He was going to be down the drain, and old Ted never give credit, not even on the Old Pal's Act.

Opposite a sort of gardens, He come to a big cinema where people was queued up waiting to go in. The picture looked all right, all about New York, it was, with photographs of coppers, twice life size, shooting out of guns with a couple of inches of barrel. Proper boys, they looked, and all. There was a news, and two comics, and one of them science doings in colour, so it looked all right for a couple of hours, any rate, and He had enough of walking about for a bit.

Counting up, He had Three and Sevenpence all told, and it was One and Three to go in. So that left Two and Four to come out with. So He could still have something to eat, and get some fags, and still have enough for His fares to get home. That settled it.

Queueing up was a bit of sport and all, because you could watch everybody going by who was unluckier than what you was, and taxis come up and blokes and brides got out, and you could size them up a treat. You could tell from the way the bloke paid off, and the bride's face, what he thought he was going to get from the night's outing. It was dead funny. Besides that, there was always a chance of getting off with some bride in the queue. But most of them had their blokes, as per, and the rest of them was all ninety five or thereabouts, so it come a bit hard even to give them a look.

It was a treat to go inside the glass doors, better than even the biggest local at home. He heard about these West End cinemas before from Len and some of the lads what was in the money, but He never come in His self. After all, you could see the same picture a month or so later, round the local, so it was all the same, except you saved your fares up and back, and that was a packet of fags in anybody's money, so it had to be looked at.

But the darkness inside, and the warm of a lot of people breathing in and out together was just the same, but the seats was high up, almost in the ceiling, and the screen was the size of a penny stamp, so it come a bit of a disappointment, after all He heard. He got too used to the tanners at home, and looking up at a big picture.

This lark of squatting up at the back made Him feel proper out of it. There was too much space either side of you and a great big round black hole underneath you as made you want to do a high dive all the time. Not only that, but when the people laughed downstairs, you could hear them afore you started your own laugh, and sometimes them laughing stopped you hearing what was being said, so there you was, stuck up there, like a pross at a christening, out of it, sorry for it, and none too sweet about it neither.

But He kept on thinking of Ma, and the more He thought, the more He knew He would rather die than go home and tell her He got the sack. Besides, He made hundreds of promises to her what He was going to do for her when He come out of His Time, and started getting proper wages. Taking it by and large, He must have owed her pounds and pounds.

But now, here He was, out of work, and she always told Him He would, if He kept on going in late. It never seemed to matter then, but He was kicking His self, now. It seemed so easy, sitting there, to get up of a morning. All you had to do was open your eyes and shove back the clothes and grab your trousers, and there you was, out of it.

But somewhere or other, somehow, it seemed to come a bit harder of a morning when you come to actually do it. Different story altogether, it was.

Come to a finish, He never see nothing of the picture. New York was a bit too far away. The comics was about blokes on a farm, and another about sailors, and He never see much in either of them. He got proper impatient with His self for not knowing what He was looking at, because of His One and Threepence in the box downstairs. But what with Ma, and the way He was sitting, and knowing He was out of work and it was all His fault, He started feeling kind of hot, and proper queer, and He knew it was fresh air or flop out, so He got up and walked down the soft carpet and traipsed all the way round and round stone stairs, and found His self at the back door, out in the yard. He thought to His self it was the proper door to come out of, and all.

So there He was, walking about again, fed up, far from home, and feeling proper sorry for His self.

One of them quiet dark nights it was, up above there, not too cold, with the bright blue lights shining on the bald white heads of the buses, with all their rows of eyes shining between the red top and bottom, and cars and taxis flashing up and down, and thousands of people all rushing about enjoying their selfs along the white pavements, and the shop lights shining on their faces, and adverts all splashing and dripping away in all sorts of colours, like Old Nick's palette, and traffic lights down the length of the road, like showers of big yellow diamonds changing to rubies, changing to emeralds, and back to yellow diamonds and rubies again.

There was fur coats in the windows, and yards of marvellous shoes, and suits and overcoats, and furniture and clocks, but it was all the same to Him. He looked at the people what was all looking in the windows, watching their faces and hearing them talk, but they was like a lot of foreigners, talking a different language, and when He tried to listen to them, there was Ma again, telling Him He was out of work.

It was no good of being a artist if you was out of work, that was a dead cert. It was all very well some blokes saying artists was blokes as lived in attics and wore red shirts and had candles stuck in a bottle, but they had to have a job of some sort to keep them going.

But He was out of work, and everybody seemed to know it, because nobody so much as looked at Him, and even the lights seemed to shine whiter on Him than everybody else.

Looking at windows after a bit just turned Him up, because there it all was, for the asking, and all you wanted was the nicker, but a bit more than Two and Four. That there Two and Four was like a little wall between Him and a big black space as He could see plainer than a bus. It come up every time He thought of what might happen when that Two and Four was spent.

He had nothing, only His self, as you might say, so the answer added up the same. Just the bare nixey.

His clothes was just about ready to drop off out of being tired of it all, His shoes was nigh wore down to the lace holes, and there was nothing in His pockets except a bit of pencil, some fags and matches, and a knife with a busted blade what old Josh gave Him, to get shut of.

Ernest Verdun Mott, the artist, in all His glory, and bar a mouldy Two and Fourpence, not a bleeding sausage in the whole of the world, nothing a pawnshop would look at, and not a friend, not even Ma.

Just His self.

The big blue world, with straight bright lines of lights flashing away there, all shining with coloured neons, and full up of people, was chucking Him out of it. It, nor nobody else, wanted Him.

They was all against Him, the lot of them. He was only Ernie Mott, the artist bloke, the bastard of the world, and everybody's mug.

# CHAPTER XVII

"WHAT ARE YOU laughing about, son?" somebody says, and He sort of come out of a dream, quick, thinking it was a copper trying to be funny, or something.

"Eh?" He says, ready to say anything.

It was some old bloke in a grey top hat, sort of crashed in, and a high collar with one of them sort of folding over ties as cover up all your shirt. He had a swallow tailed coat on, and striped trousers, and the biggest boots He ever see on a bloke in all His puff, with the toes all poked up in front, and turned out duck footed. In one hand he had one of them doctor's bags, and a walloping dirty great big umbrella, nigh as big as his self, in the other.

"Know all about me now, do you?" this old bloke says, laughing he was, but having a joke, not nasty. "My name's Henry Twite, and I'm Lord of the Manor of Tookover. Sorry I can't present you with a couple of my cards. They're down the labour exchange. Been there years. Who are you?"

"Ernie Mott," He says, and the old bloke was so kind, and sort of cheerful, He started wanting to howl. "Ernest Verdun Mott, that's me full name."

"Verdun?" the old bloke says, thinking a bit. A bit like Pa Fitchett, he was. "How d'you come to get a rare old title like that, eh?"

"Me father was killed there," He says. "In the last war. I was born after he rolled up."

"Oh," says the old bloke. "After he rolled up, eh?"

He was looking at Him dead straight, and the shop lights caught him aside the eyes, so they looked like little balls of cracked glass, all white and shiny.

"And what's his boy doing, standing in the middle of the pavement looking as if He wanted to roll up, and all? Eh?" this old bloke says, turning the brolly round.

It was no good, here it come, and it was no use of trying to stop it. Hot water come up and drownded everything, drown over drown, down and down, deep and wet, hot and soppy, all the lights getting like coloured waterfalls and everything sloshing about in everything else, reds, yellows, purples and greens, blues and whites, a proper right old mess all round, standing there shaking about like a vinegar bottle over a two-penny hake and two pennyworth of chips.

"Ah," says the old bloke, "that's different, that is. Suppose we scarper down this here little crack, here, while I transact a bit of business, eh? It's me last call for the night afore I repair to the baronial eyrie. It'll give you a chance to give yourself a rub down, and all. Sweating like that on a night like this here, you'll catch your death of double ammonia. Then the band won't half play."

The old bloke goes tearing down the road a bit, and turn into a kind of narrow lane between the shops. Pitch black, it was, down there, so He just followed the clumps of the old bloke's hoofs, not knowing where He was going, or what they was on, and trying to get His face cleaned up a bit.

"Just here," the old bloke says, cheery voice he had, come to think of it, "mind how you fall down these here bleeding stairs, now. They're all wore hollow in the middle, so if you pick your steps very careful, and grab hold the banisters, you won't do so bad."

The old bloke was tapping about with his brolly, trying to find the stair edge.

"If you start slipping, lay down and slide it," he says. "If you come in here of a wet night, it's a proper sod, I can tell you. You're arse over tip before you know how. I've thought of suing the boss here a time or two, but he's in and out of Dartmoor every other year's end, so it ain't much good of trying to serve him a bit of paper, is it?"

"Dartmoor?" He says. "You mean he's a crook, this bloke?"

"Crook?" the old bloke says. "What do you mean, crook? Eh? Because a gent goes away to the Cornish Riviera for the good of his nerves, now and again? Crook? What about them dear old dears capering about in Bath? It's only a few miles away. Doing their old guts a bit of good in high class hotels, smoking fat cigars, eh? They crooks, too, are they?"

"What's this bloke do to get his self knocked off, then?" He says.

"Ask no questions," says Henry, "hear no lies. Ever see a nanny goat poop pork pies?"

"Oh," He says. "Keep me mouth shut, eh?"

"The shutter, the better," says Henry, and goes down as if he was treading on his own corns all the way, using his dirty big brolly to prop his self off of the other wall with, and grunting something alarming.

"That's it," he says, sort of satisfied with his self, down the bottom, "I've done them again. You want to see old Ma Frobishy come down here of a Friday. It's a proper pantomime, I can tell you. She's twenty one stone of hand reared Shoreditch, and she's arse first every time." Henry hit the floor with his brolly, serious as a judge. "That there woman's language, my boy, has been knowed to stop the Underground railway, just below here. Roman Catholic, by profession, she is, and the finest oysters, shrimps and winkles in the market. Pity this ain't Friday, as a matter of fact. I could go a nice shrimp or two."

"What's this place, then?" He says, because they was standing in a mouldy sort of passage with doors going off, and you could feel the railway shaking you about underneath.

"This is Tiger Collis's place," the old bloke said. "Ever hear of it? The before and after dinner haunt of the better class bohemian. Every artist of note spends his leisure hours here, and old Tiger Collis looks after their comforts."

"Well," He says, proper in His glory, "I'm a artist, too." It hit Him aside the ear, all of a sudden, He might be too young. "Only perhaps they won't let me join? I've never had the chance to do much, see? And today I come out of me Time and they give me the sack. But me father was."

"Now look here," says old Henry. "You don't want to start sweating again, else they'll all think I been chasing you up and down the road, or something. There's artists and artists. What sort of artist might you be, when you're at home?"

"Painting," He says.

"Ah," says old Henry, "very interesting. Well, some of these blokes ain't quite in the same line, and they're very touchy who they talk to. So keep your old North and South sewed up, and you'll go down a treat. What sort of painting? House, or cart and barrow?"

"Oils," He says, feeling proper put out. "Proper artist, I am. Faces and things. You know."

"Oh," says Henry, "oh, ah? Oils, eh? Well, as long as we know, like. Come on. In here."

They went in a double creaky doors and got wedged in a lot of chairs and tables stuck just inside. Warm as a barber's shop it was, with fried bacon and kippers fighting curry and shag for top niff, in thick smoke what the hanging electric bulbs come through like near holes in a blind.

"They always put this bloody lot here," the old bloke says, climbing over and squeeging round a lot of this stuff, "I have the same old game every time I come."

"Why don't they chuck it out of it, then?" He says, following on.

"Case some bright herb comes down here in a bit of a hurry," says Henry. "Wouldn't get far, would he?"

"I catch on," He says. "Coppers, eh?"

"Coppers or silver," says Henry, grunting like a van horse. "They wouldn't get a lot of change down here, I can tell you." He got out on the free bit of floor and dusted his self down with his top hat, bashing his self about and beating a bom-tiddley-om-bom with his brolly to keep time, finishing up with a bom bom when he put the top hat on again.

"Tiger?" he yells, smack in the smoke. "Where are you, me little old brown 'un? The Lord and Squire of Tookover to see you, with his incumbent, the Reverend Verdun Mott, some-time Fellow of All Souls, now a bloke of many parts." He goes a bit further in the smoke. "Where are you, you scruffy old bastard, you?"

"What's all the bleeding excitement about?" some bloke says and comes through the smoke, about two solid ton of him, from the looks of things. Straight up, once round him twice round the gas works.

"That you, Henry, me old China?" this bloke says, in a voice like a baby doll. "What're you standing there, rorting about, eh? Anybody think somebody was after you. Come on in, for Christ's sake. Who's the bloke?"

"That's my young vicar," says Henry, and gives Him a slap on the back. "He ministers to my sins in me private chapel, He do. Come round one Sunday afternoon, Tiger boy. He'll turn you inside out."

"I should shay sho," says Tiger. Closer to, he stood about six foot, shaped like a fat egg, with a small head, hardly no hair, a big moustache and a twitch in his right cheek as made him look as if he was always winking at you. A nice handful he looked, and all. "More than likely turn me pockets inside out, and all, by the cut of His jib, to say nothing about bashing me brains out, on the quiet."

"No man may do what the Lord ain't provided for, Tiger boy," says Henry, "so your brains is as safe as what your virginity is. How do we look for a bit of grub?"

"In here," says Tiger, winking away in the fog, up and down, up and down, like a line of clothes left out all night.

"What's all this here smoke in here?" Henry says. "Having a louse out?"

"No," says Tiger, proper shirty. "There's something gone wrong with that there God blinding chimney. I reckon somebody's using it for a dunnigan up there. There's some very queer things fell in the fire, lately."

"Oh, lord love us," says Henry, looking serious, "you want to watch that, Tiger boy. Why, Christ, you don't know what to expect next, do you? It might be a bird, though, come to think of it."

"I'd only just like to catch one of them pissing about up here, that's all," says Tiger. "I'd rake the guts out of 'em, fore and aft, quick."

"I mean a stork, Tiger," Henry says, laying it on a bit, "a stork, you know? One of them there funny birds as brings little babies round over Christmas. You might have one of them squatting up there, reading the paper, sweet as a nut."

Tiger give up, winking away like one o'clock. It was all right to listen to these two having a go at each other and stop hearing Ma saying I Told You So.

"I might have knowed you'd have something bleeding sawny to say, you old twerp, you," he says, kind of cheerful. "Get some grub down you, for Christ's sake."

"Two sirloins and chips, and two halfs'll just about settle our hash, won't it, mate?" old Henry says to Him. "Here, Tiger, why don't you get the chimney give a sweep?"

"Because the sloppy looking bleeder can't find it, that's why," says Tiger, blowing up a fine old fit and all. "Cost me fifteen bob last Saturday morning, it did. Prancing about the place with a bloody great armful of brushes, he was, nigh took the eyes out of a round dozen of us, cavorting round the roof, there shouting and screaming, poking about, filling the place of soot and do you think he could find that there hole? Not him, boy. Not him. And as for them there stairs, there."

Tiger had the frying pan in one hand, and a knife cutting foot long steaks off of a bit of beef nigh as big as him, in the other. He stopped in the half cut, and looked over his shoulder.

"If he comes down them there stairs once," Tiger says, thinking about it, "he must have come down half a dozen times, brushes and all. They was making a book on the time it took him to say what he thought of the place. Time he'd had a go down there, and poked a couple of brushes up, and frigged about a bit, I couldn't hardly keep me mitts off of him. So told him to mizzle."

"Would you believe it, eh?" old Henry says, nigh breaking his heart, he was. "All that going on, and there am I, up in Highgate cemetery, eh?"

"You ought to stayed there," says Tiger. "What, was you seeing somebody off, was you?"

"No fear, boy," says Henry. "Only I'm running a new line

in funeral ornaments, now. Very paying and all. Tell you about it later. How much you got?"

"Done all right," says Tiger. "Been a bit busy over the weekend. Had all the lads down from Brum."

"Oh ah?" says Henry, and he takes a big parcel of newspaper off of Tiger and opens it up. Full of fag ends, it was. Thousands of them, all sizes, just ordinary fag ends.

"Marvellous, Tiger boy," he says, joyful as if they was cigars two foot long with diamond rings on. "I got nigh a couple of pounds of gold tipped ones round the Clubs this morning, so we'll all have a packet of Henry's specials tonight. What's this go? Eight pound?"

"Scales over there," says Tiger. "Bet you half a dollar it's nearer nine?"

"Bet you a dollar it's nearer seven," says Henry, and he was over at the scales, fiddling about with weights and things afore you could look round.

"Seven pound twelve ounces, all but," he says. "There you are, Tiger boy? Talking out of turn again."

"I could have swore it was more than eight pound," Tiger says, proper kicking his self. "So instead of my nice little nine bob, I get a lousy four, then?"

"That's how she goes at the moment," says Henry. "And if you don't watch out, you'll be paying for our suppers in the bargain, me fine fat tosspot."

"Go on out of it," says Tiger, having a go at him with the carver, "and take your bleeding parson with you. Parson? I doubt if He ever said His prayers in His life, except when the coppers was chasing Him."

"You get on with them there steaks," says Henry. "I'll have you know my friend, the Reverend here, was unfrocked when He was three year old, and He ain't been guilty since. Come, Verdun." He goes through the smoke next to the fireplace and turns round in a low doorway.

"Get a move on with that there grub, you gee gutted old baa lamb, you," he screeches.

Tiger's raspberry helped Him along, after Henry, inside a

room with a low ceiling, not so smoky as the other, but nigh as foggy with tobacco, windy grey puffs coming out of the lids of about half a dozen barrel stoves, with their stacks strung across the ceiling like a spiders legs and all going up one spout in the middle. There was blokes in wood bunks round the wall, sort of piles of sacking on the floor what blokes was kipping on, chairs made out of beer barrels knocking about anyhow, and a long table, covered in plates and knifes and forks and bits of grub. There was three or four electric bulbs hanging up, so white they made your eyes ache, and over on the edges, where it was darker, in some of the bunks, candles was alight, and proper homey and orangey kind they looked, and all.

All of a sudden He tried to think to His self how He come to be in this lark at all, and it come back, proper wallop between the eyes. He was out of work, and Ma was waiting for Him now, all right, and no larks, neither, because it was a couple of hours after His getting home time, so His supper was just about fried black. So even if He went home straight off, He was never going to hear the last of it about His supper, never mind about the job. Paying out good money, working my fingers to the bone, standing here sweating my guts out, He could hear it all, so plain.

"Now then, Reverend," says Henry, "I'm just going to take me daisy roots off and cool me poor old plates." He shot one boot off with the toe of the other. "Ah. What a joy, eh? They call them there black blokes cannonballs for rushing about in their bare webs, don't they? I reckon they're sensible, meself. There ain't a corn amongst the whole lot of 'em." He pulled the other one off, and patted his toes as if he was bribing them. "You just have a kiko round a fine old Christian collection of blokes, like this here, and have a screw at their tootsies." Old Henry held up his finger as if he could hear somebody giving money away, somewhere. "They've got corns, warts, calluses, hobs, nobs, bunions, and in fact, Reverend, me old pal, everything except turnip tops, spring greens and a young radish. Why? Because of being too bloody superior, Reverend. Boots, that's why. Crippled of bleeding boots. They reckon they got to fit tight, in case they might think they hadn't got none on. It's marvellous to me, it is, straight."

With his top hat off, he had longish stiffish white hair all brushed forward, just parted in the middle, so it sort of shot off his head at you, and his eyes was shining away there, proper little white crushed glass balls.

"It's no good, Reverend," he says, proper in the dumps, "the longer I live, the more I see, the more I'm sure of it."

"What?" He says, expecting to hear something.

"We're all barmy," says Henry. "We're all Charlie Muggins. Joe Soaps. Soft. Daft. Sloppy. Off our onions. Up the bloody pole, the lot of us. We're insanitary."

"There ain't much doubt about you, any rate," some bloke says, and Henry turns round to dekko.

"Well, God starve the bleeding Khedive," Henry says, "if it ain't the Bishop of Paddington Green. How's your old belly off for spots, Jim boy?"

"Not bad," says Jim, just about seen in a lot of sacks on the floor over by one of the stoves. "I'll take a Two, if you've got one?"

"Make one up for you, afterwards," says Henry. "How's the old dear?"

"Gone in the Royal Free," says Jim. "Had a rare old time with her all last week."

"Sorry to hear it," says Henry. "What's up with her?"

"Down the bandstand in Green Park it was," Jim says, sort of far off, and not too sure of getting back. "I made a little hutch with the chairs and made her all right for the night. Then this here pain got hold of her. She'd had half a bottle of meth to keep her quiet, and all. So I went for a copper and he got a ambulance."

You could tell, without looking up, how everybody in the place was listening to him. Even blokes what breathed hard and made little whistles with their noses stopped it for a minute or two.

"Yes," Jim says, "I had to smack her on the chin before she went in. Scratched their bloody eyes out, she did. So I had to chin her. And the look she give me when she see I done her. I ought to cut me throat, I did, Henry. Cut me bastard throat."

"You done right, Jim, boy," Henry says, and the whole place come out in a sort of low Yes. "She'll thank you for it after, you'll see."

"Ah," says Jim. "I hope so, Henry boy. I hope so. Don't forget my Two, will you?"

"I'm making up a few soon's I've had my supper, boy," says Henry.

"Want a spit and a drag, chum?" somebody says, nigh Jim, in the dark.

"Shan't say no, mate," Jim says. "Ain't had one since yesterday. No heart for it."

"Here you are," says this bloke, and slings a fag over.

"That's Jim Burdkin," Henry says, quiet like. "Bishop of Paddington Green, we call him. Runs prayer meetings round the parks, and up and down the gaffs, you know, races, and what all. Don't do bad, but he got too fond of the bottle. The old girl's been with him thirty years, as I remember. Fine bit of stuff in her time. Pity. All the old ones are going."

"What's up with her?" He says.

"Old age, cold nights, no grub and wet grass," Henry says, "chuck in a nice East wind and a lump of cancer, and you're just about right. To say nothing of the meth. Sends you blue in the face, it do. They call her Ultra Violet. She used to drink pints of it. I don't go a lot on it, meself."

Tiger come in loaded down of plates and a jug of beer. The steaks looked a bit of all right, nigh buried in chips, with big doorsteps of bread and marg wobbling on top.

"There you are, Henry," he says. "Poke this lot down your old guts, boy. Come out a new man, you will. There's no glasses so you'll have to make do with the jug. Them bleeders broke them all yesterday, rough housing. Had a rare do down here, I can tell you."

"Many of them?" Henry asks, showering salt over his steak careful as if he was afraid of bruising it.

"About thirty," Tiger says. "Bert Marks lot. They went

down the White City. Done all right, and all. Took about a couple of thousand quid back with them, anyhow. I'm expecting Sartorelli's lot in here fore the night's out. Him and Bert had a battle yesterday, so I've got a couple of the lads here to keep me company, like."

"Christ," says Henry, and he starts shovelling it down for all he was worth. "Come on, Reverend. Get it down you, quick."

Tiger starts laughing a bit, but he was dead serious, just the same.

"I don't mind what they do, or how many of them," he says, "I can handle the lot of them, but I don't want no fuss with the police, that's all. I got a couple of new boys down here I don't want seen, see? That's the bother."

"If I can put your lodgers up any time down Tookover Manor," Henry says, chewing like a cement mixer, "you only got to say the word, Tiger boy. Plenty of room, clean beds, bring their own grub and fleas. Can't say no fairer, can I?"

"It'll be all right," says Tiger. "And if I ever get one good bash at that cowson Sartorelli, God Christ his self'll cry for the bastard."

"I'm crying for him now," says Henry, finished, and shoving his plate alongside all the others. He pulls a packet out of his inside pocket and opens it up. Full of fine shredded fag tobacco, it was. He picks up the fagpapers atop of it and starts tearing them off.

"Ever rolled cigarettes, Reverend?" he says, and Tiger piles plates one atop the other and carts them off next door. "Because that's how you're going to sing for your supper tonight. See this little machine do you? You put a fagpaper round there, like that. Then you put your tobacco in here, see? Then you turn this here little knob, like that. Then you give the edge of the paper a lick, like that. But don't go and gob all over it. Then you open the lid, and there's your fag. See? Easy, ain't it? Lump of treacle pudding when you know how."

So while Henry was walking round the room talking to blokes and taking their money, there He was, making cigarettes for all He was worth, and proper sweating on the top line, case this Sartorelli bloke come rushing in. He knew all about Sartorelli and his gang in the newspapers. Razors, choppers, carving knives, sandbags, anything to lay blokes out quick.

Listening to these blokes, and laughing at them when they was looking the other way, was all very fine, but it looked like having a serious finish, one way and another. He wished He never come in the place. Besides, if the police copped Him down there, He was proper in the dripping, because it looked as if it was a doss house for crooks, and here He was, out of a job, Two and Fourpence in His pocket, not a hope in the world, nor nobody to even give Him a good word, so there was sweet fanny adams He could say to them, even if they wanted to listen.

Them cigarettes rolled out by the dozen. He was sweating all over, what with the heat of the place, and the thoughts of Sartorelli, and the police, and one thing and another, but He kept on thinking of Ma at home, there.

He knew she was waiting, going to the stove to look at His dinner going dry, and not doing nothing about it out of spite, and then going to the door to listen if that was Him walking down the road. He see her so plain.

And them cigarettes come up in a big pile, more than He ever see at one time.

"God stone the bright lights of Blackpool," old Henry says, and he runs his dukes through the pile and sorted them out real professional. "That's enough, Reverend. You must have been born in a harem, the way you roll a fag. Put a hand full in your sky rocket, and count out tens over here, will you? Then we'll be finished for the night and we can shift out of it. This Sartorelli bloke, and his flash boys and bookies, all plastered hair and pointed shoes, they puts cobs on me, they do."

Old Henry had a double handful of packets all made out of newspaper, full of fags, proper clever, it was, the way he done them. He bent across the table and stuck his dial so close, his whiskers tickled.

"But I'll tell you what, Reverend," he says, whispering quick, "he won't half catch a bleeding cold down here with Tiger."

His eyes come up a pair of big size O's, and his mouth was just like a button hole ready for the button.

"Tiger's a case, he is, boy," he says, frightened of his self, almost. "He's done about twelve year, all told, for grievous bodily harm, he has. Eat half a gross like Sartorelli fore breakfast, he will, and never know what he got in his teeth. The two he's got, that is, like. Get hold of your hat and let's hop it, quick. I don't want to be here when they start singing the bloody hymns."

He went tearing off all round the room dropping packets here and there, and blokes was saying Ta, Henry boy, and sort of being pally as you like. When he finished, he picked up his brolly and knocked his bom-tiddley-om-bom on the floor.

"All paid, all weighed?" he yells. "Every gent got his evening solace and mornings cheer? The Viscount Twite, Baron de Beef, Commodore of the Serpentine Fleet, now weighing anchor and setting course for Tookover Manor, with his clerk in holy disorders. Are you all done?"

Everybody, pretty near, it sounded like, worked him a good old raspberry.

"Twenty one guns, correct," he yells, and off comes his top hat, and he bows as if somebody give him a bunch of flowers. "Good night, you scabby nosed lot of bleeders," he shouts them, and tears out through the double doors, and they was all hollering after him and laughing proper loud.

"So long, Tiger boy," he shouts. "Keep your sheets clean. Back tomorrow."

"So long, Henry, me old cock sparrow," Tiger yells, from the back there, somewhere. "Take care of your bleeding self."

"Not half," Henry shouts back, starting to climb over all the furniture. "Give that there hokey pokey blokey a nice French kiss for me, will you? Not too hard, though."

He was grunting so much of getting caught up on legs of chairs and such, he could hardly get his breath.

"I don't wish the bleeder no harm," he says, "but I hopes to Christ he gets proper stuck in this here lot. I don't see why it should always be me."

He went grunting and climbing and shoving about a few more yards, and stopped to get his breath and pull his self together. His top hat just come over the top of a pile of chairs rolled anyhow over long trestles.

"If there's any bleeding hard luck going spare," he says, proper down on his luck, "I always seem to cop out, somehow."

"Never mind, Dad," He says, lighting up, "it don't last."

Outside, they went very careful up one side of the stairs, till they come out in the narrow crack, and made for the lights.

"Ah," says Henry. "Fresh air. What a treat, eh? Good old fresh air. Well, Reverend? What do you go on old Tiger, eh? He's a lad, ain't he?"

"Yes," He says, still looking round for signs of this here Sartorelli merchant. "And he's got a proper funny sort of cafe there, and all. We might have got our selfs proper landed, there, you know? Specially if the coppers come in."

"Yes," says Henry, thinking a bit, he was. "It's a proper bright hole, ain't it? But what are you worried about the coppers for?"

"I'm on the floor," He says. "I'm out of work."

He was a bit surprised how the words seemed to fit in the wide dark night and the bright empty street. Something cold in the wind, the pale dust ringing round on the pavement and the buses galloping home on a glad last trip all seemed part of it.

"Out of work," He says, looking up the road, hearing His self, "that's me. Out of work."

He could see Ma looking at Him, saying it all again.

I Told You So.

# CHAPTER XVIII

HENRY COME TO a dead stop. They was just passing under a red traffic light, so his top hat and him was red as a apple and his eyes come up a bit strange, not knowing whether to laugh, or sing his self to sleep, it looked like.

"Out of work?" he says, as if he never heard nothing like it in his life. "What do you mean, out of work?"

"I mean," He says, getting a bit narked, "I've got the sack. I'm slung out. I've got me pictures. Got me cards. See? I ain't got a job."

"Well, God stone me eyes right and fours about," says Henry, and he leans up against the traffic light and just looks. "Don't you know you're one of the luckiest blokes alive? Out of work? No job? Why, Reverend, you're in heaven, if only you knew it. Think of all the worry and messing about you've give away. You're free. Do you know your luck? You're a free man. And you're standing there moaning about it? Well, well, well."

It sounded proper barmy, but Henry looked as if he meant every word of it.

"Look," He says, "all jokes a one side. I got my Ma to think about, see? And she's been keeping me in this apprentice job for nigh on five year. So I got to go home and tell the old dear I'm sacked. And she can't afford to keep me. So I got to find a job. See?"

"No," says Henry, flat as that. "Listen, son. You're looking at a bloke seventy four years of age. Wouldn't think it, would you, eh? Born on a roundabout, I was, and I been going round ever since. My father was the engineer, and me mother had a job on a stall. Here, do you know that?"

"What?" He says, and Henry gets hold of Him by the collar, getting a grip on Him.

"I was a young feller me lad like you, a long time ago,"

Henry says, dead serious, no larks. "I had ideas, see? No more fair grounds and gaffs for me. No more living in a caravan in amongst beer bottles and a lot of nasty blokes slinging their weight about and knocking women over every time they felt like it. Oh no. A nice, steady job for Henry, I says to me self. I started off one cold morning in April, it was, and my dear old Ma, she give me a sovereign and a bit of good advice. On her last legs, at the time, she was, poor old dear. She says to me, she says, son, she says, never let 'em get you down, she says. They'll boot you, they'll bash you, and if they can't shove you out of it that way, they'll try knifing you with their dirty tongues. One way or another, she says, they'll try and get you down. Don't let 'em, son, she says to me. Just get on with what you've got to do, but never, never let 'em get you down, see?"

Old Henry took off his top hat, and the traffic light poured a lot of shining green all over his white hair. He pointed a green finger up at the stars.

"One of the sensiblest women as ever put her foot inside of a slipper," he says, half sort of whispering. "She's sitting up there on the Right Hand Side, she is, son, bless her heart. And I've still got her sovereign, and all."

He dug about in his waistcoat pocket, and up come this here little gold kind of shilling poking out of his finger tips, covered in yellow light.

"A good breakfast, a bit of good advice, and a sovereign in gold," says Henry. "Who ever had a better send off? And what happens? I gets a job in the packing department of a drapers. Thirty two year, one hundred and twelve days, I was there. One Saturday they come up to me and give me a week's wages extra. Making a change, they said they was. Getting a younger man. Thirty two year, one hundred and twelve days. They give me one week's wages. Two pound, fourteen and a tanner."

Old Henry was all in red again, looking down the road. All the lights was reaching out and smudging their selfs in raggedy streaks along the smooth shiny top of the roadway, and the cars shot past, fair blinding you with headlights, very nigh, but not caring if they did or not. Nobody in them was worrying about a couple of blokes under a traffic light, nor worried about nobody else, for the matter of that, except their selfs.

"Yes," says Henry, talking down the road, with the back of his head like one of them red paper bells what you hang up Christmas time, "they made a change, all right. I walked about this here town that night, I did, trying to find out what had happened to me. Sacked. All me life, pretty nigh, never a minute late, in one room, eight of a morning, till half six at night. Then the rest of the day's yourn, and you can go home. I thanked Christ my poor old Mrs had gone a few years before, else I don't reckon I could have stuck it. Lucky for me, though, I could hear my old lady telling me, Don't Let The Bleeders Get You Down, Son. They'll try heavens bloody hard, they will, but don't let 'em. And if you don't let 'em, you've got the lot of them stone cold."

The old bloke turns round and starts laughing as if it was the biggest joke out. On goes his top hat, right on one side, and he sticks his brolly under his arm. The yellow light clicked on as if it knew something, and covered him in bright gold leaf, and he pulls his waistcoat down, comic as you like.

"God perish the starving rooks," he says, "hark at us. Standing here getting perished of cold, telling you the old, old story, eh, Reverend? Ain't it a bit of all right, eh? Come on, let's get cracking. I hear the call of Tookover. This way home, Reverend, if it's on your way, like?"

# CHAPTER XIX

"I AIN'T GOING home tonight," He says, getting proper frightened all of a sudden, after they went along a bit. He knew,
quick as lightning, He never had the guts to face Ma, not
tonight, any rate. What she might say, and the way she said
it, was more than He could abear thinking about. She might
be better when she slept on it a bit.

"Perhaps I won't go home at all," He says, coming over
brave; "not till I get another job, any rate."

"There you go again, Reverend," says Henry, and the pair
of them was tearing along there like a couple of Brighton walk-
ers. Old Henry shifted his self when he started, all right. "I'm
surprised at you, after what I've told you. You don't want to
get in their clutches again. I've been a free man for nigh on
twenty year, now, and it's lovely. That's what it is. Proper
lovely. There's nobody can come round me telling me what to
do. I tell meself. I ain't got to be nowhere, any time. I can
do what I like, when I like, how I like it. Ain't that lovely?
It's the life, Reverend, it's the proper life, so help me Christ,
it is."

"That's all very well," He says, getting narked again, because
it was no good of listening to all this while He was thinking all
the time of Ma. The two of them was miles apart. "You're
You. You got nobody to worry about, you ain't. I've got my
Ma, and we got to live."

"Well, I'll go to my bleeding tea," says Henry, and stops,
right outside of a shop full of women's things. There was half
a woman with a skin tight pink kind of corset on, with a couple
of beauties just like Ada. It give Him a funny sort of twist in
the guts somewhere, sort of happy sick, wanting to be with her
and touch that hot shaking air as come off of her, and smell
the breath of her hair.

"What do you reckon I do, then?" Old Henry says, agra-

noyed, too, and all. "I might tell you I've got a town and country residence, and estates, and a lot of people working for me. They've all got to be kept going, ain't they? Think I'm one of the lilies of the field, do you? Have another dekko, Reverend. This is hard working Henry Twite talking, first Baron Tookover, Lord of the Hackney Marshes, and don't you forget it."

"Then you've got a job, then, ain't you?" He says, not wanting to have a row, but feeling His temper coming up. "There you are, then."

"Job, me big fat arse," says Henry, hollering out loud. People was turning round and getting nosey. "I ain't got a job. I had one. But I swore I'd never have another. I'm me own governor. I work for me self. Easy, ain't it?"

"Easy for you, perhaps," He said. "But I ain't even out of me time. I ain't got a trade nor nothing, have I? What use am I?"

Henry stopped dead again. All the laughs had gone, and his brolly slid out of his arm as if he never had the strength to keep it there.

"Look here," he says, and he shoves his top hat right on the back of his head. "I don't know how you was dragged up, I'm sure, but I hope I had a bit more guts when I was your age. Some of you young bleeders don't even know you're bloody well born, it strikes me. Pull your sloppy self together, for Christ's sake."

He had two minds to get out of it and leave the old bastard to swear at his self. He thought He was being sensible and arguing the business out cool headed, and here He was, getting a dogs life give Him as if He was a luny. This was the second time in one day, and all.

"Look here, Reverend," the old bloke says, a bit more easy. "Don't forget I had to start all over again when I was what you might call a old man, you know. Old enough to be your grandad, I was, any old how. And here you are, a young feller full of muscles, don't know your own strength, shouting the odds before you've even got the cradle marks out of your arse.

If you want a job all that bad, all you got to do is get up tomorrow at half four, and waltz your self down Billingsgate, or Covent Garden. You'll find a job all right. A couple of mornings wheeling a few sides of beef, or shoving a barrow of spuds about'll do you a world of bloody good, it will. Might wake your bleeding ideas up for you."

"Ain't the sort of job I want," He says, proper narked this time, and just about ready to tell the old bleeder so, too.

"Ah, well," Henry says. "There we are, you see. What sort of a job do you want? That's the next question."

It was proper funny, now He come to think about it, how He never knew His self what sort of job He wanted. The road come up kind of like one of them catherine wheels going off on Guy Fawkes Day, rushing round and round in all sorts of colours, making a sort of fizzing noise, everything rolled up in one, like a ribbon threaded through one ear and pulled out the other. Something to do with artists, anyhow, whatever it was.

"Artist's job," He says. "Any kind of artist's job. That's my job. I been working my time nigh on five year. Can't waste all that, can I?"

"What sort of artist was you going to be, did you say?" old Henry asks, and the pair of them was tearing down the road again, nigh on skidding round corners, they was, and He never knew from one minute to the next, where they was, or where they was off to, and He never cared, neither.

"I told you," He says. "Oils. Oil paintings. Faces, and people. You know. Pictures, like."

"Well, ain't that your job, then?" Henry says. "What do you want to start finding one for, if you've already got it?"

"I ain't," He says. "I've just been telling you I got the sack."

"But you can't get a job painting pictures?" old Henry says. "Can you?"

"Not exactly," He says. "You got to do most of it in your own time, till it starts paying. You got to have a job to keep you going, like. It ain't like nothing else."

"Sounds too much like school kids home work, if you ask me," old Henry says. "I don't hold with it. Worse than just having the bare job, that is. Coming home dog tired and then pitching in to another job. Life ain't worth living, not at that rate. Sides, you can't do two jobs at the same time? Can't be done."

"So how do I go on, then?" He says, feeling He ought to lash out at him.

"Just be a artist," says old Henry, easy as oiling a bike. "If you want to be a artist, don't mess about with a job. Be a artist, and have done with it. Like me."

"Like you?" He says, and He wanted to scream the place down of laughing.

"Certainly," says old Henry, and he pulled up again in this here narrow road what they turned down, with a face as come out of the dark like a dab of the rubber on a heavy patch of pencil shade, no end to dark or light, just a smudge, but his eyes come up there, like a couple of packets of pins heads, all tied together. "What do you reckon a artist is, then? Let's have a basin of that, for a start."

"Well, a painter, or a drawer," He says. "A bloke as does anything to do with pictures and things. That's what a artist is?"

"Don't talk so bleeding wet," the old bloke says. "A artist, let me tell you, is a bloke as tries to find the best of things so as to get the best out of them. That's all. The blokes you're talking about are only painters and sketching blokes. I know the kind. They squeaks if you treads on 'em. You want to make up your mind what you're talking about, son."

"Well, I ought to know," He says. "My father was a artist. So am I. And that's it."

"I see," says Henry. "When father turns, we all turns. Is that it? What do you find about being a artist as does you such a lot of good? Make you feel a bit higher, or a bit more different to the other blokes round about you?"

"Look here," He says, proper hollering. "You look after your business and I'll look after mine. I don't know why I'm bothering with you. Anybody think you was doing me a favour."

"I'm only trying to see if I can help you," says the old bloke,

hollering too. "You sloppy lump of half bake, you. You're walking about half asleep, you are. Don't know you're alive, that's
what's the matter with you. Artist, me arse. Sides, that ain't
for you to say, anyway."

"What you want to say you was one for, then?" He says,
and He reckoned He proper had him there a treat.

"Because I'm old enough to know what I'm shouting about,"
the old bloke yells, and you could have heard him right down
the road. "And I'm too old to worry if I'm wrong or not. But
you ain't. So help me Christ, why, there's more artist in old
Ma Frobishy's little finger, than there is in a dozen gross like
you. You want to see her fruit stall, sometimes."

"I'll hop it," He says. "I've had just about a gutser of this
for one night."

"Where you going?" the old bloke says. "It's no good of
you trying to find your way back out of here. You'll get lost,
then where'll you be, eh?"

"What you want to bring me down here for then?" He says,
and He starts getting a bit of a shake on. It was all very well
of a daytime, walking about, but night time was a different do,
altogether. Pitch black it was, only a couple of lights here and
there down the road, and not a living image knocking about
anywhere. They must have come miles, jawing away there. It
hit Him, all of a sudden, He only come with the old bloke to
get away from the thoughts of Ma, and having somebody to
talk to. Besides, he was just like old Pa Prettyjohn or Dad
Fitchett to meet, ordinary, but down here in the dark it was
different. He started wondering what kind of a lark He let His
self in for.

"Look here, Reverend," the old bloke says, sort of more
friendly, "I never asked you to come. You just come of your
own accord, you did. So you and me better dodge just round
the corner here, and meet the household of Tookover Manor.
That's always providing you don't want to walk about all
night?"

"Okeedoke," He says, but only because He was a bit too
tired to say much else. "I might as well, I suppose."

"Ah," says the old bloke, crashing his brolly on the pavement and wheeling off. "You're a proper artist, Reverend. Don't care what happens to you, do you? As long as there's three square meals and a bed on the end of it, that is. Tell you what? All you want's a coloured handkerchief round your neck, and a pair of them purple corduroy trousers, no wash or shave. Oho. What a boy, eh? What a lad. What a artist. Here. Do you know what?"

"No," He says. The old bloke come to a dead stop again. A newspaper come skating along and stuck round the end of his brolly. Just as he was going to swipe it off he thought of something, and started folding it up.

"Come in nice and handy, that will," he says. "Look here, Reverend. You get this in your nut. There ain't a job in the world as you can put your tongue to, where you don't have to work full time to come out on top. You can start forgetting all your home work ideas. It won't wash, Reverend."

Off he goes again down this here dark road and shoots round a corner, and He come tearing along behind, not caring much where they was going as long as He could get a sit down, and a smoke, out of the cold wind.

"And another thing, Reverend," the old bloke says, puffing away, he was, and he carries his brolly like some of the blokes in the picture was holding their spears, sort of tucked under his arm with the point in front. "I've heard a lot about this here artist business one way and another. If you'd been the proper solid article, you wouldn't have been standing in the middle of the pavement when I first clapped me mince pies on you, would you? And second, you wouldn't have come out in a sweat when I give you a shout. A real artist, Reverend, is sure of his self from the time he's pupped. He ain't sure he's a artist, but he's sure of his self. You can't get him down just because he ain't got a job, or if there's no grub, or the rent ain't paid. No fear. Else he wouldn't be a artist, would he? Artists ain't got the time to worry about them sort of things, Reverend. They're worrying about something else all the time."

"What?" He says.

"If you was a artist, be name and nature," says old Henry, "you'd know."

It was just like punching a rubber wall. You never seemed to get no further, nor it never done you no good, neither.

Walking about with this old bloke on a dark night, cold as ice, clonking along empty pavements, in and out of balls of light as made the roads come up a sort of browny pink, it was hard to get His self thinking except about Ma, down there, waiting for Him, or else she was in snore, or perhaps she might have gone round the copper station and kicked up a row about Him.

But it was hard to get thinking about anything, after a bit, even about her. All in all, it was a piece of cake not to think about nothing, but just go on like He was going. It all come the same in the finish, whatever He done, seemed like, anyhow.

But what old Henry said kept on coming up inside of Him like the hiccups when you hardly knew what to do to get rid of them. He tried to see where Old Nick fitted the picture in this artist business and funny enough, he fitted right down to the ground as far as He could see. So Old Nick must have been right when he said all he had to say, although half of what he said He forgot.

Here He was, with everybody, even Ma, not wanting Him to be a artist and all of them saying every blind thing they could to stop Him trying to be one, and yet something inside of Him kept on saying He was a artist and nothing else would do.

It come a bit hard, wanting to be a artist when not a bastard alive would do a hands turn to help you, or even let you live like a artist, with paints and canvas and a palette and things, and sort of just go about painting.

Not that He could paint much, either, because everybody knew that had to be learnt you by somebody, but He never knew nobody to get even a match off of, never mind about a painting lesson.

So He give it up, at last, and just looked at the road and felt cold, without thinking about nothing, except how it would be to have a smoke and sit down. It was easier. And He felt a lot better for it.

"Here we are, Reverend," the old bloke says, "we've been and crossed the frontier. The Squire of Tookover's home, and nigh in kip."

They was standing in the pitch black, not a move, nor a light, nowhere.

## CHAPTER XX

Black as the ace of spades it was. The tops of the houses was a bit blacker than the sky, that was all, else the dark would have been all the same piece, and come to have another look, there was no sign of a lamp even round the corner. Proper give you the creeps to look round you, case something started jumping, or rattling half a ton of chains.

"Here," He says, "half a mo. What's all this? Where are we?"

"Tookover," says Henry. "The Manor. This is it."

"Where's the lights, then?" He says. "Come to that, I ain't seen lights for I don't know how long, never mind about people. Where are we?"

"How many times you want telling?" the old bloke says, proper complaining. "I'm showing you over Tookover Manor. You're only on the estate where you are now. Let's get out of this here wind. Creasing me, it is."

Away he goes again, straight through the dark, banging his brolly every other step.

"This was all condemned by the Borough, see, Reverend?" old Henry says. "And one night, me and my mate was coming along here from our country place, down Greenwich way, and we come across this here big board. Some development stunt or other. You know. Pull down a couple of decent looking places, and shove up a line of them there chromium and concrete concerns, where you live one atop the other and you don't have to buy a wireless because there's two hundred of 'em outside the window all playing different, you know, and a bloody great big picture palace for the silly sods to go and get rid of the rest of their minds in."

They come to another stop. Old Henry got a grip on Him again as if he was afraid He might fly off.

"Do you know what, Reverend?" he says, trying to see Him in the pitch black. "We been here nigh on three year and they ain't touched it. They turned all the people out, and condemned the lot, turned off the water and gas, and let it go to the rats. So me and my mate picked out the best, and took over."

He turns round and gets on the pavement and starts going up some steps.

"Here you are, Reverend," he yells. "Welcome home. Welcome to Tookover Manor, London residence of Henry, first Earl Twite of Kennington Horns. The dollop millionaire. By Christ, if the horse buses was running now, I wouldn't half show the fag trade a thing or two."

The front door was big enough to get a horse and cart through and when the second doors inside was opened, the size of the place give you a right smack in the eye. It sort of went up and up, with a big stairs, like in the picture cemetery, with gold baby angels flying about, and glass in all the doors, and a real plasterer's joy all over the ceiling and round the walls.

There was another old bloke standing there, as if he was waiting for them, with some old duck standing one side of him, and by the fire of bits of planks, as lit up everything a jumping yellow, there was a bride about in her twenties. When she turned round, He see she had a big sort of ragged splash of purple all down her face.

"Marjoriebanks," old Henry yells, "this is the Reverend Ernest Verdun, just down from Cambridge. Come by the bus, He did."

The other old bloke come over the black and white squared floor light as a bouncing ball, in shoes with little black bows on.

"This is Marjoriebanks, Reverend," says old Henry. "Rescued him from the knacker's yard, I did. Butler and bailiff to Tookover Manor, he is. Be profession and likings, a burglar."

"Hi, cock," says Marjoriebanks, opening a mouth like a empty doorway, big enough to get your foot in, no teeth, so his chin was nigh in his nose end, and when he talked, his tongue sort of shot out by accident and made a funny kind of spitty noise. "Where's your holler boys, holler?"

"Eh?" He says, and looks at Henry, as if he knew.

"Ah, come out of it, Reverend," the old bloke says, "anybody think you didn't talk the language. Holler boys, holler?"

"I catch on," He says. "I just come from work. I don't wear one."

"I don't know if you know we're standing here, like two of cheese, listening to all this?" the oldest of the two brides says, right up her nose, looking at old Henry like she would something hanging off of her boot.

"Ah," says Henry, sort of coming to life. "The distaff side, Reverend. I clean forgot 'em till half of it opened her trap. Allow me?"

He give the old girl his arm and come down proper fancy, like they do on the pictures when some bloke, in a bum freezer covered with gold braid and cords, takes some tart in the ballroom for a rush round.

"Reverend," he says, pretending he was eight foot high with a pouter chest, "permit me the honour of introducing Dulcie, Dowager Duchess Tiddledraws. Comes of a fine old French family. The Hors de Combat. Ever hear of 'em?"

"I wish you'd give over," this old freezer says, and pulls her arm away. "You don't want to take no notice of him," she says, and gives old Henry the thumb. "I'm Mrs Sitram, if you want me, see?"

"If He wants you, Dulcie," says Henry, "there's something wrong with Him. This one here," old Henry says, getting hold of the bride with the stained dial, "is Persephone, not Telephone, Persephone. She can't talk, nor can't she hear very well, neither. What a wife, eh? Her Ma drunk a drop too much port in her time, didn't she, Perse?"

Perse was laughing away, looking at Henry as if he was solid bar gold.

"There you are," he says, giving her arm a bit of a pat, "See? She's laughing, Reverend. I found her on Blackfriars stairs, just going to make a bed in the river. People had been so bloody kind to her all her life, just because she was give a bit more colour in her cheeks, natural, than what they could smarm on out of a box."

He turns round and grabs Marjoriebanks.

"This bloke's full name is Cholmondeley Marjoriebanks," he says, "without no short cuts. You want to see him with his teeth in, Reverend. We got 'em out of some bloke washed up down Barking Flats when the tide was out. Fit him a treat, they do. Handsome? Charlie Peace ain't in it."

Perse come up with a brown velvet coat as shone yellow where it creased, all red padded inside. A round pill box hat, with a tassel, was over one eye, so she had to hold her head a one side to keep it from sliding off.

"Ah," says Henry, and he slips out of his coat, letting it fall on the floor with his brolly. "The Squire of Tookover disrobing, Reverend. I got it down the Cut a few Sundays ago. Three bob. Bit of all right, eh?"

The top hat got chucked at Marjoriebanks, and the cap got stuck on his head, with a bit of elastic behind his ears to stop it falling off.

"One Squire, correct," he shouts, and give Ma Sitram a fine old slap across the bott, "I suppose you had your suppers, eh?"

"We been waiting on you, that's what we been doing," says Ma Sitram, and although she was rubbing her backside, she never said nothing about it. "You been skating round the tiles again, have you? Ought to been in bed hours ago, you did, your age."

"Duchess talking," Henry says. "Take my tip, Reverend, never get mixed up with a lot of distaff. Nag you skinny, they will, and starve you in the bargain. I suppose we got to eat a bit more, have we?"

"I got it ready in the parlour," she says, and off she goes, with Perse following up after she give old Henry a wave.

"Parlour me hind legs," old Henry yells. "How many times you got to be told, Dowager? The drawing room, you soppy old mare. Parlour? Anybody think we was pigging it in Streatham, or something. And it ain't supper, neither. It's dinner. Give it a bit of bleeding class, Dulcie, for Christ's sake."

He turns round proper sorrowful, shaking his head and tutzing with his mouth.

"She ain't used to it," he says. "It's no good. It gets her down. She done ten years hard out of twelve, I think it was, for clouting some bloke as mucked about with her daughter. Wakes up screaming in the night, sometimes, she do. I found her outside a doss house a couple of years back, poor old cow. They slung her out for screaming the place down. So she's been here ever since."

"What did you bring me here for?" He says, and He starts feeling proper queer again. All the candles was waving about and so was the fire. Nothing kept still, and what with being a bit tired, and Ma popping up inside like a nail in your boot and old Henry shouting the odds, He come over a right packet of grief, like a shower of live worms creeping about cold inside of Him.

"Well, I'll tell you, son," Henry says, quiet as you like, no larks this time. "Me own boy got killed like your dad did, last war. And I didn't like you saying he rolled up. That ain't the way to talk about 'em. They was too good. See? Even if they wasn't, we'll say they was, see?"

"Okeedoke," He says, and He starts up a fag.

"What the bloody hell is okeebloodydoke, when it's let out for a run?" old Henry yells, going up in a rare old flash. "Talk something we can understand, can't you? Going to them there rotten pictures too much, that's what it is. New kind of lunatic asylum, that's all they are, Reverend. Make it your bleeding church, some of you. Couple of hours spare? Pictures. Barmy, the lot of you."

"Oy," says Marjoriebanks, down in the doorway at the end. "Supper up."

He starts crashing a brass plate with a drumstick.

Old Henry shoots down there and grabs him by the arm, gripping the stick, looking at him nigh speechless. Marjoriebanks dropped the plate, not knowing which way to turn.

"Where's your gloves?" old Henry says, and you was ready for the ceiling to fall in, any minute.

"Upon my blinking sam," says Marjoriebanks, and out come his tongue, "if I ain't been and gone and left 'em in me sky again. Sorry, guv."

"Sorry?" old Henry yells, and starts pulling him about, feeling in all his pockets. "You're always doing it, you shower of tom tit, you. Always leaving his turtle doves in his sky rocket, he is. Too much trouble, see? There."

He pulls these gloves out and shoves them in Marjoriebanks' fists.

"You know you didn't ought to announce nothing without your gloves on, you pudding headed old git, you," he says, tired, real tired. "Walking about without your gloves on? Never heard nothing like it."

"Well," Marjoriebanks says, and he puts these here cotton gloves on, very careful, all out at the fingers, they was, and just about coal black. "I thought, being it was supper, stead of dinner, like, we could get down to it a bit more easy, see guv?"

"He's a right 'un," says Henry, looking at him like he might do at something fancy in the pet shop. "Supper? Look here, Marjoriebanks, how often have I got to tell you that when I come home, it's dinner? I don't care if it's four of a morning, it's still dinner, and it'll still run a pair of gloves. See."

"Well, all I can say is," says Marjoriebanks, and his tongue come fair popping in and out his face in showers of spit, "it's a bloody fine old time to have your dinner, that's all. I told you before I don't like these here gloves. They gets in me way, they do."

"Eat with a knife and fork, then," Henry says. "Stick your fingers in your mouth, and you're bound to catch 'em some time or other. Anybody think you was butling a coal barge. It's no good. I try, but I can't run a mansion. The flesh is too weak. Look at it. It's rotten."

"I got a clean pair for him," Ma Sitram says, out of the

doorway. "But do you think he'll wear 'em? Not him, he won't. Too much bother, that's him."

"Hark at her," Marjoriebanks says, nigh howling he was, "always trying to get me into more trouble, she is. You wait, you old fleabag, you. I'll get me own back, you see if I don't."

"Ah, shut your row, the pair of you," old Henry says. "Ain't it marvellous, eh? They're just like school kids. A bloke of sixty eight, mind, worried about getting into trouble? It ain't them in the asylums what's barmy, Reverend. They got a thick wall round 'em to keep the rest of us out."

"I'm glad to hear it," says somebody, and old Henry jumps as if he been give a good inch of hat pin.

"I often think I'd like to end me days in one," says this old man's voice, as you could almost see the silver on, "and I probably will."

Henry grips Marjoriebanks down by the ends of his waistcoat, almost half way to his knees.

"You mean to stand there, you lop sided muggins, you," he says, sarky as you like, "letting me shout me guts out while I got a guest in the manor? Ain't you got no eighteen pence, you sloppy old cheesecake, you?"

"Now, now, me lord, now, now," says this somebody, and the doorway come over dark with him standing in it, looking at them with his hand on Ma Sitram's shoulder. "Gently, now. A gentle word, perhaps?"

# CHAPTER XXI

VERY SMALL, smaller than Ma, he was, in one of them there long cloak things as monks wear, with a rope round him and a couple of big knots in it. His hair was clipped short all over, and with the light behind him, it looked something like a chalk drawing when you rub your thumb round it to soften up. His eyes come at you a real startler, what with being sort of grey, light, like old Henry's, only sort of more bossy, as if he knew a bit more about your doings than what you wanted knowed, or knew your self, even. Old Henry sunk inside his self a bit, not much as you could see, but like a lump of blotting paper does when you look at it soaking up a blob of ink, kind of gentle, or something.

"Hullo, Father," he says, pleased as Punch, he was. "I never thought you'd be round here this time of night? If I thought you was coming, I'd have been round here all dolled up and bob's your uncle, hours ago."

"And where is the reverend gentleman I was hearing about?" says this monk bloke, laughing a bit, and coming out. His cloak thing was black and white, close to.

"This is Him," says old Henry, shoving Him forward. "Reverend Ernest Mott. Oxford, he is. Followed 'em on His bike as far as Hammersmith Bridge every year since '98. Ain't you, Rev, boy?"

"Are you one of his lordship's apprentices, Mr Mott?" says this bloke, easy as you like, and still laughing.

"No," He says, "I just come back for the night."

"Artist, He is," old Henry says, "bit of hard luck at His job. They shot Him out of it today just when He was coming on man's wages after finishing His time. So I brought Him home to talk to Him. Know what, Father? You'll make a better job of it than me. You have a go at Him. You're used to the lark."

143

"If I can do anything, I'll be glad," says this bloke. "What sort of artist are you? What's your medium? Pen or brush?"

"Oil painting," old Henry says. "One of the coming blokes be all accounts. Ain't you, Rev?"

"I'm not too good," He says, wishing He could find His self a nice little crack to slip down and get rid of His self, "but there's bags of time for me to learn."

"That's the spirit," this monk bloke says. "Are you studying in a school or under a master? Or how are you working?"

"On me own," He says. "Never had the chance to go to a school. Can't afford it."

"So you're not influenced by any movement, then?" this monk says. "Perhaps it's as well."

"Would you mind getting your selfs sorted out, here?" Ma Sitram says, a bit scratchy, she was. "This here grub's curling up, what with one and the other of you."

"Blimey," Henry yells. "The grub. Come on, Father. Reverend, over there. Marjoriebanks, just hop about there, will you? Walking about there with your little brother on your back. Now then, Dowager, where are we, eh?"

"Salmon," says Ma Sitram, "and lump it."

"I got it this morning off of a pal down the Gate," says Marjoriebanks, a bit anxious. "Fresh caught Wye, it is. Give him a tanner for it, and some winkles what we had for tea. Any complaints?"

"Bet you scoffed all the bloody lot, didn't you?" says Henry, digging in this here flat pink fish, not like the tinned stuff, in a round lump, "knowing how I love my winkles?"

"Touch his guts and you touch his rotten soul," says Ma Sitram, coming up in a rush with boiled spuds. "No, we ain't ate 'em all. I saved yours for you. I don't know why."

"Distaff again," says Henry, giving everybody a wink. "What you doing down this way, Father?"

"I've come to see you about Mrs Gomm," says the Father. "Wife of Harry Gomm, the pavement artist, you remember?"

"Course," says Henry. "Harry the Screever. What's up with his Mrs?"

"Five children," says this Father. "Her husband's sick, she's a bad tempered landlord, and her purse is empty. A brave woman, too, what with children about her feet and no coal or hot water."

"That's Harry's fault," says old Henry. "Always poured his takings down his Duke of Teck, regular. He could have been as comfortable off as me. Always had a good pitch, he did."

"Drunkard he might have been," says the Father. "But he's sadly in a way at the moment. I wondered whether we could start a whip round for them? Or they'll be on the pavement by the weekend."

"No, they won't," says Henry, taking a three inch bone out of his front teeth, "they'll come to Tookover if there's any larks like that. Leave it to me, Father. I'll settle that, all right."

"Then there's a little matter of John Haffley's children," says the monk. "Haffley, the organist. Three girls. They could go to one of the orphan schools, of course. But I'd as soon put them in a barracks, or the dogs home, meself."

"Dowager," says Henry, flashing his knife at her, "your job in the morning. Go over and collect 'em. Then we'll find out what they're fit for. What are they? Ten, eleven, twelve, I suppose?"

"The awkward age," says the Dowager, looking as if she bit on a bit of stone.

"So was Jim Haffley awkward," says Henry. "Married three times, knocked eighteen kids out of the three of 'em, one after the other, without giving the poor mares time to have a look round, hardly, lost the wives and all the kids, bar three, and then went and fell down the tube stairs and broke his neck. If that ain't awkward, I'd like to see it."

"It was that there harmonium falling atop of him as did for him," says Marjoriebanks. "Ain't too clever, that ain't."

"What about the Reverend, here, Father?" says Henry. "He's sitting there looking very how's your father, ain't he? He's afraid to go back and tell His Ma He's sacked."

"Where are you living?" this monk says, looking all right.

"Off the Kingsland Road," He says. "I'll be all right. Straight up. I'll get through it."

"Well, eat your salmon, then," says Ma Sitram.

"Can't," He says, "I ain't hungry."

"What sort of subjects are you interested in?" this monk bloke says. "What have you painted?"

"I'm doing one of a blond girl now," He says. "Get it in a exhibition, if I can, afterwards."

"That's where I can help," says the monk, bright as a new tanner. "I know a lot of people in that line. I'll come and see it one morning, shall I? Or whatever else you'd care to show me that you've finished?"

He could see He was shoving His self down the pan again. He knew this monk bloke would be there, brisk as a kipper one morning, and catch Him dead in snore, no picture, not even one started, nor a tube of paint anywhere. So He had to go careful again.

"Well," He says, trying to come up in a blush, "I don't want to show nobody, not till it's all over, like, see? I mean, that's how I've always gone at it. So I kind of like keeping it sort of, you know, like, a bit quiet, like, case it's a, well, case I ain't satisfied. Thanks all the same though."

He wanted to talk a bit more, but everybody had all gone quiet, like they do when somebody goes and smashes a dish, but they was eating their grub for a minute proper workman-like. Funny sort of eyes the monk had, hardly ever blinking, and when he looked up, them worms started crawling about in His guts again so He started feeling round for a fag.

"Oy," says Henry, flashing his knife again. "Nark it. No smoking in Tookover except in the proper place. I can't abear somebody blowing a gutsful about while I'm having me grub."

"Suppose He had a couple of lessons from old Harry the Screever," says Marjoriebanks, with his tongue plopping about between lumps of salmon, "he'd get learnt a thing or two, wouldn't He? And do old Harry a favour the same time."

"What sort of a favour?" says Henry, slinging his bones to the cat.

"Well," says Marjoriebanks, "let this bloke do the drawing part of it, while Harry just sits down there with the hat, and tells Him how to set about it?"

"And time Mr Bloody Gomm's finished doing his self a favour," says Henry, "the Reverend 'll be owing him money, I suppose, and paying for the tools in the bargain? He wants something where He gets a living. Sides, Harry's the King of the Coloured Chalks, not oil painting. We'll just have to think about it, that's all."

It started proper getting on His nerves, the way they was all talking about Him as if He was a bit of fish as wanted carving up. They was all so serious about it, and all.

"Look here," He says. "What's this getting you? What're you getting out of trying to see what you can get me to do? I can look after meself. I don't want no help, not from nobody. I'm all right."

"Ah, well," says old Henry. "Now we're getting a different bit of music."

"No, you ain't," He says. "I been telling you all night I just want to be a artist. That's all. You can't help me. Nobody can't."

The monk finished chasing a bit of spud round the plate and put his knife and fork together. He took a lot of time, chewing with his front teeth, and all the time everybody stayed dead quiet. The cat was looking up at Perse but she was pretending he never see him, till he put out his paw to shake hands, then she shot him a lump of salmon, watching Ma Sitram all the time to see if she was going to get copped or not, innocent as half pint of water.

"You're right," the monk says, when the quiet was getting too hot, it was making Him sweat a bit. "Perfectly right. As long as you understand that, you'll be perfectly safe. As an artist. But we're worried about you from the practical side. We'd like to help you. Isn't that so, me lord?"

"I'll help Him with a smack aside the earhole," says old Henry. "He don't even know He's born."

"Won't get far if He leaves His plate in that state all the

time," says Ma Sitram. "Ain't hardly touched it. I'll bet His Mum wouldn't half take on, wouldn't she?"

"I can't get it down me," He says. "Gone past it."

"I gets like it when I'm worried," says Marjoriebanks. "Can't look at it. It's me feelings."

"He's full of feelings, he is," says Henry. "Kick his arse, you'd knock his brains out. What did old Shakespoke say? Something, anyway. He was a boy, wasn't he, eh? Here, do you think he was a artist, Father?"

"I imagine so," the monk says, and he starts laughing.

Old Henry turns round and looks straight at Him, dead serious.

"There you are, you see?" he says. "Old Shakespoke never drawed a straight line in his life, he never, except from his house to the pub. But he was a artist. It's like I told you, see? Find the best, and make the best of it. No half larks. And you're seventy five per cent a artist. The rest's a lot of elbow grease and a bit of luck."

"What's seventy five per cent?" Marjoriebanks says, having a good old round up on his plate with a bit of bread. "I never did catch on to 'em, me self, these here per cents, I mean. How do you set about it?"

"Set about what?" says Henry, a bit too smiley.

"Per cents," says Marjoriebanks. "Look, supposing I say fifty per cent, talking big, see? What am I talking about?"

Old Henry looked at him sort of pitying, but you could see he was scratching away inside his self, trying to get it right. The monk got his face straight and started mucking about with the cat.

"Look here," old Henry says, and shoves his cap back and fore a couple of times as far as it would go, without busting the elastic. "Per cents is only a sort of way of saying something like, for instance, The Above Have Arrived. You know, that they shove in the papers when there's races on somewhere. You don't know what it means, no more than Adam, nor what they've arrived at, nor nothing else about 'em, and what's more, you don't want to. See? It's just a way of saying some thing, like Bob's Your Uncle, or Have a Banana. That's easy, ain't it?"

"Just a moment, now," says the monk. "Per cent is another name for a hundredth part. One per cent is a one hundredth part of anything. So seventy five per cent is seventy five hundredths of something. Three quarters, in other words."

"There you are," says old Henry, and you could almost see the oil dripping out of him. "Nigh on as good as what I could have done me self, give the time and place, that is."

"Half a mo," says Marjoriebanks. "What's a hundredth, while we're at it?"

"God stone the Crystal Palace," old Henry yells, "he just told you, didn't he? Chop something in a hundred pieces and any one of 'em's a hundredth, you stupid looking old crab, you."

"Stupid, eh?" says Marjoriebanks, and he give the cat a clout for shoving its nose under his arm to have a go at the salmon. "What about a bloke as chops another bloke up in two pieces, never mind about a hundred? Is he stupid?"

"This is going to turn out terrible, this is," old Henry says, holding his forehead. "Who's stupid?"

"You are," says Marjoriebanks. "You going to chop young Reverend there in hundred pieces to find out what seventy five of Him's doing of? Eh? Now who's stupid?"

"Dowager," says Henry, "put a drop of something in his grub tomorrow and send him off nice and quiet, out of his misry. Else he'll do for the lot of us one of these fine nights. He's started wandering."

"You said," says Marjoriebanks, waving his fork, "seventy five per cent of the Reverend was a artist. How do you know you ain't counted Him up? And how do you make out seventy five per cent's three quarters? A black cat ain't white, is it?"

Old Henry scratched his head and shut his eyes.

"Look here," he says, "we'd better just pull the plug out of his lot, and let it run out by itself. Can you sort this lot out, Father? I ain't got the patience, me self."

"See?" says Marjoriebanks, and sloshes the cat again. "Seventy five per cent wrong every time you open your mouth, guv. Everybody chucking per cents about all over the shop and they don't even know how they start, never mind about setting about em. How'd you know where to start talking about a bloke in per cents?"

"I don't, mate," Henry says, tired as you like. "I don't know why I started it. I don't know why I start anything while you're knocking about. Ideas graveyard, that's what you are."

"An industrious worker in the flowered field of semantics," says the monk, "or near enough."

"Sem who?" says old Henry, looking at Marjoriebanks to see if there was any spots showing signs of breaking out.

"Semantics," says the monk, giving Ma Sitram a wink, enjoying his self a treat. "The science of the nature of words. The meaning of the meaning of words. The meaning of meaning, in other words."

"Perse," old Henry yells. "Serve tea in the conservatwah. This bleeding lark's gone far enough, what with per cents and the meaning of meaning. Meaning of Meaning? I'm going stone atcha."

"You ain't, guv," says Marjoriebanks. "You've went years ago. But what about the Reverend? Is He kipping here tonight, or ain't He? I got to think about getting Him fixed up if He is."

"No," He says, so quick He was surprised at His self. "I'll be home by five or six o'clock if I start in a minute. I wouldn't bother you, straight up. I'll be all right."

"You ain't bothering nobody, son," Ma Sitram says. "You put your feet up here for tonight and go off nice and early in the morning with a good breakfast inside of you. Your Mum wouldn't thank me for sending you off in the middle of th night, would she?"

There was another wait and He just sat there looking.

"I can walk with you part of your way," says the monk. "I'm going to Pennyfields."

"What," says old Henry, "Pennyfields, tonight? Now?"

"I've an early service in the morning," says the monk, "and a little thing or two to do before. D'you mind, me lord, or have I leave?"

Old Henry looked across the table and shook his head like he might have at a champion, or something.

"What a lad, eh?" he says. "What a boy. If they was all like you, I don't know, I might find meself in bloody church one of these fine mornings, and chance it. Give 'em something to talk about, wouldn't it? The Squire of Tookover in the family pew. Eh?"

"It would give me something to talk about," says the monk, still mucking the salt about, patting it this way and that. "You might bring others in with you. Did you think of that?"

"There you are, you see?" old Henry says, and he gives the table a right wallop. "It ain't me you're after. I don't count. I'm only Henry Twite, the soppy old bleeder as sells fags here and there. You're after the crowd I'm supposed to bring in with me, ain't you? The old collection box again, eh?"

"That's right," says this monk, laughing away, and Perse was laughing away with him, but it was ten to one she never knew what she was laughing about from the look on her dial. "You don't count, me lord. It's your lordship's following I'm after. But if ever I see you on the bench in front of me one of these bright mornings, it'll be the lighted silver joy of me ministry. It's a lonely place, sometimes."

Somehow or another, it all come sort of quiet again, and you could hear the planks dying in the yellow outside.

Old Henry was looking at the salt getting mucked about, Perse was looking at him as if he was twenty two carats right in the middle of her hand, Ma Sitram was picking her teeth, with her other hand curled up in her apron, and Marjoriebanks was trying to balance a fork on a glass with the prongs on the rim, making low clongings like music going away from you.

"I'd like to, Father," old Henry says, sort of not quite satisfied, "but I can't like it. I've tried, I have, hundreds of times. I've been on the steps of churches. In fact, I have, I've been just inside the doors. But they puts me off, they do. They're so bloody dead. They even smell dead. And as to them bleeding parsons. God stiffen the bloody rooks."

"Well," says this monk, not even looking angry, "now I know where I am, me lord, eh?"

"Not you," says Henry, "you ain't one of 'em. Else let me tell you, you wouldn't have come through that there door. You're all right, Father. But this here lark of going to church ain't. I can't get nigh it, somehow. Kneeling down there, grousing away to some bloke you can't see? It ain't sensible."

"Hark," says Marjoriebanks, looking up at the ceiling with his tongue stuck out like a big wet strawberry. "What was that?"

"He's off," says Henry. "He can hear 'em. What, come for you at last, have they, Cholmondeley? What they playing? Harps, or rummy?"

"I heard a couple of knocks," Marjoriebanks whispers, holding his hand to his ear and pulling his dial about to tell Henry to pipe down. The whisper done it. Even his tongue looked as if it had ears all over it.

Henry piped, listening with one eye shut.

Something was chasing itself all round Ma Sitram's guts, creating a rare old row, bubbling and squeaking away there, having a fine old time, up and down, round about.

Two knocks, quiet, and proper shivery, from the back there, somewhere.

"My two guests from the Grand Hotel Collis," says Henry, shifting. "Let 'em in, Marjoriebanks, and put 'em in the modern wing."

"Ask 'em if they'd like a bite," says Ma Sitram. "It's cold down in that there rotten cellar."

"They've had their grub at Tiger's," says Henry, standing at the door and listening to Marjoriebanks going along the hall, "and if they take a bite out of you, Dulcie, they're greedy. I'll lay odds they wouldn't take two."

Funny how Ma Sitram never took no notice of him, and just went on picking her teeth.

"Ah," she says, "that's all very well. I wouldn't give you the chance though. My oath. Not even now."

"Stopped the traffic, she did, in her prime," Henry says, still listening. "Cab horses have been knowed to say they was sorry they come out."

He shut the door and stayed there.

"Father," he says, "the coppers are out there. What would you like to do? Stay here in the hidey hole for a bit, or do a scarper through the back?"

"Didn't I hear of a cup of tea, somewhere?" says the Father, quiet as a bird.

"Next door," says Henry, going over to it. "What I like about you, Father, is the way you fly about. Nerve racking ain't in it."

All of them went next door. Perse had lit some more candles, but a dozen dozen would have lit about half of it, never mind all of it, so the four or five was like lonely little orange holes in the dark. It was another big room, full of furniture, or what looked like, but it was squarish sort of stuff, with different coloured patches in rows all over it. You had to look hard to see what you was looking at, and even then, you was as wise as you was before.

"Careful how you go when you sit down," says Henry. "Here's a chair for you, Father. One for the Reverend. One for me. The distaff can bring their own."

Ordinary kitchen chairs they was, and proper hard luck to sit in, specially when there was big arm chairs all over the place.

Old Henry see Him looking and stopped with the fags half way between them.

"What's up?" he says. "Looking at the furniture, are you? My royal suit, this is. Made 'em all me self."

There was a couple of big sofas, table to sit eight, easy, with chairs round it, four big arm chairs and a lot of desks and cupboards and things, all patching up out of the dark, and over in the corner there was a walloping great big piano with the lid open, not one of them ordinary pianos, but a big posh one, shaped a bit like a horseshoe with one side of it pushed in.

"Don't you like nobody sitting in them, then?" He says.

"Ah," says the monk, "he'd love it. But we daren't. They're not ordinary pieces of furniture, you know. Go and look at the concert grand, and see for yourself. The finest home made piano in the world, I'll be bound."

He started up His fag on the way over, and time He got the flame out of His eyes, He was there, feeling it. All them patches are labels.

It was made of matchboxes.

So was the arm chairs, and the table. Thousands of matchboxes all stuck together, they was, and you could smell the glue when you got your face nearer, but glue or not, the whole job was as solid as houses. He give the piano a shake but it never budged.

"Matchboxes," He says. "All of 'em?"

"Every blind thing," old Henry says, pleased as if they was diamonds, "all done by kindness. I've used a couple of hundred thousand one way and another all over the house. You want to see the bridal suit on the first floor. Don't he, Father?"

"He does indeed," says the monk. "On any moonlit night, so they tell me, Titania herself holds court up there."

"Wouldn't have her in the place," old Henry says. "You go it all wrong, Father. That's the Dowager prowling about that is. Looks under all the beds, she do, to see if she's going to be lucky."

Marjoriebanks and Ma Sitram was going at it hammer and tongs somewhere, and somebody else's voice was dripping in now and again, but Ma won every time.

"Hark at the barney going on out there," old Henry says, then he turned round again. "What's up with that there piano then, Reverend?"

"Well," He says, "it don't need the telling, what's up with it. There ain't a single wire in it. What's the good of it, if I can't play?"

"That's a fine, large, ripe, old joanna, that's what that is," says old Henry, coming up narked. "Can you play the piano, Reverend?"

"No," He says.

"No more can't I," says old Henry. "Can you knock a tune out, Father?"

"With one finger," says the monk, "but a very powerful amen with both hands."

"That's a bit of luck," says old Henry. "Send 'em home happy, eh? Now then, Reverend, you got a jo at home have you?"

"Yes," He says, "two of 'em. One in the shop and one in the parlour."

"Ah," says Henry, "well off, eh? Can your Mum play, can she?"

"No," He says.

"Well," says Henry, lighting up, "what's the good of any sort of a joanna to any of us, then? Bit of furniture for swank, that's all. And that's all that one is, over there. Swank. Except I did make it me bloody self, and that's more than some of you can say."

The door come open in a blow of air when you could smell them planks burning, and shut again with a long little noise like the top note in a tin whistle.

"Guv," Marjoriebanks says, all breath and splashes, "coppers all round the place. Them two downstairs are wanted for a lot of very nasty things. Shot somebody, they have."

"Oh ah?" says Henry and he give his hair a rub down, "Shocking, ain't it? They'll have to go through Banana Grove, then, won't they?"

"And the inspector's outside and he wants to see you," says Marjoriebanks, giving his self a polish round the face with his cuff. "And he's got a warrant, and he'll pinch the lot of us for aiding and abetting, and being after the facts and what all. Worked his self up in a fine old stew out there, he has. Pinch the lot of us, he will."

The worms started rushing round His guts again, this time

twice as big, freezing His skin so tight, He thought His bones was coming through. He knew He had to get out of the place quick.

"Here," He said, and they all looked round, "I'm going home. I don't want to get in no trouble from the police. I got my Ma to think about."

"Hard luck on her," says Henry. "Don't start going mad, Reverend. You'll go home all in good time. You going to take him, Father?"

"I'll put Him on His way," says the monk. "What'll you do?"

"Me?" says Henry. "I'm all right. I'll entertain me police bloke friends to a nice cup of tea. This way, Father, and mind your nut."

Marjoriebanks shoved his end of the wall behind the piano, and it all come out like a gate.

"In we go," says Henry, ducking to go in. "Marjoriebanks, go and sing to them coppers till I gets back, will you? And tell the Dowager to make some more tea, and get Perse off to bed. I don't want her frightened."

"Frightened?" says Marjoriebanks. "Her? She's having the time of her life, she is, nigh sitting in their laps."

"Yes?" says Henry, shoving this thick cardboard wall shut again. "Well, get the chairs out of it, then. Then there won't be no laps to sit in, and I'll be running a respectable house. Laps, eh? I never knew a copper had one."

They come out in a smaller room, and Henry lit a match to find a candle. Then they went through the door, down a stairs and along a passage all slated and white tiled, passing kitchens with stoves and sinks and pipes, all pitch dark and quiet except for the mice, and they was almost under your feet. Down the far end, there was a light coming under the door.

"Steady here," says Henry, and spit the candle out. "Wait while I see what's going on."

He goes down and opens this door careful as going in a lion's cage, and looks inside. There was two blokes in there and soon as he see them he turned round.

"It's all right," he says, "all friends, here. What's up this time, Chaser?"

"Ah," this bloke Chaser says, "bit of urr er barney down the urr er club. That's all, mate."

"Some geezer got bashed," says the other bloke, short and skinny, with his dial in his coat collar.

"Oh, ah?" says Henry. "Only bashed, was he? I just heard there was a bit of shooting going on. Not that it's any business of mine, like."

"Don't pay to be nosey," says the skinny bloke.

"I thought of it first, mate," says Henry. "You know the Father, don't you? Pennyfields Mission? He'll take you out."

"Let's get a move on, then," says the skinny bloke. "I don't know why Tiger sent us out here."

"If you hadn't let the coppers follow you," Henry says, "we'd be all right. As it is, they're playing the bloody band all round the house. So long, Father. Come round again, soon."

"Goodnight, Henry," says the Father. "This way home, now."

As they started, Henry grabbed His arm, a real strong pull round.

"Here," he says. "I ain't forgot you. If you get fed up of looking for a job, just come round and see me, see? There ain't much here, but it's better than nixey, ain't it?"

"Yes," He says, "Ta, Henry."

"You look after your Ma," says Henry. "See? Look after her. She's the best pal you'll ever have, see?"

"Yes," He says, and Ma come up warm beside Him, big and black, but He shoved her out of the way.

"So go straight home and stop her worrying, see?" Henry says. "And keep out of mischief."

Them white, bright, cracked glass balls was going right through the back of His head in two straight worrying lines. Henry started poking with his finger again.

"Take my tip and leave off this here artist stuff," he says. "It's no good to you, and it'll land you in trouble, see? See?"

"Yes," He says, but He was dying to be tearing down the passage after the other blokes.

"Right," says Henry. "Hop it."

So He tore out and rushed down this passage where somebody was flashing a torch. He see they was all standing round a manhole.

"Come on," says the skinny bloke, proper rough. "Can't wait all bleeding night for you. Who d'you think we are?"

"Nobody much, either or both," says the Father, and he climbs down the iron ladder. "I'll go first, then the boy, then you two. Last man put the cover back."

"Oh," says the skinny bloke, "so we're going to do all the bloody work, eh? Pair of bastards, eh?"

"That," says the Father, with his face out of the hole, and his eyes shining, "or you'll find your own way out. And don't let there be any more argument about it. Understand?"

His voice was a right surprise, strong as a bull, and banging about down there all over the place till it sounded like twenty of him all going at once. The two blokes never said another word. Down they come, and then sweated to pull this big iron lid over.

"Let me warn you, now," says the Father. His face come up a polished white colour in the torchlight, but his eyes was small half circles of hottish light blue. "This sewer is unused, and it's full of rats. It joins the main sewer further on, and that's where we'll have to be careful of gas. You've got a mile and a half to go. Keep together, shut your mouths and walk carefully."

There was a funny sort of smell coming up, like bad breath and carbolic mixed, all the way round. From the little moves of air, you might think you could get your breath in a clean bit, but whichever way you ducked your head, there the smell was. It was hard, walking on this foot wide or so ledge, with a wall curving up all round you, and your shoulders was always in the way, and getting pushed over till you nigh tipped in the dark beneath you. It sounded like thousands of them walking down there, till you got used to the echoes, then you could pick out who was walking behind, because the skinny bloke limped and the other one was humming now and again, but the Father was going on in front there, steady as if he was out in the garden for a blow of air.

What with the smell, and being dog tired, He was just about done up. He wanted to sit down and have a smoke, but the smell was right in His mouth and making Him feel a bit sick, and there was a hard lump as kind of stuck in His forehead, although when He put His hand up, there was nothing there.

"We're coming to the main sewer," the Father says, and it was a bit strange, because now there was no echo at all. Just flat sound, and far away. The ledge was curling round, left and right, like a big double S, and the torch began picking up white flashes off the tiles going round and round the tunnel, getting darker and darker. The stink got worse, sharp as a pair of knifes going up your nose, nearly hurting you to breathe, almost making you wish you was dead and out of it for good. He jammed a corner of His coat against His mouth but it only seemed to make it worse.

They come to a corner and the Father turned sharp right, taking the light with him. He fell over His self to catch up, proper thankful to get round and see the black shape ahead. It was easier going, because the ledge was wider, but there was water somewhere, slopping along, and the light bobbed up and down in front, bringing up everything nearer to a strong white, grey beyond and then black. But the light caught up on the top of surprised water about three foot down below, waving about like bits of white rag.

The Father stopped and struck a match. It burnt whitish, fat, a bright leaf rounding up to a point that smoked a hair of grey, up and up. The blokes behind come up and stopped. Chaser was coughing, deep down, as if everything inside of him was running over a washing board.

"No gas yet," says the Father. "When there is, we'll have to run for it. There isn't much further to go. If you see me get down and start crawling, follow suit. Or you'll regret it."

"Cut the lark, and let's get out of it," says the skinny bloke. "I'm browned off with this."

The Father never said a word. But the hot pale blue of his eyes sort of come to a point and stuck. The water was dribbling and dripping, going strong, black everywhere, except for them white rags here and there.

"If you feel anything round your feet," he says, quiet and ordinary, "it'll be rats. If they bite at you, don't kick them or they'll jump at you. Just shout, and I'll turn the torch on them."

"Trying to kid us, are you?" says the skinny bloke, going sharp and clever and squaring his self up. "Think rats are going to worry us, do you? Go on, get your body out of it. Bleeding parsons, you're all the same."

Coming out of his coat collar, his face give you a nasty feeling inside your self. It was thinnish, with shadows all over it, and the bones stuck out white. The chin part seemed to come out more than the top half, and it was black with whiskers. His eyes was black, no colour nor light in them, staring wide, blinking as if there was weights top and bottom of his eyelids, and his mouth was dry and cracked all the way along, no wet on it at all.

"Urr er, half a mo," says Chaser. "Don't start coming the urr er bleeding acid, for Christ's sake, don't. Urr er, we got to get out quick. Ain't we?"

"Shut your gab," says the skinny bloke, and give Chaser a dig with his elbow as nigh winded him. "I'm talking, see?"

"Come along, Mott," says the Father, taking no notice, and off he went. The other two was arguing it out behind there, but not much come out of it because of the noise of everybody walking, and the other sounds, especially the water. It was getting stronger and it sounded as if there was a lot more of it, sort of deeper.

He see the rats about the same time as the fight started, but He never knew which of them to be frightened of first. The light caught them on the moving, jumping brown fur of their backs, and made their eyes like hundreds of orange slits, near to, and then pale yellow points further back in the black, where the light never went. Hundreds, thousands of them, whispering, and squeaking like a pair of shoes sometimes do, only not so loud, showing pink feet like little hands.

But Chaser and the skinny bloke was fighting. The sound of the punches come up like slapping your leg, only deader, and it hurt just to hear them landing.

"What possesses those two?" the Father says, sort of saying it to his self, but he kept the torch on the rats.

"They're having a bundle, sounds like," He says. "Nothing much we can do, is there?"

They was fighting quiet, which was worse. Not a sound except fists going home.

"Let me cross over you," says the Father, trying to shove past. "I'll separate the fools."

"And leave me in amongst them rats?" He says, and blocked the way. "Not if I know it. Let them have it out. We can't do nothing there? You ought to know that."

Chaser was coughing and trying to shout at the same time. You could hardly hear because of the slopping of the water and the squeaking and smoothing of the rats. You could even smell them through the other smell.

Suddenly there was a big splash and it sounded like a woman screaming.

"Let me by there now," the Father shouts in His ear, and the torch come by in a big white flash, lighting up the skinny bloke leaning against the wall, nigh beat, with his mouth open and blood all over his face, looking down in the sewer. Chaser was down there but only his face, and that went under while they watched.

"Help the man," the Father shouts, "help him, dear God." But the skinny bloke only looked down, and the Father was shoving his way along the ledge. "Get out of it," he was yelling, "get out of it. Help the poor devil."

The rats was jumping up His legs all round. He was crawling all over, expecting to feel their teeth any minute.

"Watch the rats," He shouts, and shoves the Father back,

grabbing for the torch. But the Father was strong, and kept Him arm's length away, shoving Him on toward the skinny bloke.

Chaser come up, and his hands come out a pair of sticky, shiny, muddy claws. His face was black and shiny and his eyes was big bright white balls with a staring black spot in them. Screaming, he was, only this stuff run off his face in his mouth, choking him, and he started going under again, very slow, with his mouth open.

The skinny bloke looked round when they was only a couple of foot away. The light made him pull his self together. He wiped his mouth over with the back of his hand and spat down at the bubbles where Chaser had gone down, and turned full round on them.

"Get out of it," he says.

"Help the poor devil, quick," the Father says, nigh howling he was, all trembly. "He's drowning, you awful brute, you. You bloody coward, he's drowning."

"He kicked me," the skinny bloke says, and he starts trying to stand up straight.

"Reach down for God's sake," the Father says, and he kneels down, but the ledge was too narrow. "Give me a hand, and I'll go in. Keep these rats off me."

The rats was jumping on his shoulders. But where the light caught the top of the water, He see there was hundreds of them in swimming. Their heads looked like fat floating leaves with orange specks in them.

The skinny bloke aimed a kick at the Father, and missed him.

"Come on," he says, in amongst the blood, "fore I do for the pair of you."

"You can't leave the poor brute," the Father yells. "You can't. You've murdered him."

"He kicked me," the skinny bloke says. His eyes was queer, sort of covered, not with tears, but like thin net, greyish, and there was lots of froth both sides of his mouth and dribbling down his chin. "Let's get out quick. I want a doctor. He done me. Oh, he done me."

The skinny bloke started crying like a kid, only quieter, but the rats was going mad. They was sliding off of the ledge in the water, some jumping, some doing proper dives. The top of the water was bumpy with their heads, and they was swimming like blokes learning the breast stroke, though some of the bigger ones was going over the others in front as if they was playing leap frog.

"Almighty God," says the Father. "It can't be. No, it can't be."

"Let's get out of it," says the skinny bloke. Kids asked their Ma for a halfpenny sherbert stick in just the same way, half way crying and hoping. The Father was just looking down in the water, not even bothering to hold the torch proper.

"Let's get out of it, I tell you," the skinny bloke yells, all of a sudden, and he come off of the wall, feeling in his coat pocket. "I can't last out much longer."

"I'll not help you," says the Father, not looking at him. "You'll go every step of the way yourself and I'll hand you in charge when we get out. Cold blooded horrible murder, nothing else."

"You open your trap again," the skinny bloke says, and from what was coming up, he must have been bleeding inside, "and I'll give the pair of you a share of this."

He had one of them flat black guns pointing at them, one to the other.

"I'll do the boy first," he says, "then you. Now get out, will you?"

The Father was a sensible bloke and started off without a murmur, and He was only too pleased to be following. He could feel all the bullets going through Him, and He caught one good look at Ma having a laugh and saying Serves You Bloody Well Right. He see her plainer than the light.

He never wanted to be home so much in all His life. All He wanted to do was just go home, open the door, sit down in the kitchen, and have a smoke, nice and quiet. He swore blind if ever He got outside, not even Christ his self would ever shift Him out of the Kingsland Road again. He made up His mind so much, He could even feel it in His chest, all tight and wrapped up.

"Here," says the Father, and stopped, flashing the torch up another iron ladder, "you go up first and shift the cover. Careful how you do it."

"Will there be any coppers out there?" He says.

Their faces was only a foot apart. Them pale blue eyes had something in them He could hardly give a name to, yet they made Him feel a inch high, no more.

"No," says the Father. "It's a yard. Wait for me when you get out, and give this creature a pull. I'll come up behind."

Up He went, only too glad. He was proper laughing inside, to be so near getting out. The tired part of Him seemed to pack up and leave Him fresh as a daisy, so it took no time to push the lid up and slide it over, making a noise like banging a anvil.

But coming out in the dark air was like somebody slinging a heavy wet sheet over Him. He got His head and shoulders over, and then all His strength went out, and He nigh slipped back in the hole again. But He managed to claw along the roadway, pulling His self out flat, and He laid there, shivering, trying not to breathe because it hurt. But it was lovely without the stink.

"Mott," the Father was shouting down there, and the light come shooting out whitish blue and strong through the hole. "Give me a hand, here."

The skinny bloke was hanging half in and out, and getting bumped about from below. Swearing, he was, but without opening his mouth, so there was no proper shape in the words. A couple of jerks got him out and on his back with his head on the manhole cover.

The Father got out and breathed deep.

"Thank God," he says. "Pick up his head."

He lifted him, and the Father put the cover on the hole, and picked up the skinny bloke's feet.

"Go to your right," he says, and away they went. "This man's seriously hurt. We'll put him beside a phone box and I'll let the police know. That's the best. Otherwise it means getting Henry in awful trouble."

They put the skinny bloke down just behind the phone box out of the wind, and the Father listened to him for a minute. Then he went in the box and dialled, and when he come out, he went through the skinny bloke's pockets, and took out every single thing, gun and all.

"Just in case there's anything there to trouble Henry," he says. "Now let's be off, quickly. Which way are you going?"

"Anywhere you like till it comes morning," He says. "Then I'm off home."

"I'll take you there, now," says the Father. "It's the best place, and always was."

"No fear," He says. "You don't think I could face my Ma without a walk round and a bit of a think, do you? She's going to ask where I've been. I've got to get the story right, ain't I?"

"That's a horrible fellow we left behind there," says the Father. "He'll hang one of these days, you'll see. Try and not get mixed up with such. They'll lead you down till there's no rising."

"What about old Henry, then?" He says, trying to keep it chatty, because the Father sounded like crying any minute. "He's all right, ain't he?"

"In his way, none better," says the Father. "But only in his way. He's too ready to treat all alike, and that brings trouble. He does good, but not always in a good way."

"Why did you want to leave that bloke out there?" He says. "Why didn't we wait till the coppers come? He might die."

"He might, indeed," says the Father. "And no loss to himself or the world. I'll do nothing to help such. As well expect a doctor to help disease."

"I thought monks helped everybody," He says. "Don't they?"

"Perhaps they do," says the Father. "But I'm not a monk, you see? I'm doing a little in my own way in Pennyfields and elsewhere. But I'll do nothing for horrible creatures. There's too many good ones needing help to waste time and effort on them. And by helping him back there, we might easily have put Henry in prison along with ourselves. And I've had enough of it."

"You ain't been in, have you?" He says, and the morning wind blowing up was all that colder.

"Ten years hard labour," says the Father, and he come to a stop on the corner. "I went in when I was twenty two. The best years of my life. I stole money, that's why. Everybody wants to steal money, sometimes. Especially when they're young. But most of them never do because they can't get hold of enough to make it worth while. I did. But I was caught. So be warned, son. Keep your fingers off what isn't your own, and your nose out of another's business, and your tongue away from things that don't concern you. Away down there you'll come to Holborn and Oxford Street. I'm going through here to the City. Which way will you go?"

"Oxford Street," He says, quick, because He wanted to be on His own.

"Then be on your way, and keep out of trouble," says the Father. "And say nothing of tonight to anyone. Goodbye, now."

He went off without another word, so black, with the hood pulled over his head, he was a bit of the dark moving along on rubber.

Putting His hand in His pocket for a fag, He found the pocket half full. And in the other was a piece of hard paper. It was ten shillings. He could just see the colour by the lamp down the road.

It might have been Henry, or the Father, or even Ma Sitram, but whoever it was, they done Him a right favour. At least He could get some breakfast, and go home all right, and later on, see Ada down the Fun Fair without a care in the world.

The very thought of her come off of the street like a tune played soft.

Even sore eyes never meant much, thinking of Ada.

The streets come up pale blue almost while He was looking, and all the buildings come up deep brown, or a grey, almost spring green, and the top of the road shone purple in between silver powdered pavements, with the wind blowing all the bits of paper about in rings, proper mad.

The sound of His shoes was talking to each other across the road, and when He went tip toe to deaden it, they whispered, but the squeaks was like the rats, so He turned it in, and started whistling, still walking quiet, and trying to put each foot inside a paving stone, like playing a game of hop scotch.

But when He see the two coppers having a smoke on the corner, He started walking loud again, in case they got nosey and asked questions. He tried to look like a bloke going on early work, but He hoped His face was cleaner than what it felt. They looked at Him out of the doorway, and He looked back at them, but they never said nothing, so He just walked on, regardless, though His heart was doing double shifts, knocking the breath out of Him.

The early buses looked proper homely, coming along all red and solid, and making the old row they always made, and leaving behind the smell they always left. He could have kissed them all over. Full of blokes, they was, and blue with smoke on the top deck, bright with light down below.

The blokes in the All Night cafe was all coats off and swilling down, or cleaning the carpets, when He went in there. A couple of old girls was washing the marble stairs down, in water almost like the stuff Chaser went down in. He had a twopenny wash and felt the better for it, and if He could have screwed up the guts, He might have had a shave from the barber, but everything looked so posh, He thought it might have come out more than He could afford. And anyway, He could go another day, easy, before his whiskers started tripping Him up. Besides, Ma might ask questions if He looked too clean.

It was a right treat to order eggs, bacon, kidneys, chips, toast and coffee from a waiter. He never done it before, and He was a bit worried what the waiter was going to cost Him, although He could afford it and not miss it. But there was some posh bloke at the table in front as got up and left threepence by the side of the plate, so He knew He was all right again.

This big room with all the lights, and the carpet, and tables with proper cloths on, was a real bit of all right. Warm and sort of pally, it was, and you could have everything if you had the money. But He wanted to sleep more than anything.

He come over that tired, He nodded off, and got jerked up out of it by the old waiter giving Him a shove, none too nice, neither.

"You can't sleep here," he says. He was old, and his face was yellow, all cracks, and his eyes was sleeping even if the rest of him was moving about. "They won't allow you to sleep here. If it was me, you could sleep. But it ain't. So you can't."

He put a orange bill on the plate, folded in half, and picked up his big round tray.

"The old man's got his eye on you," he says. "If you go off again, he goes to the porters. They'll shift you."

"I'm all right," He says. The old bloke lifted his shoulders and let them drop. He walked off with his toes turned out, as if his feet was hurting him, and his grey bald head hardly come over the top of his back.

He changed the note at the desk and rattled the change about in His hand, giving the bride in the desk a wink. But she was too tired to worry about Him. He went down the Gents again, put a penny in the slot, closed the door, and sat down on the seat. It was bigger than the one at home and real comfortable.

It was warm down there, lovely and warm, His guts was full, He had plenty of money, He was seeing Ada later on, and He was that there sleepy, He could hardly open His mouth to yawn.

Some machine was saying pumble chumpa, pumble chumpa, deep down below.

# CHAPTER XXII

HE WAS LOOKING at the light making long patterns on the wall, and some bloke in his shirt sleeves, with a brush, was standing there banging on the open door, looking at Him.

"Come on," this bloke says. "I want to clean out."

"Okeedoke," He says. "Shan't be long."

"Out of it," says the bloke, "else you'll get your bloody feet wet. Give you two minutes."

There was a stiff ring all round where He had been sitting. He could hardly stand up, and He was shivering cold. He tried to button His coat, but His hands was soppy with sleep, His eyes was bunged fat, and He was itching all over.

Out in the wash place He had another wash with His coat off, and a cup of tea upstairs just about put Him right, even though the waitress looked at Him as if He fell off of a dust cart. Outside in the street it was warmer, and full up of people and traffic. It was more kind of pally, there was more of everything and it felt happier. Blokes were selling buttonholes off of trays and the paper blokes had a right collection of stuff to sell, all spread out on the pavement and in doorways.

Looking for a penny for a paper, He come across Miss Wilmore's card. It was just what He wanted for a tale to tell Ma. So He shot across the road and got the bus, handed over His fare, and started reading the paper, just like a rich bloke, not a care in the world, and all His cash tied up safe in the bank.

Some old bloke come in and sat down aside of Him, nigh shoving Him through the side of the bus. He was going to say something, but the morning was so sunny, and things was working so nice, it hardly seemed worth while, and besides, nobody could help the size of their arse, however hard they tried.

"See the paper this morning?" He says, trying to get things going.

"No," the old bloke says, "why?"

"Oh, nothing much," He says. "They're still mucking about with it, that's all."

"Who is?" says the old bloke.

"The Government," He says, as if everybody ought to know.

"You don't want to worry about the Government," the old bloke says. "A boy your age didn't ought to be mucking about with that sort of thing. You want to leave it alone. It won't get you a copper or two, you know?"

"Well," He says, "we got to see what they're playing at, ain't we?"

"Whatever they're playing at," the old bloke says, "don't make no difference to us. They ain't worried about you, nor me, neither. So why should we waste time with them? We're all right. They're all right. So leave 'em alone. You can't do nothing, whichever way you look at it. I been living three times as long as you, and I know."

It seemed to be sensible enough, looked at that way, so He give over. But He tried to think what the Government was. One way or another, He heard a lot about it, what it done, and what it ought to, and the blokes on politics aboard the Workmans was always chewing the fat about it, but nothing never come of it. It seemed like a sort of firm, or something, only far way. Anyhow, like the old bloke said, it never meant nothing, after all the talk, so it was best left alone.

Walking along the road Miss Wilmore lived in, He was surprised how the houses was just like round His way, only they was cleaner, and most of them had coats of paint and canvas blinds. But they was the same shape outside. He rang the bell at Miss Wilmore's black front door, and some bride opened up. She was in grey, with a apron and a white cap.

"Yes?" she says, very snotty, looking Him up, down and sideways. She was a good looker, too.

"Miss Wilmore," He says. "And I ain't got a lot of time, neither."

"What you want?" she says, still the same way, only worse. But her legs was too thin. "She's busy."

"So am I," he says, "so get cracking."

"Who are you?" she says. You could see where her corset stuck out round the top of her legs.

"Mr Verdun Mott, the artist," He says. "Now, how do we go?"

"We'll see," she says, and shuts the door.

He sat down on the step in the warm of the sun and put a fag on. It was proper funny how people treated each other, He reckoned. If He come up there with a posh suit, and one of them black hats and a umbrella, He would have gone inside and the skivvy would have tore about all over the show. But like He was, He was a little bit of poop what you kicked about till you lost it.

The door opened again, and the skivvy come out, looking down at Him. He see that only her ankles was thin. They come out in a lovely bulge higher up.

"Come on," she says, none too nice, but better than the first time.

"Ah," He says. "I thought the old girl would see me."

"Not so much of the old girl," she says, proper mouthy.

"You know what you want, don't you?" He says. "You want your arse smacking. And I'm just the boy, and all."

"You?" she says, "and how many more like you?"

"Just the bare me," He says, and He knew He was all right. She knew the game. "And I could go it a treat. Do you a bit of good."

"Drop us a card," she says. "Straight through, last door on your right. If you know which is your right, that is."

He looked at the top of her apron.

"I know which one of them's right," He says. "No error, neither. Every satisfaction guaranteed."

"Saucy bleeder," she says, and they both started laughing.

"See you later," He says, and went on down the passage.

It was full of animals' heads sticking out of the wall, and cases of birds, and coloured chimney pots full of everlasting grass. He went through the last door on the right, and come out in the sun.

All glass, the roof was, and Miss Wilmore was in a green pinafore, standing in the bright white with sunshine all round, painting.

"Hullo," she says, and her piano keys come out all spit again. "I wondered if you'd remember. Now, what can we do for you?"

"I don't know," He says, feeling a bit down.

Here was a artist, at last.

She was dressed like one. There was as much colour on her pinafore as there ever was on Old Nick's trousers, and there was dozens of tubes of paint chucked all over the floor. Canvas squares in all sizes was stacked six deep round the walls, and she was painting a big one on a proper easel, like you see on the pictures, with a big jug full of brushes down at her side, and a marvellous palette, boiling up of every colour as ever come in your mind, nigh as big as a meat dish, stuck on her thumb.

She was a proper artist.

Painting a landscape, she was. Not that it was much good, what He could see of it, but then it was hardly started, so you had to give it a chance.

"You paint, don't you?" she says, and He could see she was trying to get Him chatting. It looked to Him as if she was a bit put out, Him coming at all, so it started Him off feeling a bit uncomfortable.

"Yes," He says. "Not much, though."

"What have you done?" she says, and she give Him a fag.

"Not much," He says.

"But what sort of things?" she says, a bit impatient.

"Heads," He says. "And fishes."

"Fishes?" she says, and the piano keys come out twice as big. "Oh, that's lovely. What a lovely idea. What sort of fish?"

"Japanese rainbows," He says, thinking hard and trying to remember all the jobs they done in the firm for the fish books. "And all sorts of gold fish. And crabs, and things."

"I'd love to see your work," she says, interested as you like. She was younger than He thought she was, and not bad looking, if you left off the glasses and forgot the piano keys. "Couldn't you show me something? When could you bring it?"

"Ah," He says. "That's it. I've had to sell it, see?"

"Oh, bother," she says, proper funny, she was, though she was serious as a judge. "What a shame. Were you so broke, or something?"

"Broke?" He says. "I'm always broke. I've got my mother, see?"

She looked real pitiful. It was almost a shame to look at her.

"Oh, I say," she says, as if the place was coming atop the pair of them. "Who did you sell it to? Have you an agent?"

"No," He says, going slow. "Some bloke on the firm got rid of them for me. But now I ain't there, I'm proper up the spout, see? No pay, no paints, no pictures, see? It's hard, but that's how it goes."

"What are you going to do, then?" she says. She took smoke down just like a man, and it come out sweet and heavy, making Him breathe deeper to try and get it.

"I don't know," He says. "That's what I come for. I thought you had some ideas."

"I was going to offer you a job cleaning the studio," she says. "But I can't think what made me think of it. And I'm going away at the end of the week. I was wondering who I could send you to."

"Look, Miss," He says, and He got up. "I don't want sending nowhere, see? I ain't the parcel post. I'm just a artist, that's all. And life's hard enough without getting chucked about all over the shop. Thanks all the same, like."

"Don't you be silly," she says, and she pats the chair for Him to sit down. "Look here. I'll tell you what we'll do. You come here next Saturday about three o'clock. I shall be gone, so you'll have the whole place to yourself. Rivers will be here, so you can go in and out as you please. And you can paint away till I come back. There's plenty of canvas and all the paints you'll need. How's that for help?"

"That's marvellous," He says, thinking of Rivers. "Who's Rivers?"

"The maid," she says. "She won't worry you. I'll take care of her. You just come whenever you like. If you want to sleep here there's a sofa and rugs over there."

"Okeedoke, Miss Wilmore," He says, keeping it down. "That's just what the doctor ordered, that is. Thanks. I'm dead lucky."

"On one condition," she says, and she holds up her finger.

"What?" He says, and everything come to a dead stop resting on the finger.

"You leave your work here for me to see," she says.

"Okeedoke," He says. "Done."

"Right," she says, and gets up. "Saturday, after three?"

"I'll be outside the door, queued up," He says.

"Good luck," she says, and shook hands. "Straight along the passage, and the door's in front. Goodbye."

"So long," He says, and He got out, thankful to be somewhere where He could have a good laugh.

The skivvy come up the stairs when He was just about level with them.

"I'll be here on Saturday," He says. "She's going away. I'm using the studio."

"What," she says, real cocky, "painting it out, or cleaning the windows?"

"Painting inside of it," He says, just looking at her. "You'll get your orders, don't worry. And I'll clean your windows, if you ain't careful."

"That'll be the day," she says, but He knew He was all right. There was something about the look in her eyes. Very straight, they was, blue, proper blue, and wide. She was a right bit of stuff. He wondered if she knew what was going on inside Him.

"See you Saturday," He says, and started to go.

"If you're lucky," she says.

He got out on the front step feeling proper pleased with His self. Everything was going marvellous. The sun was hot on Him, He had a pocketful of fags, plenty of money, and a proper good tale for Ma.

But walking along the road it come on Him all of a sudden

how Saturday was a long way off, and there was no pay day
in the week. Never mind how good the story was, it had to be
a lot better before it would cover up Friday, and no wages to
take home. Slapping paint on canvas was all right to think
about, but not much good without the roast and boiled.

It hit Him a right wallop, while He was watching all the
people tearing about buying things, and old girls doing the
shopping, and a bloke on a stall screwing up apples in a bag
and putting half a dollar between his teeth to dig for change.

He was forgetting something. He forgot it for hours. But He
remembered now, and it made him sickish, and He come over
so dog tired, He could have sat down in the gutter.

He was out of work.

He kept saying it over to His self. It was like as if everything
all round Him was empty. It never meant nothing to all these
people. Nobody give That Much for Him.

The sky came over darker and the light sort of went out of
the day and people seemed to feel Him there and look the
other way, not wanting to be bothered, or afraid He might tap
them for a copper or two. He felt as if He had a card round
His neck saying I Am Out Of Work So Look Out.

Out of work, that was Him, out of work.

Even the buses was saying it to Him as they shot past. He
was proper frightened at the space all round Him, as if the
back and side walls of His life had been tore out, leaving one
wall in front, with all the people for Him to look at, and be
afraid of.

Out of work. If He was blind He could rattle a mug, and
people would any rate be sorry for Him.

But not now, not as He was, because He was only out of
work.

And Ma was waiting at home.

He started feeling angry about everything again. After all,
take it all round, it was no good of getting worried. Thousands
of other blokes was out of work, and not so well off as Him. He
had a home to go to, anyway, and there was grub and fags and
a warm bed. After all, He could have been a thousand times

worse off. As it was, He had enough money to take care of things for the next couple of days, and Ada was waiting at the Fun Fair. Like a tune, she was, thinking of her.

Somehow, He started to feel more cheerful, and by the time He had a fag going, He was whistling away as if He was right in the money, rolling in it, and like old Henry said, just a right lucky bloke, without a care in the world.

Except Ma.

## CHAPTER XXIII

THE ROAD WAS busy when He got off of the tram. He never see it busy in the week before, ever since He grew up and went to work, anyhow. It come a bit of a surprise that all this had been going on day after day, all these years, and He never knew nothing about it. The shops was full, people was thick as flies, blokes was hollering out what they was selling, and everybody was getting a living, or else spending a bit of it. All except Him.

He felt more Out of It than ever, specially because He used to look down on the blokes as worked in local shops, instead of getting on the tram every morning, like He did, and going to work in the City. He used to think they was mugs. But it was proved who was the mug now. There they was, comfortable as anything in good jobs, hardly a step from home and no fares to pay out, and there He was, Out of Work.

He could feel them looking at Him as if they thought He was the scum of the earth. So He pretended not to notice anything, and just whistled His way down the road. The fish and chip shop had a queue outside, mostly kids from school waiting for their dinners. That was something else He never see since He left school.

Len Tate was serving them for all he was worth, and so was Ma Tate and the two girls. The shop was steamed out, and the lamps looked like dead marigolds coming through, but Ma Tate's face come up a howling red, nigh purple, at the back there, under the silver roof of the fryer. Len's hair was falling round his face while he chucked more chips in the fat, pulled out twopenny pieces, wrapped them up in sheets of newspaper, and slung the money down to Ethel, working the till, sliding the vinegar bottle down the counter, all at the same time it looked like, while he held up his hand to stop too many shouting at once.

Quick on the job, busy, smart at it, and earning plenty of

nicker, that was Len, and the business was his when Ma Tate rolled up, so he was just about laughing.

And there He was, tired and hungry and out of work. It never seemed right, what with the heavy steam of fish fat and the raw smell of hot chips warming His dial, and all.

He tried to whistle, but it was no good. The tune seemed to have gone out of Him and the sight of The Shop made it worse.

The furniture was on the pavement, as usual, but there was a different look about it, somehow. Ma put it all out herself, every morning except Sunday, and if the whitewashed prices was rubbed off, she drawed them all on again, with her big figures, the 2's as looked like swans and the 8's like cottage loafs.

The Shop, and the furniture, and even the pavement looked different, because it was dinner time of a weekday, and emptier, duller looking, sadder, somehow, specially because He had no right to be there. He ought to have been at work, by rights.

He see Ma's hat before He see her, and before she see Him. It give Him such a shock, He stood still, watching the black ostrich feathers creeping about their selfs just over the top of a yellow grained chest of drawers, trying to get hold of His self, so as to be ready when she got her eyes on Him.

He could feel this big hole in His self. He could feel where He had to say He was Out of Work. But there was no good reasons why He should have been sacked, except the ones she been yelling about for months, such as always being late, and not going in of a morning, and sometimes staying away for a day at a time. I Told You So, He could hear her saying, shouting it louder than the engine whistle.

He was dead afraid of going in and seeing her. He was afraid of hearing her say I Told You So. He could bear anything, or put up with anything, but not her saying There You Are, I Told You So, and He knew she would, loud as she could get it out, for hours on end.

He watched the curtains blow about in Ma Chalmers's front

room where she was giving her plants a airing, gentle and lovely, like a dancer's legs, up and down.

"Hullo, son," Ma says, even though she was sitting behind the chest of drawers, aside a bookcase, and soon as He heard, He could have kicked His self. She always put a looking glass where she could look in it and see up and down the Road. It was half the joy of sitting in the front of the shop.

"Ah, Ma," He says, and went round the bookcase, sitting on a kitchen chair marked half a dollar.

"Where you been?" she says. He could feel her eyes, but He was looking down the road.

"Oh," He says, "just having a look round."

"Heard you got the sack," she says. She was cutting up cabbage and chucking the leaves in the bowl.

"That's right," He says, and though His heart was bashing away, He made His voice as slow and easy as you like.

"Where did you get to last night, then?" she says, ordinary, no panic. "I got a bit worried in the finish."

"Went down a friend of mine's studio," He says. "Where he paints."

"Look as if you had a rough kip," she says. "Nick Falandora was here last night."

"Oh, ah?" He says, nigh dying for air, but not showing it. "What he say?"

"Said you was looking for something else," she says. "So they give you your notice."

"That's right," He says, feeling better, and watching her.

"What you going to do, son?" she says, but there was Something Up with her voice.

"Well," He says, having a go in the dark, "I wouldn't mind helping you in the shop for a week or two? There's plenty I could do till I can find something else."

They both looked at her hands cutting up the cabbage leafs, listening to the crack of stalks getting tore off, and the wettish whistle of the knife going through the leaf.

"What you going to look for, son?" she says.

"Don't know, Ma," He says, trying out the ground. "I'd like

a decent job, where you don't get sacked when you're nigh out of your time."

She waited for the train to blow itself past.

"What sort of job?" she says, same voice, but He knew there was Something On.

"Anything you like," He says.

"I mean," she says, "like what you been doing, or something else?"

"Something else," He says. "I'm fed up of mucking about. I want a real job where I can do me self a bit of good."

"Oh," she says, "do your self a bit of good, eh? How about being a artist, then?"

He see very plain where Old Nick must have been talking. He got proper angry all of a sudden.

"I ain't a artist," He says, before He knew what He had in His mouth, but when it was out, He knew it was true. That was funny, because if anybody else said it, He knew He would have argued against it blue in the face. But now it was out, He knew it was Gospel. He could feel it inside of Him, and in some way or other, it made everything that much easier.

He felt the fat lump of crayon as never did what it was told, and heard the trams moaning round the corner. Everything come lighter, brighter. Even His clothes seemed to weigh less.

"Oh?" Ma says, giving the leaves a swish round and banging her hands on the rim of the bowl. "You ain't, eh? What are you then? I thought you wanted to be like your father?"

"No fear," He says. "I've had enough of that lark. All I want's a good job. I'm sorry I ever went there. Just wasted a lot of time, that's all."

"Give this stuff out here a rub down while I get the dinner, will you?" she says, and she got up. "I meant to do it first thing."

"Okeedoke, Ma," He says. "How long you been having dinner on the sly?"

She started laughing, going in the shop.

"I ain't," she says. "But I knew you'd come home hungry gutted, so I got a bit of steak."

He set the furniture out there as if they was all the things He ever liked. He give them a proper polish up, and arranged them a bit more artistic than what Ma done. When He finished, the shop looked all right. But the sign wanted painting again, so He got the idea of tackling Ma about it. He heard her calling and went in.

"Here, Ma," He says, "what about painting that there sign out there? You can't hardly see what you're looking at."

"It'll do," she says, "I can't afford no signs."

"I can paint it," He says. "It'll cost a couple of bob for paint, that's all."

"All right, son," she says. "See what you can do."

They never said nothing right through dinner. Ma never got much grub down her any time, so He made up for the pair of them.

"Suppose I get you a job in a solicitor's?" she says, when He was half way through the afters.

"Okeedoke," He says.

"You'd have to wear the proper clothes," she says. "You'd have to look the part, I mean."

"What sort?" He says.

"Well," she says, as if everybody knew except Him, only nice and kind, "you know. Black coat and trousers. And a bowler hat, or else one of them grey velours. You'd look all right."

"When could you get me in?" He says.

"We'll see," she says. "Look under the vase on the right hand side, and you'll find a ten shilling note. Get the paint and keep the change."

He nigh fainted.

"Okeedoke, Ma," He says. "Blimey, I shan't know me self. Bowler hat and ten bob? They'll take me for a split, or something."

"I nearly went round there, last night," she says, "but I can't like a copper station."

"No copper could have found me," He says. He see Chaser going down plainer than the sugar bowl. "I was safe enough, Ma. You don't want to worry about me. I'm all right."

He got the ten bob note and went out in the kitchen for a wash and brush up. He come back feeling marvellous. Ma was still picking her teeth by the window. Her little finger went in, right down the back, digging away there, finding all sorts of things from the sound of it.

"Shan't be two ticks, Ma," He says.

"Don't rush it," she says. "Take your time. That was the trouble with your father. Always tearing about, he was."

"Am I anything like him?" He says.

"The dead spitting image," she says. "I can see him every time you turn round. That's why I been afraid."

"Afraid of what, Ma?" He says, and He knew there was Something On from the sound of her voice.

"Well," she says, looking round for the way to say it. "Afraid you might be like him. Artist, like. They was all over him, one time. That was what got him on the drink. And drink was what finished him. He died drunk."

"But you told me he was killed in the war," He says.

"Wherever he was killed," she says, "he was drunk. You can take that from me. I had years of it. That was why I was always against this artist lark. It don't do nobody no good. Just gets you into trouble, that's all. People as don't know what they're talking about making a fuss of you, and getting you thinking you're God Almighty. I listened to them for years, round him. He could never see through 'em. I could, though. But he wouldn't be told."

He started seeing a bit of light, at last.

"I always had the idea you never liked me, Ma," He says. "Is that why?"

"I only never liked what I see of him in you," she says. "Always afraid you'd grow up like him and lead me the same sort of dance. In and out the pubs all day and somebody else's bed half the night. That was your father. Artists? My oath."

"Well," He says. "That's one worry off your mind, any rate. I wouldn't mind a clean collar, if I could get one, Ma?"

"I'll see," she says. "Don't hurry back. There's plenty of time."

"Okeedoke," He says.

So He got outside in the road feeling like a brand new bloke. Something lifted square off of His mind. He was no artist. That was something He found out, for a start.

But the question was right in front of Him, plain as the sign He was looking at. He had to be Something, if not a artist. All the other blokes was Something. Len Tate was a fish and chips fryer. Bert Clively was a lorry driver. Art Taylor was a boot machine hand. They all had their trades except Him.

But he was going to be a solicitor, in a posh suit every morning, so that was better than all of them. He found His self liking the idea of a solicitor even better than a artist. After all, a solicitor was a bloke you had to look up to. A artist was a bloke you sort of felt sorry for, in a way, now He come to think of it. Perhaps that was why the other blokes always treated Him a bit rough.

Thinking of the blokes still working on the stones, back there at the Firm, He felt sorry for them. They were going to be standing there all the rest of their lives. Standing there drawing, and stippling, and watching Old Nick pull proofs, for year after year.

No wonder the old man got drunk all the time.

He thought red and yellow with a black lining would do a right job for the sign. Gold leaf might cost too much, and He never knew how to handle it, neither. Besides, the less the paint cost, the more change there would be.

You had to use your loaf about things like that.

# CHAPTER XXIV

HE GOT DOWN in the Fun Fair almost as far as the shooting gallery, when He had the idea of His life. It stopped Him dead, looking over at the peep show of Lizette in Paris, where some bride was looking in the peephole and laughing, while the bloke with her tried to shove her out of it.

He could take Ada to the studio. It come on Him like a ton of bricks.

Why it never struck Him before, He never knew. It was so easy. It was like eating your dinner.

Soon as He started tasting the idea, life come up a proper treat. Everything started being lovely.

He see how the Fun Fair was full of blokes and brides all having a rare old game all round, and when He come to look at them a bit closer, they all looked the same as Him, somehow. There was Something About Them.

And it proper hit Him, all of a sudden.

They was Out of Work, too.

You could tell it from their clothes and the way they looked at you, and they all felt the same about it, not caring if it snowed ink. There they all was, all in it together, enjoying their selfs on The Dole.

Everybody down there, pretty nigh, was on the Dole.

He never thought of that, neither. He was all right for the Dole His self. His cards was clean. All He had to do, was go round the Green Shop, and sign on. That was about seventeen bob to draw every week, to the good, more than He got for His self by working, now He come to look at it that way. It was a lump of cake, all round.

It was toffee.

Seventeen bob a week for nothing. A little present from Aunty Somebody, and just enough to do Ada grand, besides what He got from Ma. In fact, looking at it all round, as you might say, He thought He ought to think twice about taking this solicitor job. After all, by the time He finished with fares and odds and ends, seventeen bob was more than He could get out of most jobs, so it had to be looked at very careful.

What with one thing and another, He was feeling a right boy by the time He got nigh the big room.

He knew how much He missed the music as soon as He heard it. It come on loud and sweet, and the saxes sort of made a trellis work round and round His guts. Almost as good as being in bed, it was, making you think of things as never got on your nerves, nor worried you. It ran out of your mind and down your legs, making you want to dance, or any rate, shift your feet about, and then you had to start singing.

"Buh duddy doh, buh duddy dee, oh doh," He started singing, along with a couple of other blokes round the crane. "Boh doh, did did dee ree, dee doh."

"Voh vuh duh ree, duh duddee," the other bloke sang.

"Did did dee ree, dee doh," his mate cut in, turning the wheel.

"We ought to stick together," He kids the other bloke. "We might put a few of 'em out of business."

"Yes," says the other bloke, trying heavens hard to get the crane going the way he wanted it, "might put us in hospital, and all."

"Sounded like a case for the police," the bloke with him said. "Wouldn't bother about it if I was you, mate."

He went on down, through the imitation rocks along the passage, and the music, as got a bit bent when you passed too close to the square loud speakers, and the busy sounds of the Fair, all the machines going, blokes shouting, money rattling, bells ringing, light all on and flashing about through the looking glasses, happy as a king amongst all of it.

There she was.

The sight of her always seemed to stop the world going round.

Still in red, still reading, still with her hair down one side of her face, still shining pale gold, still the loveliest, marvellousest bride out, Ada, the one and only.

All her machines was full, and there was four blokes waiting for a go on the one nearest to her, so He was at least half hour too previous.

He had a feeling of not knowing what to do with His legs. All He wanted to do was look at her. But He knew He might look a mug standing there just looking, so He had to do something.

Then she looked up and see Him.

He could hardly believe His eyes.

She was laughing at Him, waving to Him, proper lighted up from inside to see Him. There was a light inside of her while she was laughing. She was all gold and red, laughing away there, with her teeth showing up and ripping out bits of light, and her red beetles flashing in a wave at Him, and then going to push aside her hair.

"Hullo," she says, through her laughing teeth, "where you been, stranger?"

"Doing a bit of night work," He says, knowing all the other blokes was looking at Him. "What you been doing?"

"Oh," she says, coming along the ledge to talk to Him. "Just quiet, you know. Been painting again, have you?"

"Yes," He says, "what you doing Saturday night?"

"I'll be here till gone ten," she says. "Why?"

"Thought you might like to come down the studio," He says. "Watch me do a bit of painting, like."

"Where is it?" she says, a bit doubtful.

"Only down Chelsea," He says. "Not far. We could get a bus back, easy."

"I was going dancing," she says.

"Where?" He says.

"Down the Palais," she says. "I generally do. Makes a break, stuck here all the week."

"I come with you?" He says.

"Course," she says. "Ten o'clock outside, Saturday. We'll have till twelve."

"Okeedoke," He says. "How about before? All right to-night?"

"Don't think I'd better," she says. "Make it Saturday, eh? I have to see to things at home, see? Don't matter so much on Saturdays. I get the lay in of a Sunday."

"Good old Sunday morning," He says. "I come and bring your breakfast in bed, shall I?"

"Wish you could," she says, laughing away there. "Egg fried both sides, and toast."

"Okeedoke," He says. "Leave the back door open. I'll be there."

"Then after that, you'd paint me, eh?" she says.

"All over," He says, getting so cocky He was nigh falling over His self.

"See you ten o'clock, Saturday," she says, still laughing, but kind of pulling back, as though things had gone far enough. "And don't come wasting your money round here, see? I don't like seeing you in here. Artists don't fit in."

"What's up with it?" He says, surprised as anything.

"If you'd been here as long as I have," she says, "you'd know. Wasting their money, that's all they're doing."

"They have a bit of sport?" He says, but He see it was no argument.

"Sport?" she says, as if it was something you scraped up on a shovel. "Call this sport? This bleeding nonsense?"

"What are you here for, then?" He says.

"Because it's a job," she says. "That's all. Just a job. I got to go now. Saturday, ten o'clock, eh?"

"Okeedoke," He says. "Take care of yourself. Nice to seen you."

"Same here," she says. "So long, Ern."

Watching her go away up there on the ledge, He see the lovely shape of her legs, and the marvellous balloon of her hips, going in to her waist, and coming out to her shoulders.

It brought Him up that stiff, what with being tired and all, He could have cried. But there was nothing He could do, only walk away, slow, in case somebody looked at Him, and stand there leaning against the back of the shooting gallery, hoping it would soon go down and stop aching.

The thoughts of going to bed was a real marvel. All of a sudden He see that a cup of tea and a nice kip would put Him just about straight. So away He went, giving Ada a wave, and getting one back, before He went up the steps.

He was living in Saturday, all the way down the High Road.

He went in Dad Prettyjohn's for the paint, picking out a couple of pots from the pile while Dad was hanking about in the back, looking for hairpins for some old dear.

Dad was on a crate, ferreting about in amongst a lot of boxes of shoes and odds and ends of linoleum and lengths of curtaining. He had a little rock garden full of different sorts of prickly fat leaves all over the show, so wherever you looked, little pots of these spikes stuck up, looking proper out of the joke, and knowing it, especially one in a saucer perched on top of the margarine.

Dad's hat for the day was one of them funny long ones, like Admirals wear, only without any gold on it. All his other hats was on a shelf at the back, and there was lots more all over the shop.

"I got the bloody things here, somewhere," he says, "I only had me dukes on 'em not twenty four hours past. Can't make out what happens to things, lately. It's a proper scream."

"Put 'em where you can find 'em, then," this old dear says, proper sniffy from waiting. "I don't know how you ever get through a day. It's a right old glory hole, that's what this is."

Pa looked at her over the top of his glasses.

"How long you been finding that out?" he says, cooing like a cage bird. "Don't you like what you're getting? Perhaps you'd like a couple of bloody shopwalkers prancing about, eh?"

"No," says the old dear, getting her toes dug in, "all I want's my hairpins. That's all."

"Is that all?" says Dad, loving as a two year old, "just your hairpins, eh? And the nasty old man can't find 'em for you, eh? I suppose you want me to turn every bleeding thing in the place out in the street just to find you a packet of bloody hair-pins, eh? What am I?"

"I don't know," the old dear says. "The label's fell off."

"Well, I never," says Dad, giving his self a scratch. "Fell off, eh? You never had a label, have you?"

"No," says the old dear, "nor never been near getting one, neither. I never come nowhere near a madhouse, that's why."

Dad turns round and looks at Him, proper sorry.

"Hear that?" he says, but his eyes was far away, looking out for words. "Course, you know how lunies all say they ain't mad? Oh, yes. And they never did admit they lived in a barmy hutch, neither. They call it a Home. You got a Home, have you?"

The old dear nigh on lost her glasses, out of the way he hollered at her.

"Yes," she says. "Course I got a home, and you're keeping me out of it, and all."

"Ah," says Dad, and he rubbed his hands as happy as a sand-boy. "Well, suppose you got back to your Home in amongst the other lunies, then? They must be looking out for you, by now."

"You give me my hairpins," she says, "and not so much of it, you silly looking thing, you."

"Go out, you stupid old bitch, you," Dad yells. "D'you think I care if you get your hairpins or not? D'you think I live off of your packet of bloody hairpins, do you? Silly looking thing, am I? Glory hole, eh? Getting worse, is it? God perish Gravesend Pier, what a bleeding neck, eh? Coming in here, slinging your weight about? Anybody think you owned the place."

"If I did," she says, "I'd sack you, for a start. And I'd be doing you a favour, and all."

Dad looked round proper helpless, and sort of pulled his self together, quick.

"What you want, son?" he says, rubbing his hands, acting as if the old girl never come in the place. Proper merry and bright, he was, scratching his self two hands at once.

"These two pots of paint," He says, holding them up.

"Ah," says Dad. "Two and ten the two."

"Not these two ain't," He says. "This one's tenpence, and the other's one and a penny."

"One and eleven, a gent," says Dad, "same difference."

"I want my hairpins," says the old dear.

"You've had 'em," says Dad. "That serves you right for getting so bloody excited."

"I stay here till I do," says the old dear, and she put her self down in the chair, umbrella, bag, and all.

Dad leaned over the counter and stared her straight in the eye, but she never shifted a inch.

"You're here for the night, my girl," he says. "And I might tell you we got a breed of mice here bigger than bleeding cats. They'll learn you a thing or two, I know."

"If they ain't no bigger than you, I shan't worry," she says, calm as they make them.

"If I didn't know you," he says, nigh strangling his self he was, "I wouldn't half tell you your fortune. Here," he says to Him, and come out of the counter down to the door. "I hear you've just left your job?"

"That's right," He says, surprised, flashing His mind all round.

"Your Ma was in here, just now," he says, saluting some bloke up the road, "nigh on bought me up, she did. Going to have a do about it, are you?"

"Not as I knows on," He says.

"Ah," says Dad, "well, you'll soon find out. Now, look here, Ernie. If you want a job, and I mean a job, mark you, and one as'll pay, you come in here along of me. There's prospects here, son. I shan't last forever, you know?"

"Thank God for that, any rate," says the old dear, back in the shop.

Dad laughed over the top of his gold half moons, and give his hat a shove, wearing it like Napoleon.

"Mouthy old cow, ain't she?" he says. "I'll sit her there till she's more browned off than what I am. She's the same every time she comes in. Don't forget what I told you? Prospects, don't forget?"

"Ta, Dad," He says. "I'll talk it over."

Ma was inside the shop with a customer so He went in the back way and got a right shock. Most of the old furniture in the kitchen was out of it, and new stuff was in its place. There was a couple of arm chairs by the fire, with lovely tassels hanging off of the arms, and a new carpet. He hardly knew the place.

But when He went upstairs, He got a bigger shock still, because His room was changed right round. There was a new bed, one with a oak headboard all carved round in colours, and a dressing table with a big round looking glass, and a cupboard for His clothes, and a table, all the same style, new curtains at the windows and a round arm chair to match the furniture.

But the green plaster girl was gone. It seemed to have something to do with the new furniture, as if she belonged with the cracked washing stand and the crumby birds, and it made Him angry, right inside His head, to think of her being treated like junk. It was no good of Him going downstairs and kicking up a row about it, or else it might come hard when He tried to borrow a bob or two. But there was a ragged hole round the place where she ought to have been, and a sore place somewhere inside of Him.

"Like it?" Ma says to Him, downstairs.

"Blimey," He says, "I reckon it's smashing. Proper smashing, it is, Ma."

"That's all right, then," she says, and He could see she was pleased with herself. "Been meaning to do it a long time, but I never seemed to get a minute."

"What's happened to my statue?" He says.

"What statue?" she says, pouring out the tea.

"The green one," He says. "What I got down the shooting gallery."

"Oh, that," she says, "didn't think you wanted it no more?"

"Why not?" He says. "It was a prize, wasn't it?"

"Funny sort of a prize," she says, and He could feel her eyes while He was spooning the sugar. "Thought you said you was giving all that stuff the go by?"

"All what stuff?" He says. "All I'm doing is find a job where you don't get treated like a pair of wore out boots, that's all."

"I don't reckon it's right," Ma says, and she shoves her hat pin through a different place, like she always done when she had to say something she never wanted to. "I never liked it, any rate. Ain't decent."

"What's up with it?" He says. "It's never done me no harm, has it?"

"That's all very well," Ma says, "but it's a bit too much like your father to suit me, thanks very much. He had that sort of thing all over the house here, once. Couldn't get his mind off of it. And I won't have you going the same way, see? Not now, any rate."

"Now?" He says. "What's happened now, then?"

"Well," she says, as if it was a fact. "You ain't going to be a artist no more, are you?"

"What's that got to do with it?" He says, proper surprised.

"Well," she says, "it's one thing or the other. If you're going to be a decent, hard working, respectable man like I want you to be, you can't go mucking about with no statues. You won't have no time for it, for one thing. And it won't do you no good, for another."

"But that statue's got nothing to do with being a artist," He says, narked as anything. "I won it for a prize. What's up with that?"

"I told you," Ma says. "It ain't decent. That's all there is to it, and that's it."

"Where is it?" He says.

"In the dustbin," she says. "Best day's work I ever done. I want to see you make something out of yourself, not start getting into trouble through a lot of stuff like that. I've seen it happen before, but it ain't going to happen again. Not if I can help it."

He wanted to try and explain that the statue was no more

to do with being a artist than fly in the air, but He knew if He tried she might go off in one of her loud fits again. Besides, even though He somehow knew what He meant, the words never seemed to come out right. It was like the crayon in His hand. He knew what He wanted to do, but He never knew how to get it done. There was nothing He could say to shift her. It was like being in a room with only three walls, and everything blowing in without being able to stop it.

"It's no good of you looking like that, son," she says, but not nasty nor nothing. "The happiest night of my life was last night when Nick said you was fed up of it. I always knew you had a bit of sense about you, somewhere. But I never knew you'd find it so soon. So I made up my mind to do the same by you. That's why I've changed the place round a bit. You start living decent and respectable, and so will I. That's a bargain."

"But, listen Ma," He says, trying to see through fog, "I can't make out what you mean. Wasn't I decent and respectable before? Did I ever come home drunk, or anything? Or shout the odds? Anybody think I was a proper rotten lot, or something, wouldn't they?"

"The way you was going, they wouldn't be far wrong," Ma says. "I see your father in pretty nigh everything you was doing. You was both off on the same road. And you was getting worser every day. Getting up in the afternoon, and borrowing a couple of bob whenever you could, and then blueing it on some woman or other outside. I've been through it too many times. You can't tell me. And that's it."

He see them red beetles crawling about all over the place.

"I ain't blued nothing on no woman," He says. "I never had the chance, did I?"

"I see to it, and all," Ma says. "But what about that cheap bit of stuff down the Fun Fair, eh? What about her?"

Quick, it ripped right through Him boiling hot, and He see it, easy. Len Tate told Ma Tate, and she went and told Ma. He could smell the fish fry in Len's clothes, and see Ma Tate's screaming red dial.

"Ah, well," He says, "I mean, she's just, well, you know,

I mean, there's nothing in it, Ma. If you ever meet her you might like her."

"You bring her round here," Ma says, taking two bites out of spite, "and I'll brain the pair of you. She'll waltz her arse out of it a sight quicker than what she come in, I can tell you."

"But listen," He says, "you don't even know her, do you? How can you say it if you don't know?"

"I been down there," Ma says. "I see her, all right. You take my tip. Keep away from her. There's plenty of decent girls knocking about, without getting landed with a bit like that."

The gentle heat coming out of Ada was getting tore up, like a navvy sticking his boot through a lot of lace. He see her face, looking tired after a day of it, and He heard the hopeless sound of her voice, even under the swearing, where she could see no finish to it.

"Look here, Ma," He says, "it might be a surprise to you, but Ada is a decent girl. The decentest one I've met, any old how. And she's keeping her Ma, and doing the housework when she gets home of a night. Now, then. Can't be much wrong there, can there?"

"I'll see it proved, first," Ma says. "But the fact is, you're going to be something decent. You've stopped being a artist, so you better stop your artist ways. Once you're a solicitor, you'll have all your work cut out, my boy. You do your share of it, and I'll do mine. You'll have a nice home, and you'll have the proper clothes. You'll be something. And you got to be something before you can do anything. See?"

"But listen, Ma," He says, and He could have cried, out of temper, and not being able to tell her where she was so wrong. He could feel it so plain, but the words was missing. "Artists are something, ain't they? People look up to them, don't they? They got whacking great exhibitions and things, ain't they? They are something, ain't they? But where's the solicitors' exhibitions? They've been at it a good long time, ain't they? What they got to show for it?"

"In the bank," Ma says, as flat as the lino, and proper laughing at Him. "That's what. In the bank, son. That's where you want it. Sticking it up on the wall don't get you nowhere. Look at your father. Pictures galore, and what did he have when he kicked it? I had you coming along and not a fadger in the world except me pension. Don't tell me, son. I know too much about it."

"The bank ain't everything," He says, but she sounded so right, it was no good of arguing. "I've never been bothered about it, any how."

"No?" Ma says, looking inside the teapot as if somebody was in there. "Never wanted to borrow a few bob here and there, eh? No use for a bit of dough, now and again? Where've you always come when you've wanted the nicker?"

"Well," He says, and He see He was proper up the spout. "I mean, I was growing up, wasn't I? I wasn't out of me Time, was I?"

"Out of your Time?" she says, and she starts laughing again. "Perhaps not, but you had your tales ready for the telling, didn't you? You was grown up enough for that, wasn't you? You was getting about as big a bloody liar as what your father was. And that's saying something."

"Here, well, half a mo, Ma," He says, and he starts feeling real hard done by, nigh crying somewhere, He was. "What tales have I told you? Eh? Be fair, Ma?"

"Fair?" she says, and she leans back till the chair cracked, laughing proper out loud. All the ostrich feathers was shaking about against the window glass, looking as if they was laughing, too. "Stone me. Fair? What about that catch about the paints, eh? There was a bit of your father, if you like."

"What paints?" He says, and then He remembered Old Nick, and He could feel His face coming up red as a bus, and burning hot. "Oh, them? Well, I shan't be wanting 'em now, shall I?"

"You never did want 'em," Ma says. "And Nick never had

'em to give you, neither. That was just a tale to get a few bob on the sly. You come straight to your bank for it, though, didn't you? Me. The bank."

"But if you knew it was a tale, then," He says, "why did you give it to me?"

"Well," she says, "it was so much like your father, I never had the heart to say No. That's why."

"But look here, Ma," He says, trying to fight it, "how did you know it was a tale? How did you know it wasn't true?"

"Knowing your father before you," Ma says. "Think we was all born yesterday, do you? Ain't so long ago since I was washing out your napkins, was it?"

## CHAPTER XXV

THE DAYS WENT sliding by in soft soap, it seemed like. Working in the shop was a real lark, He found, and He often wondered why He never tried it before. Not that there was much work about it, all said and done, but the time went by just the same, giving odd bits of furniture a polish up, and painting the sign, and stacking the hundreds of old books and prints to get them a bit tidier. The books was a proper dry lot, all history or some other fine thing, and years old. He had a look at them all, to see if He was missing anything, but they was all about the driest stuff out, so He just give them all a kind look, and forgot them.

The prints was a funny lot, and all. Old views and blokes in armour, and what all, not much cop to look at, and cheap at half the price. Ma only kept them because she thought they might come in useful, sometime, and she heard of people buying them for collections, and, of course, they come in useful for wrappers.

Mostly the people come in to put something in for the week, or to take out what they put in the week before. Chairs come in at half a dollar, and it cost them three and a kick to get them out. Mangles come in at ten bob and went out twelve and a tanner. Ma made a nice thing out of it, by and large, because if the stuff was left over a month, she sold it to a dealer, generally old Ike Buzgang, for a nice profit, so she was always on the winning side.

Then she ran a borrowing club, lending half a dollar for three and six over a week, or five bob for the month, and she done all right out of that, too. With that, there was the Clothing Club, and the Boot Club, and the Christmas Club. So all day long, old dears and kids was coming in to pay in a tanner here, and a bob there, and Ma done nothing but fill up their books and put the cash in the different boxes.

He never see that cash before, and He wondered where she kept it. But He never found out, because she always hopped it while He was shutting the place up, and when He finished, she had the supper ready, and the boxes was missing. Nor she never let Him mark a book, nor take the money, neither. But after all, it was her business and He was only just learning, so it was natural, and He never worried about it.

"Ernie," she says, while they was having breakfast, Thursday morning, "I'm going to do a bit of business in the City, today. Don't know how long I'll be, but I want you to take charge of the shop, see? Let's see how you go."

"Okeedoke, Ma," He says, and He felt proper proud, but so surprised, He never even tasted His breakfast. Thursday was always a bit busy with old girls popping things in all day for a bit of nicker to see them over till pay day. So He opened up with a good heart, and give everything a good shine, arranging things so as they looked nice, drawing the prices in careful, and generally enjoying His self for once. He had a marvellous feeling of being His own boss, and it was just like living in a different world. He thought of old Henry a lot, but He thought more of Ma, what she said at breakfast, and how she said it. He kept on feeling as if she said it with her eye on Him, as though she was afraid He was on the crook and ready to do her down, and she was giving Him a chance to see if she was wrong.

They started coming in as soon as the kids was in school, carrying chairs, best coats, fire irons, china, anything worth a bob or two. He just looked at the book to see what Ma always give them, and doled out the halfs and dollars, not saying too much and not even smiling. He felt it was a bit too serious for having a lark, or even half a one, because if He made a mistake there was no knowing what Ma might say, or do. They seemed to think so, too. Specially the younger ones with babies. So the morning passed off, and He shut the shop at one o'clock and went up to Ma Tate's for His dinner.

"Settled down in business for yourself, now, have you, son?" she says, picking out a big sixpenny bit and piling on the chips.

"You'll do all right for yourself, there. Lot better than mucking about, ain't it? Yes. It's safe, that's what that is. Safe."

"That's right, Ma," He says, giving the vinegar and salt a good old shake, but He was thinking about her telling Ma about Ada, and hating her face, like a round red bag with two blue slits, wet as if she washed without wiping, and laughing without meaning to.

"See you round the cafe tonight?" Len says, giving Him the wink, while he was giving the chips a stir round in the whistling fat. The steam clouds come up making his face a yellowish smudgey silver one side where the light caught it and his hair flopped down like black fingers crawling about.

"Okeedoke, Len," He says, and He was somehow pleased, because for the first time in His life, Len had spoke as if He mattered. It all come of owning your own business and being your own boss, it looked like. They was both all that much different since He stopped being a artist and started being sort of ordinary, like them, and it made Him feel a bit more pleased with His self.

The shop was filled up to the door with kids and women all yelling the place down with orders. The kids had to be served quicker because they had to get back to school and the women had to get back home with the grub for the old man and their families, and between the lot of them, the Tates was just about going barmy. He took His plate up in the corner and slid along the bench, up against the wall, well out of the crush, and started to get it down Him. The fish was fried in a heavy batter, just how He liked it, and the chips was just a nice hot gold, so what with the vinegar and salt, and a fresh white roll, He done His self all right.

It was too hot to sit there very long, and any case, He was too excited, even wanting to get back to work before the dinner hour was over. He had to shove His way through all the kids to get to the door, and pulling His self out of the crush and getting free on the pavement was like stepping out of a fist, but it was all right, feeling the coolish wind blowing all round Him and up His trousers legs after the steam of the shop and all the yelling and the arms and legs and wriggling shoulders of the crowd.

Ma Sedgwiss was waiting outside when He got back. She came up to His shoulder, no hat, hair in paper curlers, and a brown coat made out of a blanket, with the green stripes all running down one side, so it looked as if she was always standing up on the skew.

"Hullo, son," she says, proper chatty, "where's your Ma? Gone out, has she?"

"Yes," He says, trying not to be too nice, in case she tried getting a extra bob or so off of Him. "What can I do for you?"

"I brought Joe round again," she says, and waves the canary cage. "I'll have him out again, soon as I draw me pension. Your Ma always goes three and a tanner on him."

"Don't say so, here," He says, looking in the book. "Half a dollar, that's all."

"Can't be looking right," she says, and her eyes went wide as open windows. "Three and a kick, I give you my dying oath, son, never a halfpenny under."

"Half a dollar, take it or leave it," He says, and shut the book.

"Now, look here, son," she says, putting on a lot of the Madam, "you just let me tell you something. It might be half a dollar in the book but it's never been nothing else but three and a kick in me hand. Your old Ma's one of the old school, she is, like me. So just you pay up and not so much of it."

"Half a dollar," He says. "It's no good of you shouting the odds, Ma. I'm in charge, here."

"More's the pity," she says. "You don't care what happens to a poor old woman, do you? You got your home, and your Ma to look after you, and all the grub you can eat, and all your pleasures, and everything, and here's me starving for a crust. It ain't fair, it ain't. Ain't fair. Ain't fair."

Then she starts howling. Proper sloshing about in it, she was, with her tongue hanging out and bubbles coming up and popping off every other second, and her hands trying to wipe away the spit and tears at the same time, till her face come the colour of salt beef and her eyes was all floating about under flashes of light.

"No good of you carrying on there, Ma," He says. "We're used to it by now. Half a dollar, or don't waste me time."

"I'll tell your Ma about you," she says. "You wait. I'll tell her. She wouldn't allow it if she knew. You young blokes, you're all the same. No feelings, nor nothing. Don't matter to you what we have to go through, do it?"

"Half a dollar," He says, but her voice, and the way her front flopped about while she was howling made Him feel proper rough inside of Him, somewhere. He knew it was all put on, like she put it on round the police court every time she got run in, but just the same, He found it coming hard on His feelings.

"What can I do with half a dollar?" she was yelling, as hard as she could. "Shilling for coals, and I got one and six. What can I get for one and six? Couple of pennyworth of scrag ends and some potherbs, and what about tomorrow? Eh? What about some tea and milk? And the gas? And bread? And how about my rent? Eh? Do you know? Do you care, do you?"

While she was going on there, He tried to look anywhere else because her eyes was so sorry for their selfs, wet through they was, slopping about the shop through lonely water, not even grey any more, but just old and tired of it.

Joey was laying on his back in the sand, taking things easy by the looks of him, with his head against the brass railings, and his eyes closed, just like some old bloke having a nice forty winks after his dinner.

"Half a mo," He says, trying to stop her turning the tap on further. "Supposing I take him? How do I give him his grub till tomorrow? What's he eat?"

"I got his birdseed here," she says, holding up this screwed up paper. "Your ma generally lets me take him home again, though."

"Ah," He says, smelling the catch. "But I ain't Ma, see?"

"Don't have to be told," she says. "Now what about my three and a tanner?"

"Half a dollar," He says. "And how do I capurtle on the grub stakes?"

"If you don't know," she says, "you don't know much. Put it in his seed box, down there, and give him his water in the other one. If it was much easier, you wouldn't have to do nothing at all, would he, Joe boy?"

"How much can he eat?" He says, making her talk sensible. She was giving her dial a good old polish off with the back of her hand, and drying up a treat. "And what time's he like it?"

"As much as he can get, when he can get it," she says, "and that ain't too much, nor too often, neither. Specially when there's blokes like you hanging about. Now give me my three and a tanner and I'll go out and get me self some grub. Then we'll both have a treat, won't we, Joe? Eh? When he gives us the three and odd?"

"Half a dollar," He says, looking out the door quick, proper fed up of His self for saying it, but not wanting, somehow, to be bested in the argument. He thought she was going to start howling again, but she never said a word. Not only that, but it sounded as if she was holding her breath.

It come over proper heavy quiet in there, all of a sudden, and He got the idea she was getting ready to slosh him. But He never turned round, even though His hair come up like rows of railings.

"Joey?" she says, as if she seen a ghost. "Joey? What's up with you, ducks? Eh, lovey? What's up, then, eh?"

She had the cage in one hand, holding it up, and the other was flapping about inside trying to make him take a bit of notice, but Joey never even give her eye room.

"Joey?" she says, while her finger was stroking his waistcoat, "Joey? What's up, boy? Eh? What's up?"

He see her eyes through the shining brass railing go a sort of darkish queer colour, and her breath come in, long and slow, like as if she was never going to stop filling her self, but Joey never said a word nor moved a inch.

"Oh, Joey," she says, "Joe boy? Joe? Speak to your Mum, Joe? Speak to her, ducks?"

She started to cry just like a train coming out of a station, one puff, another puff, then another, and another and another, another, another, but so quiet, you had to listen to hear it.

But Joey never budged.

"Here, Ern," she says, holding it all back, looking at Him bluish through a long white road full of lonely water. "Do you reckon he's all right, do you? Don't say he ain't, Ern boy?"

He put His hand in and touched a leg, but there was no kick, and the feathers was cold. He picked Joey up, a cool yellow nothing, softer than skin, with a floppy head as hung down and swung about, pecking at the air, knocking against His finger, making Him feel a bit funny.

"Looks like it, Ma," He says.

She shoved both her fists in her cheeks and her face split in half, proper split in halfs, all her mouth showing while she screamed with her eyes screwed shut.

Scream, scream, scream, the shop was filling up of screams while He was looking stone cold at Joey, and then the floor shook about and the screams was out in the road, curving down, going away.

Joey had his thin feet stuck up in the air with the claws curled round, just like Chaser held up his hands when the rats was jumping at him.

Listening to Ma Sedgwiss yelling and snivelling down the road there, He suddenly got a lonely feeling His self, deep down somewhere, nagging at Him like the itch, only deeper. Although He knew the shop was empty, He could feel all the people as ever used the furniture all standing there, in the dark somewhere, looking at Him, even spitting at Him, some of them. Chaser bobbed up again, staring, and He felt the slack of His skin getting screwed up in cold little jerks when He thought what might happen if the Police ever got to know, and started asking a lot of awkward questions.

Ma Sedgwiss was still lolloping down the road, though, and

the sounds of her loud howling was making the people come out of the shops and turn round on the pavement to look at her.

His thumb somehow got under one of Joey's claws, and He seemed to hear a bright yellow voice somewhere, asking Him to be a sport and give her the extra shilling, and chance what Ma might say.

He found His self running down the road just like getting out of it in the morning when you do it without wanting to, sort of surprised at yourself. Something was telling Him as people could go in the shop and pinch what they liked, and something else was saying it never mattered. Only the old blanket coat with the dark green stripes all skewy round the bottom, howling away there mattered, nothing else.

"Ma," He says, "here you are, old girl. There's your three and a tanner, and there's Joey."

He held out His thumb and the canary dropped off of it, on top of the half crown and shilling lying in her hand.

"Don't say I never done nothing for you," He says, trying to make a joke out of it, so He could get a laugh out of her. But it was no go.

Her face was a picture, what with her hair hanging down, and mixing sweating and crying. She never seemed to get her mouth straight enough to say anything, and He see her gums was all puffed up round her front teeth, and there was little tadpoles of blood swimming about in her spit. She shoved Joey inside her blouse and held him down there, as if he was doing something as hurt her proper cruel.

But people was coming up and poking their snitches in, so He turned round and come out of it, feeling He done His self a world of good, in a rotten kind of way, somehow.

"What's up now?" Pa Prettyjohn shouts Him. "Pinched something, has she?"

"No," He says, "canary's kicked it."

"Oh dear," says Dad, and gives his self a scratch in a new place, "ain't too comic for the poor old mare, is it? No more pennyworths of birdseed, eh? Nobody to give her a bit of a tune of a morning."

There was nobody in the shop when He got back and everything was just how He left it, which done Him a bit more good.

The brass wire cage was shining in a patch of sun on the floor, a bit of Joey's white waistcoat was rolling about in the sand, and the little door was wide open. He could feel them claws round His thumb, tight as wires.

## CHAPTER XXVI

When Ma come home she was loaded down of parcels, and laughing all over the show.

"Go on, hop it," she says, "I'll tot the books up. You get off to the pictures."

"Okeedoke, Ma," He says.

Going upstairs, He thought it was dead funny the way Ma sort of changed herself about the last few days. He never see her laugh kind of all up in the air before. Her voice was more cheerful, and her eyes was different somehow, although it was hard to tell how, but they never seemed to look so dark at Him, under the hat.

In amongst the new oak furniture, He tried to make out what He was getting at, but it never come to very much except Ma was different, and that was all there was to it, seemed like.

The big round glass, as no flies had a chance to skate over, give Him a good light squint at His self for a change, and it come a right smack in the eye to see His self so plain. His suit was proper rolling round Him with wrinkles, and there was deep creases and bags at both elbows, making His sleeves pull up over the tops of His wrists. A couple of buttons was hanging down, looking proper fed up of their selfs.

He looked at His face again, seeing the pimples had cleared up a bit, but it was queer, never mind how hard He tried, He could no more get His self to keep His self looking His self in the eye than fly in the air. Somehow or other, His eyes would keep sliding off and looking at something else.

"There's chitlings for supper, so don't be too late home," Ma says, downstairs. "Stick this in your sky, and see how you like it."

"Ta, Ma," He says, sticking the ten bob note in His waistcoat. "You're a toff. Me nose'll bring me back, don't you fret."

He come out in the royal blue evening, with everything going a sort of marigold shine inside and all round Him, and them ten red finger nails was having a rare old game all on their own.

He was feeling that there pleased with His self, He reckoned He ought to go down and give Ada a shout for good luck, and see if she was still in her red jersey. He could feel that sickish, half smiling, dying feeling washing round Him again, and He liked to feel He was entitled to it, seeing He was like Len Tate, now, with His own business when Ma rolled up, and a pocket full of cash.

Down in the Fun Fair it was just like getting home again, lights up, flags out, band playing, everybody laughing away there, proper pleased to see you. The place was crowded out with the usual Thursday mob, and He could just about see her red jersey over the tops of their hats and between their heads, dodging up and down there, she was, through a lot of blue fog as made her sort of float. So just to pass the time away, He had a couple of goes on the crane again, but keeping an eye out for a player leaving her lot of machines.

He was going all out on His second tannersworth, when a bloke come up behind Him, looking over His shoulder, and He see in the glass where he was wearing one of them starched double collars with sharp points, a blue sort of silk tie, and one of them blue suits with a white stripe in it. So pretending He was playing it real scientific, He got over one side a bit, going very slow with the lever, and give this bloke a good look up and down, without too much being noticed.

Proper smashing he looked. He had one of them black smooth hats on, with the brim all curled up tight, tipped to the right on the back of his head, and his face was powder smooth, pink and pale blue where you could almost see the barber rubbing the cream in. What with the shine of his collar, the pearl in the silk of his tie and his brown shoes, fair laughing with polish they was, it proper made your mouth water wanting to be like him. He was a proper good looking bloke, but if you looked at him for a bit you never knew why, except he looked clean, pink, pale blue, and a smell of hair oil come off of him, a bit louder than Old Nick's, and better.

"Hard things to conniver, ain't they?" this bloke says, matey as you like, shoving his fag round the other side of his mouth without even moving his chin.

"Yes," He says, feeling, He never knew why, as if this bloke had give Him a dollar. "I reckon it's a catch, me self."

A couple of coloured sweets tapped into the cup, the engine whizzed inside, and the crane swung back again, all done.

"There you are," He says, "that's all I get for a tanner. Fadgersworth of sweets, and a lot of bleeding excitement."

"You got to be wider than that, mate," this bloke says, not even looking at Him. "Ever see these?"

A lot of little round bits of celluloid was in his hand, and he puts one in the coin slot, pulls the lever, and the crane swings into position.

"Now then," he says, like as if he was in a armchair, "just you watch this."

The engine whizzed and the crane swung over, pretending it was going to do miracles and pick up wonders. The bloke started turning the little wheel, and his fag shot a narrow grey rope clean up his snitch, and while He was watching the cloud blowing out, the bloke give Him the wink.

"There you are," he says. "Easy when you know how, ain't it?"

He see the crane had its lugs in a alarm clock, picking it up and holding it. Them lugs opened up just above the trap, the clock dropped down the hole, and slid out in the brass cup just like going to roost.

"It's a piece of meat," says the bloke, shoving it in his pocket. "Easy as eating your breakfast."

"Well, stone me blind," He says, "I ought to paid to see you do it."

"It's just a matter of knowing how," the bloke says, and he holds out a big handful of these celluloid tanners and pennies.

"Here you are," he says, "have a go with these. Won't cost you a sausage."

"Blimey," He says, rattling these things about in His hand, heavy as nothing. "Ta. I must have spent quids down here, one way and another. I'll get a bit of me own back, now."

"That's the idea, son," this bloke says, and still the ash on his fag never fell off, even though it had curled round almost as much as one of Joey's claws. "Couldn't do with a couple of quid as well, could you?"

He looked at the pink and pale blue of this bloke's face, wondering what was coming off.

The loud speaker started playing one of them tunes like loads of dark blue plush curtains curling all round you, with thousands of silver stars shining in it, and you could hear blokes whistling quietly to their selfs, as though they was proper pleased with the way things was turning out.

The heavy blue plush sound waved up and down, like Ada when she walked and the deep beats and curving notes of the tune somehow settled down lovely and quiet somewhere inside your head, making you feel as if you just wanted to lay down and think of something nice.

This bloke fingered two flat, clean, quid notes out of a case made out of a sort of squared red leather, with gold all round the edges.

"Between you and me, this is," says this bloke. "So long."

He stood there with the two quid slipping about between His thumb and finger, watching the black curly brim going away behind all the caps and bowlers, and grey velours till it went behind Madame la Zaka's.

Something was telling Him it was all wrong and never ought to have been, but something else inside of Him, not a voice, nothing He could put His finger on, was telling Him that two quid was two quid, and there was plenty of things He wanted as two quid would get Him.

Like a big orange flash in the eye, wallop on the back, He see one of Ada's tables was empty. So He stuck the two notes as far down His waistcoat pocket as He could get them, and got there just in time to flank somebody else, turning off what was going on inside of Him like screwing off a tap to stop it dripping.

"Hallo," she says, looking proper surprised. "What you doing here?"

"Just having a look round," He says, and He give her the ten bob note, feeling as though He just grew up all of a sudden. "Ain't I allowed to, then? Change us half a bar, will you?"

She Ada'd away to get the change and He see them two round shiny patches where she sat down, going from one side to the other, all soft and wavy, like, sort of beating time to the music. Her hair fell round her face when she bent to get the change, and all of a sudden He got a nose bleeding, sweating, dry mouth hate for the bloke playing her machines, because He knew he was looking straight down her blouse, and meant to. The hate was so big, He come over proper sickish and then He started getting cold, and His knees sort of rattled about in their holders, nigh coming loose and letting Him fall.

She come back throwing her head up, getting her hair out of her eyes as shone Him smiles and made Him feel all right again.

"Don't want you staying here too long," she says. "There's enough mugs about without you starting."

"I come in here to see you," He says. "That's worth a tanner or two, ain't it?"

"Give them to me, then, not the machines," she says. "Just come in and put them in my hand. I can do with them."

"That's on," He says. "How long have I got for looking at you?"

"Go on, cunning," she says, laughing away there. "You're giving yourself away, you are."

"How?" He says, wondering what He done.

"You look at yourself," she says. "Don't have to ask."

"Well," He says, feeling the red powder blowing up hot all over His face. "I only come in to see if we was all right for Saturday."

"Course we are," she says, proper nice, bending her head forward and giving Him all the soft part of her voice. "Ten o'clock, Saturday, outside, with the gardenias."

"The what?" He says.

"Gardenias," she says. "My favourites, they are. Send me off, they do."

"Okeedoke," He says, "gardenias. That's on."

"Don't waste your money," she says quick, as if she was sorry she spoke. "I don't want none. Straight up, I was only joking. You save your money."

Blokes was tapping the glass all over the shop, like hail on a greenhouse, it sounded like, but she was still looking at Him.

"You'll get your gardenias," He says. "How do we get to this place?"

"Bus," she says, "fourpenny ride from here."

"How about running down the studio in the afternoon?" He asked her.

"Can't," she says. "I'm on all day."

"Okeedoke," He says. "See you ten o'clock, then?"

"That's right," she says, and looks away at the machines, proper sorry. "Listen, I got to go now, before these bleeders break all the glass in the place. So long. Don't forget my gardenias, mind?"

"Okeedoke," He says. "Take care yourself."

It was all very well saying gardenias, but getting them was a different story. He went through the motor boats, hearing them all bash into one another, seeing the big blue sparks come off like splashes off a wheel, and brides sitting back laughing their heads off, but they was all sort of smudges in front of His eyes, not real things or people. The only time He ever see gardenias was when some bloke on the films give a bunch of them to some tart or other, and it looked so nice the way he done it, He always wanted to do the same. But now He had the chance, it come a bit hard. The only bloke He could think of was Charlie Pool down the market, him in the grey bowler, and the big white moustache, and a fourpenny flamer with a red and gold band on it, as slid down while he smoked, till it got down to the last half inch, and then got itself smoked in the bargain.

Dad was just beginning to lash the stall up when He got there, and his grey bowler was on the canvas roof where he always put it when he was afraid of getting it knocked about or trod on.

"What cheer, Ernie boy," he says, taking a lump of string out of his mouth. "How's Ma?"

"She's all right," He says. "Something I wanted to ask you, Dad. How do I go about getting my self a couple of gardenias?"

Dad stopped bagging the sprouts and clashed the brass pan back on the scales.

"Gardenias?" he says, as if he been asked to have a bottle of beer. "Easy. Any time you like."

"Saturday morning?" He says.

"Bring them back with me," Dad says. "Here be eight o'clock. Cost you a few wheels, though. Might get them for half a dollar? Perhaps more? Depends on the market. Who are you taking out?"

"Nobody in particular," He says. "Just the same, I'd like it kept between me and you."

"Bloody sure they wasn't for your Ma," says Dad. "Waste of time and money, gardenias. Couple of lovely bunches of grapes, same price. Never seen no sense in flowers. Never done nothing with them. Something to handle, something to taste, something to swallow, that's me."

"Some people like them," He says.

"Well it ain't me, thank Christ," says Dad. "Come round Saturday, midday."

"Okeedoke, Dad," He says. "You're a sport."

Walking through the market, watching everybody pack up their stalls, He got the idea He was a cut above most of them, because He had a shop and a good business to look forward to. Stalls and barrows was all right, and so was standing in six inches of paper, straw, and squashy fruit, when you wanted something on the cheap, but when it come to doing a bit of decent shopping, you had to go to a shop.

He never thought of it like that before, and all of a sudden He see why Len Tate and the rest of them had always sort of looked down on Him.

A artist was nowhere near as good as a stallkeeper, nor never earned as much money, and a stallkeeper never took near as much money as a shop, so there was no wonder why Len and the rest of them treated Him different since He stopped being a artist.

It was a bit too late to go in the pictures, if He was going to be home early, and there was nowhere else to go except the cafe, so He strolled down there thinking it all out and getting the new idea fixed up inside His mind.

The usual crowd was standing round the pin tables, and Len give Him a shout soon as He come in the door.

"This is on me, Ted," he yells. "Cup of coffee and a double nelson, a gent, forward."

"Coming up," yells Ted, and starts pulling the urn handles about and getting a bit of steam up.

"How does it feel to be a business man, Ern?" Len says, pulling up and making a bit of room. "Get your books right, did you?"

"Okeedoke, boy," He says. "I took a bit of dough too."

"I should say you would," says Len. "One of the best little gold mines in the district you got there. Even Ma says so. You do it right and you'll be branching out before long, you will."

"That's right," He says, as if he had all the arrangements in hand. But He got the idea, and though He was watching the ball knocking up the pink and white lights, He could see all the other blokes looking at Him very quiet, and He knew they was all taking their hats off.

He got that feeling again, only more of it, of being a cut above them, same as He had about the stallholders, and He knew why it was that all the blokes sort of looked up to Len.

They was in jobs but he had his own business.

Now, they was looking up to Him.

What with a couple of quid in His pocket, and this new feeling of being Somebody, instead of just being a artist to be kicked about, and swore at, and sacked whenever anybody felt like it, He started feeling proper kind to people. And it hit Him like a ton of bricks as Len felt exactly the same way.

The both of them knew they had a good home to go to, bags of grub, plenty to spend, and a solid business behind them, safe as houses for years and years.

It was easy for the pair of them to feel kind to people, and have a laugh here and there whenever they felt like it. They could afford it.

# CHAPTER XXVII

"Ern," Ma says, while He was still reading the paper after supper, "I make you four and eightpence out on your cash. Have a nine course dinner, did you?"

"No," He says, "I went down Ma Tate's for one and two-pence, and Ma Sedgwiss had three and a tanner."

"Where's Joey, then?" she says. "Ain't put him in the coal hole, have you?"

"Well, it was a bit off, like, see, Ma?" He says. "She come in here and started her larks, saying you always give her three and a tanner, see?"

"She's a liar," says Ma, looking at the ceiling.

"So I told her," He says, feeling on the right side at last. "I made the bid half a crown or nixey, see? So she started howl-ing, and carrying on there something chronic. Then it turns out that Joey's rolled up, see?"

"How do you mean rolled up?" says Ma. "Been healthy enough these past few years, he has?"

"Well, he's kicked it this time, anyhow," He says, "and soon as she see it, she sort of went barmy and rushed off down the road, screaming the place down, see?"

"Oh, I say," Ma says, sitting up and looking proper grave-yard, working overtime with the match. "Poor little cow. Where's the three and a tanner come in, then?"

"I tore out and give it her to stop her howling," He says.

Ma stopped digging about her back teeth and starts laugh-ing.

"I could have told you that before you started," she says. "That's your father all over. Tell him a hard luck story and you could have the shirt off of his back."

"Ah, that was because he was a artist," He says. "I ain't. Not now I ain't, anyhow."

"We'll see how long it lasts," she says, and she sounded none too pleased.

"Here, Ma," He says, trying to work up a bit of interest, "did you ever see Dad's painting in that there gallery, wherever it was?"

"What painting?" she says. "There was millions of them."

"This one's in that gallery up the road somewhere," He says. "Old Nick was telling me all about it. It's the real stuff, be all accounts. Something about a girl, ain't it?"

"Millions of them, too," she says. "Don't know nothing about it, and don't want to. Never liked it from the start."

"What sort of a bloke was he, Ma?" He says. "I never ever see a picture of him."

"Look at yourself in the glass," she says. "That's your father."

"Where did you find him, Ma?" He says.

"Never you mind where I found him," she says. "Getting bloody nosey all of a sudden, ain't you? Was that the knocker?"

She said it so quick, and she looked so queer about it, He started going cold all the way down, and He could feel a big hand freezing His face.

"I didn't hear nothing, Ma," He says, just about getting it out of Him.

But there was the knocker, going again, doing a double post mans.

"That don't sound too healthy," she says, and pulled herself up, shoving the chair away. "I'll go."

While she was gone He see Chaser come up with his hand in hooks over his head, all going curled up and stiff, dripping with thinning mud, shining a bright pale blue light.

Ma come in so quiet He never heard her, and her feather was a proper surprise. Behind her He see a couple of coppers, one with a flat hat and a black loop on his belt, and another one with three or four white stripes on his arm.

"This is about Ma Sedgwiss," Ma says, as if she was doing somebody a price.

He was so sure they was going to talk about Chaser, He forgot all about who Ma Sedgwiss was.

The bloke with the flat hat sat down and opened out a notebook.

"All friends here," he says, "I just want to know what happened when she come in the shop, that's all."

He was surprised to find His self pouring out word for word without thinking, or anything, and all the time He was talking this bloke was writing. When He come to the part where He was coming back to the shop, the copper puts his pencil away and shuts the book.

"Right," he says. "That's the four sides of the picture. No need to bother you any more, Mother."

"What about a little drop of something before you go?" says Ma.

"Not for me, thanks," this bloke says. "We've got to go round and take charge of the body. Sorry to give you all this trouble. Wouldn't mind dropping in some other time, though?"

"Any time you like," says Ma, following the pair of them out in the passage. "This is open house, you know that. Harry Freeman's, that's us."

Rushing, blinding, ripping round and coming back again, pictures of Chaser coming out of them shiny white rags in the sewer, and the little orange slits of the rats jumping over their selfs all round him, smudging up in shining brass wire bars, with a open cage door and Ma Sedgwiss screaming, shoving her fists in her cheeks and screwing the sides of her mouth together.

The place shook about and the table jingled while Ma was coming back, but instead of sitting down, she went to the fireplace.

"What she want to go and do that for?" she says, right on the floor, from the sound of her.

"Do what?" He says, knowing all right, but wanting to be told to get His face right.

"Poor bitch's been and give herself a gas supper," Ma says. "Won't want much breakfast, will she?"

It come a bit hard to think of that old blanket coat, with the green stripes cut on the skew, not carting all that fat about no more. It come strange to think the voice He could still hear screaming had gone off on its own, somewhere, in two penny-worth of that funny sort of tight smell of gas.

"I don't blame her one way and another," Ma says, still looking in the fire. "I've been just about going to do the same thing many a time. I would have done it too, I give you my word, if it hadn't been for you."

"Hope you wasn't worried too much about me, Ma," He says, giving her the wink.

"Not too much," she says. "Just about enough, though. I couldn't abear thinking what was going to happen to you if I wasn't there to see you all right, see? No more worries. No more wondering where the next halfpenny was coming from. No more arguing with the bloody rent collector. No more bailiffs smoking their bleeding pipes in the kitchen. Just a nice long sleep, that's all. I tell you, it sounded all right, once upon a time, like."

"What made you change your mind, Ma?" He says, a bit surprised at the springs bouncing up and down in her voice.

"You," she says.

"Why?" He says.

"Too many dimples in your fists, I suppose," she says, giving the fire a couple of digs as nigh on shoved the bricks in the alley. "You slept too quiet, and all. I hope you're going to be worth it, that's all. Goodnight, son."

"Night, Ma gel," He says, feeling a bit shamefaced, though He never knew what for. The table jingled again when she went out, but everything got a shake on while she was going upstairs.

Sitting there, listening to the gas trying to whistle tunes through the mantle, He started thinking of Henry, and Chaser, and Old Nick, and all the lads on the Firm, but it never seemed to come to nothing, except He was lonesome, just sitting there in the greenish up and down of the gas, thinking about things. Not one of them blokes was ever going to come nowhere nigh

Him, and if they ever give Him a word, it would only be because they thought He was a bloody young fool. Not one of them would ever stick up for Him as a friend, and now He come to think of it, He was a bit surprised to find there was nobody He could call a proper friend, to go out with and talk to, nor even nobody to give Him a leg up sometimes, never mind about a kind word.

He began to feel things getting Him down again and the kitchen started getting too hot to stay in, what with the walls getting closer and the ceiling coming lower. He started feeling like He done down the sewer, all gone at the knees and gasping for a breath of fresh air.

Out in the backyard, the moon was shining white along the clothes lines, giving Him a feeling like one of them songs down the Fun Fair. He was a bit sorry He never went in for music, because He often felt He wanted to have a band, and stand in front of it, flapping His hands and beating the time, in one of them dancing suits with silk fronts and a white waistcoat cut square all the way round, like a skin tight sweater.

He went through a hole in the fence, up the alley way and got in the road, in two minds whether to go down the cafe again or just have a walk round, but thinking about the cafe and the blokes somehow seemed to put Him off.

Walking down to the corner looking at the pavement, He knew where He was going because the smell of shaving soap come out of Pa Floom's, and carbolic soap started fighting paraffin yards and yards away from Dad Prettyjohn's. The church bells started clonking out the quarters to twelve o'clock, some now, some then, just arguing it out between their selfs, sounding as if they was proper sorry they had to do it. The last tram moaned by the top of the road, splashing its lights all over the show.

He leaned up against the black of the lamp post, with the pale blue ring drawn round Him, listening to the tram grousing its way on again, and the quick flat clap of blokes feet, just got off it, going the short way home.

He knew it was Aggie Hunner as come round the corner,

because of that big sort of fiddle in the thick green bag what she carted about on her shoulder. He see the white of her face turning towards Him, and seeing Him standing there, she pulled up a little bit, as if she expected He was out to do a bit of bag snatching.

"Okeedoke, Aggie," He says, "it's only me."

"Oh," she says, "you put the wind up me. What you doing out at this time of night?"

"Bit of fresh air," He says. "Carry your bag for you?"

"Shan't say no," she says. "But don't drop it, whatever you do."

He lifted it off her as though it was going to weigh three ton, but it was like lifting a heavy feather.

"I don't often meet a cavalier on a dark night," she says. "I've just finished playing at a club dinner, and you know what they're like."

"No," He says. "What?"

"Oh, just a lot of men smoking their annual cigars, and getting tight, and showing off." She put her hand through the letter box of the pea green door and pulled the key out on a bit of string. "I get sick of it," she says, opening up.

"What you do it for, then?" He says, putting this big fiddle down in the pitch dark of the passage.

"Half a mo," she says. "I'll get a light on."

When a match fizzed white and the candles started poking their tongues out, old Henry started banging his brolly, and Chaser come up again, but when they was all alight, and it looked like dozens of them, it come a bit more homey.

The place was done in yellow sort of whitewash with the same pea green doors and furniture, a flat sort of sofa with a back and sides, with some purple cushions on it, and a couple of arm chairs.

"It's not much," says Aggie, wagging the smoking match about nigh twice as hard as she needed to. "But it's home and there's nothing like it. Like some coffee?"

"Ta," He says.

"It'll keep you awake, then you won't be able to get up," she says, watching Him with her head down.

"I don't go to work no more," He says, while she was opening up the cupboard, "I'm helping to run the shop."

Aggie looked round at Him quick, as though she was a bit sorry for Him, or something.

"Why?" she says. "Ma ill, is she?"

"No," He says. "I got the sack. Last card in the pack."

"Oh, dear, dear, dear," she says. "What they want to go and do that for?"

"That's easy enough," He says. "I was just coming out of me time, see? They'd have had to paid me a man's wages, see? So they give me the boot, quick."

"Oh I say, what a shame," she says, meaning it, and all. "Haven't got another job in view, have you?"

"No," He says, "and I ain't going to try, neither."

"What are you going to do, then?" she says.

"Help with the shop till the right sort of job comes along," He says. "I'm going to be a solicitor."

"I reckon you ought to think this out very carefully, if you ask me?" she says. "Get the cups out, while I put the pot on, will you?"

While He was pulling these pink, thin cups off the hooks, she was taking one of them long tin coffee pots out of the oven, and putting it on the hob.

"Won't take long," she says. "Think you'll like being a solicitor?"

"It'll be a change," He says.

"You may not know it," she says, sort of far away, "but ever since you were a nipper, I've had an eye out for you. Your father was a great artist. You know that, I suppose? I thought you were going to be one, too."

"I found it ain't much cop," He says. "You get shoved round a bit too much to suit me. People think you're a slop, and they treat you like one. So I'm going to be a solicitor and get a bit of me own back."

"It's a nasty breed," she says, "courts on one side of you, prisons on the other, judges in front, and bailiffs behind. Earning your living in a lot of misery. I know. I've had some."

"Well," He says, "it's a living."

"What does your mother think about it?" she says, bringing up the milk and sugar.

"She likes the idea," He says. "She says it's respectable."

"I should have thought she'd have been the first to cry her eyes out," she says, and she pointed to the cups. "What about the saucers?"

While He was getting them, so thin He could feel the warmth of His finger meeting His thumb through them, she started nattering away, fifteen to the dozen, about artists, what they did, and how they brightened your life, but it got sort of hard to understand, like the politics blokes first thing of a morning. So He just let her natter away, and nodded now and again, looking in the fire. He kept on seeing blokes in the coals, Old Nick, and Bert Clively, and the bloke as give Him the couple of quid. They all got jumbled up together bobbing their heads out at Him saying a few words and kind of going away.

"The one thing I've always wanted to do was go and see your father's pictures," He heard her say. "But I've never seemed to have the time."

"What do you want to see it for?" He says.

She come up proper surprised.

"Why," she says, "I reckon every artist ought to go and see what the others are doing. Specially your own local man. We've got to help each other in this world. There's precious few'll help us, you know? If us artists don't stick together there's nobody else to do it for us."

"You ain't a artist, are you?" He asked her.

She put her cup down and started laughing.

"What do you think I am then?" she says. "It's my living, isn't it? I had twelve years practice before I was any good, and even now I can't play like I want to."

The minute she said it, and the way she was looking He was dead certain He knew her feelings, and a queer sort of idea about her come over Him. Like He thought about Ada, it was, only different.

"I get it just the same, with a bit of chalk and paper," He says. "I know what I want to do, see? But I can't seem to get it out of me self, somehow. Queer ain't it? I mean, it don't sound like sense, do it?"

"Ah, well," she says, sort of playing it big and using both hands. "I mean, it's practice, isn't it? Practice and patience, that's all you want. Every time I pick up my bow, I've got nearly twenty years practice and professional playing behind me, and it's bound to come out in my music, isn't it?"

"I've never heard you play, Aggie," He says. "How about it, some time?"

"Of course," she says. "Come up to the hotel one night, and have some dinner. That reminds me, I've got to get my collars washed for tomorrow. When do you start this solicitor's job?"

"Sometime the next fortnight," He says, and got up, seeing her a bit itchy. "Well, I'd better make a move, before I get my collar washed."

"Come over again," she says, kind as anything, "soon as you like. And you give that solicitor's job a good going over before you do anything about it. It's nothing to do with me, mind, but if you're an artist, you're an artist, and I don't see any sense in being something else, and making things hard for the rest of your life."

"Okeedoke, Aggie," He says, "I'll think it over."

"That's right," she says, going through the passage. "Mind, it's dark out here."

Going through the dark with His hands out, He bumped into her with His finger ends and felt them sink in.

"Sorry," He says, but He kept them there, looking in the dark where He could hear her breathing, feeling the inch raise and drop in time with it.

Her hands came on to His elbows like a couple of kittens jumping up, and the more she pulled, the deeper His fingers went in till His hands was resting flat on her soft, hottish, sort of silky, slippery pair, and He could feel bands of stuff across the tops of them. His elbows was stopping Him going any closer, so He shifted His hands under the curves, round her waist, and she pulled Him close in, proper grinding herself up against Him, making Him wonder all of a sudden, what was coming off. But she was so strong, and getting a bit choky and breathy, He got a bit of a shake on in case He done something. If she fell down in a fit, or fainted, or some other bright thing, and He got found there, He might have to answer some nasty questions.

"Half a mo," He says. "Ma'll be waiting up for me."

She let go, quick as that.

"Didn't frighten you, did I?" she says, as if she frightened her self. "Just wanted to say goodnight nicely, that all."

"Okeedoke," He says, opening the door. "See you later, Aggie."

"Come over soon," she says, in the pitch black. "Goodnight, Ernie."

"So long," He says, and closed the gate.

He went across the road on tip toe, climbing up the long, skinny back of His shadow, wondering if any nosey parker see Him coming out of the pea green door.

When He got back again in the warm of the kitchen and looked in the glass, He see He had that sticky red stuff all over His mouth again, and He shook hands with His self as Ma was in bed.

Up in the bedroom, it was colder than ever in the new oak furniture, and the candle was in a new white enamel holder, to keep the grease off of the wood.

He give at the knees when He see three suits laid out on the bed.

There was a black coat and waistcoat, and striped trousers, a nigger brown with a link button, and a blue serge. He never undressed so quick in His life so as to try them all on, one after another, and though the light was a bit orangey, He see where Ma made no mistakes. They was proper smashing, the lot of them, and fit Him as if He had been poured.

There was half a dozen shirts, a couple of fancy ties, and some socks. Down by the bed, there was a pair of brown shoes, and a pair of black, all tissued up, and not a crack in them.

He never wished so much for morning. What with shaking with excitement, and shivering with cold, He hardly knew how to get into bed.

He got such a proper nice feeling for Ma, He was in two minds whether or not to go next door and say so. He only thought better of it, because the last thing He wanted to go and do, was to go and do it all wrong, and rub her up the wrong way by waking her up. So He give over and spit the candle out, looking up in the dark, just shoving the hours out of His way.

## CHAPTER XXVIII

SATURDAY CAME UP fine, and Ma was in a real nice way with her self, singing all over the place, and out on the pavement while she was washing down, giving everybody a shout and a wave, and generally handing her self a good fat lump of the morning.

He was proper surprised the way she was taking things. She was even changed in the way she dressed. Where she always wore the old black blouse and apron, now she come out in a coloured dress with lots of flowers on it, and different sorts of aprons, and two new hats, like the old ones only not black, with white feathers. She looked a treat, and what was more, she knew it.

The morning was a real winner, what with everybody paying in, and the books getting crossed off, and everybody the better off for it. Just before dinner, Reg Taylor, down the gasworks, brought his bride in to have a look at some samples, and pick their stuff out.

"This is the one I'd have, if it was me," Ma says, pointing to a fourposter with brass railings. "Always get your money on this if you wanted to get rid of it, that is. Lovely springs, and all."

"But look at the price," his bride says, with her voice pegged up on the kitchen line. "I'd be afraid to get in it."

"You'd what?" Reg says. "Not if I was behind you, you wouldn't. I'd take a running jump, I would."

"Go on, sauce," she says. "You wouldn't get the chance. You won't half catch a cold if you try any of them larks on me, let me tell you."

"Hark at her," Reg says, looking at Ma real surprised, but you knew he was only playing his cards. "Larks, eh? You've never had a lark yet, me fine ripe old strawberreehee. I reckon we ought to have it, me self. We couldn't half have a game in that. Half way line, penalty area and all. And change over half time, eh Ma?"

"That's right," Ma says, having a laugh too. "Want anybody to rub you down, give us a shout."

"No fear," Reg says, as if he just had a dollar took off him. "I'll do all the rubbing down in this family, ta. That's what I'm getting married for. Ain't it, gel?"

"I don't know," says the bride, flat as a dinner plate, her face was, but she was half way blushing and trying heavens hard not to show it. "And would you mind getting on with the business? We come here to do some choosing, didn't we? Keep Mum's dinner waiting, and you won't half get told your fortune, me lad, you will."

"Oh, Christ," says Reg. "Quick. Here. What else we want? This bed'll do, Ma."

"We want tons of other stuff, and all, don't we?" says the bride, getting a right old scratch on. "What about a washing stand, and things?"

"The bed's the most important," Reg says. "I'm happy. We can't kip in a bleeding washing stand, can we? Use a bit of common."

"I'll get you a set of stuff put together, dearie," Ma says to the bride, shoving her arm round her. "You'll be all right. Got all your kitchen stuff, have you?"

"No," the bride says, talking to Ma as if Reg just flew off of the earth. "That's what's worrying me. Mum's giving us a bit here and there, but we'll have to buy most of it."

"You'll have to start a book," Ma says. "Pay in so much a week so it don't come hard on your pocket, see? And get everything you want, all the same time. Leave it to me, dear."

"Ta, Ma," Reg says. "Call in Monday night, eh?"

"I'll have the list ready for you," Ma says.

"Don't forget the oil can for the springs," Reg says, and gives the bride a smack across the bot. "Don't want to keep the neighbours awake, do we, gel?"

"I wish you'd give over," she says, proper wild, and bending her self over backwards to try and miss him. "Soppy looking thing, you."

"Oh, getting personal, eh?" says Reg, and starts chasing her. "I'll learn you, you little bit of cord, you. So long, Ma. I'll train her. Git up, there."

Ma watched the pair of them arguing down the road, laughing all over.

"Make a lovely match, they will," she says, pinning her hat again. "Nice, sensible head on her, that girl has. And he's a proper case, ain't he? But he's steady, for all that. Have a happy life, she will."

Over dinner she never said much, nor did He, because He was thinking about the studio, and what He was going to do when He got in front of the canvas. She had her usual couple of forkfuls and started picking her teeth.

"You ought to think about getting married yourself, son," she says. "Coming on twenty, soon, you know? You'll be all right for money, and I'll see you fixed up for your home. I'd like to see a nipper or two fore I get took off."

"Eh?" He says, when He could get His breath. "Me, marry? What for?"

"You ought to," she says. "Sooner the better, I say. Then you'll have somebody nice to look after you when I ain't there. Shan't be here always, you know?"

"Go out," He says. "They'll have to shoot you. Who am I going to marry? Who'd have me?"

"I don't know," Ma says, coming out in a laugh. "You ain't bad looking. You'll have a business of your own, and your solicitor's job. You'll be a nice catch for the right girl. You have a look round."

"Okeedoke," He says, having a look all round it.

Something inside of Him started liking the idea, specially if she was a right bit of stuff. Them red beetles started chasing about again, and He could just see Ada walking through the kitchen, side to side, pushing her hair out of her eyes, giving Him one of them looks. She got in the oak bed upstairs like a hot water bottle, pushing up a lovely swelling in the blankets where her bot stuck up, looking at Him, all bare and ready, with them red beetles clawed up and itching to scratch Him to pieces.

"Do it," Ma says, pulling herself up. "Don't just think about it."

"Okeedoke, Ma," He says, "I'll see what I can do. I go off now can I?"

"Course," she says. "Find your money upstairs, on the dressing table. And just use the ash tray a bit more, will you? You nigh on burnt a hole in the chair, you did."

"Okeedoke, Ma," He says. "Sorry."

"Did you know young Percy Floom's getting married the end of the week?" Ma says, as if it never mattered. "He's a good year younger than what you are, and all."

"Good luck to him," He says.

It took Him a good twenty minutes to make up His mind which suit to put on, what with hanging them up and taking them down, and putting them on, and hanging them up again. Then He had to find out which shirt went best, and by the time He tied His tie, and untied it to tie it up higher, and then a bit lower, and looked at His self to see the difference, and put both pairs of shoes on to see what looked right, He was in a good hot sweat, and wishing He was back in His old clothes again without the worry of it.

But though everything was a bit tight under the arms, and smelt new, that funny sort of new smell you get out of shirts straight off the shop shelves, by the time He got a fag going, He felt like a millionaire, and He had to admit as He looked the part, and all.

"You're worth the money, you are, son," Ma says, and He could see she was jumping over herself. "You pay for the dressing, straight up. You look a real treat, you do."

"Do I, Ma?" He says, coming up a fine large red. He never heard Ma talk or look like it before. She come over proper sort of young, not like herself at all as He always knew her.

"What's up with you lately, Ma?" He says, coming it a bit.

She was holding her blouse together with both hands, looking at Him as if she wanted to eat Him.

"What you mean, what's up?" she says, a bit surprised, but laughing.

"Well," He says, thinking fast, "you're sort of changed, or something, ain't you?"

"So have you," she says, starting a proper big laugh, but not like she used to, sort of shouting the place down and making you frightened to look at her, but proper laughing, so you could have a laugh as well, even though you never knew what you was laughing at. "It's like I told you. You change, so will I. You stop your capers, so will I. A bargain's a bargain, ain't it?"

"Okeedoke, Ma," He says. "I catch on."

"That's it," she says, proper giving it big licks, screaming the place down as if it was the biggest joke out, till her face come nigh the colour of Ma Tate's. Then she give herself a wipe over, and tried to get her breath.

"Go on," she says. "Hop it. Be the death of me, you will."

She sort of give Him a shove to get Him out of it, not hard, nor hard meaning, but a sort of shove like you give the cat to get it out of the chair. But no sooner she see Him rock off his balance, she done no more, she grabbed Him. She had Him like being in a big crowd, where you try to move and you feel warm people all round you, pressing against you, squashing you, till you wonder where the next breath is going to come from, and wishing you stayed out of it.

"Ernie, boy," she says, with her hat shoved over, the way she was gripping Him. He could feel all her front sort of soft, like heavy half blowed tires, and how hard her corsets was. "Been wanting to make a fuss of you a long time. Love your old Ma, do you?"

"Course I do," He says, not knowing where to put His face.

"Give us a nice big kiss, then," she says, and she turns her face to Him. So He give her a smacking big kiss, just on the fat part under the eye, and she turns round again and give Him one, a real beauty, taking a lot of time over it, and squashing Him till He had to set His self to get some air down Him.

"Now we're all quits," she says, pleased as punch. "Now clear off, and don't come mucking about round here no more today. Go off and have a good time, go on."

"Okeedoke, Ma, gel," He says. "But what about the doings? There wasn't none upstairs."

"Go and have another look," she says, like as if she just had plenty to eat. "Have a good look, this time."

So He shot upstairs and started tearing things about, and under the shoepaper He found a little square parcel done up in tissue and tied with a bit of satin tape. There was a silver cigarette case inside of it, with twenty fags in two broad white rows, and three quid notes, crossed flat on top of them. To my darling Ernie boy from his loving Ma was wrote on the card, in red ink, so He knew Ma done it while she was totting up the books last night.

The case was long, and thin, with square corners, and sort of frilled about all over it, with E.V.M. in a ring in the middle.

He reckoned, sort of standing there hot, there was something He ought to do for Ma, and He tried to think what He could get her, but He kept on thinking more what the lads would say when He flashed it in front of them.

He never felt so rich in His life.

Here He was, three brand new suits and everything to match, silver fag case, nigh on five pounds spending money, and two places to go to.

The way things was coming round His way was a marvel. He could hardly believe it was Him, looking at it all round. He could even feel the very air sort of giving Him a laugh and a smack on the back, and He wanted to get out in the road and whistle all sort of wobbly, like you do when you feel proper pleased with your self.

Downstairs Ma was talking to Ma Fitch and a couple of others about Ma Sedgwiss, so He put His head in the door and give Ma the wink.

"All right, son?" she says, and her feathers give Him a real old fluff round for luck.

"Proper smashing this is, Ma," He says, holding up the case. "Shan't forget you. So long."

"Have a good time, son," she says, as though nothing happened, but He could see by her face as He done it right for once.

He was a bit disappointed He never see nobody as knew Him while He was on His way up to get the gardenias. When He went in Ma Crann's for a box of matches He never wanted there was only Ma Crann, still looking palish and darkish green in the up and down of the gas. So it was no cop, because even if He had a suit of diamonds on, she never see nothing a yard away from her, not even with her glasses on.

He tore down the road to the market, going through the rotten smell of greengrocery with sharp sweet whiffs of apple breaking through, dodging round old girls shouting for their kids, same time trying to get two handles of a nigh on bursting shopping bag with a pink and yellow head of rhubarb hanging out one end, in one fist without busting the lot, and got to old Charlie Pool's just when he was trying to get rid of a pineapple.

It was a funny thing about old Charlie, but he was too posh in his ways to be like any other greengrocer. Best class and top price was what Charlie always said he stood for. He only made a living because he sold from a stall and never had to pay nothing high in the way of rates and taxes, getting rid of the stuff to the people what still wanted it the best, never mind if they could afford it or not.

"God give us pineapples, but Christ alone knows who shoved tins round 'em," he screeches. "Fruit, that's what this is. The sweets of nature. The riches of the orient brought right to your front door. No trouble to you. You ain't got to worry about picking 'em, packing 'em, or putting 'em on the stall, here. All you got to do is eat 'em. Anything hard about that?"

The old girl wagged her head, not knowing how to take him, but saying yes for the sake of it.

"Course not," Charlie says. "Put it on your Sunday's table, cut the lovely, juicy rounds off, and lick your chops. Lovelyhee. Nature in the raw. Sweet as a woman. Charge you two bob for this one, and think your selfs bloody lucky I take the bother with you. Who wants it, another lovely little pine?"

He shoved it under some old bird's snitch in the front row.

"Here," he says, "smell it. Do your self a favour. Living like a bloody lot of white ants, that's what's the matter with some of you. You don't know what's going on, half your time."

"Get my gardenias, Pa?" He says, calling round the side.

"Four and a tanner," Charlie says, quick as light, throwing Him a box.

"Okeedoke," He says, paying up. "Save us a pine, and some of them peaches for Ma, will you? Call round Sunday for 'em."

"A pine, and half a dozen glass grown peaches, pride of the Kentish gardens, a gent," hollers Charlie. "Looking after His old Ma while she's still here to be looked after. A dutiful son. Wish I had half a dozen like Him. I'd be on me arse inside a week."

He come away hearing Charlie starting on the grapes, and shoved His self through the crowd, watching the blokes about His age helping in the stalls, and getting that bossy sort of feeling about them, proper glad and shaking hands with His self because He had a decent shop to lean back on, instead of mucking about with a barrow and a lot of canvas.

Upstairs on the rolling tram He felt proper cock of the walk, high up and far from everybody, handing His fare over, feeling almost sorry for the conductor, with that shiny sort of corn on his left thumb, where he nicked the tickets as rang that little bell.

He was afraid to cross His legs in case He shoved a bag in the knees first time out, so when He got off, they was like a couple of knife blades. He done up the coat on the inside button, rolling the flap back very careful, sticking his hand in the pocket, breezing His way along the pavement in and out of people, rattling His dough about, and puffing away there, for all the world like a millionaire.

It took Him real funny, how a week changes things about a bit. He could see His self coming round this same corner, the week before, feeling like a spewing cat just because He was out of work. It hit Him a right bash what old Henry said about how lucky you was when you was out of work, and He could almost hear the umbrella knocking it out on the pavement.

He give the knocker a good old doing, and Rivers whipped the door open in two ticks, looking as if she expected a dozen telegrams, all bad news, and half the family clubbing round for the black.

Soon as she see Him, she come over proper shirty.

"What's your lark?" she says.

"Making sure you could hear me," He says, and walks past her, inside the passage.

"More sauce than a bottling factory, you have," she says, coming up behind Him.

"That's right," He says, "noted for it."

In the studio, it was that there quiet and sunny white, it was just like coming inside of a little church. A new canvas square was on the easel, and the big palette had all the colours squirted out on it, right round the edge, proper pretty.

As soon as He see Rivers was going to start talking, He started taking off His coat.

"All right, all right," He says, "I know all about it. I knows exactly what I got to do, and what I ain't, and what I can do, and what I can't, see? Now what have you got to say?"

"Nothing," Rivers says, "only if you want tea or coffee, make it yourself in the kitchen. There's some sandwiches cut for you. There's some fags in the box over there. There's a drink in the cupboard, and make sure you shut the front door when you go."

"Okeedoke," He says. "Now we know where we are."

"I reckon you've got a bloody fine old sauce, me self," she says. "And if I didn't like the job, I'd tell you a bit more, and all. I reckon the old girl's off her onion, if you ask me."

"What's it got to do with you?" He says. "Mind your own business, and go and make me a cup of tea."

She looked so ready to sling something, He got ready to duck, but she turned round and went out like a lamb, giving the door a push to that nigh bounced every bit of glass in the place out of the frames.

He was left in the middle of the white, warm sun, looking at this rough square, and all the pretty colours frilled round the palette. Digging back in His mind, pulling out everything He ever see the lads do in the way of fish, trying to remember the colours of them rainbow trout, the same shape as kippers, with long hairy fins and things on them, He started off to draw one in, then He got busy with the paints.

This oil painting lark turned out to be a bit harder than what He thought it was, and before long He was sweating harder than a navvy. The colours went on all right, but they took a lot of brushing in, and He was soon wishing He took a bit more notice of Old Nick. The brushes took a bit of cleaning, and all, and there was nothing handy to wash them in, except the pot on the floor, and that was full up of brushes. So by the time He used all the clean ones, and most of them in the pot, He was up the wall for a brush, and starting to get smarmed from head to foot in paint.

Rivers came in with the tea tray, and put it down on the little table.

"You going to pour out?" she says.

"No fear," He says. "That's your job."

She give the painting one look and started dropping sugar in the cup.

"What's up with it?" he says.

"Nothing," she says, without looking up. "You're just about as good as what she is, that's all. And I don't go too much on either of you, me self."

"What's up with it?" He says.

"Don't suit my book," she says. "I like something to look at. Old Fanny paints with a knife and fork."

"What you mean, paints with a knife?" He says.

She pointed to the little flat trowels on the table.

"There you are," she says. "She dabs a bit of paint on with that, and then streaks the rest of it over the cloth. You have a look."

She got hold of two or three of these paintings stacked round the walls, and turned them round. They was all farmhouses, and apple trees, and sort of purple flowers growing up the walls. But instead of looking like proper flowers, they was just big blobs of purple paint, and a right mess, at that.

"She get her living at this, does she?" He asked her.

"Course she don't," she says, proper turning up her snout. "She makes lampshades. This is only a hobby. I guarantee you don't get your living doing no paintings, neither, do you?"

"How do you know?" He says.

"How do I know?" she says, proper cocky. "I reckon you want to start making lampshades, and all."

"Well, here you are," He says. "Supposing you show me how?"

"Come down the workroom," she says, and went out.

They went downstairs into a big sort of cellar, and when she switched the light on, He see there was work tables all round the walls. There was piles of square sheets of thick paper next to a heavy press affair, and hundreds of lampshades of all sizes and colours, all scattered about anyhow.

"There you are," she says. "This is the work, and the play's upstairs."

Some of the lampshades was very pretty, all painted up, and tassels hanging off of the corners.

"Do you know how to make these?" He says.

"Course," she says. "Easy."

She took a bit of squared paper, twisted it round, put the two joins under a boney kind of sewing machine, stitched the thing along, and put the bottom ends under a kind of cutter, just twisting it round. Before you could look up, there was the lampshade.

"That's natty," He says. "Let's have a go."

He made half a dozen as easy as winking your eye, and she

finished them off with tape round the top and bottom, putting in a wire frame to fit on the holder.

"This is a lump of cake," He says. "This ain't work, it's pleasure. Make a good thing out of this, does she?"

"She's rubbed along so far," she says, "and she don't hurt herself at it, neither."

He noticed she watched Him all the time, like a moggie after a sparrow, not looking dead at Him, but a little bit off, taking in all He done out the sides of her eyes. It come strange to be standing there in the yellow electric, looking at a lot of paper shapes with this bride standing next to Him and neither of them saying a blind word. But He felt something sort of creeping about in between them, as if their feelings had soft hands to touch each other with, coming tickling about all over the place, round and round and up and down them.

"Thinking about?" she says, still looking at the lampshades, all going up and down like a line of mountains.

"Same as you," He says and give her a pat on the bot, soft as He could, ready to duck in case she shot a wallop at Him.

But she stood for it like a lady, and never done nothing, not even look.

"What's that for?" she says, as if she was asking the price of spuds.

"Talking," He says. "Get some more if you're not careful. Somewhere else, and all."

"Mm?" she says, starting to swing her bot about a little bit. but still looking in the same place.

"Course," He says, and a kind of red hot sticky ball of spit come up in His throat, making Him choke a bit.

"All right, behind?" He says, and put His hand square on her, surprised how He come over trembling.

"You're cake," He says, but He wished He could get rid of the stuff in His throat so He could talk proper, instead of having to swallow half way through saying something.

"What you think you're doing?" she says, and He tried to make out why she sounded so quiet, as if He was the only one in the party, and she was on top of a tram.

"Having a look round," He says.

"Funny sort of a look," she says, and whipped her self round, leaving His hand in the air, facing Him dead on. She was laughing proper saucy but her eyes looked queer. "What you shaking about for?"

"I'm frightened," He says. "Why are you?"

"I ain't," she says, laughing away there, and she held up her arms. "You feel."

He felt the heavy round shapes through her dress, lifting them, and letting them slip slowly through His fingers, and smoothed His hands down her waist to the swelling fat, but when He started pressing her, she shoved Him off.

"Half a mo," she says, cutting it off the crusty part, "not so fast."

"What's up?" He says.

"Nothing," she says. "Only that's as far as we go. That's all."

"Ah, come on," He says, surprised how He never had no voice at all. "Be a sport."

"My oath," she says. "Some of you blokes think you know it all, don't you?"

"I never said so," He says, and He tried to get hold of her again to kiss her, but she shoved Him off a bit harder.

"This is where you go back to your painting," she says. "That's more in your line."

"What are you, then?" He says, and He could have bashed her.

"A bit too good for you, mate," she says, making a real joke out of it. "We can always put your kind in their place, you know?"

"You teasing mare," He says, feeling like howling, He was that weak. The pain in His guts was just about creasing Him, but He was trying hard as He could not to show it.

"That's all right," she says. "Tease or not, it'll learn you not to come it another time, see? We ain't all barmy, you know."

"You hop out of it, fore I crash you one," He says, and He could feel a bursting hot red boiling up somewhere inside of

Him, making Him want to jump on her and knock her teeth out, one by one, not just to hurt her, but to try and reach the part of her what was so far away from Him.

Looking at her, standing there looking at Him, with a laugh all over her dial, He see the fat and flop of her, and thought of Ada in the same place.

One thought, a second of it, only just a little scratch of them shining red beetles, and the clean light of her hair and the smiles of the pale blue water with the stars blowing over it was enough. Ada won with a smile.

"Okeedoke," He says, and went for the stairs, "I don't know why I took the time. I'll know what to call you next time I see you, you rotten teaser, you."

"Yes?" she says. "You get them pimples off your dial fore you talk to me, mate."

He felt His face on the way back, and the pimples come up like mountains, sore to touch. He started getting the feeling it was no good of living, what with the pain, and the thought of what you had to put up with, what you never seemed to be able to do nothing about.

He got back in the quiet, warm white of the studio, standing square in front of the canvas, trying to see how He was going. But the colours was all streaky, and none too good for shape, though looking at the pictures Miss Wilmore done, something said if she never had to be particular about the shape of the houses, there was no reason why He had to start getting fussy about the shape of a fish. So He done no more, He got hold of this sort of little trowel, scraped some blue and green together, sloshed it round on the palette a bit, and started painting all over the white part of the canvas, so by the time He finished, the fish was finding its own way out, proper blinded with science. He had to stop, at last, because the sun was coming a brownish light blue through the glass, and what with the light going, and this chronic pain in His guts, He thought it was time He packed in.

Rolling His sleeves down, going through the passage in the half dark house, He felt proper glad, in one way, that He had

His chance of having a go at this artist business, and finding out about it. Standing there, buttoning up His coat, feeling the quiet bricks building up all round Him, He reckoned He was dead lucky He give up the idea of being a artist. Sloshing paint about was all very well till you started doing it, then it turned out to be a proper messy sort of a do, and it looked as if you had to wait a long time before anything happened. He come over real glad He was going back to the shop and Ma.

He come outside, and felt His mind shut out the artist lark with a slam as loud as the varnished black door. He thought it was a right puzzle, the way He was thinking the last time He come down the road, that afternoon, and the way He was thinking on His way back, now.

Somehow or another He never seemed to get hold of the right end of the stick, first go off. First, He wanted to paint, then He never wanted to see a brush again. Then He thought Miss Wilmore was a toff, now He never give fourpence if she fell down and broke her neck. And every time He thought about Rivers, He kicked His self black and blue for being such a mug. He thought it was dead funny how you kind of think things, and always seem to get them wrong, but all of a sudden, at last, they seem to come out right, and you wonder why you never see it before.

So He got on the bus, feeling very man of the world, and He reckoned, all in all, taking it by and large, as you might say, He was growing up, and learning things every other five minutes.

# CHAPTER XXIX

No sooner He got near the back door of the Fun Fair, swinging this little box, than a bloke called His name out.

"Hullo," He says, a bit worried.

"Ernie?" says Ada's voice, a bit one side. "Here we are."

He looked through the dark, seeing the polished mud guards of a car, the same time as somebody switched the light on inside.

Ada was leaning out the window, with the flat of her hand whitish in the light, and He nigh fell down when He see the Celluloid Tanner Bloke laughing at Him behind the wheel.

"We got a lift," Ada says. "This is Jim Mordinoy."

"Yes?" He says, a bit surprised the way things was turning out.

"Get in," says Ada, "ain't got much time. Brought your lunch with you, have you?"

"No," He says, while the car starts off. "Something for you."

"Don't believe it," says Ada, grabbing this box and ripping off the string.

"Oo," she says, two feet in the grave, "you got them. You remembered."

"What's He done He never ought to?" says Jim, trying to turn round and keep his eye on the road, same time.

"Got me my gardenias," she says, nigh crying.

The sound of her voice like that sort of sent creeping fingers soft inside Him, making Him come over proper soppy, till He could have got down and kissed her feet, and proper made a mug of His self.

"Gardenias, eh?" says Jim, as if they was the business. "He's after you, Battler, girl. He's after you. And He's started the right way, too, and all. You want to watch Him. He's a boy."

She held these white hard flowers against His nose. All the icy scent of lemony loneliness breathed up in His head, and right away, far back inside where nobody could touch, He knew why she loved them and nigh cried when they was give her.

"Ain't they?" she says, still with that voice, nigh crying, but laughing, aching in a place as never hurt. "Ain't they? I don't know what to call them. Gardenias ain't good enough. Oh, Ernie. You're a lovely feller, ain't you? Eh?"

"Don't know," He says, red as a traffic light, trying to play it down.

"I'll see you right," she says, and there was a little gold bubble in her voice, jumping up and down like one of them little balls on the jet in the shooting gallery down the Fair.

"Watch out, Ernie boy," says Jim, and He could tell he was having a quiet laugh. "She's a killer when she starts."

"Wait till you know, big mouth," she says. "You ain't got a chance, anyway."

"Me?" says Jim, trying to be surprised, and cutting his self. "Never thought I had. Not with Clem blowing away there."

"You can leave him out of it, and all," she says, throwing her self into it. "That's all over, and you know it."

"Yes?" Jim says, meaning no.

"Yes," she says, meaning half a no.

He got a nasty hole opening up in His guts at the thoughts of some other bloke getting her. It was opening and letting Him drop in it.

The lights of the Palais shone dotting bright red right down the bottom of the road, and Ada started getting a bit restless, shifting up and down, pulling her skirt over her knees and then holding her legs straight to look at her shoes. Every time He see the curves of her legs, the pain in His guts come on worse.

"I always get that there rotten excited, coming down here," she says.

"I know why," says Jim, driving in and out of the traffic. "The old tenor sax, eh? The pie eyed piper's calling."

Ada never said nothing, but you could feel she was just about ready to bite.

"Don't get tickets," says Jim, pulling up.

"We will get tickets," she says, getting out. "Thanks for the ride, just the same."

"If you want to spend your money," Jim says, laughing away. "I'm giving you free tickets and you're chucking them away? Too much pride, that's what's wrong with you, Battler."

"Always shall have with you," she says. "Come on, Ern."

"How long you know him?" He says, as they was going upstairs.

"Who? Jim?" she says. "Couple of years, now. He runs this place, you know?"

"Runs it?" He says, stopping.

"Yes," she says, having a smile, "and about a dozen Fun Fairs, in the bargain."

He followed her up, trying to work it out.

"Hullo, dearie," says Ada, to the old girl in the desk. "Give us two nice ones off the top of the roll, will you?"

"Hullo, Ada," says the old dear, tired as you like, with a yellow face, and eyes like two black holes burnt in by a fag end. "Ten shillings, please."

He nigh fell straight down the stairs, but He paid up like a lord, even if His face felt a bit stiff round the chops when He was trying to laugh at Ada and the old girl at the same time.

"See you inside," she says, holding up the flower box. "Just going to put these on."

"Okeedoke," He says, and went for the Gents, hearing the axes throwing it softly in and out the drum beats and the soft crash of brass plates just under the rainy wash of all the feet going criss cross and twisting round, opening and closing, all in the hundreds of warm pink lights running round the gallery.

But the white bulb in the Gents brought Him up again. He was getting His ticket, watching a bloke chuck His hat somewhere amongst thousands of others round the back there, and im come in. Off come his white silk scarf, then his posh black hat, and He see his double breast dancing suit with silk lapels

and a black bow tie, just like a photo of a big band leader,
black and bright white, pinky pale blue, and shining lines in
the curls of his hair. "What's up?" Jim says, slinging Him a
fag.

"Nothing," He says, but He started wanting a suit like
that, and a black bow tie, so hard somewhere inside of Him
He could feel it hurting. All of the feelings He had all day was
running out, and He started feeling proper poor again.

"If we keep the Battler waiting," Jim says, "we'll get our
ears wet."

"Keep who?" He says, following behind, out of the white
light and the gritty stone passage, on the carpet in the pink
lights while the swing door blew cool puffs at His black hair.

"Her," Jim says, pointing to Ada, waiting in a white dress
with the gardenias shining quiet white frills in her hair, and all
her shape in broad lines of silver pink where the light painted
it on the edges and long curving creases. Satin, or something
shiny, it was, and her two beauties was kept up by a couple
of thin straps covered in beads, all shining away like little
kitchen fires.

"Don't she look a smasher, eh?" Jim says. "How about the
first dance, beautiful?"

"Have the next one," she says, "this is His."

"No," He says, "I can't dance much."

"Here," she says, and she grabs Him by the arm. "It ain'
often I ask a bloke to dance, but when I do, I want it done,
see? Get cracking."

"There you are, Ernie," says Jim, looking pinker and paler
blue than ever. "That's the Battler giving orders. Find me in
the bar."

"As usual," Ada says. "Ought to been born a dish cloth
you did."

In her high heels, they was just about the same height, and
when He shoved His arm round her He could feel she had
nothing on under the satin. He tried to pull His self back and
away from her, but as fast as He bent out, she come in, tight
up against Him, holding Him round the neck and humming

the tune in His ear, making Him come over proper giddy. All that aching of the afternoon come banging back in time with the gentle crashing of brass plates. He could have cried, out of being so weak somewhere near His knees.

"What's up?" she says, in His ear.

"Nothing," He says, with all this soft, curving scented back and fore movement pressing close against Him, and yellow hair tickling His cheek and the hard softness of her pushing Him off and bouncing Him back on her again. "I'm all right."

"Telling me," she says, and He could feel her shaking up and down. "If you'd hold yourself up, you'd dance better."

If He had His face next to the bars of the grate, it might have been cooler. It was frying hot and the sweat come off almost like steam. He tried to pull away but she had Him tight.

His heart started bashing away and He started shaking about, even the sides of His face.

"Like me, Ernie?" she says, and put her cheek flat against His.

"Bit," He says, hating the sweat on His dial, in case it put her off.

"How much?" she says, like a warm waterfall in His ear. "All I can feel?"

"Pulling my leg?" He says, and tried to see her face, but she held Him.

"Not this time," she says, and He knew she meant it. He started shaking proper bad. The pink lights all the way round the gallery got going round faster than a roundabout. All the faces wiped over in one face with no nose or eyes or mouths. The drum and brass plates crashed and crashed louder and louder.

"What's up?" He could hear her saying. "What's the matter, Ernie?"

"I'm all right," He was saying, or somebody was saying it for Him while He listened, trying to keep His feet from walking off His legs and letting Him in the cart.

"Feeling queer?" she says. "You feeling all right, Ernie?"

"I'm okeedoke," He says, "straight up. Thought I was going to sneeze, that's all."

"Proper queer hawk, you are," she says, bending back and looking right at Him, pushing herself tighter into Him to do it. "Don't know what to make of you."

"Why?" He says, looking at her mouth, knowing her eyes with all the stars in the pale blue water was watching Him, weighing Him up, and He was afraid she was going to guess.

"Telling me you're a artist and then getting in with Jim Mordinoy," she says. "He won't do you much good, you know?"

"Why you going about with him for, then?" He says, hoping she was going to stay where she was, because she was kind of shaped into Him.

"What can I lose?" she says, surprised as anything. "He's the boss, ain't he? He's got a car, too, what's more. So I don't have to worry about getting nowhere, do I? He's never said a word out of place to me, neither, so what's the matter with me going with him? Sides, what's it got to do with you who I go with? Eh?"

"Nothing," He says, coming over chilly. "But if he's all right for you to go with, why's he going to do me a bit of no good?"

"Listen," she says, shaking Him about a bit, "you know what he is, just as well as I do. He's a flash boy. You know it. Don't you?"

"What if he is?" He says. "He's still doing me no harm, is he?"

"Noooo," she says, pulling it out like the bottom drawer, "but I notice you've got yourself a new suit since I saw you last. How much he give you?"

"Listen," He says, feeling a fast rage fly up. "My Ma give me this for my birthday. See? My Ma give me it. And a couple more, and all."

"You listen," she says, holding off a bit. "Think we're all daft, do you? Think you wasn't seen the other night down the Fair when he give you a couple of quid? I don't blame you, mind.

Get your money how you like. It's hard enough to get, without worrying where it comes from."

"Don't you?" He says.

"I didn't use to," she says, a bit tired she was, and going a bit heavier on His arm. "Don't let's talk about it, else I'll go and get blind drunk. Then Mum'll have a word or two to say."

Everything He felt for her sort of went cold, and another part of Him come real hot. He wanted to put His arms round her and keep everybody out of her way, or sing her to sleep or something barmy. He never wanted her to be hurt no more. He could have murdered every bastard as ever done anything to her to make her talk like that about herself. He started getting so worked up about it, come to a finish He nigh on started howling for her.

"Don't die on me," she says. "The tune's lively enough, ain't it?"

"Tune's all right," He says, "it's you."

"Me?" she says, and come closer, starting it all over again. "What? What, Ernie boy?"

"I'm soppy about you," He says, feeling a mug and knowing it, but there was nothing else to say. "Straight up. I can't see nobody else. I'm up the wall."

The tune stopped, and everybody started clapping. She dropped her arms but she stayed where she was, touching, so close He could feel her breathing.

He wished He could do what the blokes on the pictures always done when it come to saying it nice, but He knew if He give her any of that, it might come back on Him specially if she see the same ones, and knew the same blokes. He wanted to do it rough and sort of easy, as if He was boss of the shop, but she might know who He was trying to take off, so He just had to do it His own way and feel a mug. The words never come out right, and His hands was all sweaty, and even though some of the words was there, ready for the saying, He felt too much of a mug to say any of them.

"That's tore it," she says, sort of hopeless, only she was quiet and kind with it. "It's always the same. I don't know."

"What's up?" He says. "Listen. Don't take it the wrong way. I never said nothing, see? I was a mug to open me mouth. I never wanted to."

The brass plates crashed again, and the saxes come out in kid gloves, just loud enough to be heard and so sweet, you just wanted to lay down where you was and think it all out, specially with all this soft bumpy heat pressing against you, and the far off cold lemon of the gardenias getting up in the top of your head, making you think of things, like poetry, only not with words.

"You're a lovely feller, Ern," she says, as if she meant it. "But it's no good of me telling you the tale, is it?"

"Not much," He says, but He noticed she was still as close. "But that don't stop me seeing you now and again, do it?"

"Course not, you silly," she says, proper giving Him a shake and then holding Him all the tighter. "We can be nice friends, can't we?"

"Yes," He says, wondering what she had in mind.

"Well, then," she says, as if that settled everything. "Now let's enjoy the dance."

Just going round and round the floor in a sort of fancy walk, a turn here and there, going up and coming down, first her going forward, then Him, turn round again, pause, side step, off you go again, thousands of you at it, all close together, all thinking away inside their selfs and not showing it on their dials, except the engaged ones, and you could tell them a mile off because they was just stuck together, most of them with their eyes shut, so you had to keep an eye out for them, else you walloped into them and they woke up, looking at you as if they thought you never ought to been let off of the lead.

"I wish I could live my time like this," she says, dreamy as a pillow. "I only know how much I love dancing when I'm here."

"Can't you get a job here?" He says. "Ought to be easy, didn't it?"

"Course," she says. "But where's it get you? Sides, it's a

long story and I'll only start crying, so give over. I just want
to dance, and forget it."

The band stopped again, and everybody started talking and
you could hear the glasses and cups rattling about, and the
till ringing up in the soda fountain, while the bloke at the
piano was tickling up a little tune of his own, and everybody
cleared off the floor. Blokes was standing about watching
brides come past to try and get a good looker for the next
dance, and the brides was all looking as if nothing ever
surprised them.

Jim was sitting at a table, looking proper real in all the pink
lights, talking to a lot of people, but he shot them all off when
Ada sat down.

"Cold drinks," he says, waving at the glasses. "Hear about
Clem?"

"No," she says, looking a bit frightened, with the drink half
way. "What's up with him?"

"Taking the band to Blackpool," Jim says, "nice contract,
and all."

"Blackpool," she says, thinking about it. "Ain't far, is it?"

"Far enough," says Jim. "Suppose we go round the Club
and see him, after?"

"Don't think I'll bother, thanks," she says, like dropping a
fag and leaving it there.

Some bloke come up, all smiles, and shoved his arm round
her chair.

"Ada," he says, "been waiting years for this. How about a
turn or two, eh?"

"Glad to," she says, and got up as the plates crashed, with
the red beetles shining while she touched the gardenias and
generally pulled herself about a bit.

"Always unlucky, I am," says Jim, just smiling.

"My oath," she says. "You've got years for your dances
you have."

Jim watched her go away, and even when he lit his fag, his
eyes never blinked, or lost her till she got behind the criss crossing crowd. The band was playing low, slow, sad and sweet, till

it nigh had the same smell as gardenias and everybody was quiet, just whispering with their feet. The pink lights went out, and limelights punched pale blue, green and red arms across the room, making everybody coloured shadows moving up and down and round and round, all in time with the soft crash of the plates. Some bride started singing in the mike, doing all the actions with her hands, and her voice come up fat and bubbly through the loud speakers, just like down the Fair, only not so plain. All you could hear was love and you and a bit more about going away, then the band come up strong and took over.

"I'd give my top teeth to ride her," Jim says, just his eyes flashing up red in the dark. "You been going with her long, have you?"

"Who, Ada?" He says. "Not long, no."

"Can't get nigh her, somehow," Jim says. "Tried everything. Won't wear me."

"She ain't like the rest of them, that's why," He says.

"Telling me?" Jim says, proper sorry for his self. "I can take my pick any time I want to. And I don't want to. She won't even marry me. Trouble is, she's got this band leader in tow, see?"

"Don't know nothing about her affairs," He says. "Nothing to do with me who she knows."

"No?" says Jim. "Well, it is to me. If you can find out what she really thinks about this bloke Clem Arbiter, you'd be doing me a favour, see? And I'll see you right for it. On?"

He was surprised to hear the queer sound of Jim's voice. It was the first time He heard anything about him not hard as iron. It made Him feel a bit more important and all, as if He had Ada in charge.

"Okeedoke," He says, "I'll see what I can do."

He see it all, quick as the limes going out. Jim was in the same boat as Him, feeling the same smiling dying feeling for her, but instead of being nice about it, like she was to Him, she was playing him up and giving him a dog's life, even though he had all the nicker ever made and owned this, that and the rest, and He was just a artist. He started feeling a bit uncomfortable about the artist lark. He could still smell the paint and see all the brushes in the pot. But they was like that bit of crayon, do anything you told them, but you never seemed to tell them right.

"She seems to have took a fancy to you," Jim says, not shifting the fag, and not looking at Him. "I wish I knew why. Artist, or something, ain't you?"

"Was," He says. "I'm giving it up. It ain't a living."

"That's what I thought," says Jim, as if he just remembered where he lived. "Couldn't make it out, somehow. Ain't your Ma something in the furniture line?"

"That's right," He says, proper prickling of surprise. "How'd you know?"

"Found out," Jim says, watching the crowd. "Always do with my rivals."

"I ain't your rival," He says, getting a bit cold, and waiting for it.

"If I thought you was," Jim says, laughing away, "you wouldn't be sitting there, son. You'd be in hospital, see? Or worse."

"What for?" He says, proper getting a shake on. There was nothing soft or dying about Jim when he said it. It was meant.

"I been after her too long, that's why," Jim says. "Ain't losing her a second. She knows it. Arbiter knows it. Now you know it. So everybody knows it. That's why she ain't going with Clem. She knows if she does, I'll get working on him. Sides, he's no good to her, anyway. She's got enough sense for that."

"You going to be any good to her, are you?" He says, narked by the way he was talking, and forgetting.

"Son," Jim says, "she can have everything she wants. Everything. Every blind thing she can think of. I've only gone up the bloody pole once in my life about a girl, and she's the one. And I can't make her see me. But I'll have her. I swear to Christ I will. Nobody else won't."

Talking to his self, he was, or seemed like. Then the pink

come on again and made everybody look healthy and warm, and he looked like a ordinary bloke just talking about things, ordinary.

"Listen, while we're at it," Jim says, slinging a fag over, "you out of a job, are you?"

"Not exactly," He says, glad they was going on something else. "I got the business to attend to. And I got the promise of a solicitor's job."

"Solicitor's?" Jim says, turning comic. "Jesus. Artist, second-hand furniture and solicitor's? When are you going to start getting a living? How old are you?"

"Nineteen, nigh on twenty," He says.

"You want to start getting a jerk on," Jim says. "I had a good few quid in the bank when I was nineteen. I did?"

"Never said you didn't," He says. But He felt like a bone in the stew.

"Wasting your time," Jim says. "Listen. Do you want to start doing yourself a bit of good? Do you? I can always use a right boy? I got plenty of them working with me."

"Depends what it is," He says.

"Breaking windows," Jim says. "That's all. Just busting windows. Taking a lock off now and again. Climbing about a bit. Strike you right?"

"Sounds queer to me," He says. "I thought you ran the Fairs?"

"So I do," says Jim. "Side lines. So's this place. But I like a bit of life, see? What's there to this place? Hire a band and take their money. Fairs are easy run, too. Take a shop and shove the machines in. It's too easy, that is."

"How do you make out busting windows gets you anywhere, then?" He says, feeling hot and somehow knowing what was coming. Ada was right. He was a flash boy, and he was looking like it.

"Depends what you bust 'em for," Jim says. "If there's something behind 'em worth taking, see?"

"Ain't you afraid I might go to the police?" He says. "Suppose my Ma got to know?"

"I ain't afraid of you nor nobody else," Jim says, having a proper good laugh. "I talk when I'm sure, see? If you want the job, say so. You can earn yourself a nice fifty quid a week easy. If you work hard, that is. On?"

"Fifty quid a week?" He says, nigh off of the chair.

"Easy," Jim says. "Three little jobs'll pay you that. The more jobs, the more pay, see? On?"

"Okeedoke," He says, feeling big. "I'll have a go."

"Tattamy's Garage, Ermington Street," Jim says. "Monday morning, about half nine or ten? You can join the school, and see how you go. Fair do's all round. If you don't get on, you get out of it, see? And you keep your trap shut, see? If you don't, you'll get it closed for you. None too nice that ain't."

"Where's Ermington Street?" He says, taking it all in.

"Back of the Angel," Jim says. "Know it?"

"Course," He says.

"Half nine or ten," Jim says, "Lobbo. Here's the Battler. And she don't know nothing about this, neither. See?"

"Okeedoke," He says, and He starts feeling that there pleased with His self, He could hardly stop jumping about in the chair and chucking things round the place, just to cause a bit of trouble.

"What about me?" Jim says to her. "Do I get this one?"

"Let's get me breath," she says, and sits down. "Think I'm made of?"

"I couldn't give it a name," Jim says, not looking at her. "I'll find out one of these days, though."

Ada looked at Him, nodding the gardenias at Jim, laughing as if she twisted her ankle.

"Kids his self something cruel," she says.

"I'll go over you inch by inch," Jim says, "head to foot."

"Yes?" she says, pulling the gardenias over a bit. "I'll see you get a few nasty surprises here and there, and all."

Jim give Him half a wink to slope, so He finished off His drink and stood up.

"Where you off to?" Ada asks, looking a bit downhearted.

"Don't ask the gentleman questions," Jim says. "He don't have to spend pennies. It's free. Ain't it, Ernie?"

"See you later," He says, not knowing where to put His face.

He stayed in the Gents reading the paper for a bit, hearing the band running through the walls like hot water through a pipe, coming up strong every time the door opened, wondering what was going on outside, just chasing the words about, not knowing what He was looking at, but looking because it was something to do to keep Him there. Hundreds of blokes come in, did their business, wiped their sweat off with their second handkerchief, did their ties nice, and then pulled their combs out and set their hair for a few minutes, combing and then putting the curls back in with their fingers, gentle as if they was handling gold. Then they looked at their selfs, both sides, pulled their first handkerchief up a bit more in their handkerchief pockets so as it would show better, straightened out the corners, and pulled their coats down, all ready for the next dance.

When He went out, all the pink lights was on. Jim and Ada was missing, but He see her soon as He looked, on the other side of the band, dancing with Jim, but the gardenias was a foot or more away from his head, and her hand was just about on his shoulder, no more.

They was arguing.

He come over proper glad bright, He did, because Jim was getting such a dog's life, and He was so well in.

The trumpet seemed to think so too, proper jumping up and down in the music, it was, cheerful as you like, all on His side, laughing at Jim being give the thumb.

All of a sudden He got a funny idea that Jim was just taking Him in the business because He was so well in with Ada. He remembered the way he spoke about her, and how his voice went. The idea came, and stuck. But never mind how He thought about it, He could no more hate Jim for feeling like it about Ada than hate His self. He hated this bloke Arbiter, and He hated all the blokes down the Fun Fair, but somehow He never felt nothing about Jim.

He thought perhaps it was because Jim was so straight about it, and so posh looking in his dancing suit, and all. Or something. Perhaps He felt sorry for him, knowing they both stood about the same chance with her, when it come to a finish.

But trying to think of things without Ada, all the lights started going down. They was still pink, still hundreds of them, still shining like they always did. But they went sort of dead.

Thinking of going through the day without the thoughts of her, somewhere, made Him come over kind of not quite sick but feeling proper rotten.

The scent of her, and the softness, the shadow of her hair and the way her hand sort of curled round when she put it straight, was all little things that seemed to belong to Him, nobody else, and He never wanted them took away.

Them moaning trams was moaning again in amongst the saxes, but no more, nor no louder than what they was moaning inside of Him.

"We're going round the Club," Jim says. "Want to come?"

"Okeedoke," He says, shook up out of the dream. "Why didn't you finish off the dance?"

"Try dancing with a lump of talking concrete, sometime," Jim says, "you'll soon see."

He remembered how she been with Him, and heard her voice close in His ear again.

Some part of Him, right inside, come up ripping wide open in a big smile, but Jim never saw it.

Nobody did.

"Hard luck," He says.

## CHAPTER XXX

NOBODY SAID a blind word on the way round all the little side streets and short cuts, and it was pitch dark where Jim pulled up.

"Seems to me it's going to take a few drinks to get us standing the right way up," Jim says. "This lot runs a wreath, if you ask me."

"It's your rotten temper," Ada says, giving him nothing. "I never wanted to come here, in the first place."

"You'll change your mind inside," Jim says. "You always do."

She put her arm through His and started walking down a little passage. There was a band playing somewhere, coming through cotton wool in the dark, near by, and getting louder.

"I want to be out of it in half hour, Ernie," she says. "I got a lot to do tomorrow."

"I'll see you all right," He says. "You'll be there."

"Hark at father," says Jim, behind. "Want to watch Him, Battler. He'll get you."

"More chance than you've got," she says, and give His arm a squeeze.

They come out in a little yard, with boxes full of stuff smelling like the market of a Saturday night. There was a electric sign over a little door, like a double of dice showing a six and a one. Down the steps, the band got louder, proper crashing it out, and a porter come out, opening another door with a lot of curtains over it, ducking his nut and laughing back and front.

"Evening, Mr Mordinoy," he says, falling over his self, "full house again tonight. Marvellous business. Evening, Ada. Like old times. You're looking well?"

"Hullo, Tom," she says, and hopped off in the Ladies. "Shan't be long, Ern."

"I park the car, shall I, Mr Mordinoy?" Tom says, saluting nigh twice a second.

"Want it in a minute," Jim says. "Go and tell Rossi I want him, quick."

There was a big sign in this room where the Ladies and Gents was. Clem Arbiter and his Melody Boys, it had on it, in silver powdered letters like they have round the cinema, and all the boys photos was stuck round in little frames, with Clem Arbiter in the middle. A right looking boy, he was, with his violin, and all, and lots of dark waves in his hair, and a thin moustache, like a line of crayon, making you wonder if he shaved with a ruler to get it so straight. He looked a smashing bloke, and just the sort to start a riot among the brides.

A nasty, floating feeling, like the floor not being there, come over Him, and all He wanted to do was go home, because it was no good of Him trying for Ada, or even thinking about her, when this bloke was still kicking about. He knew exactly how Jim felt, and He started feeling sorrier than ever for him, even proper pally.

They give their hats to some tart in orange silk drawers and a little bit of stuff covering her top half, and went through some curtains to a long room with the ceiling nigh touching their heads, worse than the top of the Workmans for smoke, and stuffed full of people, all talking so loud you could hardly hear the band.

The Melody Boys was down the far end, squatting in a big open fan affair, made of glass, changing its colour all the time. They was all dressed up like chinks, with little round black hats on and yellow coats, sitting behind red wooden stands made like chink towers, with CA in the same silver letters fixed on them, and a red piano with Clem Arbiter painted on it.

The room was all hung right round in dark curtains, with different coloured lights hidden in the folds, and the ceiling was ridged over with long neons all shining different colours every other minute so it looked as if it was a cave under the water, only more comfortable. When you could see proper, there was dozens of tables, with little dull pinkish lights on

them, all crowded together, and the people was sitting round
them looking like a lot of Guy Fawkes's day masks coming out
of the dark, all jawing and laughing away, knocking back the
drinks as hard as they could go.

"The Lucky Seven, in full bloom," Jim says, proper pleased
with his self. "All I have to do is stand back and take the
dough."

"This yours and all, is it?" He says, just about giving up.
"What don't you do?"

"Get the sense to get out of it," Jim says, squeezing behind a
table the size of one of Ma's dinner plates. "Sit down."

A little thin bloke, with sideboards on the big side, came
rushing up, rubbing his hands and laughing all over his self.

"Ah," he says, and soon as he opened his mouth, He could
tell he was one of Old Nick's lot. "Mr Mordinoy, such a pleasure. Doing very nice, eh?"

"Listen, Rossi," Jim says, chopping it off the boney end.
"Who we getting in, stead of Clem? Fixed anybody?"

Rossi looked a bit fancy, wanting to talk, and not liking to.

"I had a lot of trouble," he says, going clever. "He got a contract, and he no want to go."

"Well, I want, see?" Jim says. "So make up your minds, the
pair of you."

"We doing good business, Mr Mordinoy," Rossi says, still
clever.

"We'll still do it when he's out," Jim says. "Who're you getting?"

"Suppose he don't like to go?" Rossi says, not looking at
him. "Suppose he go to his solicitor?"

"I hadn't thought of that," Jim says, thinking about it. "Tell
you what I had thought of, though?"

"What?" Rossi says, with his face like a wall, and his fat
hands fiddling about with his waistcoat button.

"The lamp duffers squad," Jim says. "Ever hear of 'em,
Rossi?"

Rossi never said a word, but he come in and started pushing
the glasses and knives and forks about to get his head nearer.

"Sartorelli is with two, three, down to the left," he says, proper bad news from home. "Clem had drinks with him."

"Any girls with him?" Jim says, laughing away.

"Three," says Rossi.

"Won't be no trouble, then," says Jim. "You get cracking on the band, see? Start them in a fortnight. I'll see Clem after the last session, tell him. Tell him about the lamp duffers, and all."

"I don't know what is, Mr Mordinoy," Rossi says, real put out, with his hands wagging and his head a one side, just like Old Nick.

"He does," Jim says. "You'll see. And get a bottle of champagne up here, quick."

"Certainly," says Rossi, and tore off round the corner.

Looking round at everybody, He tried to make it all out, but He had to give up. Here He was, in this place, sitting with the boss, and He might just as well have been home in bed for all the good it was doing Him. He felt proper out of it. Everybody else was enjoying their selfs, seemed like, yet even though the champagne was coming up, and Ada was on her way in, He could no more start feeling like enjoying His self than cut His throat. The name Sartorelli come up a nice smack in the nose, and all, but Jim seemed to feel it was all right, so He never bothered much. But it was this feeling of being out of it that made Him come over so queer. Everybody was having a good time with their brides, buying bottles of champagne planted in silver flower pots, and grub in sort of copper pans, and what all, and having the nicker to pay for it, but He was only there because a bride had took him along for a shove round at the Palais. He felt proper out of it, not like any of these people, at all.

Ada came in like a shining ghost, and even blokes at tables loaded down of posh brides all looked at her and you could see their faces turning to watch her Adaing all the way down to their table, proper carving it up, she was, giving them all a treat, back, front, and sides. "She's a bloody picture, ain't she, eh?" Jim says, and you could hear it in his voice. "Sometimes I know why I'm barmy, and sometimes I don't. I know why tonight, eh, Ernie boy?"

"My oath," He says.

"Who's dancing with me?" she says, putting her bag on the chair, giving the pair of them the benefit of a nice wash and brush up, and a dab or two of something fresh out of her little box. Proper breath of good, it was, specially in that place, and it made Him want to not exactly kiss her, but hold the air all round her with her inside of it, and kiss all that, only not even hard enough for her to feel it.

"I'd like to," Jim says, with the ash of his fag clawing round again, "but I'm so popular. Made too much of a fuss of, I am."

"Come on," she says to Him, "leave him in his misery. I'll want a glass of champagne when I get back, and all."

"It's yours," Jim says. "I don't know why. I ought to give you a drink in the river."

"Wouldn't get you far," she says. "Then you'd never get what you're after."

"Nor would nobody else," says Jim.

"That all you're worried about?" she says, and starts off for the floor, just in front of Him.

The brass plates was crashing louder than them at the Palais, and the band was hotter, just like down the Fun Fair, proper posh, nothing local about it. It fell over Him, all of a sudden, just while He was watching the lights catching Ada on her white back, with the soft bumps of her backbone going down in her dress, and the rest of her full of little muscles you could hardly see, except the shadows of them, chasing their selfs in and out, coming and going, shadow and not.

This place was just like a better kind of a Fun Fair, only instead of playing the machines and losing your cash that way, you chucked it away on the booze. And whether you did it the Fun Fair way, or had a do down here, old Jim Mordinoy got your nicker whether you liked it or not. Whatever you done, he was laughing.

"I reckon Jim's about the cleverest bloke I ever heard of," He says to her, when they got near the dance floor. "He's a proper boy. Fun Fairs and this place. Same bloke, different gravy."

But He sees she was looking towards the band, not listening, even if she heard Him at all, or knew He was alive.

All the time, this here brass plate bashing and saxes rolling about under trumpets was going on so loud, it sort of got between your teeth. Their idea seemed to be to kick up as much row as they could, as long as they kept in time. He never see a big band close to before, but He heard them on the wireless now and again when Ma Chalmers turned it on loud enough, so to see them all dressed up and playing was something to tell all the lads about. But they was nothing like what He expected to see. They was just like a lot of ordinary blokes, close to.

The bloke crashing the brass plates looked as if he was saying No all the time, wagging his head and jumping off of his chair in time to the crasha tuh, crasha tuh, worked by his foot, and the wishtywish, wishtywashty, wishtywhish of a couple of wire things he was rubbing the drum with, proper enjoying his self, sometimes having a go on the other bits of stuff all round him, but generally sticking to the rubbing business and never once letting his foot stop crashing. He looked as if he done it in his sleep. The gent knocking a walloping great big fiddle about, bigger even than Aggie Hunner's, was a proper scream. The fingers of one hand was creeping up and down the handle like a crab on the booze, and his other hand was digging away at these strings, as thick as wrapping cord, they was, making a row like a drum, only not so loud, and kind of in tune with what was going on. Laughing away there, he was, with this crab crawling about next to his earhole, and digging away there, proper dainty, as if it was all done scientific, with his music all wrote special. The trombones was all blowing together, with bowler hats over the ends to keep the row down, and all the trumpets had little bags over them. Some of the blokes playing them was all swole up in the face and proper red every time they had a go, but some of them never puffed out at all. It just made the cuts in their cheeks deeper. But they all sort of closed their eyes while they was ripping it off, making out they was feeling whatever it was something chronic. The bloke on the piano was pretty to watch, and all, tickling away there, winking at all the brides, laughing with his mouth wide open, and his eyes staring wide, like Chaser's, trying to look a real hot boy, very sharp round the corners, but his hair was so much like Len Tate's, He could almost smell the fish frying, and He knew without looking that he had a little comb in his waistcoat pocket to use down the Gents.

Clem Arbiter had a dancing suit on with hangings at the back, a white bow and a white waistcoat, and in the coloured lights of this big glass fan behind him, he looked smashing, straight up, a right smasher.

Soon as He had one good look at him, He knew why Ada never had no time for the other blokes. Here he was, famous all over the world, records by the millions, photo on all the music pieces, and placards, playing on the wireless week in and out, and all over the theatres, dressed in a marvellous dancing suit all the time, and everybody falling over their selfs to get him to give them eye room, never mind talk to them.

He got a proper rotten feeling coming over Him, thinking how some blokes got all the luck, looking proper smashing in coloured lights all the time, with brides running after them, and other ordinary blokes was sweating their guts out and never getting nowhere, or having anything.

The skitchy little bit of floor was so small it was no good of trying to dance on it, and everybody else looked as if they had the same idea. They just waited their chance and got the bride's bot in a little crack between two couples, and then shoved her in, coming up behind to give her a bit more weight, else they might have got their selfs shoved out again. It was a proper game.

Soon as they clinched to go in, He noticed she was holding Him different, not coming close like she done down the Palais, but trying to keep off a bit, even though she was getting squashed on Him whether she liked it or not. He could feel her arm was nowhere near where she had it before. Everything started going cold all round Him, like the fire going out. He wanted to go home, without dancing or anything.

"Don't let's muck about here," He says, and drops His hold. "What's the use?"

"Talking about?" she says, looking at Him three inches off. "It's a bit of a squeeze but we'll be all right once we're on. You want a bit of practice, I can see."

"Your half hour's nearly up," He says.

"It will be, when I've had a chase round here," she says, so He see it was no good.

They went in like scrag ends getting chewed in the mincer, getting their feet working in time to the band and then jogging about as if they had a screw loose. Everybody was arse to arse, so you had to go round one way whether you liked it or not, and what with dodging beefy blokes trying to do their dags, and ducking tarts elbows sharp as nails digging your ears out, and top of all that, trying to do your fancy bits at the same time, there was no doubt about it, it was a proper rare do, and cheap at half the price.

He see she was looking towards the band all the time, and He could feel her sort of half shoving and half guiding the pair of them nearer to it, so He let her, and presently they was inching near the little raised box where this tallish bloke was playing his fiddle a couple of scrapes, and then beating the time to the brass plates, turning round to all the people and nodding, laughing, ducking his nut when he see somebody he knew, and generally carrying on there something alarming.

Then he see her, and all the laughs went. The white oblong shirt was shining a couple of diamond eyes under the big white bow, and his face come over the top under the long wavy hair, but he never laughed at her while he nodded, and he looked at Him as if He was out to do a couple of murders without being too particular who it was.

Never even taking His eyes off the curls on some tart's neck in front, He could still feel her looking at this fiddle bloke as if he was Christ. He could feel her looking. Something was stretching out of her, out of the middle of her, going through her eyes and leaving her as empty as the last bus.

He could feel it, even through His hand on her back.

But the bloke never even give her a second look, never mind another nod. He shoved his fiddle under his clock and started scratching away there, looking at his music as if he could read it, making out he was doing a bit of hard work for a change and earning his money.

"Don't mean to tell me you go anything on a bloke like him, do you?" He says, not meaning to, but having to, and He had to say it loud to get His self heard.

"You keep your nose out of it," she says, and her hair come across her face the way she whipped her head round at Him, so He see just two white points where her eyes was, but He could guess the rest.

"Okeedoke," He says. "None of my business, we know. But, blimey."

"Shut your mouth," she says, in a whisper like a pair of scissors. "I do what I like, see? If you don't like it, you know what to do. So do it."

"Sit down, now, shall we?" He says, and before He knew it, He was standing there alone, with His arms out, and she was Adaing away, down to the table.

"Don't let it worry you," some bloke hollers, laughing away. "She'll come back if she loves you."

"Perhaps," He says, trying to look a bit more cocky than He felt.

"All quarrels end on the bed," this bloke yells, and the bride he was part of, give him a dig with her wrist on his shoulder, making all the little gold things on her bracelet jump about proper pretty. But she was laughing, and when he give her a nice squeeze, she leaned her head on his shoulder, so he was all right.

All the way down this darkish coloured room, people was sitting round tables sprouting bottles, like thick stems flowering the bright rims of glasses, so what with the band bashing it out, and everybody yelling and hollering, it was no worse than the pub round the market of a Saturday. The funny thing about it was the posh way everybody was dressed, specially the brides, and the way the waiters was tearing about. All the blokes was got up in their dancing suits with white ties, like the waiters, only a bit more bang about them, and all the brides was Adaed up to the nines, low back and fronts, and some of them never even had any straps to keep their dresses up, so looking at them from the back, with a chair in the way, you wondered if they had anything on at all. But it was proper smashing how white and smooth looking their skin was, like as if it been caught in the frost.

But nobody was keeping still, or just having a smoke and enjoying things. They was all on the move, banging on the tables in time with the band, or else dancing up and down the little lanes between tables, or going up to the floor, or else coming back, or arguing with the waiters, or else waving and shouting at somebody else across the way.

Proper queer to watch, it was, and funny to listen to.

"What's up with the Battler?" Jim says, pouring this bottle out in a flattish glass.

"I asked her what she see in that band bloke," He says.

Jim put the bottle back in this silver pot, and sits back laughing as if it hurt him.

"Oh, Christ," he says, "oh, Jesus Christ. See in him? She only lived with him a couple of years, that's all."

Just like being slashed across the teeth with a razor.

He got a proper guts aching blinding hate for this fiddle bloke. He only wanted to get his skin in His hands and tear it up.

"Why don't you do something about it, then?" He says, when He could.

"I told you," Jim says, having a drink, "if I can't have her, nobody can't. See? She knows it, and he knows it. If she goes with him, I start. If she goes with anybody bar me, I'll start on him. So she has a look at this bloke now and again, and goes home like a good girl. See?"

"That's a good idea," He says, "but how do you get anything out of it?"

"If I don't, nobody don't," Jim says, and lights up off of the butt end. "She'll come round, one of these days. I can wait."

In these darkish lights He see how Jim was coming out not quite so clean looking, nor so pink and pale blue as he was in other places, like the Fun Fair, and what was queerer, not as young. He kept on getting a funny kind of a feeling about him, as if there was somebody else underneath, using the pink and pale blue when it suited him, and being somebody else at other times. You looked at him, seeing Jim Mordinoy in his black hat and all the other stuff, and then you looked again and you thought you see somebody else, like seeing a bit of spit in the lamplight and thinking you was on a shilling.

"Drink up," Jim says. "We got another bottle to go, yet."

"Listen," He says, tasting this stuff like weak ginger ale, and getting the sneeze out of His nose, "what did you want to bring me round here for?"

Quick as a flash He see His self asking old Henry, and heard the brolly banging in time with the brass plates.

"You was with Ada," Jim says. "She wouldn't come without you. So here you are."

"Ah, now we know," He says, but He felt rotten. This bloke, nor nobody else wanted Him, and Ada only asked for Him to keep Jim from being too close. He see it plain as the bubbles coming up in the glass. Even having three new suits and everything to match, and a couple of quid spending money never got you anywhere, chuck in a business of your own. Round where you lived you was somebody, but up in a place like this, in amongst a lot of posh people all talking posh, and sort of queeny, in queeny sort of voices, you was just a bloke.

"Would you have give me the offer of the job if I hadn't been with her?" He says.

"Yes," Jim says. "I had me eye on you for the last couple of weeks."

"Why?" He says, a bit hooked up.

"Sort of boy I'm looking for," Jim says. "Got the sense to go after Ada, for a start. I shan't cane your knees for that. Then you was a artist, so you knew a bit about art. That goes a long way, that does. Makes you go for the right sort of things, see? You don't have to be told. If it's a jeweller's window, for instance, you'd know what to look for if you was give the chance, wouldn't you? You wouldn't grab a tray of wedding rings if there was diamonds knocking about, would you?"

"No," He says, seeing that big diamond, up in the High Road, stretching out thin blue and red arms.

"That's it, see?" Jim says. "I can get millions of blokes. But what good are they?"

"Listen," He says, finishing off the drink, "do you reckon I'll ever come in a place like this on me own? I mean, and feel all right about it? Paying for me self, like?"

Jim shoved this bottle in the pot, neck down, and come over kind of impatient.

"Place like this?" Jim says, as if he had a shoeful. "Know what it was? It was a stables. Stables of a coach house, this was. Took 'em over cheap and tickled it up a bit, that's all. Got the neons cheap from a bloke in the mantle business, giving up. Pinched the cloth out of a warehouse. Nothing very hard about that, is there? Biggest cost was the flooring and the cooking stuff and knives and forks, and stuff like that. Place like this? What is it?"

Looked at like that, it never come to very much, all said and done. But it was still getting Him down, somehow.

"What about all these posh people, then?" He says. "What they come here for? And what about the bloke down the bottom on the fiddle. I still all right, am I?"

Jim had a long drink, and so did He.

"Depends how you look at it," Jim says, watching the waiter pulling a little cage off of the cork end of this bottle. "I know how you mean, though. Far's the money goes, you can come in here any night you like when you start working with my lot. You can always pick up a bride and bring her along. If you can't, ask Rossi for one of the hostesses. She'll take care of you. But if you want to get in with the lot who come here, you got your work cut out, I can tell you. It's a different sort of bloke, see? So's the brides. I can't tell you why. I can't say two words to them, me self. No time for them."

He got the idea Jim was climbing all round it.

"Why not?" He says.

"Do I know?" Jim says, proper scorched. "I got everything I'll ever want. Except one, that is. And that won't be long. But as for this lot, you can keep them. Look at 'em."

"What you two looking so happy about?" Ada says, squashing by His knees and sitting down between the pair of them. "Fell out have you?"

"Where you been?" Jim says, looking sideways.

"If you was a lady, I'd tell you," she says. "What about getting home?"

"I'm hanging on," Jim says, same voice. "Bit of business to attend to."

"Same here," she says, and He felt five of her beetles biting Him just above His knees.

Sweating hot, crushing under, not getting a breath, and His heart rocking wide from side to side in lumping bumps, one side swinging clean over and nigh touching the other, hurting deep down inside, all the living part of Him rolling up, and swelling, and beating, bumping, bashing in time to His heart, swinging to the brass plates crashing, and the trumpets tearing about, ripping up the air, making rags of smoke, and music, building up a falling madhouse of colours, no windows or doors, just holes with faces coming out, all singing and going back in again, sliding in and out on the saxes, climbing up and down amongst the trellis of the trumpets, rushing in and out in the crashing of the plates, swinging about in the arms of the lights, all splashing round in the wet pink swim, Him and all, with five red beetles biting into His knee and telling Him something as made His guts burn and bash and stretch and suck all the rest of Him out of His self, leaving Him nothing except His ears to listen with, and this flattish glass growing a solid shadow one side of it.

"Get sick of dancing, did you?" Jim says, somewhere near.

"Dancing?" she says, right up the top. "Wouldn't call that dancing, would you?"

"It's what they're here for," he says. "They like it, I suppose?"

"Don't see why they shouldn't," she says. "They can get nice and close, that's why."

"We have a go, shall we?" Jim says.

"Going home," Ada says, and starts looking for her bag.

Jim was laughing. In amongst all the row, you could hear him laughing.

"What," she says, "you got a feather round your neck, have you?"

"Not round me neck," he says. "I reckon it's funny, what's all. There's that bloody lot up the top there, all in bed, except they got their clothes on, and here's me, paying all the bills, can't even get me self a dance. It's like having a plateful of grub and no mouth."

"You bastard " she says, "you know how to pull at me, don't you?"

"Another glass of this?" Jim says, still laughing.

"No," she says. "Come on, Ernie. Take me home."

It struck Him proper funny the way she said it, like leaning on Him. Nobody else ever leaned on Him so it come all the queerer specially in this place, amongst all these posh people all dancing about and having a good time with their selfs, because He never ought to been there be rights. Got in because of the boss, not by His self, and not paying for a blind pennyworth, even though He had a nice bit of spending money on Him and a business of His own. Somehow or other He never seemed to get it right nor do it right.

"You'll have to take Him, by the looks of it," Jim says, loud and near, somewhere by the other shadow.

"You've made Him drunk, you rotten swine," she says. "I knew it might happen. Can't do nothing decent, you can't, Jim Mordinoy. Can't even let a bloke like Him alone, leave alone anybody else."

"Listen," He says, talking to the glass because it seemed to know. "You're wrong. Pair of you, wrong. See?"

The place and the band and lights was all in one lump, too heavy to hold or look through and sort of too slippery to catch, going side to side all the time. But the glass was hard enough, and the band was still playing away there, not worrying about nobody, just playing, like Ma Chalmers's wireless, whether you liked it or not. Trouble was, the words kind of slipped about, not staying where you could put your tongue to them, ducking you all the time. You could think of what you had to say but then the words greased out, letting you in for saying something else instead, knowing all the time you never wanted to say it, but not too sure.

He give it all up. The whole affair was a bit too much of a puzzler, but it was dead funny, no two ways about it, what with Jim out of it, and Him out of it, and the fiddle bloke getting the boot even if he nodded twice as much to thousands more posh people. Out of it, the lot of them. Dead funny, it was. Out of it, laughing away there, hollering and shouting, boozing their selfs up, like that crab crawling up and down the big fiddle, all nodding and ducking their nuts to Jim Mordinoy, and he was laughing the other side of his dial at Ada, while the brass plates was crashing and the fiddle bloke was scratching and all these posh people wagging their selfs about, all standing up in bed with their clothes on.

He see Ada in front of Him, and felt her pulling His arm, but though He wanted to say something, the words was all stuck together and none of them wanted to leave, so they stayed where they was and He let them go. Walking in this sticky pink air, across tables and chairs, all tangled up like Tiger Collis's place, climbing over and feeling Ada standing Him up again, with no legs or knees, only feet under Him, and all the faces had another face growing out of them, all eyes and smiles.

"You're a bright bloke to take out, you are," she says, shoving His hat on. "Half a spoonful of lemonade, and you're bandylegged. Now pull your silly self together."

"Okeedoke," He says, but His tongue was too big for His face.

Jim was holding Him one side putting Him in a taxi, cool in the black leather and quiet dark blue.

"Ernie," he says, just over the engine doing a bit of a dance in different tunes, "don't forget Monday morning, son!"

"Okeedoke, Jim," He says. "Shan't forget. Proper decent bloke, Jim. Straight up. Shan't forget."

"Not a word to Ada, mind?" Jim says. "She ain't in this?"

"Okeedoke," He says, and leaned His head back in the cold smelly leather, slipping down a bit, wanting to sleep, feeling the new shoes making things a bit hot for His feet across the bunions, and getting worried about the creases in the knees of His trousers because they was too tight, but His hands never got hold of enough stuff to pull them up.

# CHAPTER XXXI

COMING ALIVE in this moving box with the lights flipping Him across the eyes as they bounced by, He tried to make out what was on, but He was upended. He was laying down with His top half, and off the seat with His legs, and His head was in soft heat held down by two hands. The fingers was spread like the fence with a few planks missing, warm, cold, warmer, then all cold.

He knew by the scent it was Ada, living, breathing, warm and swelling soft, Ada.

"All right, Ernie?" she says, right above Him, like talking down to a kid.

"Shall be, in a minute," He says, not wanting to shift. He could feel the deep space between her legs, and that little bright steel clip thing was sticking in His cheek, but there was another heat that was hotter.

"My legs have gone to sleep," she says, proper hard done by. "I don't know how I'll ever stand me self up."

He sat up, nigh breaking every bone in His body.

"Sorry," He says. "I do anything, can I?"

"No, ta," she says, stretching her feet and rubbing her legs under her skirt. "Be all right in a minute. Have a good sleep, did you? Ain't had a sound out of you."

"I feel all about, I do," He says, getting the fog out of His mouth, and trying to get things working. "What sort of stuff was it I had, eh? Proper put me out, it did."

"That was champagne," she says, having a laugh. "Learn you not to get too clever another time, won't it?"

"Catch me," He says. "Can't make out why they drink it. They can't like it."

"Some of them do," she says, still laughing. "So do I. But it makes you talk too much. Have a nice time, did you, Ernie?"

"Lovely," He says. "Proper lovely night out, it was. Jim's a good bloke, you know, take him all round?"

"I'd like to take him all round a nice big hole and sling him in," she says. "I thought you'd have a bit more nous."

"He's all right to me, any rate," He says.

"That's only because you're going in the school," she says. "You'll be earning him a bit more cash, that's all."

"How do you know?" He says, proper surprised.

"Go out," she says, "I know all about it. You're only wasting your time. He's caught you."

"How has he?" He says, getting cold. "I can always get out, if it don't suit me?"

"Oh, so you was going, eh?" she says, nigh shouting, tearing hold of His collar and looking at Him in the dark. "You bloody little fool, you. You was caught, was you? He caught you, eh? Easy money? I could murder you. I got a bloody good mind to go back there and scratch his eyes out."

"Keep your hair on," He says. "It's my business, ain't it?"

She let go, and sat back in the dark, bouncing up and down and trying to keep away from Him. Sometimes the light looked in and caught her hair blowing about, and sometimes it laid down white alongside her stretched legs.

"Do what you like," she says, tired as the old year. "I let you in for this. It's all my fault."

"Go out of it," He says. "It was never your doings at all, any of it. Never even seen him with you not till tonight."

"My fault," she says. "You'll do time. He'll see you will. I know you will. Oh, Christ, I know you will."

He see a tear blob on the round of her cheek, and slip over the edge, running a narrow shining alleyway down in the dark of her hair, but there was no row about it. She cried quiet, just letting it go, and yet, when she breathed, she nigh on shook herself in halfs.

"Here, hold up," He says, "turn it in, me old china. You don't want to go like that, gel."

He wanted to say all the things He ever heard of, but He somehow never had the guts to say them for fear of looking a bigger mug than what He felt. He wanted to say Ada, darling, and Ada, my sweetheart, but when He got His tongue next to them, something inside of Him started curling up and burning all round the edges. But He had to say something because that sound was driving Him all hot and sort of barmy. Everything was going further and further away from Him.

"I'll do anything," He says, "straight up. Anything on Christ's earth, I will."

"It's no good," she says, in a proper deep way with herself. "Sides, I'm not crying for just you. I'm crying for the lot of you. Somebody's got to do it for you, if I don't. So leave me be."

Then she turned her head in the dark corner, and let it all go.

It was proper real, sitting in this bouncing little box, smelling petrol, and old fag ends and leather, and hearing Ada having it out with herself in the corner, but not believing it was her, yet knowing it was her, and being cold surprised. Before, she was always sort of far away, like that diamond in the High Road, all lovely, and giving you a weak smiling dying feeling, making you feel you only wanted to look, not touch nor nothing but just look, and right down inside you knew you could only look at it, but never get at it, even if you had it for keeps.

But Ma Sedgwiss was having a go in the corner alongside of her, and all.

All broke up and smashed about, like the old washing stand, not like Ada, looking at you sideways, with her hair almost over her face and parted over one shoulder, so as the skin come out like a round white egg with a gloss on it, making you want to kiss the dent where her chin was resting, while she was asking you to have a dance and her eyes was saying something else with a smile.

"Half a mo, gel," He says, and put His hand on her, just over the knee, but it was so wide and warm and soft, He took it away again, quick. "Ain't much sense about this, is there, eh? What's it for? Eh?"

"Ah, Christ," she says, and turns round, feeling about fo

ıer bag. "Nothing, I suppose. Depends on the way it takes me. Sometimes I could laugh at the lot of you and let you all go ınd have a run. Other times, I want to cry for the lot of you. That's all."

"But what for?" He says, up in the air.

"I got something at home as'll grow up like you, I suppose," ıe says, wiping up and looking out the window, but still shakıng about a bit. "Won't have a chance. But I'll tell you this ınuch. If ever I catch him down a Fun Fair, I'll strangle him. There you see. That's what I'll do to him."

"What you want to work down one for, then?" He says, to ry to get her off of the nasty side.

"If I didn't, I couldn't keep me eye on Jim, could I?" she ıays, as if it was like going indoors. "Sides, he's always been all ıght to me."

"Listen," He says. "First you say you hate the bloke, then ıe's all right. How do you make that out?"

"I'm sorry for him," she says, as if she spilt something on ıer dress. "Can't find nothing to do, he can't. And nobody ıkes him, and he knows they don't. So he just goes on getting ıorser, like. Proper gives me the creeps, sometimes, he does."

"What about other times?" He says, trying to see her face, ıut she was sitting too far off in the corner.

"I'll have to give up one of these days, I suppose," she says, ıust like closing a window. "Can't go on with a bloke like that ıfter you all the time, can you? He's bound to get you some ıme or other."

"I give up," He says. He still had this funny sort of feeling ıanging about Him, not quite sure if it was Him or some other ıloke, seeing things a bit queer, and not quite remembering ıho He was talking about. But all the time, He was proper ıırprised this was Ada, because she was just like any other ıride, not Ada at all, really. The far away Ada in the red jerıy, as never looked at nobody, nor cared who was looking, ıas nothing like this wrinkling warm ghost in the corner, ıouncing up and down and trying to wipe her face off, with ır hair flopping about worse than Ma's feathers.

"Give up what?" she says. "What you got to give up?"

"Nothing much," He says, but not knowing why He was saying it, any more than the bloke driving. "I reckon it's proper real the way things turn out, that's all. They ain't what they look like, are they?"

"How do you mean, Ernie?" she says, kind of worried, and coming so close, He could feel all the warm of her going through one side of Him. "You mean about me?"

"Well," He said, and He wished He could get rid of this funny going round and round feeling. Somehow, He had to dig His way through it, even to think. "Why did you have to go and live with that there fiddle bloke for a couple of years?"

"Told you, did he?" she says, and went dead quiet, as if it all run out of her.

"Yes," He says, and He knew He never had to say no more. This feeling of being dead while He was alive kept on coming back. Trying to keep His eyes open was hard enough, but it was cake beside trying to think things out sensible. Even the fiddle bloke was only a bloke, like the head and shoulders of the cab driver, black in the blue glass, while the lights was reaching out and giving the three of them a dab of their whitewash brushes every time they passed.

"Never thought he'd be so mean," she says, proper half closing day, everything shut and the blinds all down. "But that's him, all right. Say it to hurt his own self, he would."

"Who's worried?" He says. "What's done's done, ain't it?"

"Yes," she says. "It's done, all right. I've got a kiddie three year old. Wouldn't be without him, though, never mind what they've said. Say it all again, I'd still have him."

"Call him Clem?" He says.

"Course," she says. This little bouncing, rattling box got full up of blokes all of a sudden. Clem Arbiter in his dancing suit with the diamonds giving everybody a nice big wink, and Jim in his hat and the silk scarf, and all the blokes in the band all playing away there, and all the blokes down the Fun Fair, an Bert Clively and Len Tate, all sitting down having a smoke and watching points, and that there crab was dancing up and down the big fiddle somewhere nigh His earhole.

"It's a proper game, ain't it?" He says.

"Played slow," she says. "Wish I knew then what I know now, though. But I was a bit too soppy, I suppose. You ain't too clever when you're sixteen, you know? Everything's so marvellous."

"I never noticed it," He says.

"Blokes are different," she says. "I had all sorts of people taking me out. Buying me things. Scent, and everything. Girls like nice things, you know?"

"Yes," He says, and He could see old Charlie wagging his head over the gardenias.

"Trouble is," she says, "once you get used to them you don't like getting rid of them. You want to keep them. A bathroom, for instance. I've cried over losing my bathroom, I have. All pink and black, it was. Lovely hot water all day. And bath salts. It's different for a bloke. But once you're used to it, you can't go back to a couple of bloody pails in the scullery. You soon get fed up of that lark, I can tell you. Sides everything else."

"What you want to leave it for then?" He says.

The cab driver shoved the half window open and tried to talk through the hole, but the wind took all the words away.

"Second on the right," Ada says. "Do us lovely."

"We home, are we?" He says, proper surprised.

"As good as," she says. "If you can call it home, that is."

"Why don't you get out of it, then?" He says. "That ought to be easy?"

"Course it's easy," she says, like having a wallop at a blue-bottle. "But what d'you reckon Jim might do?"

"Get the lamp duffers out," He says, and then He could have kicked His self.

She had Him by the arm, digging her nails in Him, right through the cloth.

"What you know about the lamp duffers?" she says, nigh howling again, all eyes and breath, pulling Him about.

"Only what I been told," He says, keeping it down to try and get her to rights. "What you worried about them for?"

She let go of Him, slinging Him away from her like rolling up the paper after she had her fish and chips. He see the tears was on again, but He made out He never see them.

"Here?" the cab driver says, and pulls up.

"Okeedoke," He says, and opened the door.

"Fare's fixed up," the cab driver says. "Mr Mordinoy see me fore we started."

"Okeedoke," He says, and lobbed him a fag. In the orange light of the match He see this bloke watching Him proper chancey.

"What's up?" He says, none too nice.

"Nothing," this bloke says, going for the gears. "Only used to drive Miss Ada home many a time. Not round here though. So long."

"So long," He says, not too sure He liked the way it was said, as if it was a proper old come down for all concerned.

She was right down the road when He looked round for her, just like a tall white ghost going away from the lamplights but only a black shape in between, so it come a bit hard to think was Ada He was running to catch up with. He kept on seeing that red jersey.

"Didn't you want me to see you home?" He says. "You only had to say so."

"Now don't you start," she says, not looking round, and He could see she was just tying a bit of string round her self, like "I've had just about the lot for tonight, thanks. I don't want hear another blind word out of nobody, else I'll scream th bloody place down."

He slowed up alongside of her, feeling like a kid trotting his Ma, hanging on the shopping bag and trying to keep up Everything seemed to have gone all cold in between ther There was none of that kind of soft voice about her, no smile no holding hands, and the beetles was all in their hutches. started Him off feeling proper rotten again, hating everythin

He could see and feel and hear, and everything He knew, even her, because she was so far off.

It come over Him, while He was looking along the road at a little white light, right down the end, on the corner. Only a little white light, it was, winking away there, proper saucy, pretending to be a diamond, shooting out sparks, and long bright feelers all round it, just like the couple the fiddle bloke had in his shirt.

"Listen," He says, "why don't you go back to that fiddle bloke and chance it?"

"Think I want him bashed?" she says, quick, in a right old tear. "Think I left him for? Fun?"

"Well, go to the police, then," He says. "They'll take care of him, won't they?"

"Ah, shut up," she says. "You know Jim'll do what he says he will. I only left him to save him getting bashed. That's why he won't look at me. He knows."

"Why don't the pair of you go away out of it, then?" He says.

"Gone too far, now," she says. "Too late. He's got over me. Sides, he thinks I'm living with Jim."

"He must be a mug," He says. "I bet I wouldn't let no Jim talk me out of nothing. And if he tried duffing my lamp, I'd set about duffing his. That's fair, ain't it?"

"Listen," she says, so tired she could hardly stand up. "The lamp duffers are a dozen to one. It ain't just a case of getting bashed. They'll do for a bloke. Shove him over a bridge when they've done him, and all. Don't tell me. I know."

They turned off the High Road, going down a little road with trees either side, all pale green where the lamps shone through them, making raggedy yellow and black patterns on the pavement. Up on the right, a big block of flats come up square black against the sky, chopped up by some of the lighted windows.

Watching a light up in a top floor, He got the idea again, twice as strong.

"Listen," He says. "Supposing this fiddle bloke goes to Blackpool. You be any happier, would you?"

She never said nothing for a few steps, and then she stopped, and leaned against the stone ledge with her back on the short railings.

"How can I be happy?" she says, and here come the water-works again. "I can't bear to see him, and I can't bear not to. While he's near, I want to be with him. If he goes up there, I'll go mad and have to start chasing up there, too, I suppose. But only to see him. If he was anywhere else, it'd be the same. If he was dead, I'd forget him. Oh, Christ, I'm sick of my rotten self, I am. I do, I wish I was out of it."

Tearing her self in halfs, she was, with them iron spikes digging in her back. He see all the rounds, and ins, and outs of her, where them shadowy bumps was, under her coat, and where they rounded in to her waist, and then come out, and out, and out, all round, and dropping in again, down and down in pouring shiny white.

But He kept on seeing that diamond light, even where the lamp reached out, painting a big grey V below the flat bulge of her, dabbing a couple of grey splashes under them two little clip things on the tops of her stockings. But the in and out round shape of her where her coat fell away sort of reached inside Him, and poked at Him, making Him feel all sloppy and shaking about, even though all the time He see them sparks of the diamond in the nick of the backsight getting covered over with that little black bit on the end of the rifle.

He knew He could do it. He could smack five of them little grey holes all round any one of them diamonds any time of the day or night, easy as eating your dinner. He come over all kind of hot and boiling over inside, proper sure of His self for once in His life, feeling as if He just grew a new skin twice as big as the old one, full of muscle and all of it yelling to have a good go.

He went up to her, standing flat against her, putting His hands on the tight warm waves swelling out below her waist, feeling without pressing how steady it was, no flop or fat, but just steady swelling rounds as went from side to side when she walked away from you.

"Listen," He says. "Don't get worried about no lamp duffers. Do a bit of worrying about yourself, for a change. If you don't want to marry Jim, hop off out of it. There's plenty of blokes ready to lay down and let you walk on 'em."

"What about my kiddie?" she says, quiet as a mouse. "The only job I can do and earn anything like decent money's down the Fun Fair. I don't want to go down the club again."

"Why not?" He says. "If that's what you like?"

"Only end up one way," she says. "It don't take long, you know? And once you're in, you can't get out. The only other thing's a maid, or office cleaner, or something in that sort of line. Work your self skinny for a few bob a week. What for?"

All the pale green leaves in front of the lamp light looked as if they was smiling away, nice and quiet, sure as He was. Even when the wind come blowy and roughed them all up, it still kind of smiled away up there, just as sure.

Five little grey holes all round the diamond.

"But what you worried about me for?" she says, a bit shirty. "You got enough to do to worry about yourself, I should think."

"Take care of me self." He says. "But it ain't fair on you, this ain't."

"What ain't?" she says.

"Well," He says. "All this business. You know, Jim, and that there bloke, and what all. You didn't ought to be worried like that, you didn't. You ought to have a nice sort of place of your own. Done out proper. Decent bit of furniture, like, and things. Somebody to take care of you. Bash the first bastard even looked at you."

She got up off of the railings and leaned warm against Him for a couple of ticks. He was so done up with what was going on inside of Him, He never knew what to do for the best.

"Let's get somewhere softer," she says. "That there railing's corpsing me. Round here."

He could feel all them beetles on His hand where she had

Him, taking Him down a dark little cut between the flats. There was only a narrow band of darkish blue over the top where the sky was pasted on.

"Can't go up," she says. "Might wake him up, then Ma'll wake up. Then there'll be another slanging match first thing in the morning."

"Why didn't we go down the studio?" He says, proper kicking His self. "Bags of room all to our selfs. Tea, sandwiches, everything."

"And a nice big sofa for getting painted on," she says. "Don't tell me, I knows all about it. That's why we never went."

"What you grousing about, then?" He says, a bit put out, because she was on the ball too fast every time.

"I don't like to be took nowhere just to get painted, that's why," she says, as if she was pulling His leg, and He could see the smiles was there. "If there's any painting going to be done, I'll have a hand in it, see? But I don't like nobody telling me the tale, nor I don't want taking nowhere to have it told. See? Now what you got to say?"

"Nothing," He says, and all of a sudden He wanted to go home and get shut of her, even though she was Ada, leaning up against Him, putting her bare arm round His neck, clipping it in a cool, soft scarf, as seemed to have a bit of rubber in it.

"Now what you going to do about it?" she says, and that warm waterfall was pouring again, wearing away all the sharp bits inside of Him.

"Going home," He says.

"Give us a goodnight kiss, then, just for luck," she says, and there was sort of millions of little gold bubbles in her voice, cracking it up, and He could feel how warm her face was, even though she was a inch or so away. Standing against her got like being part of her, fitting into her all the way down, except from the knees, so want to or not, His hands come out of His pockets without being told and found their way round her waist, under her coat, feeling the steady curving warm of her, pressing the soft give of her weight flatter to Him.

He felt the gentle surprise of her cheek and the tip of her nose when He turned His head, and the dry edges of her lips was almost sharp, but all of a sudden they opened in a warm yawn and come down flat on His mouth in a hot O with a cool rim all round it.

Holding her, with her scent burning the air sweet all round, a sort of sleep come over Him making His eyes shut, not because He was tired, but for going kind of dead and wanting to die with her, like they was, both together, so close, He could hardly think how they ever got on without each other, like two halfs of a apple going brown out of heartbreak.

The dreams about the green plaster girl was nothing like this, because she only stood there looking up at the sky, not at you, letting you do what you wanted, but here, somebody else was doing what she wanted to do, and that little cherry as kept on playing hide and seek with His tongue seemed to be asking Him to try something on His own.

But when He moved, she lifted her head and He felt the cold air on the wet round His mouth.

"Ain't a lot of sense in this, is there?" she says. "Just making it worse, that's all."

"I don't mind, if you don't," He says, a bit disappointed, because she sounded as if it was like something for tea. "I'm cushy."

"Ever been in love, Ern?" she says, looking down this passage way in the dark.

"Only with you," He says, feeling a proper mug.

"Yes," she says, both feet, only laughing with it, "they're all in love till they've had you in bed. Then it don't matter. You like that, are you?"

He wagged His head, because He had His mouth against the soft of her cheek with her hair blowing all round Him, and He never wanted to let go.

"It's a proper game," she says, and pulled Him in closer. "I don't know what to make of it. If we was two other people, we'd be all right. But I'm no good to you and you're no good to me. We're just wasting our time, that's all. Ain't we?"

"I ain't," He says. "Wouldn't shift for a million pound, not a inch."

"I like you," she says, while the beetles was scratching round the back of His neck, and He knew she was having a smile from the crack in her cheek. "You're quiet and you don't chuck your weight about, do you? Eh? Just nice, quiet little Ernie boy. With a look in His eyes. I ought to be kind to you, didn't I?"

Her voice was changing, going off to whispers as got mixed up in the sound of her hair blowing about, and the warm rounding and rising shape as fit Him was moving sort of inside itself, as if all them little muscles, shadow and not, come and go, was all having a game on their own.

"What you got to be kind to me about?" He says. "I'm all right."

"I know," she says, like telling somebody to go to sleep. "You're all right. So's my little bloke upstairs, there. But I'd like to know somebody's going to be kind to him one of these days. You get in such a state on your own, sometimes. Don't you? Eh, Ern?"

"Don't you?" He says, not quite sure what she was at.

"Course," she says, same voice, but laughing again. "That's why it's such a game. You don't want to, and yet you've got to, somehow. Go round for weeks and weeks all screwed up. Afraid somebody's going to touch you the wrong way, and start you off. Think I don't know?"

"What about Clem?" He says.

"What about that other swine?" she says, and He could have kicked His self, because she went all stiff again, and almost got clean away from Him. "No use thinking about him. I've done too much of it. Only it comes over me sometimes. Then it's hard."

"Like now?" He says.

She nodded, looking down the passage way, and He felt her shake only a little bit, but He knew she was crying again, quiet, just letting it run.

He let go of her, leaning against the bricks, feeling them pull at His new coat and not caring, looking up at the dark blue road above the house tops. The thoughts of her being like she was just about made Him go proper mad. He could feel it inside of Him. He wanted to put His arms, not only round her, but all round where she was ever likely to be, or go, like a thick wall, keeping everybody away from her, stopping her getting hurt, never letting her cry again or knowing even what tears was.

"Still," she says, "it's no good of acting about like this. I always was a silly mare. Only, I don't know. Something comes over me. What you standing over there for?"

"What you do, when it gets too hard?" He says, staying where He was.

"Chew the sheets," she says, as if it was just ordinary. "Get up and make a cup of tea. Read. Anything. What you do?"

"Have to be told?" He says, but not wanting to.

She come at Him like a clawing black wind, grabbing Him, both arms round Him, half biting, half kissing, and there was cold between her pressing weight till it started getting warm again, but the beetles had gone and her fingers was holding His head, both hands tight, and her cheek was denting His, hard, between the times she kissed and turned and kissed and turned, then both her hands was over His ears and she was looking at Him.

"Let's find a place, quick," she says, whispering through the funny dull noise in His ears, rocking His head about like a ball. "Come on."

She let go and put her arms tight round Him in a right squeeze, and when He breathed, He got the weak salt taste of other tears.

This large white flash hit Him a blinding smashing bluish wallop bash in the eyes, same time He felt the inch more grip of her arms and the stiff straight stand of her.

"What you think you're doing?" some bloke says, not too loud, so He knew it was a copper behind the light.

"Nothing," He says, trying to look, but it was too whitey blue.

"Funny kind of nothing, ain't it?" this copper says, still with the light on. "Where do you live?"

"Here," Ada says, shaking like with cold, but not shifting, with her back to him.

"I could hear you right down the bottom, there," the copper says. "You want to be more careful. Where do You live?"

"Off the Kingsland Road," He says, loud, wanting to have a go, quick, and kick his voice quiet, but her arms gripped Him that much more.

"You want to get off down there, then," the copper says, and the light went out, like a smack across the face. "Just get it over, and get off home."

He heard the rubber feet go by, like squeaks with a weight on them, squashing out the sound.

There was a dribble of water down a drain pipe somewhere, but the dark blue road still run quiet along between the tops of the flats, and everything else was just black.

She shoved her self away from Him, holding Him off with two strong straight arms.

"They won't let you alone nowhere," she says, proper letting go and not worrying who heard, "even among the bloody dust-bins. Even down here. Can't even kiss, or say goodnight, nor nothing. I don't want to live. Christ Almighty. I don't want to live."

She was going up the stairs, pulling her self up the iron railing, and He could hear the soft ding of it as her hands let go and went on up, in front of her scraping feet, and the sound of her pulling the breath back in her throat, and the roughing of her walk through her dress.

The door shut, and that was the lot.

He was left in the dark, not knowing where He was, and not caring, but His guts was so sore, He had to laugh at His self trying to walk. Come to a finish, He was proper killing His self of laughing and down in the little road, where the leaves was still smiling pale clear green through the lamp light, He had to sit down where she sat, and Him and the leaves and the lamp light all had a laugh together.

He see the funny side of it, somehow, though He could see how He ought to be feeling sorry for His self, and Ada, but the more He tried to see it, the more He had to chase it, till He give it up and let it go.

But He see that diamond with five little grey holes round it clear enough, and thinking of it seemed to make things that much better, so He started off home in a good heart, even though He had to walk pretty slow.

But in amongst a lot of messing and playing about, He see it was a job He could do, and write off, without no arguments, no hanking about, no worrying or any of that stuff.

Them five little holes would clear it all up, like cabbage water going through the strainer, and the sooner the better.

It was on.

# CHAPTER XXXII

MA WAS YELLING downstairs when He woke up, sweating hot, with the blankets all anyhow, so He had to fight to get His self out, wondering if He was late for work or if there was a fire, and wishing He took His clothes off before getting in bed because of the fluff all over them and the bags and creases in His trousers.

"Aggie Hunner's just sent across, Ern," she was yelling. "Ern? You wake, are you? Hear me, Ern?"

"Who wouldn't?" He shouted her, in a right old fit, seeing His self proper sprat eyed in the round glass.

"Well," she says, as if she only wanted to know, "wants you to go over and see her. If you get time, she says. You going?"

"Don't know, yet," He says. "What's she want?"

"Do I know?" Ma yells. "You just crawl out of it, and find out, my lad. Your breakfast's ready."

He leaned His head again the wall, just like He always done ever since He was little, in the same darkish place nigh the pillow, feeling sort of weakish, as if He slept a bit too long, looking up at the fag ends stuck to the ceiling, hanging down like little teeth with black tips. Soon as He started thinking a bit, He wanted a fag, so He pulled the butt ends out of His waistcoat pocket and picked out the longest, getting a match out of the candlestick and scratching it down the wall a few times till it come up a light. He always found the first few drags at a butt end, first thing of a morning, was proper tasty, even if taking it down too deep made everything slide round and round and bob up and down, sort of giddyish.

"Don't hear nothing shifting up there, yet?" Ma yells, out of the kitchen. "Got the cramps, have you?"

"Give us a chance," He shouts, up at the fag ends. "Ain't got four hands, have I?"

"Use two," she screeches back. "You won't do so bad."

He never knew what to say back, so He just give her a ahhh out the side of His mouth, had another drag at the fag, got it set just nice between His thumb and middle finger, and shot it up to join all the others on the ceiling. It give Him a right treat to see it stick there steady as if it been nailed.

Then it come a job to get out and take one suit off, and put the other on, so He made it the nigger brown, and changed His tie, give the brown shoes a polish round on the end of the bedclothes, and hopped downstairs, making as much row as He could to let her know things was happening.

"Wonder what she wants?" He says, while He was having a sluice round. "Bit queer, ain't it?"

"You don't want to go getting too pally there, if you ask me," Ma says, as if she could niff something a bit ripe. "See what she wants and let it go at that, I would. See?"

"Okeedoke," He says, but He was thinking about the way she said goodnight.

"In late, wasn't you?" Ma says, pouring out, while He was dipping bread in tomatoes and bacon fat.

"Had a look round up the West End," He says.

"Won't find much up there," Ma says. "That's a proper hole, that is. So's the people."

"That's what I thought," He says. "Still, you got to find out, ain't you?"

"As long as you don't find out too much," Ma says. "You stick to your own neighbourhood, then you can't go far wrong. Start getting yourself tooling about up there, and you'll be following your father. Then we shan't be long."

"Not me, Ma," He says, seeing Jim and The Lucky Seven a bit too plain. "I'll hop over and find out what Aggie wants."

"Anything to do with business, tell her to see me," Ma says. "Anything else, give it the go by."

"What am I going over there for, then?" He says. "Might's well stop here, eh?"

Ma started slapping the plates together, all feathers and grabbing hands.

"Might be in trouble and nobody to turn to," she says. "We don't want no more of the Sedgwiss lark, do we?"

He see two fists stuck in a screaming mouth and Chaser going down in shining pale blue mud.

"Okeedoke, Ma gel," He says, and got out the back door, glad to have a look at ordinary things and get His mind straight again.

The road was proper Sunday morningy, full of bits of paper playing ringaroses, quietish all round, and sort of lazy grey, as if even the bricks knew everybody was still in snore, or just getting their selfs sorted out. Some kids was standing outside Ma Crann's in their Sunday best, looking in the sweets window and trying to make up their minds how to spend their half-pennies, and He see His self doing it with them, years before, so He knew the arguments off by heart because they was still the same sorts of sweets in the same old saucers and glasses, and even the same old tickets.

Aggie opened the door in two ticks, as if she been squatting on the mat.

"Ernie," she says, all smiles and eyes, "didn't disturb you, did I? Hope I never, anyhow."

"No," He says. "I was mending something. What's up?"

"Like to go somewhere with me?" she says, going in the kitchen. "How about going to the Tate Gallery after lunch? See your Dad's picture, eh?"

"Course," He says, and all of a sudden He wanted to go, just to see what made people say the Old Man was a great artist. "What time?"

"Two o'clock," she says. "I'll be waiting outside."

"That's me," He says. "But we better not tell Ma. She ain't too gone on it, see? Got anything I can mend for you?"

"Couple of bows," she says, having a laugh. "But be careful with them, won't you?"

"Won't touch 'em," He says. "Just to get me in and out without a lot of awkward questions. That's all. So long, Ag."

She give Him a couple of thick scrapers out of a case in the passage, and a pat on the back for luck, and in the feel of her hand He got the same feeling as when she said goodnight, but He never let on.

Outside, old Charlie Pool was coming along on his Sunday round with the pony and cart, leaving little round lumps of blue cloud behind him from the flamer, going strong, as per. You could have seen them miles off for polish and paint, to say nothing of the ribbons in Lady's hair, and her straw hat with rosettes on it what her ears poked through. Proper proud of Lady and the cart, old Charlie was. Dressed his self up of a Sunday and come out to sell his fruit round the pubs, doing a rare old trade, and all. People liked to see him, because you could tell there was a lot of hard work in the turnout. But it paid him, and if you wanted proof, you only had to look at the driving seat, and you see all the prizes he won at the Horse Shows, specially up Regents Park, nailed in lines from side to side, going back years and years.

"What, me Ernie boy?" he shouts Him. "How's Ma?"

"Okeedoke," He says. "Got my stuff, have you?"

"Think I got here, then?" he yells. "Couple of ton of bloody coals?"

"Just asking," He says.

"What, Charlie boy," Ma shouts, out of the shop door. "Ern, give these bits of sugar to Lady. How's trade, Charlie?"

"Can't grumble," Charlie says, "been worse. All right with you, me old china?"

"Ain't bad," Ma says. "Could be better. How's the Mrs?"

"One of her legs again," Charlie says, giving her this basket of stuff. "This is from your hopeful, here. Doing it proud. Don't blame Him. Like His Ma, He is. All right."

"What's this?" Ma says, looking proper up the garden.

"Half a dozen glass growed Kents, and a lovely little pine," Charlie says, puffing out fly killer. "Don't be afraid of 'em. Picked 'em out me self. Nothing better on the board of any duke. Eating the pride of the land in them, you are. Sweets of nature. Can't go wrong. Apple a day keeps the doctor away. Early to bed, early to rise, drive you straight up the bloody pole. So long, Ma."

"So long," she says, but she was looking at Him, not listening, and she looked as if she was going to start howling any minute.

"Buy these for me?" she says, looking up the road.

"Yes," He says, wiping Lady's spit off of His hand.

"Get a flagon up the corner, will you?" she says, going in. "Pay you when you come back."

But He knew, all the way up to the Off License, she no more wanted beer with her dinner than fly in the air. She just wanted Him out of it, and He felt proper pleased with His self about it. But she never said nothing when He come back, nor she never even asked how much she owed Him, so He wondered whether He was right or wrong, or how.

"Going up for my little forty," she says, after dinner. "Back for tea?"

"About five," He says, looking round the paper. "I do anything, can I?"

"I'd faint if you did," she says, and off she went, humming the same tune as Ma Chalmers's wireless.

He sat there thinking it over a bit, not making head nor tail of it, and round about two, He give it up and went outside to meet Aggie. She was on the corner, in a square shouldered black coat, with a black hat like a cone, making Him feel He wanted to walk a couple of yards away from her, so as not to look as if He was with her.

Off the bus, not saying too much, because He was thinking a lot, they went along smelling the river for a bit, then she turned up towards another kind of a church, up some steps and inside the same sort of affair as Old Nick took Him in, kind of spacey and dead, very quiet, where you felt it was Three Months Hard if you even sneezed.

"Now then," she says, proper excited, "shall we have a look all round, Ernie, or make it a pilgrimage?"

"What you said," He says. "Only don't make it too long. I ain't got too much time."

"See your father's picture and come out, eh?" she says. "All right. We come here for that, and that's what we'll do. Won't look at nothing else at all."

She went off to ask some old tart at the desk some questions while He was watching blokes taking in brollies and what all in the cloakroom, then she give Him the nod and started off.

"Down here," she says, so He followed the wobbling black of her down these kind of passages lined with pictures, wondering where it was going to stop, turning corners, pushing past people, going through big rooms, all grey light, making you feel pale, walking on wooden floors as made your feet click.

"Now then," she says, and pulled up beside a picture about two foot wide by a yard high, all greens, pinks, and yellows, with a splash of blue and bright red.

He could feel all His skin come up tight and freezing, screwing Him smaller, skinnier, going dry inside, making Him scrape round for a drop of spit to wet the sand in the back of His throat.

The bloke in the flat hat pulled down one side, looking in the round looking glass, was His self, in a long sort of blue blouse, painting away with a red tipped brush, looking one side at this bride, looking straight at Him, young, same size as the green plaster girl, but her eyes was nothing like He ever seen them before, a proper light blue with a big joke in them, just looking at you, laughing away there, without a rag or a stitch on her, and not worried who was looking or what was thought, and enjoying it a treat.

Without the asking, He knew it was Ma. He knew why she put the green plaster girl in the dustbin.

But He was afraid to look at her. He kept on looking somewhere else, but seeing the two big round pink flowers, and all the ins and outs of her, and not wanting to look again, and yet having to, like it or not, and all the time He never knew where to put His face.

"He was an artist, you know, Ernie?" Aggie says. "It's beautiful, isn't it?"

"Not bad," He says.

"Not bad?" she says. "It's perfect. Look at that girl's skin. It's alive."

"Yes," He says, looking at the Old Man, seeing the square tip on his nose and the grey, sideways look in the eyes. "Fancy that being my old man, eh?"

"Nice looking, wasn't he?" she says, bending down to get a better look. "Just like you. But the girl's lovely, too. Sort of figure I've always wanted. But if you start off with bad legs, you're ruined for life. You can lose your waist line and all that, but if your legs are all right, they're all right till you're ninety."

"Ain't your legs no good, then?" He says, for something to say.

"Try finding out," she says, having a laugh. "Ask your Ma who she was, Ernie. She must have been somebody interesting, I should say. She must have inspired him."

But He knew He never had the guts to even say a word to Ma about it, or tell her He been anywhere nigh the place. But He was proper knocked out how she changed. He kept on seeing her shape in the kitchen, and looking at her in the picture. It was another world. Somebody else, as borrowed a face from Ma and never give it back again.

"I could look at it all night," she says.

"I've had my share," He says. "Sides, I've got to see a bloke, soon. Won't mind, will you?"

"No," she says, but He could see she was nowhere nigh best pleased. "Let's come up again one Sunday, eh? Then we'll have a good look round and try and get a guide to take us round, and see if we can learn something. What say?"

"Don't mind," He says, but He was making for the door double time, and Ma was still a foot high, in His pocket but kicking a hole in the back of His head.

She was talking all the way back, but He never heard a lot of it. What with thinking about Ma and the way she was once, and then Ada jumping up here and there, He never had too much of a chance to listen. He got something about going to concerts of a Sunday afternoon, and hearing artists playing the piano and what all, but it sounded such a load of junk, He just sort of turned over and had a think for His self.

All of a sudden He got a proper itch to go and see Ada. He knew He been wanting to, ever since He woke up, but it was a better feeling to let it come up on its own, like, instead of just thinking about it, because then, instead of hanging about making the place look untidy, thinking about when, you just got it, and went.

"Listen," He says, cutting all the ends off, "I'm getting off here, see? Thanks for the afternoon. Been grand. See you in the week, eh? Can't keep this bloke hanging about."

"Come over when you feel like it, Ernie," she says. "Always welcome. In the week, eh?"

"Okeedoke, Aggie," He says. "So long."

Getting off of the tram and chasing down the High Road was nigh on as good as getting home late at night wondering what was for supper, but hopping down the Fun Fair stairs was better than having your grub. He see His self in the glass, surprised how posh He looked, and when He give His tie a pull round, and got His hair nice, He reckoned He was just about the last word.

He tore through the dart stalls and all the nonsense, shoving past everybody, rushed through the alley, and run through the crowd in the big room, hearing the music coming up and getting sort of drunk on it, feeling it soak in Him, and pulled up dead.

There was a different bride in her place.

He done it a bit careful for a minute or two, thinking she might be having her tea, or down the Ladies, but it was no go.

"Where's Ada today?" He says to this new bride. "Day off, has she?"

"No," she says, "ain't come in at all. Probably down Brighton, if the truth's known."

"What you mean, Brighton?" He says, wanting to slosh her one in the chops.

"You heard," she says, and went on knitting, but He knew

she give the eye to the bloke as called in the chuckers out, so He give her a good look and a spit, to show her what He thought of her, and went for the alley again.

The flat singing smack of the rifle range pulled Him up just outside Madame La Zaka's, watching the blue eyes in the skull, listening to them little grey bullets singing and smacking up and down just round the corner, and the idea come up so strong, He could hardly see where He was looking, never mind about going.

Five little grey holes round the diamond would cure everything. He heard her crying again, and see the Lucky Seven, hearing the brass plates, seeing the crab dancing about, listening to Jim and not hearing what he was saying.

But He could hear Ada.

The thoughts of her come up and drownded out the lot of them, and the music was all on His side, sort of slow and sleepy, making you want to give up and just think about laying in bed, in the warm, not caring about nobody.

The bloke running the range see Him round the corner and tipped Him the wink, so He went round, getting the idea full strength.

"Listen," He says, talking before the bloke had a chance, "we got a bloody cat or something getting in after our chickens. How about the loan of one of these? Just for a night or two? Eh? Bring it straight back?"

The bloke looked a bit umpty, turning his mouth down, shaking his head, and generally carrying on there as if it give him the creeps to think about it.

"Sorry," he says. "Ain't allowed. More than my job's worth, that is. Couldn't even do it me self, let alone you."

"Okeedoke," He says, "I'll see Jim about it."

"Jim?" this bloke says, looking at Him both eyes at once. "Jim Mordinoy?"

"Course," He says, and started to go.

"Half a mo," this bloke says, "that's all right. Only I got to be careful, see? I can give you one of the repairs. That'll be all right."

"Okeedoke," He says. "Long as it'll do the job, I'm cushy."

"Guaranteed," the bloke says. "How many rounds you want? Twenty be enough?"

"Ought to cure 'em, didn't it?" He says. "When shall I come round for it?"

"After we close?" the bloke says. "Have to go careful how you take it home, though. If a copper sees you, it's a pinch. Then how do I go on?"

"Leave it to me," He says, "I ain't worried about no coppers."

"Going to have a card?" the bloke says. "I can do a nice dollars-worth, here."

"Better keep me hand in, I suppose," He says.

"Here you are, gents," this bloke yells, "the district champion out for His Sunday's airing. Take ten to one He'll put five straight through the black. Any money you like. Learnt His self here, on this here very range. Go anywhere round the world, take care of His self and His family. Respected wherever He goes. Respected. Hear that? Respected, I said. Eyes down. Look in. Fire when you like, sir."

It was proper marvellous how that there black spot got smaller soon as you got the sights on it, and then, all of a sudden, started shining all colours, just like a diamond. He could feel the quiet, and He knew the blokes behind Him was looking at Him like He looked at Jim, thinking He was a right boy, proper knob on, knowing His stuff and doing it right. While He was flicking the lever to get the little copper case flying out, He was thinking about Ada and the dustbins, and wishing it was tomorrow to get cracking down the garage.

## CHAPTER XXXIII

EVEN THE COPPER never knew where Ermington Street was, but He soon found out it was a goodish walk from the Angel, round a lot of turnings, in and out of a lot of other streets, and the further He went, the more kids there was playing in the road, and getting swore at by the drivers, just like round His way, only somehow different.

Tattamy's Garage was in between a newspaper shop and a boot repairers, and going through the arch, over the cobbles, you got a smell of a lot of leather in the piece, creeping in and out of petrol, and the deeper, breathy smell of oily rags and drips in the road.

Jim was down there in another suit, with his hat on the back of his head, talking to a couple of blokes in dungarees, standing round a big car with the rear wheel off. A couple more blokes come out, quiet, from nowhere, giving Jim the thumb soon as they see Him.

"Customer here," one of them says.

Jim took his foot off of the fender and give Him a big smile.

"Ah, this is the bloke I was telling you about," he says. "Name of Mott. Ernie boy, this is Cosh Simmons."

Cosh, a big bloke with gloves on, give Him a shut eye wink.

"How she go, Ernie boy?" he says.

He only had a few teeth when he smiled, looking as if they was filed down, and coloured dark blue and brown to taste.

"This is Slush Yatley," Jim says, thumbing the other bloke. The other two made their selfs scarce.

"Is He a buyer, or one of the young ladies?" Slush says.

"Joining the academy," Jim says. "Going to learn something off of you, I hope?"

"Ah," says Cosh, "well, He'll have to get here earlier, then. Eight o'clock tomorrow, Ernie boy. Don't keep gentlemen's hours round here. Can't afford 'em. See?"

"Okeedoke," He says.

"Better come on round and see what's going on, eh?" Cosh says, and goes inside the garage.

They went in and out a lot of proper smashing cars, big, and all polish and disc wheels, some ready, and some jacked up with their bonnets off, through a back door and out in a small yard. A double gate, wide open, showed a lane running left and right of it, with a high wall on the other side, stuck full of broken glass along the top.

A big car was tearing down the lane, all out, from the sound of it.

"Get down," yelled Slush, nipping behind the gate. "This is it."

The driver must have put the brakes on a good fifty feet before he got to the gate, because the car screamed as if somebody was sticking a knife in it.

Four blokes come rushing through the gate, and all of a sudden He see a big sheet of glass held up in a frame at the back of the yard, with some cigar boxes and small pellets of silver paper on ledges behind it, just like a shop window.

The first bloke slung a jack through the glass, but it never went hard enough, and the glass just cracked a bit at the bottom. The bloke behind him had a hammer and a bag, the third one went to the back door and stood there, and the fourth one stood a bit away from the rest of them, just looking round.

Cosh looked at Jim as if he was just going to give birth, and took a long draw at his fag.

"Would you bleeding well adam and eve it, eh?" he says, proper giving it up. "Been at it a week, and just look at 'em."

"Ain't too bright, are they?" Jim says. "No wonder they get pinched."

The bloke with the jack was looking proper sorry for his self.

"Done it all wrong again, Cosh," he says. "Sorry, Mr Mordinoy."

Cosh give him a proper mouthful, and stopped while Jim was lobbing out the fags.

"If I've told you once, I've told you a million times to get your left arm straight, and a foot away from the pane," he says, quiet, slow, sort of knocking the words in with a mallet. "Then you bring your right arm up and over, and let the jack go, and you'll have just enough time to get your bonse under your coat when the lumps start flying about. As for you," he says, to the bloke with the little bag and the hammer, "you had a hammer in your bleeding hand, but you never did nothing with it, did you? Soon as the jack goes, you ought to be there with your hammer. Get rid of any odd bits, grab your stuff and get out. You," he says, to the third bloke by the door, "ought to have been inside the doorway, not picking your bloody nose outside. As for you," he says to the fourth bloke, "you're just bleeding stargazing, you are. You ought to be close on the wall, ready to run either way, and do the first bloke as makes a move."

"Sorry, Cosh," this bloke says. "Do better next time."

"You'd better," says Cosh. "Else you'll do ten years."

"Half a mo," says Jim. "Don't go on at 'em. Let's show 'em again."

"Yes," says Slush, "for Christ's sake, and keep your bleeding eyes open this time."

They went out of the gate, and Cosh flew straight for the driver.

"Ought to be right outside the bloody place," he yelled, "not half a mile up the road. How the bleeding hell they going to jump you, if you're right down here? Eh?"

The engine started up again and the car went past the gateway with the three of them in it, but Cosh was still yelling at the driver.

"He's a lad, ain't he?" says one of the blokes, but they all looked a bit like kids as just had a clout in the earhole off of Pa. "Starting are you?"

"Yes," He says, feeling big.

"They're turning, Knocker," one of the other blokes shouts, from the gate. "Look in."

The car got knifed and screamed again, pulling up right outside the gate as if it had been put there special. Jim come first, running so fast it proper surprised you, sticking his left arm out like a swimmer, bringing the right arm round, over his head, and the jack tipped over the top, crashing a big ragged piece clean out of the glass, same time he bent away, pulling his coat collar round his face, ducking the shower of green shining splinters spurting all over him.

Cosh seemed to dive straight in the hole, breaking the tops off a couple of sharp lumps of glass with the hammer, grabbing the cigar box and half a dozen of the silver pellets. The car revved up and got moving. Jim went for it from the crouch like a runner off the mark. Cosh followed him and Slush come up behind, so close, they was like three blokes in a dancing act, all doing the same thing.

Jim dived clean over the back of the car, Cosh vaulted in, and Slush grabbed the back and swung over in a roll while the car was doing about thirty. In a matter of seconds it was doing sixty, and the three of them was standing up in the back, lifting their hats and bowing all round, as if they just come off the stage.

"It's a lump of suet bloody pudding," says one of the blokes. "Easy as going to sleep. We ought to be doing jobs and earning some nice money for our selfs this time next week."

"Roll on," says another bloke, trying Jim's trick with his fag and doing it all wrong, burning the end of his snitch and getting his eyes wet.

Jim got out of the car as if he was going to the pictures.

"What's hard about it?" he says. "Ernie, what about showing them how it's done?"

"Ah," He says. "If I could do it like you."

"Well," Cosh says, "you can't make a bigger balls than what they done, can you?"

"Have a go," says Slush. "Can't start too soon. Go on. Have a bloody do. Show a few of 'em."

Jim gave Him the jack.

"Don't forget," says Slush, "left arm out, pointing where you want to hit, and then sling it over your head straight at the mark. It's a do every time."

"You two other useless bastards get in with Him," says Cosh.

"Except you," says Slush, to the bloke as burnt his snitch. "You come and help me with the other sheet of glass."

He got in the big Bentley, feeling like He done when He went in to see Old Nick, and the worms started crawling cold all round His guts again.

They went straight up the lane, between the wall with the bottle ends on it all streaking sunlight, and the high fence at the back of the houses in line with the garage, turning round at the top and pelting down the other way. He see the yellow arm on the little black clock in front of the driver wagging about just over the 80.

"Ready?" the driver yells, and shoved his foot on the brake, so hard, they nearly all tipped through the windscreen.

He was out of the car and through the gate before He knew what He was at, seeing the pane in front of Him coming closer, bringing His right arm over and letting go of the weight straight at the big white shine, ducking down and feeling the bits falling on Him, hearing the splash of breaking glass.

Nipping for the car, He heard the other two blokes behind Him, and done a jump just like Jim, landing head and shoulders on the hard prickles of the mat, with the other bloke falling on top of Him, and the third bloke coming in all legs and boots.

"We done it," yells the bloke on top of Him, holding up two cigar boxes, and a fistful of silver paper pellets, nigh crying, out of being so happy. "You're nigh on as good as what the boss is, you are."

The other bloke handed round the fags, but He had so much of a shake on, He just had to leave the fag in the corner of His mouth, sticking His hands in His pockets, leaning back, trying to look as if He just been out for a blow of air.

"Born for the job, you was," Cosh yells, when they pulled up.

"You're all right, Ernie boy," Jim says, all smiles, "and proper one of us. Knew it as soon as I see you. Cut out for it.

Two or three more goes to get it right and you'll be starting your own bank account. Come round the office."

"Don't stand there scratching your bloody selves," Slush yells, at the others. "Get this glass cleaned up. Put a fresh lump in the frame. Think you've give up for the day, do you?"

"Comes a bit dear for glass, don't it?" He says to Jim, going through the garage.

"Dear?" Jim says. "Don't think we buy it, do you? Nip round and get it down the warehouse. Round the corner here. Much as we like."

"Never buy your tools if you can borrow 'em," says Slush.

"Now then, me lucky lads. There's two jobs we want to do," says Jim, sitting down in front of one of them oak desks, with a sort of round shutter at the top of it, full of papers and books. "One's at Karabelnic's in the Brompton Road. There's some very good skins in there. And I ain't talking about brides. The other's a jeweller's job. You lot ready to start work?"

All the blokes nodded. He nodded along with the others.

"O.K.," says Jim, "no moon tomorrow night. Meet here six o'clock, see? We want three cars, Cosh, boy."

Cosh made an O with his first finger and thumb.

"Done," he says.

"You drive one, Slush," Jim says, "you drive the other, Cosh, and I'll take the other one. Ernie, you take the jack, and go with Slush."

"Okeedoke," He says, and Slush winked at Him as if he thought He was a right boy.

"The coppers are off the beat at eleven o'clock," Jim says, "so you'll have a good ten minutes for the job."

"Lump of duff," says Cosh.

"You'll do the job, Slush boy, with Ernie and Tug," Jim says, "and Cosh'll stand by to pick up the pieces, if any. When you've finished, you meet me in the usual place and we ditch the cars round the West End. Then I take the stuff round to Auntie's. Then we share out what Auntie pays up. All right?"

Everybody nodded, and Jim got up.

"Couple of good goes in the morning, Ernie," he says,

proper pally. "You'll have a few nice quid for yourself before
you know where you are."

"Okeedoke," He says.

"Eight o'clock tomorrow, chum," Cosh says, and He could
see they wanted to get rid of Him. So He started feeling a bit
rotten again.

"It's all right, Ernie," Jim says, slinging Him a fag, "only
we've got some other business to attend to, see?"

"Okeedoke," He says. "So long."

Going through the garage again, He come over proper
respectful because of all the big cars in there. A lot more
blokes seemed to have come in and got busy on the job, so it
looked more like a factory than a garage, specially for round
that way. He started going up the little hill under the archway
in the street, getting over one side to make way for four or
five blokes, black shapes in the sun, but when He was on top of
them, He see the nearest one was the skinny bloke, down the
sewer.

Soon as He see him, the worms left His guts altogether, in a
rush, and He come over sickish, freezing cold, but keeping on
walking even though He never knew where He was putting His
feet.

He see the skinny bloke's face turning towards Him under
his pulled down hat, with his coat collar still turned up. He
was bobbing up and down, from a hard limp.

"Oy," the skinny bloke says, stopping dead, not more than
half a yard away, "where I seen you before?"

"Me?" He says. "I don't know. I'm a stranger round here."

"I seen you somewhere before," the skinny bloke says, same
voice as usual, a sort of roughish whisper with a lot of spit in it.

"Only about the Kingsland Road," He says, "that's my
part."

"Down here for?" the skinny bloke says.

"See Jim Mordinoy," He says.

"Trunky," Cosh yells, inside the garage, "we're waiting on
you. What's up with Him?"

Trunky looked at Him again.

"Thought He might be a stooler," he shouts, "seen Him somewhere before."

"Stooler me arse," Cosh yells, proper hopping about down there. "He's a prize scholard, He is. Come on in here, for Christ's sake, and give over."

Trunky bobbed away with the other blokes, and He went out through the archway, not looking back, nigh wet through with sweat, coming out in the warm of the sun, stone cold right through, feeling as though He never had the strength to go a step further. But soon as He turned the corner He tore down the road as if He had a load of mad dogs behind Him, wondering where the strength was coming from.

Going along on the tram, He had plenty of time to have a good think, so He went all over the ground again, and the more He looked at it, the better it seemed to get. The gun in the cupboard would get rid of Clem Arbiter easy as getting on a tram. Then Ada could settle down somewhere and do her self a bit of good, and like she said, Him and her could be nice friends. The thoughts of marying her His self seemed to be a bit barmy, because first of all there was Ma, and if she kicked up rough He never stood a chance in the business, or coming in to it later on. So it had to be looked at very careful.

Going through the Whitechapel Road, He see a double breasted black dancing suit, just like Jim's, silky fronts and everything, in a tailor's shop on the corner. He stood looking at it a little while, trying to think how He could get Ma to buy Him one like it, but never mind how He put it to His self, He seemed to hear Ma saying No, and somehow or another, He knew she was right. But something inside kept on saying He had to have one like it, because after all, He was just about going to start earning His own bit of nicker, what with starting being a solicitor too, and even Ma said He had to dress the part.

Totting up what He had in His pockets, He found He was somewhere about two quid out. He could hardly go to Ma and borrow another couple of quid to see Him through the week, so it looked as if He was stuck for a couple of lousy quid. Then it hit Him, while He was putting on a fag. All He had to do was pawn the cigarette case, and buy it out again the day after tomorrow when He got His share of the job from Jim.

There was a pawnshop just down the road, on the other corner, so He went down there, through the side door with Pledges on it in gold letters nigh rubbed off, taking all the fags out of the case and shoving them in His pocket.

It was a funny sort of little room, inside, with the counter all boarded up in small partitions, like a Gents, only made of wood.

A sheeny come behind the counter soon as the bell rang, with grease patching one side of his mouth, wiping his fingers, looking at Him proper screw eyed, as if He called twice for the rent.

"Yes?" he says, none too nice.

"Want to put this in for a couple of days," He says, putting the case on the counter.

The sheeny weighed it in his hand and turned it over a couple of times, then he opened it and took a little spy glass out of his pocket and stuck it in his eye, looking at something inside of the gold part.

"How much you want?" he says.

"Three quid," He says.

"Two quid," says the sheeny.

"Make it two ten," He says.

"Two quid," says the sheeny, "or take it away."

"Okeedoke," He says, "hand it over."

The sheeny brought up a block of little green tickets, with a elastic band round them, from under the counter, and a pen, and a bottle of ink with the top all chipped.

"Name?" he says.

He suddenly see somebody taking the case to Ma, and telling her He pawned it.

"Want my name, do you?" He says. "All right. Mordinoy."

"Smith, Jones or X," says the sheeny, "but not Mordinoy."

"Talking about?" He says. "You put it down like I say. Name's Mordinoy, Harry Mordinoy."

The sheeny never said nothing, but just wrote.

"You living where?" he says, not looking up.

"Don't matter where I'm living," He says, "I'll be here day after tomorrow."

The sheeny just dropped the ticket in front of Him.

"One, seventeen, six," he says. "The half crown is for the card."

"Okeedoke," He says, and hung on for the nicker.

He had a new warm feeling inside of Him, like being brand new again.

He could feel His self inside of that suit, doing things proper proud and He knew the look Ada might give Him.

She come up a thousand times stronger, and He wanted to run to her, quick, to look at her and breathe her again.

"Come on, for Christ's sake," He shouted the sheeny, banging the counter with His fists. "Going to be all bloody day, are you?"

# CHAPTER XXXIV

SLUSH WAS DRIVING like a taxi bloke, knowing all the turns, dodging all the lights, and jumping them when he got the chance, whistling between his teeth, holding a butt end in his lower lip what he puffed sometimes and then put right in his mouth, sort of under his tongue, it looked like, blowing the smoke out through his nose, proper pretty to watch.

"This is it," he says, turning out in a wide road. "Get ready. It's on the other side where that second lamp is. See?"

"Yes," He says, seeing nothing except a lot of ragged lights through the water in His eyes, but He got His feet on the seat, and He could see the three blokes in the back, kneeling on the floor, ready to follow Him.

"I'm going to turn," Slush says, and starts pulling the wheel down hard, making somebody screech behind them, going over on two wheels and straightening up, opening out in a orhhahh soon as the bonnet was cutting straight between the lamps, slipping down in the seat, driving with his head hardly showing above the door.

"The white place," he yells, "middle window."

"Okeedoke," He yells back, seeing it coming plain as daylight.

"Right," Slush yells, giving the car the knife.

While the scream was still on He was over the side and running up the pavement. The window was bigger than the practice frame, full of wax brides all wearing fur coats, so it come just like slinging something at a crowd.

The jack went over, and He felt the lumps falling on Him while the glass was still splashing about, but when He looked up, the other blokes was through the hole with crowbars, cracking open long, white, sliding door cupboards in the back of the shop. Fast as the wood splintered and busted, the doors was booted back and furs got pulled out and chucked on blokes arms, till they was loaded high above their heads.

Out they come, shoving these wax brides all over the show, making them knock their selfs down, like skittles falling, cracking their faces in bits, and it seemed a right pity, somehow, because they was so pretty.

"Grab hold," the first bloke shouts Him, and slings this armful at Him, covering Him like a dark cloud, full of scent, warm, soft, like holding Ada without her weight.

Even when He got down to the car He never wanted to let go, but Slush grabbed them all off of Him, throwing them down the back, and the other blokes was tearing up behind, slinging their lots in.

"Lobbo," one of them shouts, "coppers."

"Look in," Slush yells, and everybody jumped for a place, while the car was moving, making the back a proper right mess of arms, legs and fur. People was shouting all the way down the road, and hanging out of windows, bells was ringing, and brides was screaming, though half of them never knew what for.

Slush went straight across the red traffic lights, just missing a couple of taxis what turned and bashed in to each other, and for yards on you could hear the pair of taxi blokes saying their prayers, right out loud, very put out about it.

"That was lucky," Slush shouts. "They've blocked the road for police cars, see? Give us just nice time."

Down side turnings, and all round squares where the lamps come pale green through the trees, making Him think about Ada, this big car shoved itself, doing everything Slush told it, till they come out in another wide road full of lights and Slush slowed down, taking his place in the traffic and then wheeling out to the right.

"Eyes down," he says, "get ready to scarper. Soon as I stop, hop out of it, you three in the back. See you down the garage tomorrow."

He pulled up in this darkish turning, and the blokes jumped for it, not saying a word. In half a tick, even the sound of them was gone.

Away they went again and turned out in another square,

pulling up behind the tail light of a big closed car with the street lamps shining off the round polished top.

"Give us a hand, Smasher," Slush says, and starts digging the coats up, but He was so surprised what he called Him, He sat there, sort of stuck.

"Come on," Slush yells. "What, you feeding the twins, are you?"

"I didn't know you meant me, did I?" He says, nipping out of it.

"Who d'you reckon he meant, then?" Jim says, coming up quiet behind. "You done all right, Ernie boy. Lovely wallop, it was. Done it a right treat, you did. In the first eleven from tonight, eh, Slush?"

"I should bloody kiko," says Slush, pushing all the furs through the door of the other car. "He's the Smasher, He is. What a lovely job, eh? Went off like I'm going to get a pint down me, in a minute."

"Everything on board?" Jim says, climbing in.

"I counted thirty nine," says Slush. "All locked up and happy."

"Take Him round the club for a drink," Jim says, moving out of it. "So long, Smasher boy. See you in a couple of hours. So long, Slush."

Slush went back and started rubbing the wheel round with a cloth, then all the tops of the sides, all the door handles, and even the leather work.

"That's just in case somebody's left any funny things behind for the narks," he says, slinging the rag away. "Another thing, Smash boy. Always do your jobs in gloves, see? Work in gloves. Then you don't leave no cards behind. Everything all Sir Garnet?"

"Okeedoke," He says, feeling as if He just started living for the first time.

"Right," says Slush, walking off. "Come on. We got a little do with some bottles and a couple of glasses, we have."

"Ain't leaving the car, are we?" He says, liking the idea of the ride.

"Course we are," Slush says. "It's a job."

"What job," He says.

"It was picked up round Saint James's Square this morning," Slush says, like talking to a sick kid. "We only took it for the outing tonight. Now we're handing it over again, and some nark'll get a nice fat reward, I suppose. You're proper new, you are."

Slush started on about everything as happened in the game, but He was a bit too full of His self to do much listening. All the way, He see His self slinging the jack again, feeling everything again, hearing it all, and on top of the lot, He wanted to have another go, quick. He could feel all His muscles hard and sort of trembly, and nothing else seemed to matter except doing another job better, and having blokes talk about Him, like Slush and Jim done, kind of pally, but taking off their hats at the same time.

He was the Smasher. He had the feeling He done something right, at last, and made something out of His self.

"Here, Slush," He says, cutting in, "how much can we make a week? I mean, going the right way about it?"

"Depends on the carve up," Slush says. "Doing about a steady sixty to eighty or so me self, lately. So's Cosh. So's a couple of the other lads. Jim's on a lot more, though. But he's got all the exes, see? So it works out fair do's, taking it all round."

"How about my share?" He says.

"Heard what Jim said?" Slush says. "First eleven. You'll be big money and all. Don't get many blokes like you, see? Lose their nerve, they do. Won't bash at the last minute. Just when you're making your run up. Christ, I've even had a couple of blokes faint, getting out the car. Shocking state, they was."

Round the Lucky Seven, Slush went through a side door down some steps, not through the big room, and they come out in a passage where blokes in high white hats was hopping about with pots and pans galore. Everybody was shouting, and there was a smashing smell of thick gravy and fresh veg rolling about in the steam, making you hungry and hot the same time.

Off the passage, they went through a kitchen full of long stoves, everything in white light, with showers of these blokes in white hats stirring things, chopping stuff, sticking forks in pots, shaking saucepans about, and generally looking hard working, and sweating something cruel.

"Down here," Slush says, going down a wooden ladder. "This is where we have a nice little bit of grub and a glass or two, then we'll go in and get our bleeding selfs a couple of decent looking bits up in the club. Suit you, Smash boy?"

"Cake," He says.

"Here we are, bears breath," Slush says to some little bloke in a black apron. "Sling it in, and make it quick. We're proper starving."

This little bloke never asked no questions. He just went off the mark and shot through the door. It was a long, low roofed place, with thousands of bottles all laying down on racks, in sort of squares, some of them with sawdust in between the layers, so it looked like walls of polished black rings all round, floor to ceiling, and down the end, half a dozen dirty big casks, same shape as eggs, with little buckets hanging off the taps.

"Blimey," He says. "There's enough booze here to start a business."

"This ain't even the beginnings, this ain't," Slush says, and takes off his overcoat and bowler hat. "You want to see some booze, you want to go round the cellars. This is only the wines. All Jim's. All ours. You're in the big stuff here, Smash boy. You play your cards right, and you're in the meat for life. Do what you're told, like you done it just now, and you won't go short of a crust, nor nothing else, see? Just box clever that's all."

It sounded proper sensible, the way he said it and He started to get the feeling He was being proper took care of all round. All He had to do was just do what He was told, and if it was as easy as the job they just done, it was a lump of treacle tart.

"Was tonight's little lot a bit easy?" He says.

"Course not," Slush says, proper surprised. "Right in the

middle of the bleeding road, and lousy with coppers? One of
the rottenest jobs we done. But we done it. I had me doubts,
but we done it. No fear. We come off very nice tonight, if you
ask me. My bloody oath, we did."

The little bloke came back with a tray full of dishes and
plates, sliding it over the table. Slush started pulling some of
it off and taking all the lids off, letting the steam out.

"Get in, Smash," he says, chucking the knifes and forks
about. "Plenty here. Come on, shortarse, where's the doings?
Eh? Where's the starter?"

The little bloke still never said a word, but he rushed down
the far end, and a lot of bottle clonking went on while Slush
was dishing up, and all the time he was working away and
laughing as if there was a right joke on somewhere.

"He's deaf," he says, in a whisper you could have heard
miles. "But he knows what's going on. Knows every bottle in
the place be name, he do. Jim's right hand, down here."

The little bloke come back with a big jug frothing full of
light coloured beer and poured it out in long glasses, proper
posh.

"Here's to it," Slush says, lifting his up. "May you never
know the pinch."

"Same to you," He says.

"Ah," Slush says, wiping it off and getting in the grub.
"That's where we come off very nice, that is. We won't get
pinched, not unless it's on the job, see? If the narks get the oil
we been on the job and come after us, we're covered, see?
Jim's got it all taped."

"How?" He says, a bit upstairs.

"Supposing you get copped doing a job," Slush says, getting
hold of this chop and proper giving it big licks, "well, you're
unlucky. It's a do. But if they only get evidence it was you, Jim
can fix it. He just pays a bloke to go inside for you. That's
all. Easy, ain't it?"

"Sounds like it," He says. "Mean there's blokes'll go inside
for not doing nothing?"

"Course," Slush says, making a job of the bone, "if they can get more be going in, than staying out? There's plenty'll do the stretch, and glad to."

He see Ma Pearson doing her little bit, plain as the string beans, hearing all her kids howling for her, somehow, round there in Basson Terrace, and old Pa Pearson getting home of a night from the goods yard, having a go at the housework, trying to steady things up a bit over night, and get them ready for school.

"Some proper queer blokes about, ain't there?" He says.

"Be in a right mess if there wasn't," Slush says, and shoves his plate off. "Come on. Let's go up the club, eh? Pick out a couple of right bits. I could do a bit after tonight. Ain't married, are you?"

"No," He says. "You?"

"That'll be the day," Slush says, giving his teeth a going over. "I'll get married when Jim does. Suit me."

"Anybody in line, has he?" He says, going for the beer.

"Who, Jim?" Slush says, and straightens out a fag. "Pick 'em out where he likes, he can. He's always got something on, somewhere. What's he want to get married for?"

"That's right," He says. "Waste of time."

"Course," Slush says. "Do 'em and get out of it. Just a bloody nuisance, that's all they are. Let's go up and get hold of a couple of 'em, eh? There's some proper right looking lays up there."

They finished off the beer and started going up the ladder again, none too steady, then up a stairs, and along a passage where the band come through just like Ma Chalmers's wireless warming up, getting louder every second, and through a door, in the club.

It was just like it was, nothing changed, nor the noise, and even the people looked the same. The brass plates was crashing away there, just like a old pal, like memory coming real.

"Here we are," Slush says, getting behind a table in the wall, "do us a treat."

Rossi come steaming up, rubbing his hands, looking as pleased as if he been give a quid for nothing.

"Mr Mordinoy is coming?" he says, and starts shoving the glasses about.

"Couple of ticks," Slush says. "Pick us out a couple of them little bits of all right, over there, will you, Rossi boy? Something passionate'll do me."

"I will see if they are free," Rossi says.

"Don't see," Slush says. "Just get 'em. Jim's coming in soon. Make it quick. I want to go home early."

Rossi went off without a word, and He was a bit surprised how a bloke like him took his orders from a bloke like Slush. Rossi was such a quiet, posh sort of a bloke, even if he did talk ice creamo and wag his mitts about.

It come all of a sudden, this feeling of being afraid to talk to some bride He never met before, and trying to keep the talk going. But the more He thought about it, the worse the feeling got.

"Listen," He says, "if it's all the same to you, I'll get off home. I got my Ma, see? All by herself, she is, and you know, might be a bit worried, like."

Slush looked proper knocked over.

"Worried about your Ma?" he says. "That's all right, Smash boy. Only you ought to finish the party off, you know? Stead of leaving me? Didn't you, eh?"

"Miss Lola and Miss Yvonne," Rossi says, right across the table, and hopped off.

They was looking up at a pair of bramahs. One was black haired, in a red dress with thin straps over her shoulders, and the other was darkish in a darkish dress.

They was just looking, no smiles, standing still, looking.

"Ah," Slush says, and moves up. "Only want one of you. My friend's off home. I ain't, though. Come on, Lola. Sit down. You off, Smash? Or you changed your mind?"

The darkish one in the darkish dress was just looking at Him, like some old girl looking at a cauliflower out shopping, wondering if there might be something else she might like better. Something inside of Him turned over at the very thoughts of even trying to talk to her, and Ada was right up close to Him again, covering Him with her self and her scent, and them beetles was scratching the back of His neck.

"No," He says, making a move, "I'll get off, if it's all the same? Some other night, eh? So long, Slush boy."

"So long, Smash," Slush says, but he was turned the other way, looking at Miss Lola.

He never looked at the darkish one again, but going for the door, He see Clem Arbiter looking at Him, and then looking away again, with the diamonds giving Him the wink, and all the time the brass plates was going as hard as they could, only not so fast.

He sized it all up a treat while He was going for the door.

All He had to do, was come down the steps the way they come in, and get up here. Nobody would ever know how He got in there, and nobody was going to hear nothing over all that row, except perhaps the bloke in the cellar, and he was supposed to be deaf.

It was easy. It was so easy. He could have started singing, only looking at that fiddle bloke turned Him up.

He could see Ada pulling herself up the stairs again, and the crash of the plates come in time with the ding of her hands on the iron rail.

He see the darkish bride going back to her table, laughing and waving her dukes at another bride sitting there, and He wished, so hard it hurt somewhere inside, that it was Ada, laughing away there and looking so pleased with herself, and happy.

## CHAPTER XXXV

"Go round and see Ike Buzgang for me," Ma says, breakfast time, "ask him what kind of a bleeding fine old game he thinks he's playing at, will you? Tell him there's no seats in them last lot of chairs, and them mattresses is all flock. That's all. Just tell him. Must think I'm getting past it, or something."

"Okeedoke, Ma," He says. "Perhaps it's a mistake, eh?"

"About thirty quidsworth," Ma says, taking it out of a back tooth, "right side of the books, ain't it? Tell him if I don't get 'em changed before the day's out, I'll be round there and blind him out of both eyes. He'll hear you."

"That'll be done," He says. "What we doing about this turn-out, tonight?"

"I got the beer in," Ma says. "Two pianos to go out, and about a dozen chairs. That ought to be all right, didn't it? Put the flags out after dinner, eh?"

"Okeedoke, Ma gel," He says, making a move.

"Your money's up there," she says, sticking the pin at the mantelpiece. "I'll make it three quid a week, till I think you're worth more. That's what Len gets, and I won't have you getting a halfpenny under. All right, son?"

"You're a proper sport, Ma," He says, nigh falling over His self. "See you dinner time, eh?"

"Don't rush it," she says. "But tell Mr Bloody Buzgang what I told you, and say it twice, case he don't hear it the first time, see?"

"Okeedoke, Ma gel," He says.

Going up the road He see where they was putting up the flags for the wedding. Right from the pub as far as the corner of the High Road, the kerb was all whitewashed, and Pa Fitchett and a couple of others was drawing squares of whitewash round all the shops, leaving little paths going up to the doors.

Pa Prettyjohn done his self up a treat, with lines of red

geraniums all round the whitewashed edge, paper chains inside the doors and windows, and lines of them little triangle
coloured flags was hanging all round the window of the shop
and up to the upstairs windows. Right across the street from
Bert Soulsby's to Pa Prettyjohn's there was a big white sheet
hung up, with Good Luck Percy painted on it in red, with old
shoes and pots and pans hanging off of the rope, clanking
about in the wind.

"Why ain't you got a bit of this down there?" Pa says to
Him, as He come by.

"Give us a chance," He says. "Got to get the furniture out
of it first to see what we're doing of, ain't we? Ma's got the
beer in, anyhow. That's something."

"Take back all I said," Pa says. "I'll go down and help her
take the bung out soon as I got me self straight here. I'm lock-
ing up at twelve o'clock, and I don't care if Jesus Christ His
self wants half of tea, he don't get it till Monday."

Ike had a big place down the Walworth Road, a couple of
shops knocked together for a showroom, and a big warehouse
behind, with his office over the top, and He went up the stairs,
thinking how He could easy make His and Ma's little business
into one like this, if He played His cards right and used His
loaf.

"Who is it?" Ike screeches, up the top.

"Me," He says, "come from Mrs Mott."

"Come up," yells Ike, and he looks over the top of the
stairs. He was in his shirt sleeves, with a pen behind his ear
and a little black cap on. He had a proper big round the
corner conk, and a suit of whiskers round his dial cut very
short, but there was more laughs inside his eyes than a dozen
blokes ever got in the whole of their clocks, mouths, ears and
all.

"Well, well," he says, "what an honour. Mr Mott, Mr Mott.
Come in. Come in. How is with Mrs Mott?"

"Bit worried about them chairs what you sent around," He
says, lighting up. "Ain't got no seats. And them mattresses ain't

sprung, neither. They're flock, see? Not like on the invoice. So she says, would you change 'em, see?"

"Mistakes, mistakes," Ike says, and holds his face like a bloke with jawache. "Oy. What mistakes. Always with mistakes. Oy."

He moved so quick for the stairs, he nigh fell over the top.

"So, Lesser?" he screeches down. "So, Mr Lesser?"

"Hullo?" some bloke yells, down there.

"So do me the pleasure," old Ike screeches back, "come to the office, Mr Lesser. Always with mistakes," old Ike grouses, "Nothing sweet. Nothing going with honey. Always mistakes. For heads, so they got empty boxes, full mistakes."

A little bloke come up the stairs cursing his self loose under his breath, so you could just about hear it if you knew what he might be saying, and he was saying everything.

"What's took on, now?" he says, trying to tie a big green baize apron tighter all round him, and giving over because the tapes was all broke off and too short. Little fat bloke he was, smoking a asthma fag, and stinking everybody out of house and home.

"So what is with Mrs Mott?" old Ike says, very quiet.

"Ah," says Lesser, like seeing something pop out of a hole. "That's the hammer. Start leading off. Go on. Just start. That's all."

"I started," Ike says. "What happens?"

"Wrong load," says Lesser. "Wrong van. Wrong order. Wrong bloke. No sense, no idea, no tongue in the head. To ask is everything. Did he?"

"It explains," says Ike, "what else I should ask?"

"Little," says Lesser, "only don't lead off."

Ike looked at Him and starts laughing.

"I should lead off with a child, still?" he says, and looks at Lesser, still squeezing green smoke out this blinder. "So do me favour, Mr Lesser. Another load, eh? Everything right, this time?"

"Everything with a kiss," says Lesser, and went out of it,

leaving the tail end of a murder behind him. "Personal, noth
ing else less from Mr Lesser."

"All right, eh?" Ike says. "Is everything all right, if you do
it right. So. You started working in the business, eh?"

"Yes," He says. "Listen, Ike. I reckon I could make some
thing out of it, if I get told a few tips how to set about it, like
Eh?"

"Any time," Ike says, coming up proper happy. "Nice busi
ness you got. For a young man, first class. Plenty hard working
people you got living round about. Plenty saving, so you go
good paying customers. Business follows good payers. You go
a business? Make it grow."

"I come to you, shall I?" He says.

"Any time, all the time," Ike says. "If help, so help. I
advice, so advice. If nothing, so pick it how you like. N
charge, eh?"

"You're about the only bloke Ma'll trust as far as she ca
sling a armful of sledge hammers," He says. "So I follow her
see?"

"You mother is first business, afterwards everything," Ik
says. "If she took advice years ago, she would be Numbe
One. But for the women, too much trouble. She wants to g
nice and quiet. You are a young man. Men are different. S
make something big, Mr Mott. Is easier to make big tha
small. Use the head. Put smiles on the head. So is everythin
with the head and a smile."

"Okeedoke, Ike," He says, looking for a way to get out, "I'
tell Ma it'll be all right. See you later, eh?"

"Any time, everytime," Ike says. "Go down quiet, steady
Take care the neck. With it, you got something. Without i
nothing. Except funerals. Goodbye, Mr Mott."

"So long, Ike," He says.

Soon as He was outside, He got a itch to go over to get th
fag case, and all the way He was thinking how it might be t
ask Ada out to the club in His dancing suit, and give her
right shock.

He nipped off of the tram just outside the pawnbrokers, an

shot inside the door with the ragged gold Pledges on it, going into one of them little partitions and banging on the counter.

A different sheeny, younger and cockier, come out and looked as though he wanted to be nasty.

"Give us me fag case, will you?" He says, putting the ticket on the counter, and this bloke picked it up. Without saying a word, he went out of it, leaving Him listening to the traffic.

Then the first sheeny, the old bloke, come in and started rubbing his hands.

"We ain't got your case," he says.

"Ain't got what?" He says.

"Ain't got your case," the sheeny says.

"Why not?" He says.

"The police have got it," he says, as if that was all there was to it.

That there stone cold hand come squeezing Him in the guts again.

"Police have got it what for?" He says.

"Because it's stolen property," the sheeny says. "We looked it up."

He looked straight in this bloke's eyes, just like a couple of black cherries straight off of the barrow.

"We'll see about that," He says.

The sheeny just shifted one shoulder forward and opened both his thumbs, making a shape with his mouth same as saying Do What You Like, It's All The Same to Me.

He shot out of the place and got on the bus, but He felt too queer to smoke, and nothing else could sort of get room in His head except the police.

He run and walked fast all the way from the bus stop to the garage, going through the strong, oily smell of the cars proper winded, and sort of heavy in the legs with nothing on top except this thin pain where He breathed.

In the office, Jim had his feet on the desk, and Cosh was sitting on the sill, looking out of the window.

"Jim," He says, "I'm in a right mess."

Jim's fag come right over the other side of his face, but he never stopped smiling, nor even moved.

"What's up, Ernie boy?" he says.

"I pawned a fag case day before yesterday," He says. "I went there to get it out this morning, and they say the police got it because it's stolen property."

"Is it?" Jim says, still smiling, quiet as you like.

"My Ma give it to me for me birthday," He says. "How could it be? It's silver. Holds twenty. She won't half say her prayers about it."

"The old lark," says Cosh. "It's been worked before, and it'll be worked again."

Jim stood up and put his black hat on very careful with both hands, looking in the glass, pushing the hair back over his ears with the tops of his fingers, looking at his self both sides, then putting his tie straight and pulling his coat down. He give his self a couple more looks to make sure he was pleased with his self, and then opened the top drawer and took out a packet of creased up quid notes pushed inside a envelope not quite big enough to take the length.

"This is yours," he says, holding it out. "Thirty quid. Might be a bit more when we get the rest of it. Happy?"

"Happy?" He says, bending this thick packet, feeling proper dented.

"Come on," says Jim. "We'll go down this place. Lamp duffers up."

"That's the talk, Jim boy," says Cosh. "Can't treat the family like that, can they? Where is it?"

"Down the Whitechapel Road," He says.

The three of them got in this big car, and Cosh drove through all the back streets proper scientific, pulling up when He thumbed him, a few doors down from the pawnshop.

"Ah," says Cosh, "I know this place, don't you, Jim? You picked 'em out, Smasher."

"Course," says Jim, as if he was just turning in somewhere for a cup of tea. "Got the ticket, Ernie?"

He give it to him.

They went through the Pledges door, and Cosh kicked it closed, almost shaking the glass out of it.

The youngest sheeny nipped in so quick, he looked as though he was on a lump of elastic.

"Now then," he says, "what's on?"

Jim leaned across the counter and grabbed him by the shirt, pulling his face right over.

"What's your bloody game, you slimy bastard, you?" he says.

"What have I done, Mr Mordinoy?" this bloke says, nigh strangled, and nigh dead with fright.

"Where's my friend's fag case?" Jim says. "Here's the ticket, and here's the money. Go and get it."

"Listen, Mr Mordinoy," this bloke says, just about howling. "I give you my honest, solemn, God's oath, it ain't here."

"All I want from you is the fag case, you pig born cowson," says Jim, and he was still smiling, "and if I don't get it, we'll smash this place up, and put you in dock. and you won't look too pretty."

The old bloke come in, proper staring white, he was.

"Listen, Mr Mordinoy," he says, in a wet whisper. "It's just like he says. I tried to get it valued already. The record says it's stolen property. So we give it in."

"You pair of dirty, connivering Kosher crooks, you," Jim says. "Nip over the back, Cosh, and have a look round. Go with him, Ernie."

They slid over the counter and went all the way round the shop, through archways of old clothes, kitchen stuff, china, bits of machinery and tools. Cosh sorted out a few odd braces and chisels and things, and shoved them in his pockets.

"Come in very handy, they will," he says. "My fee for coming."

Then they got in the little shop with all the jewellery in it, right on the corner, with the window and door in the High Road and the other window round the side turning.

"Don't go too near the window," says Cosh, pulling the door to, and bolting up. "Have a look round in here."

Inside was another little place, with a sort of workshop and a big black and green safe. All the shelves round the walls was full of stuff, ornaments and things.

"Have a look round, Smash boy, while I get the key," Cosh says.

There was hundreds of fag cases all the way round the shelves, and in drawers, but none of them was His. While He was sorting through boxes full, He could hear a proper fine old row going on in the back there, and then Cosh come in with a ring of keys.

"You got to wallop these blokes fore they see any sense," he says, fixing the key in the safe.

The black and green door come open, nigh six inches thick, and Cosh started chucking the stuff out. The case was in a little drawer at the back.

"That's it," He says, and He could have sat down and howled, He was that there emptied and filling up again.

"Sure?" Cosh says.

"Here's me initials," He says, "E.V.M. See? My Ma had it done."

"You're lucky," says Cosh, putting a lot of stuff in his pockets. In the little drawer up above, there was a lot of quid notes under a glass weight.

"Come in very handy for the Sunday's collection, this will," Cosh says, and puts the lot in his pocket. "Come on, Smash. Give Jim a nice surprise, eh?"

They went back through the archways of old clothes and stuff, to the Pledges place where Jim was sitting up on the counter, smoking, and the two sheenies was standing there quiet, just looking at nothing with round eyes.

"He's got it," Cosh says.

"Yes?" Jim says, still smiling. "Let's see."

He give it him, and he turned it over.

"Platinum, eh?" he says. "Your Ma knows what's what, don't she? I'm coming round your house, Smash."

"Anytime you like, Jim boy," He says. "But she said it was silver."

"Take my tip," says Jim, looking at Him straight grey, "it's platinum. And he give you two quid for it, eh?"

"One, seventeen, six," He says. "Half a dollar for the card."

Jim took a corner of it between his finger and thumb, and all of a sudden turned round and clouted the young sheeny across the dial with it, but he only made a funny noise and put his hands up.

"What shall we do with them, Cosh?" Jim says, giving Him the case.

"I reckon a bashing a piece would do the pair of them the world of good," says Cosh.

"Do you know," says Jim, scratching his elbow, "it's funny how I was just thinking the same thing."

He no sooner said it than he jumped down and walloped this first sheeny as hard as he could, one in the guts as got his hands away, and three or four in the dial, one after the other, and he was no slop with his mitts, neither.

The older bloke put his hands above his head and looked up at the ceiling, with his eyes shut, but it never did him no good, because Jim pushed him against the wall with one hand, and bashed him three or four times in the middle of his face with the other, till the blood was splashing about like plum juice.

The first sheeny started crying and slid down on his knees, all red from his chin down, soaking in all over his shirt.

"Don't I get a bash, then?" says Cosh, a bit put out, he sounded.

"Help yourself," says Jim, wiping his hands on the little green curtain.

Cosh picked up the first one, and his head fell right back on his neck as if he was out to the wide, but Cosh hit him three in the nose and mouth, and kind of threw him off, not even looking where he fell.

"Style's everything," Jim says. "Old Cosh'll learn you. Won't you, Cosh, boy?"

Cosh took a draw of his fag, and his face come open in a big laugh, showing them dark blue and brown bits sticking up round his mouth.

"Course," he says.

He walked over to the older sheeny and done the same to him, till the bloke slid on the floor, then he booted him somewhere in the face, and walked across to the other bloke and booted him too. They was in a right mess, laying down in the shadow all blood and piles of dark wrinkles, but not a sound come out of either of them.

"That ought to just about take care of the bastards," Cosh says, giving his mitts a rub off.

"I reckon so. Listen, the pair of you," Jim says. "You blow the gaff about this, and I'll come round here with the duffers and give the pair of you a right doing, see? Not only that, I'll find out where you live, and do your families, too. See?"

There was a shadow on the glass, and some old girl opened the door.

"Not today, Ma," says Jim. "We're closed up."

"Oh," she says. "Early closing, are you?"

"I expect so," Jim says. "What's up Ma? Took a bit short, are you?"

"Hoped I'd be able to get something on this?" she says, and she pulled a bit of china out of her shopping basket. "I only want a couple of bob on it, like, if you can."

Jim had a look and put it down.

"Soapstone," he says. "Come from China, eh, Ma?"

"My eldest boy," she says. "In the Navy, he is."

"Ah," Jim says. "Dollar any good to you, Ma?"

"Fix me up very nice thanks," she says, "I never come here before. Afraid of it, like."

"Take my tip, Ma," Jim says, giving her the dollar. "Stay out of it. We're all a dirty lot of twisting crooks in this. Else we'd never make a living. I'm giving it up, me self. Seen the light, I have."

"Oh?" she says, looking at him, proper shoved back.

"Yes," Jim says. "Going out to Zululand. Doing a missionary for the Salvation Army."

"They must be hard up," she says, having a laugh. "Like me. Well, good morning, and thanks very much."

"Morning, Ma," Jim says. "Don't forget what I told you?"

Soon as she went out, he leaned over the counter where the pair of them was laying down.

"Listen, you two," he says, "don't forget what I told you. Open your snouts and there'll be flowers coming round here only you won't smell 'em. See?"

The place was dead quiet. You could even hear the words of a song on the wireless somewhere across the road.

"All right, Ernie?" Jim says, out in the road. "Next time you want a bit of cash, come and see me."

"Okeedoke," He says. "Ta, Jim."

"See you tomorrow down the office?" Jim says. "Another job's come up. Give you a lift home?"

"I'm only a pennyworth or two off," He says. "Thanks all the same, Jim. So long, Cosh."

"So long, Smasher boy," Cosh says. "Don't take long to wipe up a couple of Three Be Twos, do it?"

"When you know how," Jim says, getting in the car.

Going back home on top of the tram, He thought to His self how easy it was to get a job done once you made up your mind you wanted to do it. He knew He never had the guts to do them two sheenies same as Jim, but seeing it done made all the difference. All you had to do was go in and bash, and you could get what you liked.

He turned in down the Fun Fair to see if Ada was back, trying to kid His self He only wanted to play a machine. Everything was going full speed as usual. But Ada come over to Him instead of waiting, and there was no smiles, neither.

"What was you doing down the club, last night?" she says.

"Meeting Jim," He says. "Why?"

"You got any sense," she says, "you'll keep away. I don't suppose you'll take any notice, but don't forget what I told you, will you?"

"What's up?" He says. "Jim ain't done no harm to me, has he?"

She looked at Him as if it was a shame to take the money, not sure whether to go or stay.

"Ah," she says, "you'll find out, like many before you."

"Can't see nothing wrong with the bloke, me self," He says, feeling the thick packet inside His coat pocket.

"Decent bloke, ain't he?" she says. "You'll learn a lot down the club."

"Ain't a bad place," He says.

"Help him out with a little job, too, I suppose?" she says, sort of not caring.

"Yes," He says. "Bit of one."

"You want to watch out how you get pinched," she says. "But you'll do the time, not Jim. He's a bit too wide. I've told you, you're dealing with a flash boy. You'll be getting one yourself, soon."

"Okeedoke," He says. "I'll take my chance."

She looked at Him as if she never see Him in her life before, sort of half laughing, as if she was too tired to do anything else.

"You're all the same," she says, "artists and all. A few quid more than you can get by a decent day's work, and you're all in the queue."

"Don't know what you're talking about," He says.

"No more don't I," she says. "I've said it too many times to too many different blokes."

"What you got against Jim?" He says.

"Me?" she says. "Nothing. He's a nuisance as far as I'm concerned, but that's only me. But it's money for jam, ain't it? He's in the business and you're only one of the mugs doing the jobs. Listen, Ern. He owns this place and a few more, and the club, and other places. He's boss of a couple of the Palais, and he's doing something about them seaside holidays camps, and all. He's got more in his pockets than you'll ever have in the bank, see? So he's doing all right, ain't he? What are you doing?"

"I might get there too," He says. "He's nigh on twice as old as what I am."

"Listen, piecan," she says, no laughs now, "I'll be poking you bananas through the bars very soon. You see. I've told you before, and I'll tell you again, take my tip and keep away from Jim Mordinoy. He won't do you no good."

The packet in His pocket was proper laughing at her.

"Okeedoke," He says. "What about a trip round the Palais again, eh? By our selfs?"

She looked at Him for a bit, not moving, nor laughing, nor nothing. He felt as if she was all round Him, taking Him to bits, wondering how to put Him all up in one piece again, the way she wanted Him.

"I didn't ought to bother with you, did I?" she says. "Not really."

"Ain't done nothing to me, you ain't," He says. "Only I was sorry about the other night. Was you queer yesterday?"

She wagged her head, still deadish, still looking, making Him want to blink a lot.

"Well? What about it?" He says. "You on?"

She looked at the red beetles for a minute or two, trying to pick a splinter of skin off the side of her thumb.

"I'll see," she says, looking at Him with her hair nigh covering her eyes.

This soft, smiling, dying feeling come up full strength, with a kind of feeling as made you want to grab her and start kissing her.

"Ada," He says, and it was out before He could stop it. "You're smashing. Straight up. I been dreaming about you, I have. Don't believe me, do you? I have, though. Let's go down the Palais again, Ada? Say Yes? Will you?"

He knew there was smiles behind her hair, and when she turned and threw it off of her shoulders, He see the big whitish flash in her eyes.

"Ernie boy," she says, giving Him the lot, making everything come out of Him. "I got to be kind to you, ain't I? You poor bloody little fool, you. Come in, tonight."

"Okeedoke, gel," He says, and beside the feelings inside of Him, the packet might as well have been a bunch of brown cabbage leafs.

## CHAPTER XXXVI

HIM AND MA sat in front of the shop after they finished dolling it up with some flags and stuff, having a bottle of beer apiece, listening to the wedding party going it hammer and tongs down the road, and watching everybody getting ready. They had about a dozen chairs out along the kerb on the white-washed line, and some tables at the back with the beer, and some plates of pork pies and what all, case they come over a bit peckish. The pianos was out in the road, just under the lamps, so as Ma Chalmers and one of her prize learners could see what they was doing of, just this side of the big sign He painted right across the roadway, MAKE IT TWINS PERCY BOY, in two foot letters.

When it come on dark, and the kids had finished playing about, all the lads started wheeling out the pianos on the kerb and getting the barrels and crates stacked where they come in handiest. Then a few of them started dodging in and out of front gardens lighting all the candles along the window sills in the road, and the old girls opened the front bedroom windows and lit up all the little dips in paste pots and jam jars up there, so by the time it was all finished, it did, it looked a proper treat, lines of little white, cheering lights right down to the corner and the road full of people all ready to make it a proper right do.

Old Pa Prettyjohn come out and made a bee line behind the beer tables, proper in his glory, bossing the lot in a big Indian's hat with blue and white feathers nigh down to his heels, no collar and a tail coat, with Dad Fitchett, standing by the crates, ready with the opener. Pa Floom come out still in his church clothes, with a white bunch of flowers half in and out of his buttonhole, and went behind the table with all the bottled stuff lined up, mostly whisky, and a little drop of gin for the old dears, trying to see what there was in the way of glasses, and after dishing his self and a few of the lads a couple of nice straighteners apiece, he busted a couple and Ma Floom shot out at a gallop and told him his fortune, so they had a bit of a barney before things was anywhere nigh getting going.

"That's the way to start it," old Pa hollered. "Have a bloody good row. Clear the air. No good of starting friendly, else it'll turn out a job for the bleeding militia. Go on, Ma, gel. Have a go."

"You mind your own business," Ma Floom yells, glad to get her mind off of Pa, "you big wet end, you."

"Hulloa," says Pa, shifting the feathers to scratch his self, "been reading my letters again, have you?"

Somebody started off a piano, and as soon as one or two got going, all the blokes got hold of the brides and went in the road for a dance round. All the pianos was going the same time, and Ma Chalmers and her learner was dabbing away there, trying to hold the music on with one hand and play with two, and Ma was calling the wind everything, and her learner, a kid about fourteen with steel specs and a bow either side of her hair, was pulling more dials than a bloke out of Comic Cuts, doing it all wrong, shoving her nose nearer the music to see if that would do her any good, till come to a finish, she just plonked away there and let everybody get on with it, like it or not.

"When's this going to happen to you?" Ma says to Him. "You'll have a better do than this, I can tell you. Ain't you got your eye on somebody?"

"Not yet, Ma," He says. There was something in the way she asked Him as cut all the laughs out. "You seen anything, have you?"

"That second girl of the Flooms', young Doris?" Ma says. "Nice, she is. Knows all about the business?"

"Blimey," He says, thinking about her. "What, that skinny bit? Sides I had enough of her at school. No fear, Ma. I'd like to find something with a bit of shape about it, while I'm at it, like."

"Don't mean much," Ma says. "Shape ain't everything."

"No?" He says, as if He never noticed how she said it. "They generally shape up afterwards, though, don't they? Sides, why pick out something just because she knows all about the business?"

"Helps," Ma says, but He knew He was doing it right.

"Don't want nothing to do with no barbers," He says. "I'd rather go in with old Pa Prettyjohn."

"Asked you, has he?" Ma says, giving her teeth a look round. "It's a paying game, that is."

"I know," He says. "You reckon I could manage this, and that the same time, Ma?"

"Not less you're packed up ready for a bloody fine old lot of trouble," Ma says. "Run one, and get a manager for the other, yes. Then you'll be lending 'em the half dollars in one so as they can go and spend 'em in the other. Can't lose much there, can you?"

"Sounds a good idea," He says. "That stops the solicitor lark, though, don't it?"

"All I'm worried about is whether you're going to be all right," Ma says. "That's all. The solicitor's game's safe. Some poor bleeder's always in trouble one way and another, and while there's trouble, it's a safe buy there'll be solicitors hanging about, somewhere. But if you've made up your mind, that's it. I reckon you'll do all right, there, son. When you going to start?"

"Don't know, Ma," He says quick. He could see He was letting His self right in the cart again. "I'd like to know a bit more about this game, first. Had a talk to old Ike about it. He's going to give me a couple of tips, and all."

"He's been a good old pal to me, he has," Ma says. "Anything ever happens to me, he'll put you right. Wouldn't trust the rest of them, not with a handful of dried peas, I wouldn't."

"Makes you keep on talking about something happening to you?" He says. "Proper gives me the creeps."

"Well," she says, "bound to happen some day, ain't it?"

"Better get you a nice big drink," He says, and went for it.

The party was going a treat. Everybody was outside, either on their own chairs or somebody elses, or they was dancing round, or having a wet at one or the other of the tables, else they was just having a look and laughing.

"Now then," Pa says. "What you after?"

"Drink for Ma," He says.

"Ah," says Pa, "now you're talking. Let's see now. I reckon a nice drop of rum in a glass of stout'll just about see her off a treat. Eh?"

"Sounds all right," He says, and Pa starts grabbing.

"Come on, Tich," he yells at Pa Fitchett, "get yourself walking about, there, will you? Pint of stout, a lady, and take your bleeding thumb out the glass. No short measures here. Nice double tot of real Jamaica. Steady on the froth, Tich."

Poor old Dad was well Down The Lane, and none too steady, and Pa was watching him like a moggie after a bit of herring.

"Leave it to me," Dad says, stretching his arms out, bottle in one, glass in the other. "Pouring beer when I was born, I was. No advice from nobody, I don't. Here we are."

The first pour went over the edge of the glass and splashed on the table. Pa looked up at the stars and shut his eyes, and then opened them and made a flying dive at Dad.

"If your Ma had poured her milk like you're pouring this," he screeched, "she'd have bloody corpsed you and saved us the worry. Get out of it."

"Pa," He says, reckoning He ought to say something pally, "when could I start down your place?"

"Monday, seven fifteen, back door," Pa says, pouring the stout in dribs down the inside of the glass. "Bring your own apron, and make your own breakfast. There's plenty of stuff there. Only wants the cooking. All right?"

"I'll see Ma," He says, wishing He kept His trap shut. "Might have a job for me Monday. But I'll let you know."

"Up to you," Pa says, holding out the drink. "I'll come over and see your Ma couple of seconds, when I've made sure this bloke ain't going to neck everything wet round here. What about taking over when I've got shut of him?"

"Say the word, Pa," He says, "but I got to meet somebody just after ten."

"Ah," says Pa. "Meet somebody, eh? Roll on. Be having another do like this soon, eh?"

"Perhaps," He says.

"I'd like to see you fixed up," Pa says, wiping his half moons. "Your Dad was about the biggest bloody lad I ever met. If he'd been here tonight, he'd drunk the rest of us in the gutter by now, been after everything broody under twenty one in the district, and you'd found him in the saloon bar down the road, there, by this time, knocking back double scotches, stone cold sober, hair parted, crease in his trousers, talking about the weather. I believe that bloke could have had Solomon's lot in the afternoon and still done your Ma a bit of good fore winding up the clock. And there wasn't nothing of him, neither. Christ knows where he got it from."

"Didn't do Ma much good," He says.

"Didn't do her no harm," Pa says. "Look at her. They'd have give their eyeballs to been her, in her time, they would. And she ain't too bad, now, taking it all round."

He looked at her, walking back careful, and Pa was right. Looking at the rest of them out there, fanning their selfs with newspapers, He had to admit Ma was all right. She might have been a bit filled out here and there, as you might say, but it was better than knitting needles, like Ma Chalmers and a few more of them, and Ma Tate, sitting outside the shop, looking like a big black bell with a radish on the top. Ma, in her new hat, with the white feathers, looked a bit of all right, and all of a sudden, He see He was lucky, specially thinking about the picture and how she used to be.

"Here you are, Ma," He says. "Don't say I never think of you. Half of stout and a double of rum. Pa'll be over in a minute."

"What," Ma says, smelling it. "Want to shove me down the drain, do he?"

"Won't hurt you," He says. "You deserve it."

"I hope so," she says. "Where's yourn?"

"Got half a beer, here," He says, lifting it. "My best respects, Ma, gel."

"Ta," she says. "Same to you, son."

The road was proper giving it big licks, what with all the dancing going on, and all the joannas knocking it out, and somebody's gramophone scratching away, everybody clapping the time, and getting lost, and clapping anyway, and cheering somebody in the family going round, or giving the bird to a few of them trying to do it a bit fancy. The yellow and green of the lamps and the shaky little white holes of the candles looked just like a garden, somehow, specially when the stars come out now and again, and what with the purple breath up in the sky, it looked as if everything was joining in to give young Percy Floom a right send off.

He come over a bit narked about it, because if young Percy could have a do like this, in a church suit and a white button-hole with a lot of fern, so could He, a sight better, and it proper hit Him a wallop how much He wanted it.

All it wanted was the bride.

But somehow He knew it was Ada or nobody.

All them beetles come back, and the yellow of her hair, the way she sort of fitted Him all the way down, the warm weight of her and the burn of her scent wherever she was, all the Ada of her, as He knew and felt somewhere inside, and never had the words for.

"Just going down the other end, Ma," He says. "Shan't be long."

"Take your time," she says. "When you going to have a dance round?"

"Going to find somebody," He says. "Keep me place warm."

He shot through the crowd, missing everybody He knew so as not to talk to them, and went down the High Road quicker than trying to catch the last Workmans.

Down the Fun Fair, it was all the same, and He got such a homey feeling, He wondered why He never stayed down there all the time. The music was going, and it was warm with plenty of people all having a good time, and the machines was all flashing up and ringing, just like it always was, sort of pally and saying it missed you, like the bloke singing.

Ada was there as per, in a kind of dark blue thin blouse, so you could see them little bumps easier, and yet not so easy, making you look even when you never wanted to, till you wanted to reach out and touch, or go barmy and make a grab at her.

"Hullo," she says, not much of a smile, though. "It's off for tonight. I'm going home."

"What's up?" He says. "Tired?"

"And everything else," she says. "Fed up. I'm leaving next week. Been here too long."

Thinking about it was just like having a couple of lumps of cotton wool stuck in His ears for a minute or two, it all went that there dead quiet, while some bloke was taking his last ball very careful and slow on the nearest machine, not noticing nothing except the lights coming up, not even knowing He was standing there trying to get His tongue to the right words.

She give some change to a couple of blokes and come over again, just leaning on the ledge, looking up the room.

"Couldn't I see you home?" He says.

"No," she says, moving about as if it was a load, "it's no good. Just wasting time, that's all."

"You said we could be nice friends," He says.

"That was last week," she says, like kicking a shoe off.

"Going back to him, are you?" He says.

"Perhaps," she says, "perhaps not. And anyway, it's nothing to do with you what I do. I'm sorry I ever see you."

"I ain't," He says. "I'm soppy about you. There you are. I don't care. I'm soppy about you."

"More fool you," she says, and went up the till for some more change, but the further she went, the more He wanted to rush after her and kneel down and grab her, hold her by them curving legs and hold them tight against Him. But there was a look about her when she turned round.

"Listen," she says. "It's no good of you hanging about here. It's all over, see? It never even started. You go off and paint somebody else, see? Plenty of them about. Sides, I'm four years older than what you are, say nothing about a kid. You couldn't keep me, could you?"

"Might surprise you, there," He says. "I've got two businesses, I have."

"I know," she says. "Painting, and Jim Mordinoy's lark. You get on with it."

"Don't you even like me no more?" He says, feeling He wanted to howl, the way she was talking. "I don't want nothing off of you. I only want to see you sometimes, and sort of, well, you know, smile, like. I don't want nothing. Nothing, I don't want. Only look at you. I got everything else, thinking about you."

"Go out of it," she says.

He never see her laughing, but she was shaking about, going along the ledge and grabbing her bag, going on down to the next bride and bending over her, shoving her self off of the ledge and going on down, all the lovely shape of her going on down the Ladies, and out of it, away from Him, the high black heels, the pinkish legs with a thin black line up the back, the balloon as went side to side and the dark blue of her back, soft to touch, and strong, as come up in little bumps of warm shadow and not, come and go, what your hands could feel moving about, yet steady, while her hair tickled your face and you felt the sharp edge of her mouth and she breathed.

The door of the Ladies let out a yellow triangle of light at the top, and that was the last of her, except her smell, chasing in and out of the fag smoke, but there was too many people looking to dodge about, trying to catch it. So He made it look as if they just had a chat round and they was both happy.

He tried to look as if He was whistling, and walked off.

# CHAPTER XXXVII

OUT IN the High Road, getting in the shadow of the lights, on the kerb away from the windows, He just let it run, because trying to keep it in hurt His chest, and made His throat feel like a long sore.

He wanted to go a walk, but He never knew where to go, and any case, He felt a bit too done up. There was too much light down the cafe and too many blokes might pass remarks, never mind the brides. A tram or bus was just the same about the lights, and sides, when He got there, He only had to get back again and if He missed the last one, He was in the cart again.

So He went down the Road, slow, looking at the black shadows of everybody dancing round down there, listening to the row, watching all the flags waving about as if they was in it, too, feeling as if He could give His self away for nixey, holding Ada one minute and giving her up the next, yet knowing all the time it was no go, and never had been.

Even though He was the Smasher to all the lads down the garage, three jobs on the slate and a thick packet of quid notes in His pocket and some more coming up, He was still just a bloke getting the go by from a bride, and nobody much here, in His own neighbourhood. None of them knew who He was, or what He done. They just thought He was Ernie Mott, working His time in a lithographers a little while ago till He packed up, and doing odd jobs in His Ma's place till He settled down again.

Looking at all the waving lines of candles and the greenish lamps making everybody black shadows with white lines round them, hopping about, like them little dolls on strings, He started hating things again and wanting to do something big, but somehow He never knew what to do, or how to set about it.

But that there gun in the cupboard upstairs come up

again. There was a job He knew how to set about. Champion
of the district, Smasher Mott, the bloke they all had to take
their hats off to, like it or not. He got the idea He ought to
start using it and show a few of them what He was made of,
shooting out the candles or knocking a couple of bottles off. But
the coppers might hear the barney, and start some caper of
their own, so it looked as if He ought to do a right job, like He
been telling His self, and go up the club with it. He had His
dancing suit, and a new black hat, something like Jim's, and
He knew the back way in, so there was nothing in His way.

Besides, there was Ada. All the time He was thinking things
out, He had her sort of just under what He was thinking about,
and when He thought about her, by herself, like, it kind of hurt
him somewhere, like the hole when you just come out the
dentist and spit dark red down a drain.

Ada was going away, even though she wanted the job,
because of the fiddle bloke, and wanting to forget him. Even
after she lived with him and give him a kid, he went and
chucked her out because some bloke said he might get hurt.
And Ada stood for it. She could even cry for him, that was
the funny part of it. But the brides always got the same sort of
idea about a bloke they was in love with, and the more you
shoved them about, the better they liked it, seemed like. You
see it in the pictures week after week, where they hung on,
and hung on, till they was walking on their laceholes, almost,
just because they was in love. If he was dead, they could forget him and start a new life, like a lot of them done, generally
with a newspaper bloke in a white macintosh, with his hat on
the back of his head, always making people proper curl up of
laughing, talking love stuff like a book, make any piano talk,
and kiss a bride, or chew the bosses knackers off, all as easy as
go to tea.

He wanted to be like it, and so did all the other blokes. He
thought of the times they used to go in a gang, Him and Bert
and Tug and Len and a few more, round the High Road and
down the cafe, generally going down the Fun Fair for a look in,
acting about like newspaper blokes after a story, or something,

they never knew what, but going at it nice and loose, sort of easy, and talking American till they run out of what they knew, then they tried to make it up but it never somehow sounded the same. But it all wore off when they got to the top of the road, because everybody knew their suppers was waiting for them, and gas lamps down a dark road of a Sunday night sort of tear anything up, like Ma Chalmers's wireless.

The road had gone all quiet while He was thinking.

First He thought everybody had packed in because of the time.

But when He got off of Ma Crann's enamel sign under the window, he see everybody was sort of in a big ring, and even Pa was standing on the beer table, looking in.

A piano made a couple of deep runs or two while He was tip toeing down there, and then He heard that big fiddle, like Aggie Hunner played, with all them low notes, rubbing it out proper deep, sort of getting you somewhere in the guts.

He climbed up on Pa's wooden stand and looked over the crowd, all watching some bride playing the piano with music and a couple of candles, and it was Aggie Hunner, with her head tucked down, letting fly from side to side, while the other hand slid up and down.

It sounded like something shivery, as you might say, but she was shoving so much into it, that even if you never liked the stuff, you had to watch her and give her the credit due for a lot of bleeding hard work. So everybody stayed quiet, and some of the old girls had a sniff here and there, and kids got a smack in the earhole for moving about, or else got shook so hard their heads nigh come off, and blokes never went nowhere nigh their drinks, case of the glasses clinking and everybody turning round and shishing them.

But while she was playing all these low notes, sort of going up and down, it did, it made you think about things, sort of dreamy, making you feel down in the dumps and not quite so sure of yourself, and then you wanted to start howling again. So come to a finish, after she had two or three goes, everybody cheered and hollered, as if they was as pleased it was over as they was about the music. He liked it all right, but it never had the juice of the Fun Fair stuff, nor it never give you no heart to whistle it, or nothing, only to try and forget it. He could hear them moaning trams a bit too plain.

"What you going to drink, Aggie?" He says, while she was bending over the fiddle bag. "Home early, ain't you?"

"Oh, hullo Ernie?" she says. "I'm glad you were here. Brought a friend of mine back to play for me. I promised Mrs Floom I would. Did you like it?"

"Smashing," He says. "What was that last bit? The one, you know, sort of make you want to give up?"

"One of my favourites," she says, proper pleased. "It's Russian. None but the weary heart, it's called. But I wish I could play it."

"You played it all right," He says. "Crying, some of them was."

"If I'd played it as I wanted to," she says, sort of half kicking her self, strapping up, "you'd have all had a cry. Do you a lot of good, too."

"What about a drink?" He says, thinking about that bit of crayon.

"I'm going in Mrs Floom's first," she says. "Come over after and we'll have a cup of coffee, again. Eh?"

"Okeedoke," He says, but He had His mind on the club.

Everybody was dancing round again, but He got fed up of it. All the brides was local, mostly out of the Road, and all of them stumers. He looked out for Ma and see her chewing the fat with a few of them, Ma Sutcliffe and Ma Tate well in front, so He knew she was safe as long as the lights lasted. Upstairs, through the back way, the whole place seemed to know what He was on, and the new oak furniture sort of looked inside itself, winking when his back was turned, not even creaking to show they was there. The dancing suit went on a treat, and after He got the black tie buckled on behind His collar, and pulled the ends out, He did, He even looked like the Smasher, never mind about feeling like it. He felt proper natty.

The hat went on the side of His head, just like Jim done it, but He wished His hair growed a bit longer so as the long ends would wave over His ears and curl down thick at the back, sort of greyish. Just the same, He was pleased how He looked, and He promised His self one day He meant doing a job where He never had to wear nothing else, only a dancing suit and a black tie and a hat like Jim's, with curly hair going past His ears. It was more dressy, and it made you feel better, sort of richer, like, and, in a manner of speaking, in the money.

The gun felt like some old pal, polished dark brown like one of Ma's best bits in the shop, and kind of cool and steady, ready to do a job without no back chat or fuss, but just the same He wished it was a revolver, one of them with a square handle to fit just nice in His back pocket. The gun was too long, and the shape never went nice with the suit.

Newspaper wrapped round it hid the shape and He went through the fence at the back, along the railway line a bit, climbing the railings on to the steps of the bridge, getting in the High Road so easy, it was like going home.

On top of the tram, nobody much got on or off, and the conductor never even looked at Him, so all the way there and dodging round the side alleys, He thought to His self He might just as well come out in His ordinary clothes for all the good it done Him. The backstairs was empty, and the blokes in the high white hats was still tearing about, and still sweating, stirring, chopping, hollering, in the big kitchen, and going down the narrow stairs to the cellar, He asked His self why they bothered.

The little bloke in the black apron was reading a paper down the end, so He went steady and got out of it without a move nowhere, going along the passage to the door of the big room, but soon as He got there, He knew there was something wrong.

Standing there, listening as if His ears was on long wires, He felt the sweat running down all over Him, like little hands doing odd tickles here and there, making Him shiver, knowing He was thinking about the job in hand, instead of just the getting there, and now He come to think about it, all together, He knew there was something wrong about the band.

He listened to Ma Chalmers's wireless too often not to know a organ when He heard one, and that same steamy rubbery stuff was shaking things about inside there, just like it shook things up at home.

Shoving the thick door open just a crack, He got the full benefit of the smell of fags, grub and the scent of all the brides in there and all the rest of the organ, with some long bloke picking the guts out of one of them stringy plinkers with a loud speaker on it, making it sound like a shower of strangled moggies, all dying slow, in time to the bloke on the drums. There was three of them at it, in fancy blue coats. But the big red piano had gone, and so had all the little red chink towers.

He let the door go, nigh getting His nails tore off, dropping the parcel on the floor, seeing the lark so plain, He never even wanted the telling.

Clem Arbiter was out, this lot was in, and that was why Ada was leaving.

First He could have howled, then He could have bit a finger off out of spite. But after a couple of seconds looking at the felt, nailed round the door, listening to the tune, He got the idea that what was done was done, and that was it. So feeling like the biggest mug out, He picked up the parcel and went back to the cellar.

"Oy," He shouts the little bloke, "mind if I put this here a minute?"

The little bloke jumped up looking two ways same time, then he nodded and grinned, so He shoved it in a dark corner, putting His hat on top of it.

"Shan't be long," He says. "Keep your mince pies on it, though."

Then the stairs started shaking about, heavy, more than one coming down, and He ducked for it, going out as if He never heard nothing, making for the door, but they was down before He was anywhere nigh there.

"Hullo?" He heard a bloke say, and He knew the voice. "That Rossi?"

But he went on for the door, and somebody was running after Him.

"Half a mo," he was saying. "Listen."

He turned round because it was Rush Millitt, and Thirsty Burrows was with him, both in the school, couple of blokes a bit older than what He was, but proper lads, always ready for a laugh.

"Christ," says Rush, nigh on top of Him. "Smasher? Here, Thirsty, boy? It's the Smasher."

"So it ain't," says Thirsty. "In His burying suit."

"His what?" says Rush. "Dinner suit, that's what that is. That's what they call it. Don't know why. Posh, ain't they? I had one. All that silk stuff in the front wore off, it did."

"Have your dinners in it, did you?" Thirsty says.

"Course not," Rush says.

"Waste of money," says Thirsty.

"What are you doing here, Smash, boy?" Rush says.

"Having a look round," He says. "What're you?"

"Just joining the Lamp Duffers," Rush says. "Just got the wire down the pub."

"Sartorelli's expected," Thirsty says. "So we got a little bit of cake for him to cut."

"Better join in," Rush says. "Bags of sport. Set that bastard to rights, quick."

"Trunky and the other lads is all waiting outside here," Thirsty says. "And there's a round dozen of the blokes in there already, so Christ help him."

He see Tiger Collis winking, away, saying nearly the same thing, hearing old Henry bouncing his brolly.

"Tiger Collis here, is he?" He says.

"Outside, now," Rush says. "It'll be plain bloody murder all round."

"What's up with this Sartorelli bloke, then?" He says.

"It's him or Jim," says Thirsty. "I say it's Jim."

"Same here," says Rush. "We've got the table just inside here, left of the band. Coming?"

"Course," He says.

"Got anything to play with?" Thirsty says. "Can't just chuck confetti at the bleeders? Get hold of a hammer, or something. Something health giving. You know?"

"That's right," says Rush, as if he was dishing out pills. "Nice, restful kip for the bastards. Nothing like it for growing lads. Grows 'em up stiff."

They went through the door and narrowed their guts behind this little table against the wall, but they no sooner sat down than this row started outside.

"Hold tight," Rush says. "This is It."

Rossi come flying down from the front, giving the waiters a sort of flip with his mitt, and they all went over to the tables where brides was, and started pulling their chairs away, getting them stood up and shifting them down towards this door to the kitchen, and another door the other side, where the waiters dodged through with the little copper pans.

"Getting the brides out of it," Thirsty says. "Good job, too. Else we'd have to crown a few of them before we finished."

The brides come down in a long lolloping line, all flopping hair and a lot of talk, waving their selfs about, gripping bags and furs, going past in washes of scent and different colours, sort of floating and curving, making you want to reach out and touch them to see what would happen, but the row outside was getting too loud to think about much else. The three blokes in the band all dropped tools together and flew for the door, too, so all the blokes in the club was left on their ownsome, looking at their selfs in the dead quiet, except for the breathing of a fan and the funny sort of dead sound of shouts and rushing about outside. Beyond a few blokes what Rossi was turfing out of it, they was the brightest looking crew outside of a waxworks He ever see, and He never needed the telling who they was, or why they was there.

They was the Lamp Duffers, and it proper give Him the creeping shivers to look at them.

Cosh come tearing down from the far end straight for their table and grabbed Him by the arm.

"Just see you in time," he says, not angry, nor nothing, while

the Duffers was all getting outside in a rush. "Go on. Hop it.
You're too useful for this lark. Tomorrow, twelve o'clock, down
the garage. Go on. Scarper."

"Half a mo," He says, feeling like a kid being chucked out
of a saloon bar, "can't I have a basin, then?"

Cosh grabbed Him by His silk fronts and He felt like jam
getting squashed out of a doughnut.

"I'll give you one," he says. "Only make up your mind.
You're too useful. Sides, one bash and you'll be in dock. Now
scarper."

He see it was no good of arguing, so He edged out of it and
tried to straighten out the silk fronts, wishing He wore His
other clothes.

"Okeedoke," He says. "But I still say I ought to be here
with the lads. I can have a bundle with anybody I like, can't
I?"

"Round your own district," Cosh says. "But not here, see?
You ain't got the first idea, you ain't. Now hop it. Fore I set
about you."

So without even looking at the other two, He turned round
and kicked the door open, letting it wimwam behind Him,
going on down to the cellar, grabbing His hat and the parcel,
rushing up the stairs, through the kitchen and out in the cold
of the dark beyond the lamp.

Round the other side where the dice sign splashed up white,
there was shouts and screams and what sounded like dozens of
blokes all tearing about, glass breaking and the crashes of
stones and stuff being chucked all over the show, and other
sounds near to, moans, as if blokes had give up and just wanted
to be let alone.

He had a squint round the corner, looking in the little yard.
It was one big shouting fight, hundreds at it, stuff flying about,
arms waving coshes and choppers, fists bobbing up full of the
pale blue ribbon flash of cutthroat razors, slashing little half
circles here and there, and in the doorway, where it was thick
with blokes under the white sign, blood come jagging up a
wicked red, and He see it was Trunky and a couple more of

them, having a rare do, all on their own, carving and bashing for all they was worth.

Copper helmets come over the top of the crowd about the same time, and soon as He see them, He was off.

Running down the alley, He could hear the fight still going on, even though everybody was yelling about the police, and whistles was going, but soon as He run far enough in the quiet He could hear somebody else was running in front of Him, and He pulled up a bit.

"Who is it?" somebody says, and He stopped dead, in the dark, going stone cold again, glad He still had the gun and wishing His heart would beat a bit quieter, case of giving the game away.

"You Jim Mordinoy's lot?" this bloke says, none too sure, and then He see it was young Knocker Gover, one of the blokes He was working with down the garage.

"What you getting windy about?" He says, strolling up and putting on a fag. "Anybody think I was Sartorelli, his self."

"That you, Smasher? Well, God perish the bleeding crows," Knocker says, shoving his hat back. "Did you see that bloody lot, did you? Christ. Tell you what? Sartorelli won't be too much good after tonight?"

"Why not?" He says, seeing another bloke further on, and listening for anything coming up behind, seeing this big round end car polishing itself in the dark.

"I see him bashed," Knocker says. "That was after some bloke got him with a razor, straight across the dial. He went down, see? All blood and snot, he was. Then they set about him on the deck. Made a right mess of the bastard, and all. What you doing?"

"Going home," He says. "What're you?"

"Me and Taz got a pram here," he says, giving this other bloke the thumb. "It's one of them big new Yanks. Smashing job it is. Brand spanking new. Picked it up round St. James's Street. Leave their mothers out, some of them would. We're going to have a do round the back of Leicester Square. Coming?"

"Okeedoke," He says, following up, "I'll put the parcel in the back."

"What, got your climbing irons with you, have you? Been birds nesting?" Taz says, coming the acid. "Out on the bash, are you?"

"No," He says, meaning it nasty, "but I can, where it's wanted."

"Whoa," says Knocker, shoving his self in, "hold it down, now. He don't mean nothing, Smash boy. Just shove it in the back, and squat in front, nice and peaceful. Christ, there's enough bleeding trouble down the road, without starting another lot here."

"Too bleeding true. Wouldn't said it if I known, like?" Taz says, and it done Him good to hear the sort of voice, as if it was known He was a star turn down the garage and had to be spoke to the right way. "Didn't mean nothing. Just joking, see, Smash? Straight up. No offence, chum?"

"That's all right," He says, getting in the front of this long, low job, but He made sure He said it the right way, so as there was no doubts about it. "Where we off to?"

"That's what I'd like to know," somebody says, and He come over proper ice cold freezing stiff, all of a sudden, half in and half out, just bent over, waiting, one foot still on the kerb, looking at His hand on the cushion.

All the noise stopped, all the night got blacker, all the lights went out, all the banging and bashing inside of Him got louder and louder and everything outside was going quieter and quieter.

This big copper was just standing there, looking at them with his thumbs hooked in his top pockets.

"Who's the owner of this car?" he says, walking round as slow as a clock, while Knocker was getting his self in the driving seat. Taz was in the back, but the door was open.

"Me," Knocker says, turning the key.

"Got your licence?" the copper says, like asking for another spud.

"Watch it," yells Knocker, and started up, tearing the wheel round, right hand down, hard.

This big thing went like a light, chucking Him in, both doors swinging about, going proper fast in a few yards, just humming sort of under its breath, like some old dear doing a bit of ironing.

Then something crashed in the window and He see the copper holding on a door handle, standing on the running board, crashing his baton on the glass.

"Shut them bloody doors, some of you," Knocker screeches, and He slammed the one on His side and went over the back and played touch with the other, pulling hard to shut it against the wind, still ice cold, and hoping to Christ they got out of it.

He see Taz winding down the side window and heard a yell, and through the glass at the back, He see the copper rolling in the middle of the road.

"Nigh cut his bleeding hand off," Taz says, wiping off on the carpet. "Go for the Borough, Knock boy. Get down there, we can take the Tunnel and nip home, easy."

"Pity the bastard got this window," Knocker says. "We could have got a nice price for this. Now they'll be looking for it."

"Can you get rid of them?" He says, not on, because the pair of them was just about as bright as yesterday's ham rolls.

"We make a living," Knocker says. "If we don't sell 'em to Jim, we take 'em down to a bloke in Croydon. We can pick up a nice twenty here and there, can't we, Taz?"

"Course," Taz says. "Dead easy, it is. That's aside of the jobs we do for Jim, like. It's bunce, that's what this is."

"What about the numbers on this?" He says. "We don't want to get copped, do we?"

"We kicked 'em in," Knocker says. "Glass, they was. Don't think we've just come up, do you? Sides, who's worried about bleeding coppers? Let them worry about us."

"That's what they're paid for," Taz says.

They was going a proper rate through the big streets, shooting lights, missing things, going between and cutting in front of buses, hearing blokes yell and brides scream here and there, but somehow, sitting back on the soft cushions, it never meant too much. Through side streets, round corners, hearing the tyres whistle through their teeth, getting in wide streets again, having a bucket full of whitish light shot on them every time they nipped past under the big lamps over the middle of the road, seeing the tram lines starting in four silver curves and bunches of people all round the stop, and waiting in the road.

Knocker pressed the button yards away, but the last of them just got back on the kerb by throwing his self there, and Taz give him a big raspo through the busted window.

"See?" he says. "Then they blame us. Standing there like a load of cheese, waiting for it. What about some grub, Knock?"

"We'll get through the Tunnel first," Knocker says, "then up the Mile End Road, eh? Go down the fish cafe, eh? Suit you, Smash?"

"If the grub's all right, it'll suit me," He says.

"All right?" Taz says. "That ain't the word for it. It's proper spagnagarous, that's what it is. Get a lump of fish nigh a foot square, see? Then some baked beans, fried spuds, tomatoes and sort of flat macaroni stuff, with a fried egg on top, lump of bread and grease, pot of chah, and a bit of, you know, this here fancy cake stuff, like, chucked in. Two bob the issue. I can go two of them, any time you like."

"Same here," Knocker says. "Smashing grub, it is. Don't know how they do it on the money."

Taz came round at them quick, chucking his fag through the window.

"Gongers up," he says. "Right behind us."

"Wrap up," Knocker says. "Trying to do? Have a lark?"

"It's a gong job, I tell you," Taz says. "Not hundred yards off. Spread 'em, for Christ's sake."

There it was, rattling like a shower of tins right behind them, the queer, weak, ringing of a police car getting its teeth in a job and coming in for trouble.

"Oh," Knocker says, looking in the little looking glass, "sorry

I spoke. Whoa. Never mind your hats. Hold your bleeding ears
on. I'm spreading me tootsies round the dinger. Here we go,
lads."

This big car went out as if another car inside of it was just
using it for garage. They was kind of smudging the dark road
in a black rush, like going head first through a long bucket of
water, without getting wet or having to flip it out of your eyes.

"More," says Taz, looking through the back.

There was a higher sound from the guts of it, going higher
and higher, till it seemed to be making a sort of squeezed out
scream of surprise to find itself doing the speed without tipping
over or blowing up.

"What's the bets I can't lose 'em inside five minutes?"
Knocker says, putting on another fag and driving one hand.
"Anything over a fiver?"

"They're right on top of you, now, anyhow?" Taz says. "I'll
take you."

"Just giving 'em a nice smell, that's all," Knocker says. "If I
can't lose a load of coppers round here, I ought to start wearing my grannies hat."

The car went rocking round corners, going in little roads
and turning out again, down little lanes and along back alleys,
brushing past bushes growing over back gardens, knocking
over clothes props and tearing away yards of line, over holes
and bumps, round here, round there, all in the dark, no lights,
only the two on the wings as never showed much, except somebody's whitish face for a second just opening up ready to yell,
and corner posts and green leaves. But sitting on cushions as
never hardly moved, it was more like being at the pictures,
watching it happen to somebody else.

"You ain't lost 'em," Taz says. "I can see their headlights.
They must have one of them big new jobs, there. One of them
super charger whatsnames. Can't half go. Ain't going to do it,
Knock, chum."

"We are, Taz, we are," Knocker says. "I know this bit like
the taste of a pint. We got the Tunnel just through here, then
we can lash out on the straight."

They come out in a road and screeched round a corner, going down through the big black O of a tunnel, all white inside with light from lamps in the roof, all splashing hot silver on millions of rings of white tiles, running down this long pipe, looking as if it been give a good old shine up by the breath of all the cars and lorries nipping past for years on end.

"Here they come," Taz says. "Have to jump for it, Knock boy."

"Can't get no more out of this," Knocker says. "I nearly got me foot flat on the bleeding road as it is. Jump at the top, eh? All right, Smash?"

"Okeedoke," He says, feeling proper up the spout, specially with His dancing suit on. "What we do?"

"I'm turning left," Knocker yells, what with the gong, and the sound of the car, and all, "I'll do a right turn opposite the second on the right, soon's we're out the Tunnel, see? Brake hard, and shove her through the door. Then we split three ways, eh?"

"Okeedoke," He says, and the worms was working double shifts in His guts.

"If I only had another three minutes I'd slip 'em," Knocker says. "Two minutes, even. They'd never find us."

He looked round through the little back window and nigh dropped down dead. This big blue car, all flashing up of polish in the light, was only a matter of fifty yards or so away and gaining every other yard, coming down the hill straight at them.

"Won't do it," Taz says, seeing Him looking. "We don't get there, Knocker. It's a dead pinch, boy. Hard luck, Knocker. Had a good try, chum."

"Listen," He says. "Suppose I let 'em have a couple of these through the windscreen. How'd that be?"

He held up the little copper and grey bullets, letting the light shine on them.

"What you going to shoot 'em out of?" Knocker says.

The parcel come up end first, and He shoved all the paper off of it.

Taz looked through the window again, and the car started dodging traffic. He was holding the gun in one hand and the bullet in the other, like a proper Joe Soap, but nobody was taking a blind bit of notice of Him.

"You've got it on 'em going up the hill, Knocker," Taz says. "They got too much weight there."

"Might do it yet," Knocker says, and the car was squeezing out a thinner scream, going through it something proper cruel, it was.

"If we was to knock one of them blokes off," Taz says, still looking round at them, "it might come to a hanging job."

"That's right," Knocker says. "Matter of fact, Smash, we might's well sling that bleeding iron out of it, up the top there. How are we, Taz?"

"Doing very nice, chum," Taz says. "They ain't come round the bend yet."

Knocker was going in and out of the traffic like some tart's knitting needle, poking in and curving out, gone again before you could look round, coming round the back of lorries and sliding in front of vans on the wrong side, making drivers yell and shove the brakes on, doing the job a proper treat, he was, smoking his fag like a lord and not caring that much for nobody.

"You've done 'em, Knock boy," Taz says, and starts hitting him on the shoulder, laughing away, there. "You old bastard, you. You done 'em again. You got 'em all proper stone cold, you have. Bet they don't half like you, eh?"

"Bit of luck it goes under the river, that's all," Knocker says, still driving like mad, but looking at him, you might think you was on a ploy down Margate, or something, he was that there cool, sitting back as fancy as you like. "It's always the hills they fall off on, them gongers. Noticed it before."

"We going down the fish cafe, are we?" He says, feeling out of it, somehow.

Knocker pulled out of the Tunnel and turned right.

"Listen," he says, "first thing. Chuck that bleeding iron out of it."

"Can't," He says, "it's Jim's."

"Don't care," Knocker says, "chuck it out. I ain't getting pinched with no bleeding irons on board."

"Same here," says Taz. "Another plate of dinner altogether, that is."

"What," He says, "you windy, are you?"

"Perhaps," Knocker says. "I don't suppose I got your guts. There you are. Don't suppose I have. But I got too much bleeding sense to let a copper catch me with one of them nigh me. Chuck it out, Taz."

"Here it goes, mate," Taz says, and there was a lot of moves in the back with a cold wind blowing through all of a sudden, and Taz was wheeling the window up again. "It's out."

"I feel like ten different blokes, I do," Knocker says, and he starts laughing, but he was still going for all he was worth, in and out of little dark roads. "Nine of 'em stone dead, and the other one paralysed."

"You'll have to square Jim about the iron," He says.

"I'll square Christ about it," Knocker says. "As long as I ain't got to square no copper about it. You'd get five years."

"Easy," says Taz. "I'd be what? Christ, twenty four when I come out, eh?"

"Don't mind getting lagged, for something I've done," Knocker says. "But no irons."

"They got to prove it, ain't they?" He says, feeling as if He was talking to the pair of them across the width of the road. "Ain't as if you done something with it?"

"Listen," Knocker says, no larks and not so pally, neither. "If we'd let you, you'd have knocked one of them coppers off just now, wouldn't you? Eh? Perhaps a couple of 'em, eh? Then where would we be? Shall I tell you? Ever heard of the Old Bailey, have you? Eh?"

"Well," He says, "what of it?"

"That's where you get your tens and twenties, there," Knocker says, same voice. "You go there on your own, chum. Not for me. Don't mind doing six months or so for knocking off a car, now and again. I can earn me self a nice living before and after. But I ain't going in twenty, and coming out forty. Not me."

"That's up to you," He says, feeling He had the say over him, although it proper surprised Him to know they thought He had more guts than the pair of them.

"Christ," says Knocker, and starts pulling the wheel while the car was screaming like a bride, but there come a big bash, with glass busting and cracking and He was flying about all over the back and the engine was just about flogging itself loose, howling through a open mouth, and then it stopped.

People was running about outside and shouting, and some blokes was trying to open the doors, chucking a bit of light all over the shop, and jiggling keys about.

"Taz," Knocker says. "You all right, chum?"

Taz never answered, and all of a sudden He see a bit of Joey's waistcoat blowing about again.

"Come on," somebody says outside. "Open this door."

"It's a pinch," Knocker says. "They got us. Taz? You all right, chum?"

Somebody had a torch dead on his face from the outside. It come up there like the ace of hearts.

"Quick," Knocker yells, "open a door. Any of 'em. My mate's hurt."

But they was all stuck tight. Everybody was rattling and tugging, but it was no go.

"Turned your petrol off in there?" somebody shouts outside, but Knocker was over the back, pulling Taz up on the seat, trying to get him to rights, but it was hard because the car was over on the skew, and he kept on slipping off.

"Stand by," says this voice outside. "I'm smashing this window. Duck your nuts."

It took a good few clouts to clear the pane by the driver's seat, and then a copper shoved his face in.

"Come on," He says. "I want all of you. Cut his self, has he?"

He got His face out of His coat and put His hat on, brushing all the bits of glass and powder off of His trousers, looking round to see if He could do something for Taz.

"Here. You," this copper says to Him. "Let's have you out of it, first. Come on. Step lively."

"Okeedoke," He says. "Don't get alarmed."

"I'll give you alarmed," this copper says. "Get your body out of it."

He was half way through the window when a couple of coppers made a dive at Him and pulled Him the rest of the way, sort of slinging Him at a couple more like a sack of spuds.

"Quick," they was yelling to Knocker. "Quick, pull him up here."

He see Knocker, head and shoulders out the window and the coppers pulling at him and then reaching further inside for Taz, and then there was a kind of little orange flash.

"Watch yourselves," the Sergeant holding Him yelled, "look out. The petrol. The petrol."

One of the coppers tried to grab Taz but he was a dead weight. He see the copper pulling for all he was worth with his eyes shut and his teeth white in the light, then the two coppers holding Him dragged Him backwards at a run while the crowd was yelling and a sort of big yellow light whoomfed up, making it come up proper warm all the way round.

"Oh, God Jesus Christ," the Sergeant said. "Poor little bastard."

The car was in the middle of a big ragged marigold blowing up running rolls of thick black smoke all round the petals.

A couple of coppers was holding Knocker by both arms and he was kicking and tearing at them, trying to get back in, screeching with his mouth wide open, but what with the yelling of the crowd and the breath of fire you could hardly hear your self, never mind him.

All of a sudden, one of these big coppers let go and grabbed Knocker by his shirt, drawing him off a burton with a solid right, splashing him straight out, cold as Monday's dinner.

"Sensiblest thing tonight," this Sergeant says, out in the cool and quiet while some more coppers was trying to get little spitting things going on the blaze.

"In you get," this Sergeant says to Him, and give Him half a shove towards the door of the police car. The other copper helped Knocker in another seat. "That's it. Now then. Fair do's. Any trouble out of you and you know what to expect, don't you? Just remember that other bloke in there, and think yourselves bloody lucky. The pair of you. See?"

"Okeedoke," He says, seeing His leg through a tear in His trousers. His hat was gone too. But it never seemed to matter. Ma was one side of Him, and Ada was on the other, and they was just looking at Him, not saying a blind word, just looking.

It was a dead pinch.

## CHAPTER XXXVIII

UP AT THE STATION, there was a lot of palaver one way and another, but Him and Knocker never took too much notice of it.

"Now, then," this big greyhaired copper says, pulling a book open, "let's have a look at you. What's your name?"

They just stood there, and let the lamps popple the answer.

"Oh," says the copper, having a little laugh. "Can't talk for fright, eh? All right. Tip your pockets out, here. Come on."

Some coppers in ordinary suits started helping, none too light neither, and bit by bit, everything they had was on the table. The greyhaired copper never touched nothing till it was all there, and all the time he just sat there holding hands with his self, happy as anything, singing a little song just loud enough for you not to hear the words.

"Well," he says, picking the stuff over very fancy, "what a collection, eh? Count them notes."

One of the coppers turned His dough out of the envelope and started flicking it up. The greyhaired bloke picked up one of the bullets.

"Interesting thing to find, ain't it?" he says, looking at Him. "Member of a rifle club, are you?"

"No," He says. "They was give me."

"Ah," says the greyhaired copper, as if he just been showed his breakfast. "Give you, eh? Wouldn't care to say who by, I suppose?"

"Don't know him from Adam," He says. "Never see him before."

"Or since," says the greyhaired copper. "Might as well get the story right. You wouldn't have slung a Two Two rifle away tonight by any chance, would you?"

"No," He says. "What's a Two Two rifle?"

"Something we had give us tonight," says the greyhaired copper. "Difference being, we knew the party who found it."

"Forty four pounds, twelve and eightpence, sir," says the young copper, shoving it all back in the envelope again. "None of the notes in rotation."

"Fancy me working hard all my life for my little bit, eh?" says the greyhaired copper, having a laugh, "and smart young lads like you running round in your black suits, eh? And earning all this? I must have been wasting my time, eh?"

He see none of the other coppers was laughing. They was all hard faced.

"Forty four pounds odd," says the greyhaired copper. "Well, well. And what have we here?"

The fag case was getting a good looking at, inside and out.

"None of that nasty cheap silver or gold stuff for you, eh?" this greyhaired copper says. "Platinum only. Just the bare platinum. No half larks. Get the pawn list, Rogers. Look through it for this."

One of the coppers in uniform started scratching about behind a partition, and the case followed him out.

"One bus ticket, and one tram ditto," says the greyhaired copper, starting to get proper on His nerves. "Cambridge Circus, eh? Get on to London Transport, and see where these were issued, and when."

Another copper went off with the tickets.

"One envelope, creased, containing a billhead, I. Buzgang, Limited. Fine furnishings. The Noted House," says the greyhaired copper, "Debtor to Mrs Who? Ring up Mr Buzgang. Find his private number. I'll talk to him."

Another copper hopped out of it.

"Handkerchief like this," the greyhaired copper says, pointing at it, "don't quite go with platinum cigarette cases, do it? That's a snot rag, that is. Take the terrible thing away."

One of the other coppers scooped it up and shoved it in a envelope.

"Now then," says the greyhaired copper, looking at Knocker.

"I suppose we're not going to have the privilege of making your acquaintance, neither? Eh?"

"You find out," Knocker says.

"That's right," the greyhaired copper says, easy as opening a door. "Nothing much in your pockets, is there? Like me, a poor man. One pound, three and nine. You two know each other?"

"Never see Him before tonight," Knocker says. "We give him a lift."

"Kind of you," the greyhaired copper says. "All dressed up and nowhere to go, so you took pity on Him. Eh?"

"We stopped to put the lights right," Knocker says. "He come up and asked us if we was going anywhere nigh the Mile End Road, and we said yes. So He got in."

"That was after you were warned to stop in Westminster Bridge Road by the patrol car?" the greyhaired copper says.

"Before," Knocker says. "By the Embankment, it was."

"How did you get down there?" the greyhaired copper says to Him.

"Walked, of course," He says.

"Ah," says the greyhaired copper, holding up his finger. "Course. How silly of me. Buses, trams and tubes all round you, and all this money burning a hole in your pocket, so you walked. In that rig out, eh? Why did you want to go down the Mile End Road, that time of night?"

"See somebody," He says. "Sides, I was going home."

"What's it matter?" Knocker says, cutting up rough. "Nothing to do with me what He done, is it? I got me own affairs to attend to."

The greyhaired copper looked at him, not saying nothing, and the place sort of went dead quiet.

"You have, indeed," says the greyhaired copper. "And you're unlucky not to have somebody else standing there, and all. Aren't you?"

"Yes," Knocker says, just looking at him.

"His Ma'll want to know where he's got to, won't she?" the greyhaired copper says. "Miss his wages, too, eh?"

"It was that bloody copper's fault what was driving," Knocker says, looking straight across this desk, head down, nigh going over it his self. "He done it on purpose. Come in the near side and shoved me against the wall. What could I do?"

"Lots of things," the greyhaired copper says, quiet as Uncle telling the tale. "You shouldn't have been in it, for a start, should you?"

Knocker was trying heavens hard to brass it, watching the greyhaired copper follow the grain in the desk with his thumb nail.

"We was only going for a ride," he says, just getting it out.

"Very old, was he?" the greyhaired copper says.

"Nineteen," Knocker says, holding on to it.

"Nineteen, eh?" this greyhaired copper says, and started looking at his hands. "What a shocking thing for his poor old mother, eh? Dear me. I wouldn't like to break the news there. Course, we'll have to put up a notice about the body. In all the papers. Outside all the police stations. Then you'll have to identify the remains at the inquest."

"I won't," Knocker says, and here it come, "I won't. Do what you like, I won't."

"Give me his name and address, then," the greyhaired copper says. "That can't hurt you, can it? And it'll ease his poor old Ma's mind, won't it? You're doing her the favour, aren't you? And you must admit you can't do him much more of a bad turn, can you? At least, you can give him the chance of a decent funeral."

While Knocker was getting his self to rights again, the greyhaired copper opened the book, and dipped the pen in the ink, holding the bit of pink blotter very careful, just where his hand was going to rest on the page. Nearly all the other coppers had come back.

"What did you say the poor lad's name was?" he says.

"Charlie Blent," Knocker says, trying to wipe his self with anything. "17, The Dale, Bermondsey."

"Bermondsey," says the greyhaired copper, writing a smashing hand and blotting up very careful. "Right."

"Your call to Mr Buzgang, sir," says a copper in the door.

"Get on to Bermondsey C.I.D.," the greyhaired copper says, and got off the stool. "Have a smoke if you feel like it."

The coppers all started pulling out the fags and He went to take one of His own off of the table, but the copper with the fair curly hair stopped Him.

"Not tonight," he says, having a laugh, and chucking Him one of his own. "They're all His Majesty's property for the moment. You'll get 'em back, of course."

"How long we kept here, then?" He says, getting a light off Knocker.

"Depends," this copper says. "When we find out who you are, that'll be halfway house. Then you might go up for bail."

"What's that?" He says.

"Asking somebody to put some money up for you. That's what it boils down to," the copper says. "Then if you don't appear in court, they lose it, see?"

"Can't see it happening to me, somehow," He says, and He could hear Ma saying the word, "can you, Knocker?"

Knocker wagged his nut, afraid to look up because his eyes was all fat of howling.

"What we going to be charged with?" he says.

"Don't know yet," the copper says. "Depends who was driving, doesn't it?"

"Why?" Knocker says, having a long draw.

All the coppers sort of sat back and looked a bit worried.

"Well," one on the end says, "a young lad's lost his life, ain't he?"

"That was one of your lot to blame," Knocker says. "He bashed into us."

"Performance of his duty," says another copper. "You were in a stolen car. You were warned to stop. You were responsible for a number of accidents on the street, and in the Tunnel, and there might be some casualties. He was ordered to intercept and stop you. By wireless."

"That was how, was it?" Knocker says. "Wireless, eh? Christ."

The lamp was having a rare old game, poppling away there, not worried about nobody. He could feel the worms having a fine old caper downstairs, making Him feel sick.

"What you reckon it might run out?" Knocker says, drawing the fag hot red and swallowing the lot.

The copper pulled his mouth down and looked up at the ceiling.

"Oh," he says, proper lights out, "that's past me, that is. Depends who was driving, see?"

"The other bloke was driving," He says. "I kept on telling him to give over, but he wouldn't. And you can't argue with a bloke what's driving, can you? I can't drive at all, so I was in a right stew. You drive, can you, Knocker?"

"Bit," he says, looking at the floor, "not much."

"See?" He says to this little ring of coppers. "We couldn't do much, could we?"

"If you don't know him," one of the coppers says to Him, pointing to Knocker, "how do you know his name?"

"That's what the other bloke called him," He says. "I never see 'em not fore tonight. But the other bloke was the one. He was a case, he was."

"You shut your bleeding trap," Knocker says, but the coppers was all round before he could shift, "else I'll put me foot in it."

"Come on," one of them says, and took his arm, taking him the other side of the big desk affair. "Don't want any fancy sparring here."

"What's going wrong?" says the greyhaired copper, coming back again, and all the coppers stood up.

"Little argument, sir," one of them says.

"Argument, eh?" says the greyhaired copper, looking at Knocker. "Ever hear of Ernest Mott, did you?"

Knocker never budged, not a inch.

"Who?" he says, looking at his fag.

"What about you?" the greyhaired copper says to Him. "Do you know Mrs Edith Mott, antique furniture dealer, do you? She's coming over here."

The worms all turned to solid ice, stuffing His guts full of them sharp lumps like what they put round fish amongst the parsley on the white slab, and He could feel His self sort of going freezing stiff. He could see Ma coming through the door, there, just standing there, looking at Him. After all I done for you, after all the decent clothes I bought you, and all the money I give you, and all the talks we had and the way we had a good laugh, and me buying things special for your supper and all, and this is what you go and do. This is the thanks I get.

He could hear it and see it plainer than everything there.

"Listen," He says, hardly hearing His voice, "don't let her come round here, governor. I don't want to see her, see? She's my Ma, all right. I'm Ernest Mott. Anything else you want to know, I can tell you. But I don't want her round here, see?"

"That's all right," the greyhaired copper says, and opens the big book again, dipping in the pen just as careful, and holding the blotting paper like a bit of gold. "Ernest Mott, eh?"

"Yes," He says, watching the pen hang it out across the paper, just like pegging up a line of smalls.

"This your address?" the greyhaired copper says, holding out a piece of paper. "Mr Buzgang give it to me."

"Yes," He says, looking at the words. It was just like dreaming something and wishing to Christ you could wake up.

"Right," says the greyhaired copper. "There's no need for you to worry about your Ma coming over here. Somebody's gone to pay her a call. Just to let her know where you are. Find out a bit more about you."

"They've gone to do your drum," Knocker says, proper taking the rise out of Him, "they give you the madam. And here was me, thinking you was a wide boy, and all."

"Go on?" says the greyhaired copper. "Why did you?"

"Way He carried on," Knocker says. "Big mouth. That's all He is."

"What's he talking about?" He says. "Doing me drum?"

"Doing your drum?" the greyhaired copper says, looking in

the desk for something or other, not even worried. "They'll search your house."

"Search me house?" He says, coming over a right shake. "What for? What have I done?"

"Don't know. Yet," the greyhaired copper says. "But there's a lot of money here wants accounting for. And a platinum cigarette case. Twenty rounds of Two Two ammunition. A joy ride in a stolen car, and a dead youth of nineteen. That's enough to be going on with, ain't it? We want to know a bit more about you. That's all."

All of a sudden He wanted to get down on the deck and feel something solid. He wanted to hold the floor. Everything was wonky, wobbling about, kind of all over the show, and there was no help nowhere and nobody to turn to. He could feel His self going sort of weak.

"Course," says the greyhaired copper. "If you're a respectable kind of a lad, you've got nothing much to fear, have you?"

"No," He says, and He see Knocker proper laughing behind his mitt.

"Take 'em inside," the greyhaired copper says. "Separate."

Somebody put a hand under His elbow and took Him out of the yellow pop of the lamps, in a pitch dark passage, turning one little blue light on, and He see this door coming nearer and nearer, along the stone of the passage and He could smell the stuff they put down the drains, and the lump, lump, lump of the coppers boots was over the lot of it, sort of smothering everything.

"I ain't going to prison," He says, outside this door, stopping dead and leaning back. "I ain't going."

"Course you're not," says some bloke behind Him, "you're just going to have an hour or two in the parlour. That's all."

The door come open, slow, as if there was a bit of weight on the hinges, and He was put inside by a couple of pairs of hands as meant Him to go in, and stay in, and no half larks about it.

The door come to, and a key went round the lock easy as putting change in your pocket.

He was in a little room with a bed covered over in dark

brown blankets, just like Ma Sedgwiss had for a coat. One little lamp with a wire cage like a ball round it slung a kind of pale brown light round the place. There was a window too high to reach, just behind there, and this big black door, all in one piece, cold to touch, so as you knew without the telling it was iron, just in front, and there was a little round hole highish in the middle of it, about where you might have a dekko through.

He sat down on this bed, about a foot wide, stone hard, trying to look at His self, but nothing seemed to be coming through, except He was cold in the guts and empty everywhere else.

He see He was in line to Do Time.

Too dry to swallow, afraid even to move His self, He heard Ma saying it all. He see Ada just looking at Him, like she done down the Fair.

Sitting there, He see the coppers banging on the door, and Ma Chalmers hanging out of her front bedroom window, asking them if anybody been run over, and then Ma coming down and taking them through the kitchen, and everybody standing in the dark till she got the gas going.

He see it all and heard it all.

He see Ma sitting down there with her black coney round her and her nightdress all bunching about on the floor, just looking up at the gas, having a go at her back teeth, while the coppers was lump, lump, lumping round the house, seeing if they could find out a bit more about Him.

He wanted to howl to try and soften the hard feeling in His chest, but there was nothing there to howl with. It felt as if it all been dried up by this lark of searching the house, hands going in drawers and cupboards, opening boxes, pulling stuff out. It was all going on, now, while He was sitting there. All them coppers was lumping about the house and Ma was sitting there, looking at the gas, while they was doing His drum.

He laid down on this narrow bed and pulled the blankets over His head to shut out the pale brown light. Nothing seemed to matter so much down there in the dark.

## CHAPTER XXXIX

HE WOKE UP stone cold on this plank affair and a copper took Him along the passage for a sluice, and give Him a mug of cocoa, but He never felt too bright so He kept His mouth shut. Then they took Him in the big room again, and there was Ike Buzgang, busy with a pen and looking proper sorry for his self in his bowler and wet mac.

"Right," says this copper, "you can go now."

So without no arguments, He just followed Ike outside, certain He was dreaming again.

Getting out on the step was better than being give a cartload of quid notes, and even though He was still in His dancing suit, all tore down one knee, and it was coming down heavens bleeding hard of rain, it never seemed to matter. The wide grey street was twice as wide, and airy, spacey, proper jumping up of places you could go to.

He was out, and all the thanks was due to old Ike Buzgang.

"Ike," He says, just under the blue lamp, "shan't forget you, mate. I don't know what you done, but I shan't forget you. Nor'll Ma."

"Listen, Ernie," Ike says, still looking proper windy, as if he just see a shower of lions, "listen very careful. I stood a surety for one hundred pounds on you. You should be at Bow Street, in the court day after tomorrow, nine fifteen. So you going to be there?"

"Course I'm going to be there," He says, feeling proper put out. "Think I'd let you down?"

"I just want you should understand," Ike says, still worried. "I will come to fetch you eight fifteen. Listen, Ernie. You not going to find everything like you should want it. You know? Is going to be hard."

"I know all about it," He says. "No need to tell me. One night in there's enough, thanks."

"Yes," says Ike, looking worse, "but not here. Home. You going to find a change."

He got that feeling of cold worms crawling about in His guts again. Every time He thought of Ma, them worms started up a rare old caper.

"Okeedoke, Ike," He says. "I know what to expect."

"You know?" Ike says, a bit brighter, like. "So, if you know, it's all right."

"Course it's all right," He says. "It won't last. She'll get over it."

Ike took off his bowler and rubbed his face round a couple of times, finishing up with a chase round and round his eyeballs.

"I don't know what kind of way you talk," he says, sort of half angry, half sorry. "She'll get over? Certainly. And one day, we all going to die. So we get over that? Certainly. But it's necessary we should every day suffer? Who benefits? Who is getting the benefit?"

"Listen, Ike," He says, seeing a argument coming up, "I'm going home. Thanks again for what you've done. I'll see you get plenty of business later on to pay for it, and all. See you eight fifteen, eh?"

"All right," Ike says, "here's enough for expenses."

He was holding out a quid note.

"Blimey," He says, taking it, "you're a sport, Ike."

"Not me," Ike says, "your mother."

"Oh," He says. "Okeedoke. Ta. So long, Ike."

Ike just nodded and pushed off up the road, opening his umbrella, and He pulled the collar of His dancing suit up round His neck, stuck His hands in His pockets, and put His head down in the rain, turning up the left, looking for a cafe and dying for a fag.

The rain was coming down like millions of thin glass rulers, all getting chucked out the same box the same way, splintering their tips on the hard road, and then going right in, sloshing the gutters full of tasty bubbling stuff, sending all the match ends and bits of paper on a right old sail, and then, while they was looking the other way, slipping them down the drain hole, giving the sewers a treat.

He started thinking about Chaser and what happened to him, and Trunky, and then Jim, but it all seemed nothing much beside what happened to Him, and He never wanted to think too much about that, neither, so He just made up His mind not to, and got on with the job of finding a place to have a plate of grub and a quiet sit down, and a spit and a drag.

Whatever He done, and however much He thought, it never seemed to make no difference, so it seemed to Him He might be doing His self a favour if He just let the whole affair get on with it. He done enough thinking about Ma all night, or till He went off to sleep, and it sort of wore off the first feelings, so now He was just waiting for her, and He had His tale all ready for the telling and all, whatever she said.

Taking it all round, He reckoned He was lucky.

He sat a nice hour of it in a big cafe, right up against the steam heat doings in the wall, had His breakfast like a lord and a couple of smokes afterwards just sitting back without a grouse in the world. Not many people looked at Him, and He see His self down the Gents, so He knew they had nothing to shout about, except the dancing suit, and the hole in His trousers.

It was about midday when He got off of the tram at the top of the Road, and it was still raining, and He thanked Christ it was, too, because it kept everybody indoors where He never had to answer no questions.

So He shot down and hopped through the alleyway, but the back door was bolted.

"Ma?" He yelled, giving the door a boot or two. "Ma? Come on. I'm soaking, I am."

The rain just went on playing ding dong tin can bells on the dustbin, and in the greyish Sunday dinnertime light, all sorts of bright white diamonds went slipping and sliding down the curves of the dark green grass.

He looked through the kitchen window, but there was nobody there. All the top windows was bolted, and there was no smell of dinner, neither.

"Ma," He proper hollered. "You in kip, are you? You all right, Ma?"

Ma Chalmers's back door opened and He heard her hopping through the wet across the concrete to the hole in the fence.

"That you, Ernie?" she says in her voice just like the things she made for tea, sort of all falling to bits before you got them in your mouth. She was always making things for tea, some·how.

"Yes," He says. "Why?"

"You better come inside fore you catch your death of cold," she says. "Come along. I got a message for you."

"Oh," He says. "Okeedoke."

While He was getting through the fence, all the tales got lost and them worms come back again, and He started thinking how Ma might have gone looking for Him, or something.

"What's up?" He says, when they was inside the scullery.

"You go in there to the fire," Ma Chalmers says, taking her coat off of her head, and pushing her hair up. "Take your shoes off if they're wet, and all. Better have your dinner here if you ain't going nowhere else?"

"What for?" He says. "Where's Ma?"

"She's gone out for a while," she says. "Go on, now. Off with them there shoes. Let's have you."

He went in the kitchen, seeing the big piano again the far wall, hating it as much as He used to when He was a kid, seeing His self squatting on the stool, trying to do scales, and getting walloped on the knuckles when He done them all wrong, till that time when He give her a mouthful, and she dropped the lid on His fingers. That stopped the practice lark for good and all.

"Been gone long, has she?" He says, trying to make it sound ordinary.

"Don't know," she says, pulling the saucepans about on the stove. "I don't know nobody's business except me own, I don't. Mr Prettyjohn come down and told me. Just said she wanted him to tell me, to tell you. That's all I know, or want to know."

"You're lucky," He says. "I'd like to know a bit more, though."

"That's a man all over," she says, "proper nosey lot. Can't the poor girl go out for five minutes on her own, without a lot of people going mad asking questions?"

"If that's all it is," He says, "I don't care so much."

"How do you know it ain't?" she says, coming in with a proper juicy looking joint.

"I don't," He says, getting the niff of roast meat with the bubbles coming through the crackling.

"Well, then," she says, as if that settled the whole affair, and starts giving the knife a bit of edge.

She carved this joint in proper marvellous looking chops, splashed on the mint sauce, spooned up the roast spuds, got the runner beans on, with a bit of butter on top to grease them up a bit, put the plate in front of Him, and licked her fingers.

"Go on," she says, "don't want to hear a sound out of you till you get that lot down you."

"Okeedoke, Ma," He says, "you won't, neither."

He started getting it down Him coming up cheerful again, thinking Ma might have gone to do a deal or see somebody, but it never seemed to tie up with Ike being down the copper station, somehow. But however it was, it just got turning over on itself, one thing going in to another, till come to a finish, He started feeling it was hardly worth the worry.

"Mr Prettyjohn wants to see you, when you finished your dinner, Ernie," she says, dropping it in the quiet like sprinkling a load of tea leaves on the mat. "I said I'd dish you up your dinner first, see?"

"Oh?" He says. "Why's he want to see me?"

"Don't know," she says, but He see there was a bit more to it.

"Listen, Ma," He says, "what's on? Eh? What's going on?"

"Don't know nothing about it," she says, scraping up the leavings. "Did me good to see you putting that away. There's some afters coming up."

"Not today, Ma, ta," He says. "I'm off down the road. There's something fishy, here."

"Won't be the worse for you going without your dinner," she says, down the dumps. "I made 'em specially for you, and all. Tell you what? I'll go down and get Mr Prettyjohn up here while you're eating it, eh?"

"Listen, Ma," He says, sure there was something on, from the look on her face and the way she was talking. "What's up? That's all I'm asking you?"

She went straight out in the scullery.

"You better go up and see Mr Prettyjohn," she says, through the door. "He'll tell you. And when it's all over, come back here and finish your dinner, like a good boy. Now, then."

He could have told her what to do about the dinner, but all of a sudden He knew something was wrong, knew it sort of inside Him, where He never had to be told. All the way down the road, from the bang of Ma Chalmers's door, right till He give Pa Prettyjohn's a doing on the bell and knocker, He never had a thought except Ma. He see her dead, or in hospital, or murdered, or in a ambulance, or knocked about.

"What's coming off?" Pa yells, inside, pulling all the bolts back and taking chains off. "What the bloody hell's going on? Eh? What's all the bleeding rush?"

"It's me, Pa," He shouted him, through the letter box. "Ernie."

"Ah," says Pa, opening up. "Different story. Come in, son. Where you been all night? Been in a right stew about you, by and large, we have."

"Where's Ma?" He says.

"Been down Ma Chalmers, have you?" Dad says, going upstairs. "I asked her to tell you I'd been down."

"Listen, for Christ's sake, Pa," He says, up the top of the stairs, hanging on the banisters, "where is she?"

Pa went in his sitting room, in front, filling up his pipe, with his braces looping down either side of his trousers, and his thumb digging in amongst the wrinkles in his vest.

"Come in, come in," he yells, while He was just looking at the doorway. "No good of standing out there."

He went in, seeing all the prickly plants in the boxes all round the walls, and the sailing ships in bottles, and the fire of kipper boxes, and what all, smelling the place out of fish and making all the screw of Sunday papers on the mat come up bright red and yellowy white.

"Listen Pa," He says. "No larks. Where is she?"

"Well," Pa says, lighting up with a lump of paper in a big blaze as made his face all yellow, "there was a bit of a do down there, see?"

"What sort?" He says, seeing worms crawling all over the boxes and round the prickles of the plants, till they was making Him sickish.

"After the wedding lark, it was," Pa says, sitting down and holding his ankles, looking in the fire and talking one side of his mouth, "I was in kip, and a copper come and knocked me up and asked me to go down there, see? So along I went, and there they was, hundreds of 'em."

"Who?" He says, getting nearer the fire to stop the shivers.

"Coppers," Pa says, not looking up. "Your Ma was just sitting there, letting 'em have the run of the house."

He see her so plain.

"So she says to me, she says, tell Ernie I'm sorry, she says, see?" Pa says, still looking in the fire. "The fag case was your father's. Had it years, she has. Insured and everything. No trouble about that. But they found some other stuff there, see?"

"What other stuff?" He says.

"Couldn't tell you," Pa says. "She never told me nothing else, except to get hold of Ike Buzgang to go and pull you out, this morning. How they come to pinch you, then?"

"Got in a car smash," He says. "But what about Ma? That's what I want to know."

"Well," says Pa, as if he was treading on his own corns,

"they took all this stuff away, see? Boxes of it. Rolls of it. Coming out of them back rooms, it was. The cars was going away loaded all night. Then Ma Sutcliffe and one or two more was brought in, and there was some others in the car, but I never see them. I heard 'em though. Poor cows."

"But where's Ma?" He says, seeing it all so plain.

"They done her," Pa says, looking at Him over his half moons, holding his pipe. "Took her last, they did."

"Done her?" He says, trying to think of it. "Done her what for?"

"Well," Pa says, holding his ankles again and looking in the fire, "if you can trust a copper, one of 'em told me they reckoned they had hold of the biggest shoplifting gang this side of the River. He reckoned they done her for receiving stolen property, or some bright lark. Mind, I'm only telling you what he said."

"You mean they've pinched her?" He says. "They've got her inside?"

"That's what it comes to," Pa says. "And she told me to tell you, don't worry, see? She'll be all right. Ike'll look after the running of the business. You do what she's been learning you, see? Ma Chalmers'll take care of the house, and such like. And I'll do what's what for groceries and all that. So it works out all right, don't it? Till she comes out?"

He reckoned He ought to be able to howl, just to show Pa how slashed about He was, but nothing come. He tried to feel tears in His eyes, but even they was off the card. He just had to sit there looking in the fire. The trams started moaning again, but somehow they got sort of mixed up with the tune Aggie Hunner played on that big fiddle, as if she was scraping it out over His guts.

"Where they took her?" He says.

"Don't know," Pa says and He could tell he was proper sorry. "They'll let you know, I suppose. Didn't half come a shock. I've knowed her, what, thirty years? Easy."

"Mean you wish you hadn't, now they've done her?" He says.

Pa spit smack in the middle of a big bit of blowing red fire and made it come up a sizzle like chips in the fryer.

"Think I am?" he says, trying to scrape a hole in the floor with his voice. "I never thought they'd get inside a million miles of her. But you never know about the police. They're a artful lot of bleeders, one way and another. They must have knew something."

"Wonder what I better do?" He says, wishing He never see it so plain.

"Yes," Pa says. "Well, she wanted you to keep on the business. Them was her words to me. Broken hearted, she was, poor old girl."

"Broken hearted what for?" He says.

"Over the disgrace, I suppose, I don't know?" Pa says, giving the baccy a poke with his little finger, looking about as if he thought somebody was going to tell him.

"Disgrace?" He says, thinking of the Tunnel and Knocker and all the lot of it in bits, just like tipping one of them cut up wriggling puzzles out inside Him. "What disgrace?"

"Well," Pa says, "I'm glad you're taking it the sensible way, son. She was only worried case it might make things hard for you, see? I mean, getting on, like. You know. If people knew your Ma done Time, like, it might hold you back, see? That's all as worried her. It's all she was thinking about, sitting there, looking up at the gas."

"Don't worry me," He says, getting up. "Who's got the keys?"

"The coppers," Pa says. "It's all tom tiddlers ground till something happens somewhere. I don't know when. But you can kip down with Ma Chalmers, or here. Which you like best."

"Ta, Pa," He says. "I'll think it over. I'll come back in a couple of hours or so, eh?"

"Anytime you like," Pa says. "Find your own way out, can you?"

"Okeedoke," He says, going downstairs, out in the rain, again.

He went down the Shop, looking at it all locked up. Even the windows upstairs had a look about them as if they closed their eyes for a bit. He started thinking about them back rooms upstairs, always locked because they was empty, and He wondered why He never even tried looking inside to see what was on. The scullery window come up in His mind as if it been built there, and He see how He could get in, coppers or no coppers.

Down the alleyway He went, taking His time, case anybody in the Road had their snouts through the curtains, under the fence, going over by the dustbin to find the old knife without a handle. A couple of pokes got the catch up, and in a couple of shakes, He was in the scullery and standing in the kitchen.

Ma's chair was just where He see it all the time.

Turned out from the table, where she could just lean her elbow on it, looking straight towards the gas, thinking of the disgrace.

It was so bloody quiet, His heart seemed to want to climb higher up inside Him, somehow.

There was only the sound of the Sunday rain, and the wind squeezing under the door.

The cups on the table, and the big tea pot, looked like a ring of coppers all standing there chatting her.

Everything else was just how she left it, after washing up before the wedding. He went through the passage, seeing the china doorknob laying on its back, still squinting at the ceiling and asking a square question, knowing it must have come off in some copper's hand. Upstairs was quieter, as if the whole place knew what happened and scrunched itself together, not to let nothing out. The back rooms was all open, and empty except for some paper and stuff and it was a bit too dark to see much else, but He see enough to know everything in the place, all over, been give a real good doing.

But it come a right smack in the mash to go in His room, hands all ready to grab the nigger brown and a shirt, and see the cupboard open, and all the drawers hanging out, empty, all the lot of them. Not a single rag was in any of them. Suits, shirts, ties, shoes, all the issue was gone. Everything He had, except the busted penknife, shining in the candlestick.

They done His drum all right.

He never had a stitch in the world except what He was standing up in.

The house come over proper cold in half a tick, almost, like snow falling and the wind coming round the corner as if it been waiting there to catch you.

Just looking round the door of Ma's room, full of the best pieces, loaded with china vases and flowers under glass, with the walls stuck full of photographs and pictures, He see the bed was turned over just how she left it to go down and see who was banging on the door. Even the dent in the pillow was still there. Her clothes was all over the chair back, and her shoes was turned on their sides where she toed them off, and He could see her taking the pins out and hanging the cartwheel hat on the bed end, just like she always done when He was a kid.

Everything was there, except her.

Funny how the whole place was sort of dead cold without her, not the cold without a fire, but the cold without people, as makes you look round quick and see what you thought might be there, and then make a bee line for the stairs to get down in the kitchen again.

He started shaking about so much He could hardly make a move, and the place was coming over dark with the grey of rain outside, making it all the harder. He see His self a kid, tearing about after Ma, hanging on to her, asking her for half-pennies and getting them, and making off for the sweets and coming back, sitting at the bottom of the stairs here, to suck them, or on the shop step, knowing she was about somewhere and not caring too much if she was or not, but knowing she was and not being afraid. He heard His self yelling the place down in the dark when He woke up of a night and Ma coming quiet through the door and giving Him a scold, and He could feel her weight pushing the bed springs down and her hand patting His feet, with the lights of the passing trains opening and closing their white fans across the ceiling.

Ma, He was saying somewhere inside His self, Christ, Ma.

He went and sat down on the top stair, shivering, not wanting to go down in the kitchen where that ring of coppers was standing all round her, afraid to go in her bedroom because it said a bit too much, just looking down in the passage, trying to find out what was going on inside of Him and all round Him, with the wind blowing cold on His knee where it stuck out of the tear in His trousers.

He never wanted to smoke, or even move a hand.

This was where He landed up, after all the talks and everything else. No job, nobody to do a hand's turn for Him, no money, no clothes, Ma inside and all that disgrace tailing Him about for the rest of His life, besides going up on Tuesday for a bit of a do on His own account. It was funny about this disgrace business. He could hardly make up His mind whether it sounded all right for Ma to be doing Time, or if it sounded like something you ought to keep quiet. Some of the blokes would think He was a right boy, with His old dear doing a stretch, but some of them, like Len Tate and a few more, might think it was something to take the rise out of Him about, and not look His way if they see Him in the street. It had to be thought about very careful. He knew the jokes there might be about Him in the cafe, so that was one place He had to keep away from.

It looked as if He was in for a proper rotten time, by and large.

Ada come up so real He could see her red jersey, and He knew how she might take it. Artist with a jailbird Ma, He heard her say, no doubt about it, and looking at Him as if she never see Him apart from the crowd. After what she told Him would happen if He worked for Jim, and then finding out about Ma, He was up the spout. The only pal He had was Jim Mordinoy, it looked like. He never had to worry about nothing while He worked for Jim, money, clothes, grub, rides, everything was all fixed up besides being big money to draw every week, and all. Not like them years at Old Nick's, nothing the first year, five bob a week the next two, and seven and a tanner all the rest of the time, and the boot when He was coming on man's rates. But He see where He was dead lucky getting out of it else it might have gone on for years, perhaps all His life.

He tried to think about His life and ask His self what He was doing with it, like Jim Mellowes used to do, after he had one or two of a dinner time.

But when you started thinking about life, it only come down to being a matter of getting round the clock as easy as you could, and sort of remembering things, but even then, nothing much ever happened to make you think about it without worrying, and if you had to start worrying, it was better to forget it, and have done with it. Beyond the time at Old Nick's, all He could remember was this house and the shop and the Road and school, and being a kid. The five years at Old Nick's was like a long way away, as if He left years ago. He could hardly remember how the place was, or which way you passed the acid tanks to get in the stone room. This house and shop was just like it always was, and so was the Road, because they was always there, like your hair and fingers. School, He could hardly remember, for all the years He was going, except the window He busted round the Infants, and the way they all used to gang up for a chase round the pisshouses in the play-time, and go tearing up the steps and in the hall with their boots all wet, and how it used to ponk in the summer.

Everything was sort of rubbed out. Nothing seemed to stick nowhere.

Except Ma.

He got that weak feeling again, where He wanted to get on the floor to hold on to something solid, but when He got down there He see the fluff blowing about and coming at Him, and it was too cold to lay there long, any case, so He got up again, but it was too quiet, and dark, and empty, and He was empty too, and sort of muddled up inside, not knowing what He wanted to do, nor nothing.

All the way downstairs He could hear Ma coming down and

going up, making all the crocks on the table play tunes of their own and shaking the light about, specially if she was wearing her slippers. But he was afraid to make too much noise because the place was too quiet, and it give Him the feeling it never liked Him. Down near the kitchen, He just took a dekko round the side of the door to see if Ma come in quiet to give Him a surprise, but the chair was still in the same place, still with that ring of cups round the table, still looking towards the gas and worrying about the disgrace.

It was all quiet, so quiet it sounded wrong.

He never heard it so quiet before. Even if Ma been having her little forty after dinner of a Sunday, there was always a bit of a row going on somewhere, even if it was only her tearing it off up there, making a low, shaking sound as come through the floor and nigh shook the place about.

It struck Him this was how it would always be without Ma. Dead quiet.

Nobody to get even a cup of tea. No dinner cooked, or supper after you come back home at night, and no extra bits in the oven, or out on the window sill getting cold to set.

And no money, or clothes, nor nothing.

Something inside of Him kept on saying Ma. Christ. Ma.

But it was no good of staying there, because it was sort of getting Him down, and any case He knew there might be a cup of something hot going next door. So He made a move for the scullery window again, and He was climbing on the table when He see the green plaster girl in the shadow of the shelf. Ma must have thought better of shoving her in the dustbin, but she put it where He never went anywhere nigh.

Just like a old pal, she was. Just like Ma in that picture, only green instead of pinkish, and little bumps of plaster on her pair instead of them pink flowers, and no big laugh, only a kind of crease in her face.

Ma, like she was before He was thought of, or wanted.

He had it in his hands, feeling it, like He felt Rivers, and Ada, and it give Him the same sort of feeling, only further away. It was too cold and hard for it to be really pally, and any case it was too small, nothing like a bride, really, just something to get your hands round, promising a lot and giving you nothing, so all you got was that there ache in the guts again, and this feeling you wanted to rush off to somebody soft and warm and put your arms round her tight, and kiss her all sorts of ways, except it made you feel such a mug, even thinking about it by yourself, though you knew you wanted to do it.

It was just like everything else. You could never make up your mind where you was, never mind how hard you tried, and the more you started thinking the worse it got, till in the finish you had to give it up.

There seemed to be three sides to this love lark. One of them was this ache, in the guts, when you wanted a bride. The second was kind of thinking about it and talking all this love stuff as made you feel a mug all round. The third was setting about it, and knowing somebody to set about.

But you had to get hold of the bride as had a part of her as cried in the warm sometimes, before you could start doing your dags, and it was odds on you could ask a couple of million, any time of the day, before you got one to own up. Then you had to start your love business and give yourself the creeps, and if that went all right, you was in.

But you had to go through all that palaver before you got what you was after, or else you just got married. Then you could have what you liked, when you liked and how you liked it, any time you liked.

It was dead easy. All you done was pick out a right bit of stuff and marry her, then you was all right. All of a sudden He thought He see what Ma was getting at all the time.

That was it.

He thought of Ada again, but it was plainer than this here statue she was a bit too bossy. He see it quick enough, once it was there. She knew too much for him. She was too wide. So it come down to finding somebody else, but the question was where He was going to set about looking for her.

Her.

Somewhere, there was somebody living and eating and

drinking and wearing her clothes, and doing up her stockings with them little clip things, and tearing about, and generally carrying on, as might suit Him right down to the ground, and she was alive.

Now.

All the time He was standing there thinking about her, she was doing something or other, near or far, but living, and just waiting for Him, like it or not.

He come over proper pleased and cheerful in a couple of ticks.

It was dead easy, because when He found her, they could get married and come and live here, and He could make a good go of this business with her to keep the books, and Him down at Pa Prettyjohn's if He felt like it, and doing a job now and again for Jim, to keep the big money rolling in and everything going nice and comfortable all round. It was so easy, He wanted to kick His self for not seeing it before.

But looking at the ring of cups, it come over chilly again because no bride would want to start getting tied up with a bloke when His Ma was Inside for a stretch.

That was what Ma meant by the Disgrace.

That was what she must have been thinking about while she was looking at the gas with that gang of coppers all round her.

It hit Him a right wallop, seeing it so plain.

He was right up the spout.

The feeling of nothing being no good got hold of Him again, and made Him feel too rotten even to be angry, because you never knew what to be angry about, and even if you did, there was nobody to say it to, and it was no good of getting your temper up if there was nobody to throw it at, so all you could do was kick something or sling something.

No sooner said than He slung the green plaster girl again the far wall, but while she was going a pale green half moon past the window light, He was sorry He done it.

It was just like a basin splattering and then there was a shower of little hard, cracky knocks when the pieces of her fell on the floor.

He wished He kept her. Seeing her on the floor in a lot of small ragged green and white lumps, it reminded Him somehow of Ada, all in bits as nothing on Christ's earth would ever get the same shape again. He tried to see why He see such a lot in her, but it seemed to slip past Him, somewhere. There was only this feeling about her of wanting to be took care of, and the soft shape of her as fit you so warm, and the scent, and the way she said things, and looked sometimes when He found that part of her He was always looking for, the part what chewed the sheets and got up for a cup of tea. It was all there in that splash of lumps on the floor.

He looked round the quiet kitchen again, feeling this headache and the pain in His guts, not knowing what He wanted to do or where He was going, or even what to think about.

Ma, this voice inside of Him kept on saying, just sit down where I can see you. Please, Ma, I wish you would.

It come driving up inside like the scream of a big car that He had to see her, wherever she was, however many coppers was round her.

He was by His self, else.

That was the lark.

That was it.

Lonely.

Somehow, somewhere, He got a sharp flick of thin fright, enough to make Him look round quick, though He never knew what for, because He no sooner felt it than it sort of went, and He was just standing there looking in the kitchen again.

Nobody to look out for Him, or cook, or anything Ma done.

By His self in the place, day in and out, and nobody to light the fire of a morning, nor nothing.

There He was, just the change of a quid in His pocket, the rest of it down the copper station, and a tore dancing suit, and no hope nor nothing.

"Ernie," He could hear somebody calling, and He nigh fell off the table thinking it might be Ma. "You there, dear? Come along. Ernie?"

It was Ma Chalmers hollering through the fence.

He got out through the window, knowing if He said any
thing, it would be either a mouthful, or else He might star
howling.

"There you are," she says, pleased as if she been give ɛ
treat. "Don't like you walking about and no coat on, young
man. See Mr Prettyjohn, did you?"

"Yes," He says, getting through the hole. "How did you
know I was in there?"

"See you go in," she says, hopping the puddles. "Heard you
on the stairs and all. Nearly hear you parting your hair, some
times."

"Listen," He says. "Where's Ma? Where they got her?"

"Holloway," she says. "I was going to tell you when you
finished your dinner."

"Think they'll let me in?" He says. "Let me see her, will
they?"

"No harm in trying," she says. "And cheer up. No good feel
ing sorry for yourself, is it? Have a nice cup of tea. Then go
eh?"

"No," He says. "I'm off now, ta, Ma. Thanks all the same."

"Listen," she yelled after Him through the passage. "Key'
under the mat. I'll make your bed up on the sofa in the parlour
See?"

"Okeedoke," He shouted her, feeling it was doing things big
going off quick without His tea, because it showed He though
something of Ma. He wondered how it might be, if He wen
without grub for days and died of starving His self for grief
It might show a few of them He was made of something a bi
different.

When He got to the top of the Road, Aggie was waiting for ɛ
tram with a bride, so He pretended He was off down toward
the town hall, but she come after Him. The thoughts of talking
to people somehow give Him the creeps.

"Ernie," she screeches, so He turns round as if He never seer
her.

"Ah," He says. "Hulloa, Aggie?"

"I heard about Ma," she says, chasing up, looking sorry

nd winded together. "I had a good cry. Really I did? Look,
ell you what? Come over tonight for some food, and we'll
alk things over, eh? You'll need all your friends in this."

"Ta, Aggie," He says. "What time?"

"Say eightish?" she says. "There's the tram. See you
hen?"

"Okeedoke," He says, seeing her hopping down the Road.
There was just as much shape and curve up and down about
her, in fact her legs was twice the size of Ada's, and the same
round shape, but there was a lot more of her, without that
unny thing Ada had, when you wanted to put your arms all
round her and bash everybody as even looked at her. Aggie
never had it, nor did a lot of others. But Ada did, even when
you just thought about her.

It was a queer thing to think about, but thinking about it
sort of brought her back a thousand times as strong, and for all
what He told His self about her, there was something in this
smiling dying lark as stuck to you, whether you wanted it to
or not.

Without thinking, just walking, He was down the Fun Fair
again, and soon as He see the lights and all the colours coming
up in the machines and the blokes and brides all enjoying their
selfs, He sort of come over more cheerful too, ready to sling all
the worry outside and give His self a treat.

The music come up slow and sad, getting down so far inside
of you, it was no good trying to do nothing else but let it,
and sort of lay down while you was standing up, letting the
tune curl round the trellis in your guts and send you off to
dreamland.

He see Ada about the same time as she see Him, and down
went her book, flat. Instead of coming down the steps further
on, she jumped off the ledge, coming straight for Him, making
a few blokes turn round, wondering what was on. She was in
her jersey, but the look on her face never give Him a chance
to look nowhere else.

"Got pinched then, did you?" she says, and grabs His arm,
pulling Him just inside the little space between Madame La

Zaka's and the peepshows. "What I tell you? Believe me now do you?"

"I'm out, ain't I?" He says, getting a shake on because her face was a queer colour and she was staring hard. Then He got it when she come nearer. She had a few, and it kind of weighed her breath down one end, sort of sourish, nothing like her at all.

"Out?" she says. "Course you're out. Bailed out. And what about Tuesday? Thought about it?"

"How do you know about me?" He says, trying to get away, but she was there.

"Jim's been in," she says. "He knows all about it. Where you going to say you got all that money from?"

"My Ma, of course," He says.

"I wonder if you got the sense to say it, and stick to it," she says, looking at Him like something crawling out of a boot. "Else you'll do a twelve month, you know?"

"What do you care?" He says, narked by the way she was carrying on.

She just looked down the big room, and the lights was making a shining line down her nose, in the red wet of her mouth and the bulge of her chin, giving her hair all the soft yellow there was, and making that feeling come out of her, where you wanted to hold her and make a mug of yourself saying things.

"Thinking of your Ma," she says, in amongst all the donging of the bells and the sounds of the machines, while the music was coming up strong in drums, and He could see Ma looking at the gas inside of a ring of coppers.

"I'll be all right," He says, knowing there was something going on inside her, just like something went on inside Ma, as you knew about, but never quite got your finger on, so there was nothing you could say or do to help.

"If I thought my little bloke was going to be anything like you and a few more," she says, still looking up the room, "I'd do for him. Straight up? I wouldn't give me self the bother of him. And I wouldn't give him the bother of going through it. It ain't worth it."

"Plenty of time to sort it out, any rate," He says. "I ain't doing so bad."

"Look," she says, looking at the red beetles, "I let you in for this lot. See? Shut your trap and listen. Jim'll have a solicitor there for you, Tuesday. Ask for Mr Nathan, see? He'll put you right. Don't go down the garage at all. Keep out of it. You can live on that money till it's all over, can't you? And if you get broke, come here and ask for Jerry, up at the office. He'll know all about it. See?"

"Jim know all about this?" He says, going cold again. It sounded as if He was out.

"He told me to tell you," she says. "They was round your house twice this morning. He's got to lay quiet, his self, over this do last night. There was two of them died in hospital."

"Down the Lucky Seven?" He says, remembering the blokes moaning, seeing Trunky flashing that razor, and the faces of the Lamp Duffers in the pink lights.

"It's in the papers," she says. "Jim's gone away for a day or two. So's everybody who didn't get pinched."

In the middle of all the music and the homey sound of people giving their selfs a treat, He got this feeling again of being on His own. Everybody was going away, or slung their hooks off somewhere and left Him to it.

He was on His own.

"What about me, then?" He says. "What am I supposed to do? I take the can back, I suppose?"

"What you expect to do, you soppy looking thing, you?" she says, and nigh flew at Him. "What you think I been wasting me time for? Eh? Christ's sake get out and make something of yourself. This is your chance."

"Chance of what?" He says, knocked over and trying to see, but her eyes was all big, and staring straight through Him, putting Him off. "What am I going to do? What with?"

She shook herself like throwing something away.

"Ain't there nothing you can do?" she says, and He sees the tears there. "You're a artist. Surely to Christ there's something you can do? Can't you go down the docks and go on a boat, or something? You got to stay here, have you?"

"I got my Ma," He says.

"Poor cow," she says. "I can hear somebody else saying it

one of these days. I can. I can hear them very words. Listen, Ernie."

She had hold of Him by them silk fronts, and she was strong, with blue eyes all dark in her hair.

"Go away," she says, nigh gritting her teeth, and shaking so much she was making Him shake, "get out of it. I can't help you, except I can give you a few quid. But get out of it. Go away. Don't let them shove you inside. Don't let 'em. You'll be in and out all your life. Go up on Tuesday, see? You'll get off. Jim swears you will. Then get out of it. Else get out now. Go now. Get on a train. Go anywhere. Only get out of it. See? Get out of it."

She was shaking Him like a mat, and people was getting nosey, stopping and looking, closing in, asking what was on.

"I'll be all right," He says, trying to put the laugh in it. "Don't you worry. They won't get no change out of me. Straight up."

She let Him go, like dropping a hot plate, sending Him up again the wall.

"What's the use?" she says, not caring who heard, nor nothing. "Talk till you're wore out, and what do you get?"

"Well, all right," He says, knowing He had to say something because of the blokes all looking in and having a laugh. "Why you down here, then, if you're so clever? Eh? Thought you was getting out of it all of a sudden?"

"So I am," she yells, and He thought she was coming for Him. "Never see me again down here, so don't think it. I'm off out of it, and bloody good riddance."

She went out of it shoving through the little crowd what was getting bigger. He see His chance while they was all looking at her, dodging round the side, up the steps past Madame La Zaka's, feeling the empty space all round and behind Him, glad to be out of the looks of them, knowing they was all going back to the machines wondering what was on, all getting a different story, and all of them wrong.

"Half a mo," the bloke on the rifle range shouts Him, and He could have kicked His self for going past.

"What's up?" He says, making it new.

"What's up?" this bloke says, nigh fainting. "What about the rifle you was supposed to keep so quiet, eh?"

"Listen," He says, quick, shutting it all up, "don't tell me. I know. We had the burglars night before last, see? Lost Christ knows what. But my Ma's queer, see? So I never knew what went or what was there till today. What's up, then?"

"They found the bloody thing down Coldharbour Lane copper station," this bloke says. "They was round here this morning wanting to know everything. So I said it was pinched yesterday afternoon, see? From here."

"Thank Christ for that," He says. "So I shan't say nothing, see? They can't get nothing on me. And they can't get nothing on you. So we're all right, eh?"

"Yes," this bloke says, but he had a funny sort of look on his face. "But it might have lost me a licence, just the same."

"Well, it didn't," He says, "so it's okeedoke, ain't it? So long."

He went out of it as if He had something on somewhere, but He was half way up the stairs before it hit Him about Ma.

It stopped Him dead between the looking glasses either side.

There He was, thinking of that ring of cups, wanting to see Ma, feeling He come off none too well with Ada, sort of hurting somewhere inside of Him knowing there was a big tear in His trousers, and a bit of a barney waiting for Him on Tuesday, but in amongst it all He was trying to think how He could get down to Holloway.

Them grey stones in blocks going up behind the trees what you could see from the top of a tram, sort of far away, making you shiver inside of yourself and look round at other people, glad you was your self and outside with everybody else, going anywhere and pleasing yourself.

Them grey stones of that sort of big castle place, with the little windows, like cracks in the walls, what they looked through, all iron barred.

Where Ma was.

## CHAPTER XL

IT WAS LATE when he got there, coming on dark, and He started thinking they might chuck Him out.

All the houses either side of the road never seemed right. They looked too big and posh, and full up of people as never knew them grey stones was so near, even though they could see them out of their back windows. What with the bushes and flowers in their front gardens, they looked too happy.

He went down this here little road, and see this big gate, right across, like a half circle of hard luck.

But He see Ma in a ring of coppers and she was calling for Him, and inside of Him, that voice was yelling for her, so He went on, even though He never wanted to, getting a shake on again, trying a couple of times before He shoved the bell.

A bit of the gate opened inwards and let out some lamplight.

"What do you want?" some bloke says.

"Mrs Mott," He says. "My Ma. She come in last night. I got to see her, governor? Only just found out where she was."

"You're too late, son," this bloke says. He had buttons, and all, and a little pillbox hat with a big peak.

"I got to go to work first thing in the morning," He says. "I wish I could see her? Just once?"

This bloke looked at Him a minute holding the door wide open.

"Half a mo," he says, proper kind, and he closed up, leaving Him out in the dark. The leaves was all breathing away, as hard as they could go, and there was that smell of earth and caterpillars just like the back yard at home, and the lamps was slinging yellow slashes through all the little trees. This door opened again.

"Come on, son," this bloke says, having a laugh. "Mrs Mott, did you say?"

"That's right," He says, a bit surprised.

"He'll take you down there," this bloke says, thumbing another bloke outside this little office place. "Got any proof you're Mrs Mott's son, have you?"

"She'll tell you when she sees me," He says.

"You'll do," this bloke says. "Follow him. You've got ten minutes."

"This way," this other bloke says, and away they went across the yard, towards these big black shapes, all dark against the night, with up and down edges round the tops, like old castles.

"Been bad long, has she?" this bloke says, going through a door and along a passage.

"Who?" He says.

"Your Ma," this bloke says, turning round a bit surprised.

"Never been bad in her life," He says. "Had some pains now and again. Don't know what a doctor looks like. Why?"

"Sure we got the right name?" this bloke says, pulling up. "Mrs Mott?"

"That's right," He says, getting this cut of fright again. "Why?"

The bloke starts off down this wide passage, going slower, and kind of spreading his moustache down his mouth.

"You're in for a bit of a nasty smack, son," he says, meaning it nice, as if he was right sorry. "The divisional surgeon's been in to see her twice today, and the second time, he brought some other bloke along. Specialist, I reckon he was. She's on the danger list. She's in the hospital."

This cold slash of fright got thicker, nigh making His teeth knock.

"What's up with her?" He says.

"Ah," says this bloke, holding his hand up. "Something I don't know. But the sister'll tell you, I expect. Here you are. Good luck."

"Ta," He says, and went inside this door, in a little passage.

"This is Mrs Mott's boy, sister," this bloke says to a nurse. "Ten minutes. I'll hang on."

This sister was looking at Him proper chancey, weighing Him up, not quite smiling but ready to be pally if she thought He was worth it. He started worrying about His shoes and that tear in His trousers, but before He could do anything, she came towards Him.

"You know your mother's very ill?" she says, quiet, but kind of between us two. "You mustn't worry her, and you mustn't, whatever you do, upset her. You see? I want her to sleep."

"Shan't say a word," He says, getting this flick again, starting them goose spots coming up. "What's up with her?"

"Well," she says, looking out in the dark and going back on one leg, "she's very ill. That's all I can tell you for the moment. Promise me you'll be quiet? You won't upset her?"

"I'll take my honest God's oath," He says, and she turns round, going down the passage, and He followed her dark blue woman shape with this sort of white cloth waterfall over her hair. She stopped outside a door and went in, taking everything careful, not like just opening a door and going in ordinary, but thinking about it.

"Come along," she says to Him, and went in to this palish light.

"Mrs Mott," she says, "here's your son to see you. Just ten minutes. That's all. And you mustn't upset yourself. I want you to have a nice sleep."

He stood in the doorway, looking at Ma in bed, and this sister went outside.

She was sitting up with pillows behind her, leaning again them. Her hair was down in a couple of plaits, just like she was first thing of a morning before she put her hat on.

"Hullo, Ma?" He says, not seeing too much to worry about.

"Hullo, Ernie," she says, just like any other time. "Where you come from, then?"

"Just thought I'd pop round and have a look at you," He says, going over to the bed, squatting on the blue blankets, careful not to sit on her feet.

"See Ike this morning?" she says.

"Yes," He says, feeling for a fag. "I got in a bit of hard

luck with a car smash. But I'm all right. No bogey, Ma. Straight up."

She was looking dead at Him, and He see she sort of got smaller, somehow. She looked bigger in her clothes.

"That's all right, then," she says, but the way she said it, He see she was thinking of something else. He see that ring of coppers all round her again.

"I see you had a bit of hard luck, too, Ma?" He says.

"Yes," she says, but a bit too tired for her, "but that's as far as it'll go."

"How do you mean?" He says. "Think you'll get off?"

"Easy," she says, tipping Him the wink. "Watch me."

"What they got you in for, Ma?" He says. "How they come to do you?"

"Don't know," she says, picking at the sheets. "They come and asked me about you, first of all, see?"

"Yes?" He says, seeing how blackish she was round the eyes, like fog dirt.

"Then I told them about that fag case, see?" she says, quiet as somebody on tip toe. "Showed them the insurance. He had it years. Give to him be some fly be night or other, it was. That was all right. But while I was talking to a couple of 'em downstairs the rest of them was all round the house, see? Then they reckoned they'd found some stuff, see? Then they got hold of all the books."

There was something up with her. She was looking at Him and not seeing Him. She was looking through Him and past Him, and now He got used to this light, He see her face was sort of salty, dry, not so fat and shiny, kind of bluish round the mouth, and her hands was a queer colour, not reddish like they always was.

This slash of fright come whipping round Him again.

"What's up, Ma, gel?" He says. "What you in here for? What's the matter with you?"

"I'm all right," she says. "Having a bit of a rest up, that's all."

"Sure?" He says. "I don't want to be worrying me guts out

about you if I know you're all right, do I? I got the shop to attend to now, you know? Till you come back there again."

"That's right," she says, looking one side of Him. "You look after it. If you get into any trouble, see Ike. He's a good bloke. Been a good friend to me. You got a lot of friends round you. Pa Prettyjohn take you in any time. Tell you that, did he?"

"Yes," He says, thinking of the Disgrace. "But I'll be sweating on you coming out of this hole, Ma. I got to get married, don't forget?"

"That's right," she says, still looking past Him, and her eyes was big, kind of dragged down in front, and red. "You'll have to get married. Find a nice girl to look after you when I ain't there. Get hold of a good girl, son. Somebody nice, with a good head on her. Can't go wrong."

"That's right, Ma," He says. "I was only thinking about it this afternoon. That's what I'll do. Eh? Then we'll have a right do, eh?"

"You must," she says, nigh hollering, trying to get off these pillows, sliding her mouth about. "You got to. I blame me self. It was all my fault. But I was afraid you was like him. Got to find somebody what'll take care of you."

"Okeedoke, Ma," He says, up the wall, the way she was taking it.

"Ernie," she says, and she starts howling her eyes out. "Oh, Ernie boy."

The door come open in a rush of cool wind.

"There," this sister says, looking at her proper narked. "After all I told you, see what you've done? You've been and upset yourself. Told you, didn't I?"

She give Him a touch on the shoulder.

"Outside," she says. "Say good night and get off home, quick."

"Good night, Ma," He says, but this blue sister and the white waterfall was bending across her, where He never had a chance to see what He was on. All He could hear was Ma sobbing her heart out for something, so He done no more, He got out of it, quick.

This bloke was in the passage, waiting for Him.

"All right?" he says, as if it was.

"What's up with her?" He says. "That's what I want to know? What they been and done to her?"

"Search me," this bloke says. "She was bad when she come in. Had a rare job with her. She's a very heavy woman, she is, you know?"

The sister come out, closing the door very quiet.

"You still here?" she says, like knocking dust off of the window sill. "Time you went home, isn't it?"

"Half a minute, Miss," He says, going up to her. "What's up with her? Why's she in there? What's making her like that?"

"Like what?" this sister says, looking at Him as if she knew that much more.

"Like that," He says. "She's different. She don't look the same."

"Now, you'll have to be a brave young man," this sister says, in her fattish voice, coming out of the dark blue, sort of quiet and dropping over everything slow and lightish, like that white waterfall as waved so slow up and down when she walked, and looking at a lot of little white pots and bottles in a cupboard. "Your mother's seriously ill."

Big lights turning round over their selfs, all colours and no colours, just turning round making the same scrunching noise as boots on gravel, turning round and coming back with this waterfall thing looking thin and clean white, sort of stiff in the middle of it.

"Very seriously ill," this voice says, building it up till the lights all changed to rags getting twisted round and round their selfs, till everything looked like twisting rags making a sliding noise.

"In fact," this voice says, quiet as the night, when no trains was going past and the rain stopped, just after Ma made the bed rattle of spitting the candle out and He was close again the warm of her, "you'd better start thinking of not having her very much longer."

He was looking at one of these little white pots with a red label on it, trying to think what this sister was on about, and He could hear Ma downstairs getting the breakfast ready, trying to hear what Ma Chalmers's wireless was playing, and running rings round it. It was like talking about something new, far away, a sort of fairy tale you made up as you went along. Trying to think about not having Ma was like having that bit of crayon back in His hand again.

"Mean she's going to roll up?" He says, hearing His self talking.

The sister picked out a couple of pots, and took a leather box out, opening it and holding a little shining silver thing up to the light, spurting drips out of this long thin needle.

"Your mother's got just enough strength to know you," she says, looking up at the needle, "but she's sinking. It may be a week's time. It might be tonight."

But there was nothing to hang on to somehow. This sister with a narrow black and gold ring on her little finger cocked up outside this needle affair, and the bare walls holding this hospital smell, making you think of knifes cutting you up and bandages and stuff, and the quiet bloke in the blue uniform looking up at the sky outside, and Him standing looking at it, all in this shaded green light. It was just like thinking of something happening when you was somewhere else.

"I come to see her tomorrow, can I?" He says, still hearing His self getting it out and wondering where He was standing.

"Depends on whether she's awake," this sister says, in a voice like going to sleep. "She's in pain. So she'll be sleeping quite a lot. You'd better telephone the office."

"Okeedoke," He says. "Ta."

"This way," this other bloke says, and not wanting to, He tailed on.

Out in the cool blue, it was hard to think He just left Ma, because she ought to been at home, across them houses, reaching right over, in the Road.

"Hard luck, son," this bloke says. "They all go one day,

though. And if she's in pain, you're better off and so's she. Cancer, ain't it?"

"Is it?" He says, and He could see Ma Crann in her little black hat, and feel how wet her hand was. "Who told you?"

"Sister seemed to think it was," this bloke says. "Only don't say I told you. I thought you knew?"

"Never said nothing to me," He says, seeing Ma again.

"They let it go on for years," this bloke says, going along the passage. "Then it gets bad and you can't do nothing for them. Always the same. Frightened of it."

He see Ma with them pains, getting about the place holding on to chairs, going downstairs one at a time, leaning again the wall, holding her blouse in front, and never saying a word.

"Might hurt too much," He says.

"That's it," this bloke says. "My old dear went the same way. It goes on and goes on, and they don't say nothing. Then they get past it. Then it's all over, bar the shouting."

They got to the gate again, and the other bloke opened the little door.

He could hear them trams moaning past just outside, and all of a sudden He wanted to go rushing back to Ma.

"Couldn't I stay here?" He says, to this bloke. "You know, case anything happens?"

The two blokes looked at each other, wagging their heads the same time.

"Wish I could let you, son," that first one says. "Wish I could. But it's against all the regulations, see? You only come in tonight as a special favour, like. See?"

"Phone up in the morning," the other one says. "We'll tell you how she is. And if she's awake, you can come along. Best way ain't it?"

"Yes," He says, and went through the door.

"Don't think we ain't sorry, just because we're behind this lot," this bloke says, knuckling the gate. "But it's all we can do, see, son?"

"Ta," He says. "But it's proper lonely out here."

He never knew what for, but a sore bubble sort of went off a soft crash inside of Him, and He started howling. But He got away out of it too quick for this bloke to see Him, making for the lights where the trams was running by, seeing them in yellow splashes going past bump a dee bump, bump a dee bump, moaning inside of Him, and outside, as hard as they could go, rocking along them silver lines like long ships with a big white eye.

He turned up the Hill, knowing how Ada felt when she let go, not wanting to, but having to, and not knowing what to do for the best. It was just like some other bloke taking charge inside, not taking no notice of you nor nobody else, just leaving you to try and wipe up, and dodge the lights, case anybody see your dial.

He see Ma in bed again with them two plaits, and it made this pain inside of Him that much worser. He knew she was by herself, right on her own in that little box of a place, when all she wanted was to be in her chair in the kitchen at home.

Thinking of her being back in that place with the up and down edge all round the towers, behind that big gate, along the passage, in that little room in bed under them blue blankets, sitting there crying, with her eyes all dragged down red and her hands that colour, He tried to see her in the picture again, all pink with little shadows all over her, looking at you, still laughing at a good joke, not worried about nothing, but too happy to last. Seeing that pink girl in bed alongside of Ma, He tried to think how the change come about, from one to the other, trying to make them both a fit. But nothing come of it. He could only hear Ma crying, out loud, when she must have cried quiet all her life.

Going straight down this long road between white lights bursting out of the dark like big wet gardenias right in His eyes, there was no room for thinking or feeling anything except about Ma. Even thinking about Ada never made Him feel nothing much, because there was no space left behind there, and He never even felt hungry nor nothing.

He looked back, not seeing too much except the lights here

and there, wanting to reach out over the roofs, and tear one of them towers out, and Ma with it. But it was no go.

Somehow or other He knew He see the last of her. He knew He was never going to phone up because He was afraid of what they might say. He knew He never had the guts to go up to that there gate again for fear of what they might have to tell Him.

He could bear it if He never heard it.

He sat on the kerb with His back again a lamp, feeling the cold of it coming through His coat, seeing His knee sticking out pale through His trousers, proper letting it all go and glad to, and a bit surprised what a lot of row He was making.

But this thin cut of fright come whipping back and stopped it in a tick, like turning off a tap. He see if Ma was going to roll up, whether them blokes told Him so or not, He was going to be right on His own, not just for a while, like now, but all the time.

On His own, day in, day out, all by His self, with the wind blowing cold all round Him, and nobody to give Him even a light.

Sitting here in the gutter, He got this fright so hard, it nigh choked Him. He looked up and down the wide, dark road, having a funny feeling He wanted to run away from His self, seeing a tram just moaning to a stop. Without worrying about how He looked, He tore after it, wanting to look at the people, sit next to them, even though He never knew who they was, even if they was with somebody else and He could only listen.

But He had to be with people, and hear them, touch them, be part of them. The thoughts of knocking about on His own was paralysing Him. Soon as He got a fag going, He felt a bit more like it, though He still had a shake on.

But thinking about it, He see where He was all right. There was that cash due Him down the copper station. He had His job with Jim when the Lucky Seven business blew over, a lot of pals down the garage, and plenty of earnings when the big stuff started again, to say nothing of the business at home, and Ma Chalmers putting Him up.

Taking it all round, it looked as if He was all right, so He wondered why He been howling. He could have kicked His self.

"More fares, please?" the conductor yells.

"Where we going?" He says, holding up a tanner.

"Tottenham Court Road, this one," the conductor says. "Why? Don't you know where you're going? Ain't you got no home?"

"No," He says, and that come a shock, too, and all.

"Take you as far as the buffers," the conductor says, ripping off a ticket. "Cost you two nice fresh pence. No home, eh? You're lucky. Ain't got the worry of it, have you? Foot loose and fancy free. What a chance, eh? Wish it was me."

That little bell on the ticket punch sounded just like some old pal.

Joinya there, so it'll come a nice supper, be for the pair of you, I hope."

The inside door come open and Tiger shoved his head in. "Here," he yelled, "none of that. Where's Mrs. Clamhous holding up the ceiling, "here a lot of pals you got. I must say.

# CHAPTER XLI

HE WISHED the club was open so as He could go and get some grub. He passed a coffee stall, but He was looking for a plateful not a handful, and it looked as if everything in that line was either closed up, or a bit too posh to wear Him. That was when He thought of Tiger Collis's place. No sooner He thought of it, than He shifted, following the bus route till He come to the corner. Down the little alley He went, taking His time in case of trouble, looking down the stairs, sniffing the cooking smells coming up, feeling His guts falling over itself to get at some grub, but making sure everything was all right, first.

Down the bottom of the stairs, He could only hear the trains going by underneath, not a sound else, but He was too hungry of thinking about them steaks to bother very much, so in He went, going over the furniture as if He been doing it for years.

"Who is it?" Tiger yelled, down the end.

"Me," He shouted him, "come in with Henry. All right, am I?"

"Let's see you," Tiger says, coming out of the dark. There was a piece of brown paper tied on the other side of the light so all the hard white of it was right on His dial, not giving Him a chance to see nothing for His self, but He felt His self getting winked at, plain as if He could hear it.

"Ah," Tiger says, close to. "What was your handle again?"

"Mott," He says. "One of Jim Mordinoy's lot. Ask 'em if they know Smasher. Just ask 'em."

"I know you without all that," Tiger says. "What you want?"

"Some grub, if I can get it," He says. "Ain't had nothing since this morning. I'm out on bail, see? Got done for a car smash."

"More fool you," Tiger says, going away, none too sweet. "See what I can do to poison you. Get in the saloon, here.

Henry's there, so it'll come a nice surprise for the pair of you. I hope."

The inside door come open and Tiger shoved his head in.

"Henry," he yells in this little voice, like Ma Chalmers hollering at the milkman, "nice lot of pals you got, I must say. One of 'em here, out on bail. Don't know what this bleeding place is coming to, I'm sure."

"What's up with you, you big headed oont, you?" Henry says, and in He went, seeing him over on the table with a big pile of fags one end, and a couple of blokes round him, looking in. "Who is it?"

"Me," He says, going in, seeing it was nigh empty, and getting up close, "Ernest Mott. Remember?"

"God perish the bleeding Khedive. It's the Reverend, His self," Henry says, and gets up, holding out his arms, proper pally. "Sit you down, Ernie boy. This is the Reverend Ernest Mott, this is, lads. Clerk of the Works. Soaked in knowledge, He is. Wet as they make 'em. How she go, Reverend boy?"

"All right," He says, sitting down.

"What's this about bail?" Henry says.

"Oh," He says, wishing He kept it shut, "got in a bit of accident with a car. I was only having a lift, so it's nothing to do with me. I'm all right."

"That's the spirit," Henry says, making these fags for all he was worth. "You're all right. I'm all right. Don't matter about nobody else, do it? Done any painting lately, have you? Off the ladder, that is?"

"Not much," He says. "Been too busy."

"Ah?" says Henry. "Makes nice hearing. Been doing? Selling lost property, have you?"

"No," He says. "Helping my Ma."

"How did you get down here tonight?" Henry says, scooping up the fags in tens and twenties. "Off your beat, ain't it?"

"My Ma's been took queer," He says. "Cancer, they reckon."

"Oh, Christ," Henry says, and stopped packing. Them white pointed crushed glass balls come at Him proper sorry, with the light sort of going out of them. "That sounds like a drop of bad, son. Don't often come out of that, you know? Been queer long, has she?"

"Must have been years," He says, hearing them slippers coming downstairs one at a time. "But it's only just got her down, like, see?"

"Always the way," Henry says. "Trust a woman. Won't say nothing for fear of doctor's bills, and worrying the house. More guts than a bleeding battleship, they have. Fact? Go on till they bloody well drop, they will. And they do. Where is she?"

"In hospital," He says, feeling proper sorry for His self. Henry talking like that, and these two blokes looking at Him all kind of soft hearted made Him feel a bit heavy for Ma.

"Ah," Henry says. "Well, they'll look after her, there, son. Give her a little drop of bye bye now and again to knock the bleeding nails out."

"What nails?" He says.

"My poor old dutchie used to say it was just like hammering in a handful of nails," Henry says. "What you going to do about a bed? Going home, are you?"

"Don't fancy it," He says.

"Bit lonely, eh, son?" Henry says, setting about the fags. "Don't tell me. I know all about it. Best pal you'll ever have. It's like a light getting blowed out. Never come on again, neither."

Tiger come banging through the door carrying His plateful and a mug of tea.

"Here you are," he says, shoving it across. "Make a new man of you. And I hope to Christ it turns out a better job than the first lot."

"Go on, you baldheaded old cowson, you," Henry says. "Time you turned over a new leaf, and all. We're sick and tired of the old one, flapping about, there."

Tiger was looking at him, wiping his fingers on this raggedy apron, trying to think of something to say, winking away and making his ears jump up and down.

"If you was anywhere nigh a man's size," he says, "I'd tear

the livers out of you, and lose me hands in your blood. There you are."

"Ain't he a little queen, eh?" Henry says, picking all the packets up. "Be selling love pills down here, soon, he will. Kissing everybody as comes in. With a butcher's cleaver."

"Here, that just reminds me," Tiger says to Him. "What's happened to Jim? Gone barmy, has he?"

"Why?" He says, a bit knocked over. He see Henry was looking back, listening.

"Heard he's getting spliced today," Tiger says. "One of the blokes was in this afternoon. Slush Yatley. Know him do you?"

"Old Slush?" He says, seeing Henry just one side of His eye, still looking. "Course. Old pals."

"Well, him," Tiger says, picking up plates. "He reckoned he was off for a couple of weeks honeymoon up Blackpool, till this lark round the corner's got cleared up a bit. Can't see him making much of a job of it, me self. Do 'em and run, that's been his motto."

He knew, better than being told, what was on.

Like a weight hanging on Him, He knew it was Ada. He see why she been having a few, and getting staring white excited about leaving the Fun Fair. He see her in that shining pour of dress again and heard her voice when He give her the gardenias, but somehow, He could no more get her in mind, solid, than get rid of being afraid of Henry knowing He had something to do with Jim. He wanted to think of Ada by His self, to try and find out what there was about her as made Him feel all sort of scratched about somewhere inside.

Henry was coming back, and this was it.

"Know Jim Mordinoy, do you, Reverend?" he says, too quiet, with a lot there.

"Yes," He says, shoving this grub away, feeling a bit sick. "Knowed him a long time."

"Suppose this bail do ain't one of his little larks, is it?" Henry says, looking at the other two blokes and balancing all these paper cones on the bend of his arm.

"No," He says. "Told you. It was a car smash."

"That's all right, then," Henry says. "Because Mr Bloody Mordinoy's going to be boss of these parts, fore very long."

"Boss?" He says. "How? What's it got to do with me?"

"He's got rid of the Sartorelli mob," Henry says. "That don't break my heart neither. But it makes him the boss. Boss of the lot. Make you, or break you. And he's going to be looking for young gents like you. The easy money lark. You know?"

"Don't know what you're talking about," He says, looking at Tiger, winking at a handful of eating tools. All of a sudden He wanted to get on His own to think about Ada.

"Just have a look round," Tiger says. "This ought to be a busy night. Ain't hardly had nobody in here, all day. Know where they are? All up and down the country. All laying doggo. Know why? Because a couple of blokes got laid out. Know why? Because your pal Jim Mordinoy said so."

He see Jim sitting back in the chair, planning the whole affair, putting his hat on in the glass, combing the long ends of his hair behind his ears with his finger tips, looking at his self two sides to see if he was pleased with his self.

"Good luck to him," He says. "None of my business."

"That's what we hope," Henry says. "Don't mind the old 'uns getting in the soup. But we like to see the young 'uns out of it. Don't we, Tiger?"

"I don't know so much," Tiger says, going out. "Couple of years inside 'll do some of 'em all the good in the world, what I can see of it."

"Listen," He says, proper narked. "Can't I do what I like, then? I got to ask you, have I? If I want to work for Jim, I can, can't I? What's going to stop me?"

"Nothing," Henry says, and starts shoving these cones in his pockets. "Only if you start working for Jim, you can't come down here whenever you like, see?"

"Why not?" He says, surprised enough to feel empty.

"Don't cater for you," Henry says, flat as that. "This is for blokes getting their selfs a living out of the rough, see? Sometimes they have to do a job and get their selfs in hot water. We don't mind that. It's human nature to go getting in the dirt, now and again. But not picking it out, both eyes wide open. Not crooks. Don't like 'em and never did."

"What about Trunky and that lot, then?" He says, seeing that razor going.

"Trunky?" Henry says, putting his top hat on, "Trunky? Ah, yes. Trunky. Know how he got his name? Carved up some poor bitch in a trunk and left her in a station. Couldn't prove it on him. Nice bloke, ain't he? That the sort you like going about with?"

"I've never had no dealings with him," He says, "bar that time down your place."

"That was because they was after him," Henry says. "Can't hand a bloke over just because somebody says so. But we don't like 'em, just the same. You got a lot to learn. But you can't learn much in the jug, I can tell you. Except to behave yourself."

"Why ain't you talking to them two like this?" He says, thumbing these other two, as never said a word all the time.

"Two good reasons," Henry says, pulling his top hat off. "First is, they're both a good few years older. They don't need no advice. Second is, they're coppers."

Everything started going round like them boats in the Fun Fair, crashing and banging, all sparks and flashes. Then it went steady again, and dead quiet. These two blokes was just looking at Him like they might at somebody on a tram.

"Go out," He says. "Coppers?"

"Pair of narks," Henry says. "Waiting to do a few likely lads. You hanging on here, or you coming my way? If you ain't wanted, that is?"

"Don't want Him," one of the coppers says. "But we'll know Him again."

"There you are, Reverend," Henry says, banging on his brolly. "They'll know you. See? That's fame, that is. You're in the same class as Crippen and Charlie Peace. That ought to give you a bit of heart, didn't it?"

"Where you bailed?" the other copper says.

"Coldharbour Lane," He says. "Go up Bow Street, Tuesday."

The pair of them just nodded, not taking that much notice.

"Coldharbour Lane, eh?" Henry says, and shivered. "Horrible looking hole, that is. Come on, if you're coming. Night, gents."

"Night," one of them says. He followed Henry out in the other place, seeing Tiger in the little room behind the kitchen, taking eggs out of bits of newspaper, setting them out proper fancy on a dish with long rashers hanging over the sides.

"One of these days," Henry says, shaking his brolly, "some big hairy man's going to come in here and catch you at this lark, Tiger. Then he'll buy you a new costume, and marry you. Look a proper dream, you will, with a flower stuck in your bonnet, and no drawers on."

"What I won't do to you, one of these bright days," Tiger says, feeling the weight of a egg. "Leave them two all right, did you, matey?"

"Happy as a pair of corpses," Henry says. "But I'm taking the Reverend out of it before He starts really opening His north and south. Proper made my blood run cold, He did."

"Why?" He says. "What was up? Why didn't he tell me they was there fore I went in?"

The pair of them looked at Him as if they see something behind it all. Henry shook his brolly out and give it a banging.

"Listen," he says, "I'll give you a little tip. See? Shan't charge you nothing for it. Always keep your mouth shut. Never tell nobody your business. Don't talk about nobody else's business. Have a joke and have a laugh. But don't talk, not even to yourself. See?"

"Okeedoke," He says.

"There He goes again," Henry yells. "Okeedoke? It's a disease. Go on, hop it. I got some flowers want picking up, sides a horse and cart to collect. My parcel there, Tiger boy?"

"Here you are, mate," Tiger says, handing over this big basket, all tied up. "Leg of lamb, a chicken, couple of pots of jam, and some chutney. All right?"

"What about some bleeding eggs then?" Henry says.

"Inside the bleeding chicken," Tiger says. "Anything else you'd like?"

"I'd like to give you a pair of twins," Henry says, getting ready to go.

"Gone past it, now," Tiger says. "Sides a couple more like you'd be murder. Three of you? Christ. One bastard after another."

"Always talking about his own family, he is," Henry says. "Well, think of me, Tiger boy."

"No fear," Tiger says, winking away there. "Rather be healthy, I would. So long, Henry, mate."

"Come on, Reverend," Henry says, coming after Him, "fore he finds out I ain't paid me owings. Get 'em talking and they forget they're running a business."

"I ain't forgot, you old twicer, you," Tiger screeches, "I got it all on the board inside there."

"That was before I rubbed it off," Henry yells, climbing for all he was worth. "You want to get up of a morning, you do."

Going over the furniture, listening to Tiger blinding old Henry, He knew He wanted to get away on His own. He wanted to get somewhere quiet to think about Ada.

"What's about the time?" He says, when they was going up the stairs.

"You'll see in a minute," Henry says. "What you want to know the time for?"

"See if I can catch me last bus or tube," He says.

"With a split on your tail?" Henry says, out in the alleyway. "Going to take him home, too, are you? I knew you was feeling lonely, but not all that much."

"What's a split want tailing me?" He says, getting this whip over Him again. "I ain't done nothing? They know I'm out on bail, don't they?"

"Suppose they think you might be going straight round to Mr James Mordinoy, Esquire?" old Henry says. "Think they might follow you?"

"The splits looking for Jim, are they?" He says, getting it cold right up the neck.

"What you think they've been sitting down there for, the last couple of days? Fun?" Henry says. "There's been three blokes kicked the bucket out of that do round the back there. Another died tonight. Razored. Think the coppers are going to let all that go? What do you reckon they're coppers for? Holding up the traffic? No bloody fear, Reverend. They want to have a nice little chat with a lot of funny people. You might be one of them, for all you know?"

He could hardly stand still, He had such a shake on, and everything got stone cold again, all of a sudden. He see the coppers getting hold of everybody and finding out everything. Specially them little jobs with the jack. He could hear it said who done what, and who got the name of Smasher, and all about that rifle, and all.

He could hardly breathe for this tight feeling of even the very shops and houses being after Him, and He found His self looking round quick to see if there was any coppers anywhere about. Even the blokes in the road looked as if they might be splits in disguise.

"What you reckon I better do?" He says, all of a nitter. "I got to go very steady, I have, with this bail lark, and my Ma, and one thing and another."

"You tack on with me, Rev boy," old Henry says, starting off. "Two minds are better than one, as the sailor said when he nipped in the fourposter along of the ginger haired sisters from Bow. I'm going down Covent Garden, first, to pick up a few flowers. Then I'm off to the Twite shooting box. It's very pleasant down there, now the weather's coming on nice again. Ain't living at Tookover no more."

He was too busy of worrying about things to listen to Henry. It seemed queer how things had sort of changed since He left the job round Old Nick's. Thinking about it made Him feel wormy in the guts again, what with Ada going off after saying all that, and then Him getting pinched, and Ma being inside and nobody to do a hand's turn for Him, besides this new caper of coppers following Him about, it was no lark.

Looking at it any way He could, there seemed to be no end to what had happened and no signs of where it might finish. That was the worst part of it. Whatever He done, it looked as if nothing was going to stop it. It was like trying to stop a bus down the road by thinking about it, or stopping ink from blobbing a cloth once it was tipped.

He got the feeling He was in for it, and He started wanting to get down on the pavement and hold on to something solid again, or dig down and get in the dark where nothing never worried you. What with trying to keep up with Henry, and all, He come out in a right sweat, but where He wiped it over, it felt cold.

"Getting the fat off of you, am I?" Henry says, going hammer and tongs down the road. "Do you good. Here you are. Bus up."

They got on this bus and sat down inside the door.

"Mind if I shove me basket just there?" Henry says to the conductor, and slung it in this little place under the stairs.

"Help yourself," the conductor says. "Don't want no telling, do you?"

"Course not," Henry says. "I've been on this lot since they was drove be horses. Ought to give me the freedom of the line, they did."

"Bet you'd like a shilling for every ride you've had, eh Dad?" the conductor says.

"I should shay sho," Henry says. "Must have spent a fortune, walking, I did. How much do you want off of me this time? Two to the Garden. This is my nephew. Ain't ten yet. Go half fare, I suppose?"

"Big lad for his age, ain't He?" the conductor says. "Go His little sister in the bag, have you? I'll take a couple o browns off of you, if you don't mind?"

Henry dropped the two pennies in his hand, one, two, and the bell went ting, ting.

"All supplied?" the conductor says. "Two pennyworths. Charge you twopence on the sun deck. Extra cushions."

"Sounds as if you been up there lately, without your hat," Henry says.

"It ain't the sun, mate," the conductor says, giving his whiskers a rasp round. "It's me pool coupons. Missed the first prize be two points last week. What a game, ain't it, eh? Bought meself a new house, I did, divorced me wife, put the kids in school, got the mother in law painfully destroyed, and I was off to the South Seas for a go of this hula hula doings. Always fancied a nice cut of that, me self. One bleeding team let me down, and here I still am. See the papers tonight? Don't look too good, do it?"

"Never read 'em, chum," Henry says. "Give it up when they started charging me to ask if me lavatory was clean. Ain't the sort of thing I'm used to. My nephew ought to be reading 'em, though. But He don't. They're learning Him not to read nor write at His school. It's a new idea, see? Saves 'em a lot of bother."

"Yes," the conductor says, looking at Him. "Don't look too knowing, do He? I look at my lot sometimes, and wonder."

"What about?" says Henry, getting down and grabbing for the basket.

"Well, I don't know," this conductor says, pulling his little board out of the slot over his head, and taking a pencil out of the leather brace, getting all his tickets straight before he started bending his knees to write, "perhaps I'm getting old, but they don't seem to be the same sort I was, their age? Take things too easy."

"All they want's a lead from father," Henry says on the step. "And a nice taste of his boot, now and again, with just a touch of the belt, here and there, see? Sweetens everything up. Proper surprising. Just here'll do, mate."

"Blimey," this conductor says, pushing the bell, "if I tried that caper with my lot, I'd come round in hospital."

"Go on?" says Henry, facing round to drop off. "What you got at home, then? A family or a stables? So long, chum."

"Mind the step," says the conductor, and pressed the bell again, bending his knees ready for the next page. "Night, Dad."

"There you are," Henry says. "Hear what he said? Everybody knows it."

"Go out," He says. "I was just listening to the pair of you. Nattering away there, you was. Ain't my fault I'm here, is it? Can't see where you done any better? I'll do what I like, if it's all the same to you?"

"That's right, Reverend," Henry says. "I shan't be here to see it, so I shan't be here to cry. That's the great thing about being a old man, Rev boy. If you don't want to take no notice, you needn't, and even if you did, you're too old to start kicking up a row about it. People just call you a bloody old fool. That's what you get for living a long time."

"Listen," He says, "I'm off. I can get home from here."

"Suppose you're stopped by a copper?" Henry says. "What you going to say?"

He got this feeling of everything watching Him again, even in the dark street. Even the lamps looked nosey.

"They can't touch me," He says.

"Can't," eh?" Henry says. "Well, here's one coming along. What about him?"

This copper come lump, lump, lump on rubber soles, testing the doors and putting his bullseye on the locks, shooting out orange balls of light as bounced back in the dark.

Henry went on past him, and He followed, on the outside of the kerb, not even looking, afraid He was going to feel that hand on His shoulder. But they got past without a word, and He knew, too well, He had to go with Henry a little bit longer or else flop out.

"Nice feeling, ain't it, Reverend?" Henry says, going down some steps in a house. "Fancy being afraid of passing a copper all your life, eh?"

"Where we going?" He says, thinking of the Smasher.

"Get some stock," Henry says. "Here we are. Anybody living?"

They was in a big kitchen place, but it was so dark at the back you could hardly tell if there was a wall there, or if it went on. A brazier was blowing little blue and green feathers out of its red holes, so warm He could feel it on His knee. It looked as if a dozen or more people was laying round it, and over again the wall, a bride was snoring with her face inside the light of a bit of candle, bringing her mouth up a roundish black hole, carrying a baby across her lap with her arms slopped aside from sleep. Her hands was turned up as if she was waiting to catch something.

The floor was piled a couple of foot high of newspapers what they was all laying on, and when He got used to the light, He see there was more blokes near to, and further on as well, all dug deep down in them, just their heads and arms showing, some of them. The snores said the rest.

"Oy," Henry says, quiet, giving some bloke a shake up. "Got that stuff, have you, Hoppy boy?"

This bloke snozzed about a bit, and then come to, all sticky eyed and scratty.

"Ah," he says, getting out of it, like coming out of glue, "thought you wasn't coming. Out here."

He went by, bobbing up and down, thumbing the bride and laughing.

"Sight for sore eyes, ain't she?" he says. "Coughs too much when she lays down. Had to kick her out of it. Keeping everybody up. Here we are."

Some cans come out of a flat barrow, and He got a whiff of flowers breathing in the dark, bringing Ada, holding herself up against him, filling His head with the cool lemony loneliness of gardenias, and almost before it went, He see Ma smelling them glass growed Kents.

"Arums, a dozen," Hoppy says, helping his voice over bumps of sleep with a couple of scrapes. "Love in the mist. Maiden hair. Mixed carns. Three colours of glads, and some roses. All right?"

"Lovely," Henry says, sniffing at them. "Carnations, eh? Here, Rev. Do yourself a good turn. Smell them lilies. Only time I ever wanted to be a fairy, Rev boy. Fancy having your daily half of old and mild out of one of them, eh? Do a few of you a bit of good to kip out here along the flowers, instead of in there, Hoppy? It's a proper ripe hole that is, you know? Thicker than bleeding cheese."

"Too bleeding parky out here," Hoppy says, shivering and rubbing his hands. "Same lot tomorrow?"

"That's it," Henry says, dropping the coins. "Where's the blood?"

"Round the corner," Hoppy says. "She's got a couple of sacks on her. Fed her about couple of hours ago."

"Ta, mate," Henry says. "Go on back and give them fleas a treat."

"Not half," this bloke says, and away he went, nigh falling over his self of yawning.

"They got forty years of newspapers on the floor in there, Reverend," Henry says, topping all these boxes up, and crumpling up paper, "besides a line of bugs as big as bloody midgets. Back answer you, they will. Only got to go just round here."

"Didn't know you was in this line," He says, picking up a couple of these flat boxes.

"It's Perse, not me," Henry says, puffing and blowing. "She's a dab hand with flowers. Gone in with Ma Frobishy, she has. Got a nice little pitch up at Highgate Cemetery. Directly I start carrying anything, I lose me trousers. I thought I was too old to buy some new braces. Didn't think I'd get me moneys-worth of wear out of 'em. Round here."

There was a strawy smell of horses about, and He heard the clack of a hoof coming down on stone.

"There she is," Henry says, laughing away, "pride of the Twite stud farm, she is. Blood, every inch of her. Half a mo."

He lit a couple of lamps, carrying them across to a little cart, sticking them in the holders either side. He see this big white eye moving about in the dark and then a horse fluffled down its nose.

"There she is," Henry says, going up to her, giving her a patting, and leading her out, "Rags, Bones or Bottles, by Sausage Meat out of Anything You Like. Nothing but blood, she ain't. Give me for half a dollar, suit of harness and all chucked in."

He stood looking on while she was strapped in the shafts, then Henry got in the cart and He handed the flowers in.

"Sort of cart's this, then?" He says, not quite placing the shape.

"The Cholmondeley Marjoriebanks Special, guaranteed not to hurt a single hair on a child's head, this is," Henry says, getting everything in the right place. "Got the mare off of a knacker down Homerton. He was going to put her out for the hide. She's blind in the off eye, see? So I done a deal with him. Then I see this on the way down to the shooting box. So one night Mr Cholmondeley put his teeth in, and waltzed down there, and back he come with this here chariot without the churn. It was a milk float. All it wanted was a scrape off, and a coat or two of paint, and there it was. Horse and cart for half a dollar, and some elbow grease. Easy, ain't it?"

They was trotting down this quiet road under purply white lights, but He missed the pull of a car. They was crawling along behind this half blind horse, so slow He was in two minds to get out and shove.

"On your left, Rev boy, what do you see?" Henry says, pointing the whip. "That's taking into account if you know left from right, that is?"

It was only a dark sort of a place, greyish and old in that light, with two big round lamps either side of the steps, looking at Him going past as if they was proper surprised the way things was turning out.

"Looks like a copper station," He says, feeling squeezed in the chest again.

"That's where you'll be, Tuesday," Henry says, waving the whip so that the float come bobbing up and down. "That's Bow Street, that is. Full up of coppers. Just shove the front wall, and you'd find narks coming out the back door by the dozen, just like tooth paste."

He had a look at this place, not because He wanted to, but because He had to, watching those big lamps, seeing the grey-ish length going away in the dark, and the cut up stones in half circles over the windows, like thick eyebrows, all looking at Him and asking questions. Somehow, He got a sort of tired, give it up feeling of not wanting to be alive on Tuesday, but same time He got angry because Henry was ordinary, like, and not worried about nothing. It never seemed fair that all this should be happening to Him, and not nobody else.

"Where we off to, now?" He says, kind of itchy inside.

"We're going to give our selfs the freedom of the City of London," Henry says, crossing his legs on the side seat, and leaning back there cushy as a millionaire. "Can't call in on the Lord Mayor, but we'll give the old bleeder a bolo when we go by his house. Perhaps if he ain't in kip, he might lean out the bedroom window and give us the time of day, if his Mrs'll let him. I suppose he's as lucky as everybody else. See his old fur coat, have you? What a draught stopper. Wouldn't mind getting in his way when he feels tired of it. No doubt about it, Rev boy. They don't half make their selfs suffer. Treat their selfs proper cruel, they do."

They was clacking along shining parts of the road, and then clumping over wood blocks, going off of one and on to the other, as if they was going under a tunnel, and the horse's head was bobbing up and down over the curly brass railing in front like something on a stick.

Newspaper vans was just starting to make a move down the other side, and in the roads going off to the right they was lined up by the dozens and all the drivers was standing about having a spit and a drag under the lights, with little softish clouds of smoke going up over their heads, something like that white waterfall down the hospital.

Ma come rushing back very strong, where He nigh on see her sitting there beside Him, making Him want to go to her, but He knew He wanted to go back to Ma like she was at home in the kitchen, not like she was down there in bed. He tried to make out why it was that nothing ever turned out like you wanted it to be. It sort of started off all right, and then started going wrong to spite you, trying to get you down where you never thought it was worth while trying to do nothing, or make something of your self, nor give you no heart. It made you feel you wanted to jack a few more windows, and hear the bash of the glass and the car scream of laughing, getting away out of it.

"What you thinking about, Rev boy?" Henry says. "I wouldn't give you a penny for 'em. I've been had before. See a bloke frowning away there, making everybody give him plenty of room case he starts picking a row with somebody, and then you find out he's only worried about the way the slugs are after his young sprouts. Ain't worth it. But what's up with you?"

"Nothing," He says. "I'm all right. Thinking about things, that's all."

"Won't do you no harm," Henry says, slinging Him a fag. "What did you say you was doing for a living?"

"Nothing," He says, lighting up. "I'm like you from now on. Ain't got a job and don't want one. Don't get you nowhere, even if you have."

"Sounds all right," says Henry, "but what are you going to do?"

"Told you," He says. "Nothing."

"That ain't what I'm doing," Henry says. "I'm just finishing my day's work, I am, and I started out half past seven this morning. How about that?"

"Thought you said you never had a job, once you give it up?" He says. "How long was that ago?"

"Listen, Rev," Henry says, "there's some things about you puts half inch hairs on me. I ain't had a job for going on thirty years. I'll never have a job again. A job's when you go up for your screw of a Friday. When you have to start sweating every time the boss comes round, case you get the sack. That's a job. I work for me self. That's pleasure. See? But I work a bloody sight harder for me self than ever I did in a job. Why? Because I'm enjoying me self. What you doing? You enjoying your self, are you?"

They was going up this hill, round a road under a place like where Ma was, only bigger, rattling about in this float like a pair of lunies out for the night. He see His self down the Fun Fair, having a right time, then off round the cinema to see a proper smashing picture, and going to the cafe afterwards for a fried supper and a bit of sport with the lads, or rushing a tart home, depending how you felt. But now it was different. With the big money rolling in, He could play the Fun Fair and never miss it, go to one of them posh cinemas up the West End, with a cigar, and then go down the club for a marvellous supper, and go up and get one of them right looking lays.

He knew He was going to enjoy His self, same as Jim and Cosh and Slush and a few more of them. It was dead easy.

"Course," He says.

"What you doing, then?" Henry says. "What's your line? Painting, are you?"

"No," He says. "I give it up. I'm doing all right, I am."

"With a lump of Bow Street on your plate, I reckon you are," Henry says. "Starting nice and early. Ain't missing nothing, are you? Next thing is, you'll be finding yourself taking a little holiday, somewhere. Then you'll laugh."

"I'll take me chance," He says, but He still never wanted Henry to think He was a mug. That there look of his, and the way he said things, sort of got down inside and itched. "I got Ma's business, see? Second hand furniture. Takes a lot of running, and all."

Henry put his feet on the floor and tipped his hat back, all smiles.

"Talking out of me turn, again, eh?" he says, laughing away. "Course. Working for yourself, I'll bet you're doing a harder day's work now, than what you ever did down that there place you was messing about in? Eh?"

"Yes," He says, "course. Open up at eight of a morning. Don't close till gone seven. Then there's me books, and the orders, and perhaps one of the wholesalers might come round. All takes time, see? There's old Ike Buzgang, like, he comes round sometimes and wastes me time jawing."

"Ike?" Henry says, pleased as punch. "I know Ike? Ike Buzgang? Down the Walworth Road? Course I know Ike. Knowed him fifty year, if it's five minutes. Proper good bloke. Do you a bit of good, he will, son."

"I can't like sheenies," He says, watching how dark it was on one side of this wide, polished road, and how light it was on their side, with a clean cut right down the middle, just like when the sun come through the bedroom window of a morning, only them little white bits was all blowed away by the wind.

"Passing the Mansion House," old Henry says, waving his hat at this place with a lot of thick pillars holding the roof up. "That's where the old Lord Mayor treats all his pals' guts. Thirty two courses for dinner every night of his life, all different. That's him. Eh? Ask for beer, you get slung out. Get blind drunk, the lot of them. If you're known, you go out on a copper's shoulder. If you ain't, you're took out on a board and tipped in the gravel bin. Serves you right for talking."

Henry's eyes come up shining like bits of looking glass in this big ball of moon, and he started singing something about wonderful love, pretending he was playing the piano proper posh on top of the flower boxes, daft as they make them.

"Well, there's sheenies, and sheenies, you know, Rev boy," he says, laying back thinking about it. "Then there's Yids, and Non Skids to say nothing of the Shonks? Then there's Three Be Twos, and Jews. After all that's over, you've got your Ike Buzgangs. And let me tell you, he's a bloody sight better bloke than you'll ever be, what I can see of you. That's funny, ain't it?"

"I ain't saying nothing about him," He says. "Just saying I can't like 'em. That's all."

"Ain't that a pity, eh?" Henry says. "Some ways, I'm glad my lad never come out of that lot, you know? He might have whelped something like you. So by this time, either you'd have broke my heart, else I'd broke yourn. I know whose heart it'd been, though. And His bloody back, and all."

Henry took one of these flowers out and looked at it in the moonlight, sniffing as if he never had enough, and while He was thinking of telling him to stop so as He could get out, a couple of coppers went over the road in front, slinging their shadows along this black glass, right under the horse.

"What me old Henry, boy?" one of them yells, and Henry made a grab for his top hat, waving it side to side, as if there was thousands all round him.

"Hi yi," he shouts them, "how's your poor old plates of meat, Sergeant?"

"All right," this copper shouts back. "How's yours?"

"Taking them home to a nice hot wash," Henry shouts, and the words bounced up and down the road. "Got my eldest daughter with me. You ought to meet her. You'd never be the same man since."

"What about your tail light, then?" one of them yells, flashing his light off and on.

Henry pulled up quick, wrapping the reins round the railing.

"Well, God chase me up and down Wapping Stairs," he says, feeling for matches, and getting his self over the side. "Forget me own name in a minute."

"How long's Lord Twite been riding in his own carriage?" one of the coppers says, strolling up, making Him nigh shiver His self out of His clothes, even though He was trying to tell His self He was all right.

"Since we left Tookover," Henry says, with this red light coming up strong in his face. "That's it. And not so much of your lord, neither. I'm a belted earl, I am. Well, not so much belted as sloshed. So long, Sergeant. Give my love to the Mrs."

"I will," this copper says. "Give mine to Mrs Sitram."

"She'll want to know your intentions, first," Henry says, coming over the wheel and untying the reins. "It's been tried, that has."

"Give you a black eye, did she?" the copper says, tipping his hat back and proper cackling away, there.

"She give me the fright of me bleeding life," Henry says, whipping up. "She was going to let me. Holdy tighty. Nighty nighty."

Off they went again, and He felt all His muscles going soft, leaving Him with this queer shake, not quite shivery, not quite steady, making Him feel right touchy and all of a jump.

"Sort of blokes I wouldn't like to get me self mixed up with, the wrong way, they are," Henry says. "Nice to talk to, show you your way home, very good natured, give their mothers all their money, drink milk, and even go to church. When they're marched there. But you start any bleeding nonsense, and see where you land up. Take my tip, Rev boy. Let this Bow Street do be the first, and last."

He got this knife in Him all of a sudden, again, coming up a proper raging temper with everything. Here He was, in this sloppy little cart with a blind nag pulling them along at a crawl, in a right patch of hard luck what with Ma gone and Bow Street coming, and everybody was ticking at Him about falling in the soup. He see as clear as the moon how the only pal He had, and the only bloke as ever give Him anything, heart or nicker, was the smartest of the lot, the bloke as could buy and sell the lot of them and never know he put his hand in his pocket.

Jim was the only proper decent pal He ever had, the only bloke as ever give Him a smile or a pat on the back.

"Listen," He says, "where we going?"

"See a bloke you know," Henry says. "Let him have a go at you."

"Listen," He says, "nobody's having a go at me. This is where I cut the lark. I'll get down here, if it's all the same to you."

"You do," Henry says, "and I'll have the first copper I see after you. You might be running your Ma's business, for all I know, but there's something about you I ain't satisfied about. Why you so afraid of coppers?"

"What you so bloody nosey for?" He says. "I ain't nothing to do with you? You go your way, I'll go mine."

"You pipe down a minute," Henry says, driving on. "Remember that bloke Trunky, do you? Down the sewer? When poor old Chaser went for six?"

"What about it?" He says, feeling something coming and not knowing where it was going to hit.

"That was a murder," Henry says, like putting a stamp very careful on a envelope, not looking at Him. "Don't know whether you know it or not? You was there. That makes the Father, you, and Trunky all guilty, see? You and the Father can witness it was Trunky done the job. But neither of you went to the police, did you? So the Father and you are accessories after the fact. See? That's as bad as the murder, that is. Know that, did you?"

The moon come whiter and the night got blacker, and the light flashing on all the window glass made it just like eyes looking at Him, and looking away again. Same time, the wind started blowing up proper cold through the streets on either side, sort of catching Him in the small of His back, besides blowing through that tear in His trousers. He come over proper queer, feeling right on the floor.

"Nothing to say, eh?" Henry says, looking round at Him. "You'd look bright if you got lagged, wouldn't you, eh? Now do you know why I'm sticking me nose in your business? Because if you lot go to chokey, so do I, for harbouring. So we're all blackbirds in the same old pud. Ain't that nice, eh?"

Whichever way He looked at it, there was nothing in it except a load of trouble. He was right down the pan. Everybody was kicking Him down.

"What you want to tell me for?" He says, feeling this sore coming back in His throat again, where He wanted to start howling. "Ain't I got enough bleeding trouble as it is?"

"No, mate," Henry says, "you want a bit more. What you got to remember is, one lot of trouble leads to another. You get snitched on one charge, and before you know where you are, you'll get done for a murder. Once the coppers have got you, they've got you. See?"

"They've got me," He says, not knowing where to turn. "Bow Street."

"That's what you're going to see the Father about," Henry says.

They turned off down a little street on the left. A couple of cafes was doing a roaring trade from the sounds coming out, and He got this feeling again of wanting to reach out over all the roofs and bring Ma back home, and get His self nice and comfy down the cafe, round the machine with the lads so as He could go off when Ted turned the lights out, and find His supper waiting in the kitchen, and everything going proper spanking.

He see what happened to Ma Sedgwiss. You got kicked about and treated worse than a dog by everybody so you just spent a couple of wheels and got yourself off out of it. It sounded easy enough, this lark of making yourself comfortable next to a gas ring and going to kip.

But somehow or other, when you come to think about it there was something a bit crawly about what happened after. All this junk about God and Heaven and one thing and another was only a tale, what you got rid of like Father Christmas soon as you see the cotton wool round his dial and his trouser ends under his red coat.

But this caper of knocking yourself off, and rolling up, was a bit different. There was nothing there. It was like going in a dark house and finding you left your matches behind, standing there listening to things creeping about, and little noises, what you never seemed to hear in the light, proper giving you the crawling itches, making you back out quiet, trying not to breathe, and then going for the door and out in the road, right glad to see all the lights, and hear people talking, sitting on the step till Ma come back from shopping.

So the gas business was no go. In fact, it was rotten even to think about, because if you died anyhow, you still had to stand in that there dark house as everybody went in and nobody come out of, except ghosts.

He started shivering, and turned His collar up.

"Cold, Rev?" Henry says. "There's a blanket down there. But we're here, now."

They stopped outside a little tin shed with a white board over the door. Pennyfields Mission it had on it, and there was light coming from the windows. Henry tied the nag to the lamp post, and put her nosebag on, and then went through the gate up this little path, stopping on the top step, pushing the door open and looking in.

It was only about forty foot long and half as wide, full of forms either side, and at the end there was a long table with a dozen or so candles burning round a big cross. He got this funny scent soon as He put His nose in, a sort of sweetish, burny smell like when Ma Chalmers was smoking up a lot of leaves of an evening, with a bit of Ada in it, only it got up in your head and made you think of things, as sort of slipped your mind, kind of no shape or size or colour, nor even feeling, but they was all there if you could only put your finger on them.

A couple of old girls was down the bottom end, talking to the monk bloke. There was no doubts about him, because the candles was shining right on his bit of hair, making it come up a white ring. Soon as He see them standing in the door he said something to the old girls and come down.

"Come in," he says, "come in. Who is it, tonight, me lord? Who's the noble guest?"

"Reverend E. Mott," Henry says, shoving Him in. "Been holding a session with the Reverend T. Collis, Canon of Soho. Just lost his surplus on the favourite."

"I'm greatly pleased to see you here," this monk bloke says, while Henry went out again. "Did you find any effects from that journey of ours?"

"No," He says. "I was all right."

"Good," this monk bloke says. "Well, come in and sit down. I'll not be long. We'll go round the back to my little cubby after the service."

"I want to get off home," He says. "I been up since early

this morning and I never had much sleep last night. My Ma's queer, and all. So I'd like to get off."

"I'm deeply sorry," the monk says. "Is there anything I may do for your mother? Or for you?"

He see this bloke finding out about Ma, and telling Henry, and then trying all this churchy business on Him.

"No," He says. "She's going to roll up, whatever anybody does. And she don't believe in all this stuff, any how. Be a waste of time."

This monk looked along at the candles with his head a bit bent.

Some more old girls, and a couple of young ones come through the door and sort of bobbed down on their hunkers, then got up and went along to spread out on the front lot of forms. This monk kind of give them all a laugh when they looked at him, but he was still having a think.

"Here you are, Father," old Henry says, coming in with these big lilies and some others, all different colours. "From Perse. Be here first thing to do 'em, so they won't do no harm like this."

The monk bloke stuck his nose in them and took it down like a fag.

"Ah," he says, "faith restored. What should I do without you, Sir Henry?"

"Buy 'em," Henry says. "No use of giving me a lot of soft soap, Father. Just because Perse likes to drop her profits. Sides, it gives her something to do."

"Of course," says the monk bloke, laughing away. "And that gives you something to do, coming so far out of your way, and it give me something to do, too. And I do it with all me heart."

"What's that?" says Henry, as if he could see a catch.

"Praise God for people such as our good friend Henry," says the monk, enjoying his self, "First Earl Twite, late of Tookover Manor, now of Tip Up Grange."

Some more old dears was coming through, and a couple of

blokes, and he was a bit surprised to see the place was coming
nigh on half full. What was funny, every one of them, even
the blokes, all bobbed down coming through the door, as if
they dropped something.

"When you say that, Father," Henry says, playing with his
hat, "you make me feel proper ashamed of me self. Don't know
why. Almost make me come inside and go through the piece.
Hark at me talking."

The monk bloke put out his arms and waved at the forms.

"Sit down," he says, happy as anything, "anywhere you
like. All the room you'll ever need, and nobody to see you.
Just say a little prayer. Only just a few words? Open up your
mighty heart, now, and pour out only a little amongst us. I'll
be selfish, then. Just for me. A little prayer only for me?"

Henry looked at this big bunch of flowers and his face come
out of the lilies proper comic. It suddenly struck Him how he
looked like one of them old blokes in the picture down the Gallery, that day with Old Nick.

"Always treading on my shirt tails, you are, Father," he
says, having a grouse. "What am I going to say? If I was God,
and he was me, and I see him coming in a place of mine, I'd
say go on, hop off out of it, you two faced old, whats name.
Go on."

"Do you hear any such Voice, now?" this monk says, taking
the flowers off of him.

"No," Henry says. "But that's only because he's tired of
talking."

"Twenty four hours in a day," the monk says, to one of the
lilies. "Sixty minutes to each hour. Sixty seconds to each minute. And you can't spare just a few of the last for a friend?
Only a few seconds for me?"

"I don't know how to go about it," Henry says, getting
worked up. "I don't know what to say, I tell you. It's no good
of me going down there and talking a lot of dripping, is it?
Sides, it'll spoil me trousers."

"I can tell you what to say," the monk says, laughing in
these flowers.

"No, look, you go and say it for me," Henry says. "But what about the Reverend, here? He's the bloke wants tackling. He's due at Bow Street, Tuesday. On bail, now. Prize, ain't He? Got in a smash with a motor."

"It won't be much," He says, trying to talk up. "They told me I'd be all right. Sides, I got a good solicitor. Bloke called Nathan."

"If he's the bloke what I know, he's the dirtiest crook in a game full of crooks, he is," old Henry says. "And he's one of Mr Mordinoy's pals, like a few more of 'em. Is he?"

"Don't know," He says. "Don't care, so long as I get off."

"Oh, he'll get you off, all right," Henry says, wagging his head about and puffing his mouth out as if he never had no doubts about it. "He'll make you out the poor little bloke, you know, everybody's pal, got His poor old mother dying at home there, calling for Him, and all that how do you do. Then he'll square the witnesses and call the coppers all the names he can think of, and generally twist and twiddle there, till you find yourself outside on the pavement again. I've see it done."

"Do you need any help, now?" this monk bloke says, looking straight at Him, and even though it was darkish, through only having them candles down the end there, He see just a touch of that hot pale blue in the eye nearest to the light, and He could feel everything inside of Him was sort of being skimmed. "I'll be at Bow Street on Tuesday, in any case."

"So will I," says Henry.

"Why don't you two let me be?" He says, getting this fly of temper again. "Done nothing to you, have I? Got to stick your noses in, have you?"

There was that rushy sound of people turning round and He see they was all looking at the doorway.

"No good talking, Father," Henry says, looking outside. "Bang your crust up again the door. Do just as much good. He don't want a sermon. What He wants is a bloody good hiding. Begging your pardon, like. Crying for it, He is."

"I'm afraid you're right," this monk bloke says, as if he

meant it. "But we'll go into it later on. I've a service, now. You'll not change your mind, me lord?"

"I ain't feeling like it, now, thanks," old Henry says. "This bloke's turned me up. See you Tuesday, Bow Street?"

"Nine o'clock," this monk says. "In the hall, there. Good night, now. And I'll say a prayer for you, instead, and one for all of us."

Henry was looking down toward the candles, where all the people was just like roundish sacks in rows, with feathers and ribbon sticking out black from the brides hats, and this goldish light bouncing off the bald heads of the blokes.

"What joy to know," this monk says, "that as the gardener planted these lovely things and knew in faith that Almighty God would send them up lilies and roses, as they were sent up last year, and all the other years, so I know that my little words will bring up lovely things in the hearts of these people of mine. This is my garden, and I'll go now and plant a few more of my flowers, please God. Give my love to Persephone and Mrs Sitram."

Off he went, gripping these flowers, starting to sing something, and all the people on the forms went down on their knees, making a fine old row, and joining in all ragged.

"Come on," Henry whispers. "Else I might find me self in there, and all."

The monk bloke was long and black, going down toward the candles with these lilies sticking their white cups out, almost like hands coming out either side of him, and the light on all the rows of heads was like water shining over cobbles.

They got outside and Henry shut the door.

"It was a Sheeny started all that, in there," he says. "Did you know? A Sheeny. One of them blokes you can't seem to like. A Shonk. A Yid. One of Mr Nathan's crew. Same family as Ike Buzgang. A Non Skid. Did you know? Funny, ain't it?"

"No," He says. "I've had enough of it, anyhow. Proper load of tripe."

"Lasted a long time," Henry says, undoing the reins, and slinging the nosebag in.

"Not with me, it ain't," He says. "I got more sense, I have."

"Do what?" says Henry, looking round at Him. "Sense? Sense, eh?"

"Course," He says, pulling His collar up. "Sides, fancy a bloke like him trying to tell me what to do? Been in the Jug half his life, he has. So he says, any rate. Got a bloody sauce, I reckon. How about a fag, fore I get off home?"

Henry felt in his pocket and took one out, holding it up. He strolled over to take it, and all of a sudden there was a quick move somewhere and He felt this blinding crash as sent a big whitish flash in His eyes with queer spiky pains through His head, and He heard His self fall flat on the pavement, feeling the hard, sloppy bump, and the wind blowing cold in His hair.

"Want a light, too?" Henry says, a long way off. "I told you you'd catch a cold one of these fine days. Now you got it. Crawl in that there cart, fore I limb you. Go on. Ever heard of a bloke getting his self knocked sensible, have you? Same name as you."

He knew it was no good of arguing, and Henry had the whip in his fist, thick end first, so He got up in the cart where He sat before, wondering where He could get hold of something weighty to crash him with, the second he looked somewhere else.

"Enjoy your smoke?" says Henry. "That baccy's very strong. And there's plenty more where it come from, so don't try none of your larks, else you'll catch a real bloody cold, let me tip you."

"Where we going then?" He says, nigh on howling again, what with one thing and another. "I want to go home."

"Suppose a copper stops you?" Henry says. "What you going to say to him? It's worse this time of night. You'd be pinched for a suspected person. Sides, I ain't having you crawling about all over the place, getting in a lot of trouble. You're coming home with me. Now pipe down."

He leaned back on the hard boards, getting his head in the corner, letting the jog up and down knock Him about, not caring what happened, and getting more shivering cold every minute, feeling sleepy, but keeping one eye open, red hot for a chance to get away and run for it. Somewhere inside of Him, He knew where He was going to get His own back for everything, whatever anybody done to Him, and it sort of made Him laugh.

The more He thought about it, the more He wanted to laugh.

It was dead funny.

Going along the river, hearing the nag clacking away, and Henry humming something to his self, like Ma downstairs of a morning, He knew He was all right.

Opening one eye, He see the moon was up there just like a football skied by some bloke with more kick than sense. Over the wall He see the water was full of black and white rags all wrinkled up, and as you might say, proper laughing silver, as if it knew all about it, and Him, and everything.

## CHAPTER XLII

HE WOKE UP when they was bumping over big holes tipping side to side, up and down, till He had to prop His self up with a stiff leg on the other seat to keep where He was.

It was still white and blue in a football moon, only there was a steamy collar round it making everything come up light, only somehow duller, and kind of tiredish.

Old Henry was still there, with his grey top hat pushed back, looking at the nag, sending her kisses here and there and handling the reins as if they was going to come in two any minute.

"Now where are we?" He says, looking round.

There was a funny sort of smell coming across, and when He looked over the side, He see why. They was going across a big dust shoot, where the dust carts tipped out. All round in this steamy bluish light, there was big and little hills of muck, stuck out with lumps of paper caught up and waving at everybody for help, and tins was catching bits of light and slinging it back again as if they never wanted it, or else standing there with their lids all peeled off, and their labels kicking free, or else gone, looking proper hard done by, getting hold of some of this light and not caring if it stuck or not.

It was the smell of stuff as had been used and got chucked away, and in it, there was that smell He got down the hospital near Ma, and a bit of the railway running behind the house, and the market of a Saturday, and Pa Prettyjohn's before he swept out of a morning, even something of Ada's hair and Jim's hair oil, and the rats down the sewer, but always the tired hard luck round about the dustbin down the bottom of the garden, where the flies went barmy.

"This is Tip Up Grange," Henry says. "Entrance to my estate. Been here going on four years, now? The borough council tips all the muck out here, so I built a place over the back there, where the carts can't come. No visitors, no rent, and no worries, and the wind's always in the right quarter. Lucky, eh?"

The night come proper light and quiet. Far away a engine was doing a crunch, crunch, and trucks was nattering and clonking, then moaning for a little while, and shutting up.

"Hulloa, there," Henry says, and pulled in, looking.

"What?" He says, getting off of His perch and trying to get His self working. There seemed to be no end of these piles of muck. They just went on and on, all round. "Where are we?"

"Middle of the Borough desert," Henry says, still looking. "We're here. But who's that over there?"

A bloke was coming through this space between a couple of these piles, right in front of them, picking his way very careful.

"Oy," Henry yells, "who's that?"

"Me," this bloke yells, and He knew it was Marjoriebanks. "Where you been? Got the place in a uproar, you have? Proper going to cop out, you are, governor."

"Get up," Henry says to the nag, and away they went. "Cop out, eh? I'd like to see 'em. That's the Dowager slinging her weight about, again. I'll learn her."

Marjoriebanks waited till they got up with him, and climbed aboard when Henry stopped, dropping a armful of firewood on the floor.

"What's up with you?" Henry says to him, "traipsing about here? Moon got you love struck, or something?"

"No," Marjoriebanks says. "I couldn't get to sleep. Tried everything. Come to a finish, the bleeding sheep was counting me, so I give it best. Who's this?"

"Don't you know?" He says, sliding up the seat to make room. "Ernest Mott. Remember?"

"The Reverend," Marjoriebanks says, pleased as punch. "Well, stone me down the Haymarket. How are you, son? We often had a jaw about you?"

"Yes?" He says, keeping His eyes open. "What about?"

"Well, you know," Marjoriebanks says. "What you was doing, like, and how you was. You had a rare game that night, didn't you? How did you get down here?"

"Come be parcel post," Henry says. "You pudding headed old slop, you. What you think He's doing on here, then?"

"Do I know?" Marjoriebanks says, with little strings of spit shooting out in the light. "You reckoned you was going to get Him to paint the panels in the hall. Is that why He's here?"

Henry took his hat off and looked down at it, proper beat.

"Yes," he says, so tired. "Only I wasn't going to tell Him. I was going to show Him, and ask Him, and get a price on it, and fix it up like that. Only you've give the bloody game away, as usual. If only you'd wear your teeth, stead of going about half naked, you wouldn't talk so much."

"I took 'em out just now to have a cup of tea," Marjoriebanks says. "Let me tell you, till you've took your teeth out somewhere nice and quiet for a little cup of tea, all by yourself, you've never lived. Best feeling in the world, that is, boy."

"You can drum us up a cup when we get in, then," Henry says. "Then we'll all take 'em out. The Reverend'll kip in the Music Room, Cholmondeley, for the time being. If He's going to do this little job, it'll take a bit of time, and we'll shift Him somewhere else."

"The Music Room's where we've got the barrel organs," Cholmondeley says to Him. "Nice collection, and all. All the old favourites. I'll play 'em for you. Roll on the winter when we trot 'em out again. Nothing like a good tune of a cold morning, round the streets. Livens the place up."

He see the game so plain, He could have laughed. They got Him here to stop Him going nigh the court, so as there was no chance of Him telling the narks about Trunky. If He did, Henry was for it, so was the rest of them, and the monk bloke. But nobody was worried about Him. They thought He was just a bloke to smack on the chin or sling a job at, whichever you felt like. Seeing His self painting again was no cop, neither, thinking about that there bit of crayon, and how the paints was just the same, easy to think about, and easy to watch when somebody else was having a go, but wear you out and drive you barmy when it come to your turn for the lark.

They rolled off of this rubbish tip and down in a field, crossing over a little bridge where He could hear water having a tiddle to itself, going over towards a lot of trees.

"Tip Up Grange, in front of you," Henry says. "Just left the Grotto, we have. This is the paddock, where the Dowager does her morning sprint. The garden's over there. That's Cholmondeley's concern, that is. He's been at it now, what, nigh on three years? He's got a couple of lovely bits of wire coming up, there, and a few pee the beds, so they tell me."

"Go out," Marjoriebanks says. "Don't take no notice, Rev. He's jealous. Look. You can just see my lot of cabbages. See? Finest cabbage in the bleeding country, they are. He couldn't even grow his finger nails, he couldn't."

All these dark rows of round heads in straight lines was just like them old dears and the blokes hollering to the monk in that little mission place. The smell of the flowers in the boxes come up, like thinking about Ada, and all of a sudden He got this feeling again, burning hot, and strong, somewhere inside Him, where He knew He had to get out of it or go barmy. He had to get away from all this quiet and the deep blue sky and the moon like a big pearl button, so close, you could almost see the holes where it been stitched on.

He had to have some houses round Him, and shops and lights and people.

The quiet, and the open everywhere, letting the wind come through like a bride trying to whistle, and the dark trees all shaking about, same as the loose hair on the nag's neck, give Him the bleeding creeps.

"There's the Grange, Reverend," Henry says, pointing the whip. "Why pay rent? Shooting box, country house and weekend cottage, all in one. If I can get hold of enough onion crates this summer, we'll build a Castle in Spain, and all. Down there by the Grotto."

"If we get as much sport building it as we did with the Grange," Marjoriebanks says, "we won't half have a time, and all. Remember when the Dowager fell off the ladder? Laugh? I nigh died."

"You did die, you toffee nosed old twimmick, you," Henry says. "We buried you over there in the marrow bed. Don't you remember?"

Marjoriebanks started picking up the firewood.

"Me own fault," he says. "Lift your plates up, Rev."

While His feet was on the seat and Marjoriebanks was scratching about on the floor, He see His chance to get out.

The feeling come over Him just like before He slung the jack.

The place, close to, was a lot of planks and corrugated iron all knocked together with some windows and doors here and there, and what He could see of it, nigh covered with creeper. There was even a couple of bushes growing round the chimneys. Flower beds was all cut out between the paths, just like Ma Chalmers, and on the side, He could hear chickens having a gurgle or two, to let it be known what they thought of getting woke up.

He see Henry was thinking about something, and though he was talking to Him a bit different, without the laughs and sort of holding off, He see he was trying to get back in His good books again, but not quite knowing how.

The rubber tires never made a sound on the paths, and they pulled up in the dead quiet just outside the big door in the middle. Henry got down, taking the nosebag, and Marjoriebanks jumped off, carrying the wood.

"Come in, Rev," he says. "Lovely fire, and plenty of grub. Welcome home."

He went at it, head down. The reins come off the railing and the whip come out the holder. One jerk and the nag was off, going proper fast, making the cart tip side to side. He could hear the pair of them shouting but the wind was going past His ears so fast, making such a row, He never heard what they said, nor cared.

Across the bridge, up this little hill at a gallop, over the top and up and down and round bends, and every time the nag thought she wanted to ease off, He give her the whip to learn her different. There was a fat sort of feeling about hearing the cord smack across her, and she had the same idea from the way she got herself moving. They come out on the main road, but she never waited for Him to guide her. She turned left, and went down the road at this sort of bumpy walk as made the cart bob up and down. Slashing her with the whip round her legs and neck got her out of it sometimes, but she kept on falling back into it as if she was tired, so He cured her by keeping the whip going in time with her legs, trying to get her under the guts and some nice slashes got in too, till the cord sort of come all lose at the end and then, pulling it back for another go, it caught in the wheel, and nigh jerked His arm out, so He lost it in the road.

The headlights of this lorry come up behind Him, and He see His way to a lift right in to the Smoke and home, so He pulled her up, getting out and slinging the reins in the back, running up to her and giving her a nice old punch in the belly to get her off out of it. She went and all, and the cart got one wheel over the ditch edge and went over, taking her with it.

The last He see of her was her hoofs all kicking away there, and one white eye rolling about, then He run off to wave the ride.

"Do us a ride, can you?" He says. "Going up the Smoke, are you?"

"Far as the bottom end of Westminster Bridge Road," the driver says. "But you'll have to drop off a bit before. I ain't supposed to take you, see? How did you get landed out here, then?"

"Been doing a bit of visiting," He says, getting in the cab. "Missed the last train. Got to be at work at half seven."

"You'll just about do it," the driver says. "Where from?"

"Kingsland Road," He says.

"Easy. Treacle pie," the driver says. "Get the tube from Waterloo, or over the bridge. Plenty of time."

"Where we now?" He says, feeling this bumping up and down and the smell of petrol sending Him off, till He felt

His eyelids was roller blinds with weights on the end of the strings.

"South of Greenwich, somewhere," the driver says, shifting his glasses down his nose. "But it don't take long in this. I do it five times a week, Smoke to Hastings, and back. Sometimes other places. Down in the morning, back at night."

"When do you get your kip in, then?" He says.

"My mate and me take it turn and turn about," the driver says, thumbing inside the lorry. "He's having His in there now."

"Mind if I have one?" He says, hardly getting it out. "I couldn't half do with a bit."

"Help yourself, chum," the driver says. "There's plenty of it. I'll give you a shove."

"Okeedoke," He says, and He stuck His self in the corner to save His head getting bumped about, pushed His hands in His pockets, and felt His self going off a treat, watching the headlights pick up some houses remembering how Knocker handled the wheel, and Taz coming up in the back, with a dial all covered sticky red.

It was coming up blue of early morning when He woke, and they was just pulling in the kerb.

"Here you are," the driver says. "Dream about her, did you?"

"Course," he says. "She was smashing, boy."

"That's half the trouble," the driver says, while He was climbing out. "Get more while you're asleep than you can any other way, I reckon. Lasts longer, and there's no arguments. So long."

"So long," he says. "See you again."

The lorry went off in front of a bus, and He had two minds to get on it, but He never see where it was going so He started walking. Then a chocolate tram came along and He nipped on the platform, standing amongst everybody else, trying to feel He was going to work again.

But the feeling was dead. He was dressed all wrong, for a start. He never had a paper, He never had His breakfast, nor

He never had no sandwiches, so it was no good of trying. But thinking about the people behind Him, He got the idea He was better off, taking it all round.

He never had to get up of a morning again as long as He lived, and soon as He had a few more jobs from Jim, He see His self getting a nice little car to go for trips in, so trams and buses would just be a nuisance in the traffic, not something to ride in, but something to dodge round and swear at. These people behind was going to be in jobs all their lives, just to earn their selfs a couple of quid, enough to keep things going without being able to chuck anything away. But He was going to be right in the big money, soon as this Bow Street lark was over.

He was going to get a suit like Jim, and a tiepin, and proper look the part of The Smasher.

He started feeling sorry for everybody going to work, because there was no need of it. If they all stayed at home, it would get done just the same, and even if it never got done, nobody would bother very much. He got the idea, somehow, He was a cut above them, in a manner of speaking, just like the blokes on the stalls, because He never had to put His self out for anybody, nor He never had to worry about nothing, or do no hard work.

He was His own boss and He would do what He liked.

The only thing was about the nicker, but if He went down the Fun Fair and see the bloke, like Ada said, He was all right, and He had a nice bit to come from the copper station, and Ma might have a bit hid away down the shop, so all in all, it looked as if He was laughing.

Everybody started getting off, shoving Him off the step along with the rest, but He never minded because it saved Him the fare, so without waiting for the lot of them to get off and on, and sort their selfs out, He started up for the bridge, thinking how different it was to when He was coming the other way a night or two back, with Knocker driving one hand and Taz laying down on the back seat with his knees crossed and his hat on the top. It was hard to think how Taz rolled up in that fire, and He proper shook hands with His self for having the common to stay in the front, where He come out first.

He found it a bit hard going up this sort of hill to the bridge, and He was dog tired, hottish and sore round the eyes, so hungry inside that a pain kept on coming, and getting stone cold through the wind, what with the big hole in His trousers, and the thin stuff.

The morning was coming up a plain brightish blue, and the river was greyish blue, silvery up the top there, all rushed about as if somebody was giving it a right old stir just round the corner, purpose to make the little boats all bob about, just like the milk cart. A couple of steamers was coming down, with big white moustaches floating away from their noses, just like old Charlie Pool, blowing big rolls of black smoke all over the show, pulling long flat barges all tied up of tarpaulin, making a proper hard job of it and letting everybody know it. The big churchy place on the other side, with the clock in the lump sticking up, looked a long way off and He started thinking of going back to catch a train because it was such a drag, and cold, too, but looking behind, the stop looked nigh as far as the other end of the bridge, so He went on, going on the top of the sort of hill in the middle wondering whether to go to the big cafe for breakfast and then go home or go back to Ma Chalmers and get His breakfast and then go to kip, like she said. He knew He was in for a good big plateful of tasty stuff, whatever He done, but He never knew how He liked it best.

That was when He see this bride coming over this rise in the middle of the bridge. She was higher than He was, coming down His way, trying to keep her little straw hat on with one hand, and hold a bag and her skirt down with the other.

The wind come through the fat stone railings, blowing everything against her down one side, smoothing her into that shape He knew the feel of, in and out, and sliding down in again, picking her red coat open and blowing her clouts up over her knees, sometimes further up, showing all the strong, roundy shape of her legs, almost as far as where she put them little steel clip things in the tops of her pinkish, shining stockings.

He see Ma again, standing there pink, with little blue shadows all over her, laughing away, proper enjoying herself, but there was a lot of Ada there, too, the way she was walking, proper picking them up and leaving it all behind.

She was all He wanted. He got this voice inside somewhere telling him to go up to her and ask her if he could take her out after she finished work, or see her home, or even meet her after she clocked out, and see her as far as the tram. Anything, as long as it was a start.

This was what He wanted to marry, a proper, right, straight up smasher of a bride, plenty of looks and shape, dress the part and look it all the time, and make the other blokes wonder where He got her from. Then He could go home and find her in the kitchen, with everything all ready, and give her a kiss, then take her out to the pictures, and come home to supper, and then go to bed and do her a treat.

The longer He looked at her, the worse this feeling was getting, sort of splashing out everything else, making His eyes run so much, He had to rub them off to see her proper, specially now she was so close.

It come over Him, while He see His self having a go, as He had to think of something quick to tell her about Ma. He could say she rolled up years ago, and He was in business for His self, and just finished a all night job. But if He took her home to have a look round and she got talking to Ma Chalmers He was in the dripping again, and she might think it was a bit queer, or something. The only thing to tell her was that He was a stranger without no family, a artist of some kind or other, and fix up all the odd ends when He got to know her better, because He was going to be in the money while it was still going on, so she might think twice about asking questions, specially if He shoved enough presents her way and made a fuss of her, like.

Then He see she was going off towards the kerb, to pass Him, while He was standing there with His hands in His pockets waiting for her, but she only come a little way and then pulled up, looking at Him sort of side eyed with her feet together and the wind still smoothing her down, as if she wanted to cross over, but there was too much traffic and the road was too wide to chance it.

Just Him and this bride on the bridge, hardly nobody else on the pavement, with the sun coming out strong and taking some of the cold out of the wind, and boats making a row like Pa Floom blowing his snitch.

She looked back the way she come, and the wind lifted her hair either side of her, nigh the same colour as Ada's, and when she turned His way again, with part of it slung across her face, she looked so much like Ada, He was in two minds to rush over and kneel down and try and say what He wanted to, and get the worst of it over, even if He had to look a mug for a few minutes in front of all the buses and trams and lorries going past.

He see how it would be to have her to come home to.

He see there was nobody He could put His arm round and have a joke with, and tickle up now and again, or take out sometimes. This was the only bride He ever see, bar Ada, as come anywhere nigh it.

He see He been by His self a bit too long and never knew it because of Ma. All alone, and used to it, and not knowing it till she went.

Lonely, like He was now, standing there, listening to the trams moaning by. It never struck Him before how lonely He was. He only see it now, because He was looking at this bramah of a bride. All the lonely part of Him was behind, where He never wanted to see it again.

Everything else was in front of Him, and this bride was only the start. He was going to find the part of His self as called Him back to the warm, and then find the same part of this bride, and be happy, and as you might say, lay back and proper enjoy His self.

She had her fist in her mouth, looking at Him, and behind

the blowing hair her eyes was like half dollars for size, and as He went to go nearer, the fist opened and He see the red beetles trying to scratch the hair away where she could watch Him, and He give her a big smile, to sort of shove the boat out.

But as He went to her, all ready for a joke, she went backwards, and then He see she was frightened.

He got a load of crawling worms in the guts again and a sort of feeling He wanted to kneel down and howl. He knew He was dust from head to foot and not too clean, with a lump ripped out of His trousers, but He never knew it was as bad as that.

"Listen," He says. "I don't want to touch you. Straight up. I wouldn't do nothing to you. Honest. I only want to chat you. Just chat you. That's all. You're the smashingest thing I ever see, you are. No bogey. I mean it. You're smashing."

He see her teeth was all white and her mouth was the same colour as the beetles, and she was doing just the same as Ma Sedgwiss.

Screaming for all she was worth.

Eyes shut, feet together, knees bent, screaming behind her hair blowing past and her clouts all flying about where they liked.

He just felt like a bloke watching a accident somewhere.

"Don't go like that, gel," He says. "I ain't going to lay even a finger on you. I only want to bloody well talk to you, that's all. Ain't asking much, is it? Eh?"

"Go away, please go away," she says, real tears, too.

Then He see it all, and it sort of cracked something inside.

She was a posh bride. She was like them down the club, with the frost on their skins. It was no go. He knew He never had a chance. It was a different lingo, never mind everything else.

Then He see buses was slowing up, and cars was pulling in. Blokes was running up the hill.

But a copper was coming over the road between the buses, hard as he could go, hollering, taking off his white gloves, flashing his silver buttons nearer every second.

He creased somewhere, like lard, hardly no strength, wanting to fall down and hold on the pavement again, feeling the hot water washing His eyes and shivers getting His arms and legs.

They was all after Him.

He never done nothing, only look at a bride He liked, and they was after Him. They might do Him for sure, this time, what with one thing and another. He see them lights poppling in the station and the door swinging in, thick.

"You sloppy mare," He says to this bride, but she was off, going for the copper. "Only wanted to chat you, didn't I?"

But He see the nark, dark blue and silver, dodging in front of the red and white face of a bus hardly a couple of spits away, and He knew He had to move.

He went the other way, over the rise, running down hill, feeling His knee coming through His trousers, knowing people on the buses was looking at Him, going for the thickest part of the traffic in the middle of the road, tearing about in front of bonnets and mudguards and headlights, hearing all the yelling and screeching behind, all clawed up and sore inside of Him, wanting to howl somewhere and yet getting angry with things He somehow never knew how to put a finger on.

The tram in front was just on the move, and He climbed aboard, just about done, holding on the brass rail and trying to get His wind.

"What's up down there?" the conductor says, shooting the stairs in a rattle of hobnails. "Somebody hurt?"

"Some bride," He says. "Not hurt. Only laughing."

"Pennyworth?" the conductor says. "Embankment?"

"That'll do me," He says.

"Thought somebody was getting murdered, the way they was carrying on, there," the conductor says, fitting the ticket in the punch. "Laughing, eh? But it takes some of 'em like that, of a morning. They see the funny side of things, somehow. Strikes 'em ticklish, like."

"Same here," He says.

Looking up at this big clock, bashing away there, knocking out the time, He see where He was going to get His own back on the lot of them. All these people walking about, all the cars and buses and trams, and the shops and houses, all the lot of them. He see it so plain, He wondered why He never see it before. All He had to do was sling that jack. Sling it hard and sling it often, and pick up His money. Then He could dress His self proper and get a car for His self, and look the part, so as no bride, posh or not, would scream if He tried to chat her.

Look the part, that was all He had to do. No bride was ever going to argue with the Smasher.

He thought it was dead funny to see all the mugs walking about there, all going to work, while He was sailing past them having a smoke on the tram, making up His mind to get His self something nice and juicy for breakfast up in that big cafe.

While the tram was moaning round the corner, making the same row as the bash of the bell up the top there, He got the sound of Aggie's big fiddle somewhere, and it sort of reminded Him of the look about Ada, as made you want to put your arms about her, and kiss the air all round her, all the part of her what He loved and never seemed to find, somehow, that part she give the fiddle bloke.

The thoughts of not having her, and never being able to hop down the Fun Fair and see her again made Him feel like howling, and the hot water all come boiling up, so He made out He got a bit of ash in His eyes.

But He was going to be all right, lonely or not, on His own or with somebody else, with Ma or without her, going with Ada or not, it never mattered. There was always somebody waiting for Him, somewhere, like the songs was always saying, and all He had to do was count His blessings like Ma said, and look round the corner, like.

He was going to be all right.